Margaret Scott was born in the English city of Bristol in 1934.

After reading English at Cambridge she worked in a false eyelash factory, taught in two schools and in 1959 emigrated to Tasmania with her first husband and their sixteen-month-old son. Although she arrived determined to return to Britain after two years, she is now addicted to Tasmania and would not live anywhere else. For twenty-four years she taught in the English Department of the University of Tasmania, retiring in 1989 to become a full-time writer.

Margaret has produced four books of poetry: *Tricks of Memory*, *Visited*, *The Black Swans* and *Collected Poems*; a novel, *The Baby Farmer*, and a collection of stories, essays and poems, *Changing Countries*. With Vivian Smith, she edited *Effects of Light: The Poetry of Tasmania*. In 1997 Margaret wrote *Port Arthur: A Story of Strength and Courage* in response to the massacre which took place there in 1996. She has also written numerous articles, poems and short stories for periodicals in Australia, New Zealand, UK and the US, and a television script for Artist Services. She is a well-known public speaker and has appeared in 'World Series' debates and on 'Good News Week' on television.

FAMILY ALBUM

A NOVEL OF SECRETS AND MEMORIES

Margaret Scott

v

VINTAGE

A VINTAGE BOOK
Published by Random House Australia Pty Limited
20 Alfred Street, Milsons Point, NSW 2061, Australia
http://www.randomhouse.com.au

Sydney New York Toronto
London Auckland Johannesburg

First published 2000
Copyright © Margaret Scott 2000

National Library of Australia
Cataloguing-in-Publication Data

Scott, Margaret
Family Album.

ISBN 0 091 84179 8.

I. Title

A823.3

Design by Gayna Murphy, Greendot Design
Typeset by Midland Typesetters, Maryborough, Victoria
Printed and bound by Griffin Press, Netley, South Australia
10 9 8 7 6 5 4 3 2 1

DEDICATION

To my family

ACKNOWLEDGEMENTS

Many people have assisted in the protracted evolution of this book by offering encouragement, advice, information and help of other kinds. In particular I would like to thank my sister-in-law and brother, Evelyn and David Russell, who gave me the seeds from which the novel grew; my daughters, Kate North and Sarah Scott; Andrew North, who told me about butterflies; Lyn Tranter, my indefatigable agent; Stephen Orgel, who gave me the benefit of his unrivalled scholarship and, like Ruth Blair, Faith Evans, Linda Funnell and Jennifer Livett, believed in the book in its more incoherent phase; Trisha Parker, kindest of keyboard experts; James Parker; Alan Andrews; Andrew Sant; Adrian Colman; Jane Palfreyman, most supportive of publishers; Debra Adelaide, most conscientious of editors; and my son, Marcus Boddy, who puts up with a lot.

Special thanks are due to Arts Tasmania for patient and generous support and to the Literature Board of the Australia Council for a Category A Fellowship.

FAMILY TREE

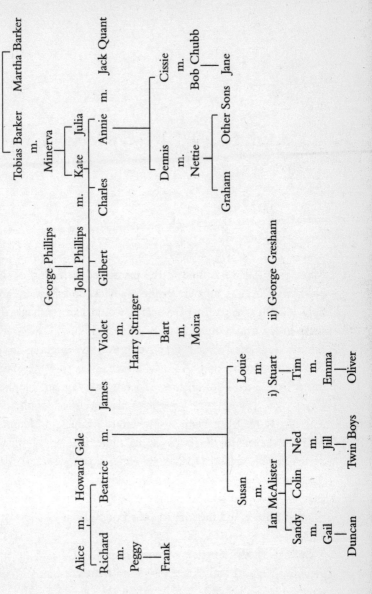

ONE

For years James Edward Phillips kept his wife and children in the dark. All through the time in the tall stone house on the corner of Howard Road, through the nights of the Blitz and the summer holidays at Brean, he let everyone think that he had never known his parents and that any brothers and sisters he might have had were lost without trace. On the few occasions when he made some reference to his early life, he spoke as though he had emerged into history at the age of six when someone in London had packed his belongings in a little wooden box and put him on a train for Bristol.

The box was still in the attic and sometimes, when she was very young, Louie would tiptoe up past Grandma Duke's bedroom, climb the narrow stairs and squeeze between the packing cases and discarded picture frames to look at it. It was a solidly made box with black metal handles and a little wheeling key. Louie liked turning the key this way and that in the lock. When she lifted the lid the smallness of the space inside gave her a terrible thrill. There was barely room for a suit and an extra pair of shoes. It made her father seem like a poor boy in a fairytale who had set out to make his fortune with nothing but a piece of bread and a few magic tokens wrapped up in a handkerchief. She would have liked very much to ask what had been in the box when her father and it were dispatched from Paddington station, but this, she knew, would be wrong, like making personal remarks or answering back.

Years later Louie could hardly believe how strong English reserve had been in the forties and fifties. People who had worked together for decades never dreamed of calling each other by their first names. Only adult relations addressed her parents as 'Beatrice' or 'Bea', 'James' or 'Jim'. Beatrice was a cheerfully inquisitive woman and, compared with her husband, alarmingly outspoken; yet, in 1920, she'd gone into marriage expecting her first child to burst into the world through her navel. She could never bring herself to say 'rats' or 'TB' out loud, and she went to her grave without ever once revealing whether or not she knew that her father had kept a mistress in Devon for thirty years, or that her brother in middle life had conceived a tremendous passion for a pastrycook.

Louie could remember only three or four times when, quite without warning, one of her parents had said something about her father's early childhood. There was one time when they were staying in the bungalow at Brean. James and Louie's cousin, Frank Gale, had got up early to go fishing. They waded along in the slopping, chocolate-coloured water of the Bristol Channel, one at each end of a net they'd found in the garage. They caught only one very small fish. James called it a 'dab' and said that Louie, who was also very small, should have it for her breakfast. She sat in the kitchen, picking the flesh off the wiry little bones while everyone else sat about drinking tea and watching her. Perhaps somebody mentioned trains or boxes or stations because suddenly James told them that, when he'd first arrived in Bristol, he'd sat on his box at Temple Meads station, alone in the smoke on the platform, waiting for Grandma Duke to come and collect him.

Beatrice said nothing at all, but afterwards, when James and Frank had gone off to have a hit with the cricket bat, Louie and Susan saw that her face had gone a violent, scalded red.

'Just fancy her not being there!' she said, hurling the breakfast cutlery into the sink. Her whole frame shuddered with rage. The two little girls, holding tea-towels, stared at her fiery profile.

'Just fancy her not being there when the train got in! Did you ever hear anything like it?'

James's adoptive mother and Beatrice were old enemies. They never clashed openly even though, after Grandpa Duke died, old Liza-Jane Duke lived in the top flat at Howard Road for twelve years. But they both had ways of making their feelings known. At supper, which Grandma Duke always ate downstairs with the family, Beatrice would talk away to her husband and daughters as though the old woman had forgotten to appear or had changed to a fat black bolster, propped in a chair. As she doled out her food she would go on smiling and chatting to somebody else and sling down the plate as though she were feeding a dog. Grandma Duke, for her part, would keep laying her hand on James's arm, asking in a low

3

voice that showed how she pitied him, if he would close the window a touch or move the fire screen or pass her another piece of the marmalade tart that Beatrice had carefully sliced into five, one for each person at the table.

Sometimes they met in the hall, one coming in from shopping, the other going out to play whist at her neighbour, Miss Wesley's, house. They swirled past each other like hussars—tall, portly women in stately hats and coats, striking their heels down on the tiled floor. Each would avert her eyes and smile cruelly as though cutting some reprobate dead for cheating at cards.

Through the years when another wider war was going on, everybody had a ration book, a tiny cube of butter to last a week, a few ounces of sugar. Beatrice put the butter rations in separate covered dishes with name tags on the lids. Every day she lifted each lid in turn to see if Grandma Duke had been stealing from someone else. She locked up her cake tins, her canned peaches and packets of jelly cubes. On the nights free of air-raids she lay awake, listening for a creak, a footfall on the stairs. Despite all her care she thought sometimes she detected a fall in the level of the sugar in the bowl, a reshuffling of jars on the pantry shelf, a missing rock cake.

One night when James came in from his ARP patrol, Beatrice made a pot of tea, opened her biscuit tin and found it empty.

'Her belly's her god,' she hissed.

Louie woke up. She and Susan had been put to bed on a mattress in the cupboard under the stairs which James had decided was safer than the public shelter. The cupboard door was propped open, bright with a bar of light from the kitchen beyond. Louie heard rattling cups, a thump on the table.

'The rest of us could starve for all she cares,' said her mother. 'I wonder sometimes how you ever managed when you were little.'

'Poor old Bert was very good,' said James. 'Many's the time he bought me a saveloy at that little shop in Silver Street. Or a bit of ham.'

Beatrice knew very well that her husband hated any prying into the secret of his origin. She suspected unhappy years in an orphanage and, in normal times, would rather have cut out her tongue than revive such a past, but the thought that old Liza-Jane, who had stolen her biscuits, knew very much more than she did about the matter drove her to frenzy. She said quite loudly, 'I wonder sometimes how she came to get her hands on you in the first place.'

Louie was aghast and so, it seemed, was James. There was the scrape of a chair pushed back. He thought he ought to slip out and see if the Freemans had fixed their blackout curtains. Last night he'd noticed chinks of light coming from their kitchen. His shadow brushed the cupboard door as he fled into the darkness. Beatrice, subdued, rattled and bumped quite softly as she tidied the kitchen so that, very soon, Louie went back to sleep. But in the morning it was clear that Beatrice's mind was still possessed by the question of what old Liza-Jane was keeping to herself. James put on his trilby and went to the watchmaker's shop that had belonged to poor old Bert Duke. Grandma Duke brooded in her flat upstairs, making tea in her kitchenette.

'All I need first thing's a cup of tea,' she would often say. 'And I wouldn't want to put Bea to any trouble when she's got so much to do getting a bit of supper for the evening.'

Beatrice refused to believe that Grandma Duke went without breakfast. She suspected toast spread with other people's butter, black market bacon and eggs. When she swept the stairs, she crouched at the top, sniffing the air like a pink and ginger pointer.

After James had gone, Louie and Susan sat one on each side of the kitchen table eating their porridge. Their mother rapped the ladle against the saucepan rim as though she had suddenly come to a decision, and addressed herself to the window over the sink.

'I sometimes wonder if she wasn't at school with Dad's mother. There was something she said once—bragging about all that drawn-thread stuff she's got—something about a needlework prize and this other girl coming second. Not that she'd have lifted a finger when the parents died, of course. She'd have let him go to some orphanage place somewhere till he was big enough to run her errands.'

Susan was a plump, slow child. People were always saying things that bewildered her. She looked sadly at her bowl, stirring a coil of treacle into the porridge. Quick little Louie, who had the extra advantage of having woken up in the night, asked, 'How did they die?'

She hoped Beatrice wouldn't be able to answer this question. She resented the dull idea of Grandma Duke's school friend and wanted it to prove too shaky to stand up, so she was glad when her mother said quite huffily, 'Well, I don't know.'

But after a moment Beatrice gazed at the window again. 'There were these people she knew that got drowned in a boating accident. She used to go on and on about it, like that time at Weston when I took you out on that boat trip. Not a cloud in the sky, she said, not a breath of wind. But over it went, she said, and sank like a stone. But then, of course, it might've been'—she silently mouthed the name—'TB'.

'Who was that Mummy said who died?' asked Susan as she and Louie started off along Howard Road on their way to school.

'Nobody,' said Louie. 'She doesn't know really.'

The thought comforted her. The boy with the little box was still drifting free in his smoky cloud of possibilities. It might still be that somewhere, hidden away, waiting for Louie to find it, lay the precious amulet his old nurse had placed about his neck, or the scroll in an unknown tongue that some faithful retainer had tucked inside his cradle.

Just before she died in the autumn of 1948, Grandma Duke gave Louie a photograph. It was the one she had kept by her bed in Howard Road among the medicine bottles and crumpled paper bags of liquorice allsorts. It had been taken, she told Louie, just after James first came down to Bristol. He was wearing a sailor suit and standing alone by a small table. His face looked soft and meek.

'I'd like you to have it, dear,' said old Liza-Jane.

The photograph was standing on her glass-topped hospital cupboard when Louie called in one day with a bag of grapes and a parcel of clean nightdresses. Louie stroked the purple velvet frame. Like Grandma Duke and everything else she owned, the lush material smelled faintly of worn coppers. The old woman lay among her pillows, slowly unwrapping her parcel with hands so fat and white they looked as though they were moulded out of lard.

7

'Did your mother iron these?' she asked, smoothing a crease. 'Dear, dear!'

Louie was taken aback at being given something that Grandma Duke prized so much. She knew very well that old Liza-Jane disliked her. She disliked all women and girls apart from humble, stringy creatures like Miss Wesley who put themselves at her service and listened in respectful amazement to tales of her affluent childhood and all that she'd thrown away when she married Bert. The only people that she seemed to like were big, jolly, handsome men, well heeled, well set up, who chaffed her and winked and threw back their heads in echoing bellows of laughter. And, although he was nothing like that, she doted on James, or at least—so Louie thought—wanted more than anything else to have him dote on her and her alone. But she'd never bothered to lay out baits for his daughters. 'A real little madam,' she called Louie, complaining to James when he helped her up the stairs.

Watching Grandma Duke smiling bitterly at Beatrice's ironing, Louie realised that the photograph was not like other presents. It wasn't meant to give pleasure. All the old woman wanted was to vex Beatrice who had coveted the photograph for years and, now that Grandma Duke was dying, was expecting to claim it for herself.

Louie looked down at the floor. Old Liza-Jane gave an elaborate sigh, bundled up the nightdresses and pushed them away.

'If you've nothing to say to me, dear, you might as well go,' she said. 'You've got lots of better things to do than bothering about what I've got to put up with.'

So after a few minutes Louie went home and stood in the kitchen watching her mother who was kneeling on a mass of damp newspapers, scrubbing out the oven. She put the photograph on the table and said, 'Old Liza-Jane asked me to give you this.'

Beatrice squirmed round to look at what Louie had brought her.

'What?' she said. 'Never in the world! She gave it to you, didn't she?'

'I don't want it. You have it.'

'No, no. You keep it. But it was good of you to think of me like that.'

She smiled at Louie, pleased at being released into generosity. She had always thought of herself as open-handed, large-hearted, fond of parties and games, jokes and dancing. Often, over the years, she had nearly wept to think how the glowering presence upstairs, crouched in curtained gloom plotting against her butter, was crushing her down into an alien shape, squeezing out of her spirit drops of obsessive malice like unholy oil.

But, as the doctor had predicted, within less than a month, Beatrice was free of her enemy. On the day after Grandma Duke's death she went through the upstairs flat like a marauding army, throwing heaps of embroidered linen onto the floor, upending drawers full of letters, snapshots and liquorice. She found a Sunday school prize awarded to James Edward Phillips in 1898, several regimental photographs, a letter that James had written to the Dukes from Mesopotamia. In a trunk in the attic, under a pile of cases filled with the butterflies poor old Bert Duke had collected she found neatly tied bundles of receipts from customers whose clocks he and James had attended. At the bottom of the trunk there were more bundles made up of letters from Beatrice's father, Howard Gale, who had acted as the Dukes' solicitor. And another photograph showing young James standing with Bert

Duke and a plump dark man with a fierce moustache, all holding butterfly nets. Behind them rose the ivied wall of what looked to be a very grand house. But there was nothing that shed any light on James's parentage or early life. It was not until the day of his funeral, thirty-eight years later, that the truth began to emerge.

TWO

Susan was standing close to the cemetery gate just inside the car park. For the past fifteen minutes she'd been shaking hands, kissing cheeks, thanking people for their floral tributes and asking all the relatives and close acquaintances to come back to Willowdene Drive for a drink and something to eat. Two large feelings stood in her mind like the decent gateposts of a well-appointed house—proper sorrow at her father's death, and grateful pleasure at the number of people who had gathered to honour him. But around these two pillars a crowd of other smaller, less decorous thoughts and feelings jostled and skipped in a way that, every so often, made her ashamed. She was worried, for instance, about asking so many back to the house. Ned, her youngest son, was in charge of the catering and she didn't want to put him out. Would there be enough vol-au-vents? Or asparagus rolls? Should they stop on the way home for another bottle of whisky? Her dark grey suit, which she hadn't

11

worn for nearly a year, was too tight. She kept wondering if people noticed how the jacket rode up at the back into fat creases. Above all, she'd start thinking from time to time about what she had to take up to the hospital today and then, remembering that all the running about was finished for good, she'd give way, before she could stop it, to a rush of relief.

A fine rain had started to fall. Umbrellas were going up. The very old, who made up two-thirds of the gathering, were hobbling and bobbing away across the wet gravel, hurried along by their solid middle-aged children. Susan could see Ian, her husband, on the far side of the car park, helping the elderly clamber into their cars, closing doors, bending forward to salute departing mourners. Colin, their second son, was standing next to his father, looking outstandingly handsome in his dark suit. How wonderful, thought Susan, that all three boys had managed to get home for the funeral. How wonderful to have the family together again even though they were all so sad about Grandad.

Ned had already left, anxious to get his vol-au-vents into the oven. The only one Susan couldn't account for was Sandy. She wondered if he and Gail had decided to take Duncan straight home. Duncan was very highly strung and Susan had been worried all along about whether the funeral would upset him. Gail had been worried too. She'd wanted to leave him at the guesthouse where the landlady was very nice and had a little boy of her own, but Sandy wouldn't have it. He always said that a child with the IQ of a genius needed all the new experiences he could get.

Susan was just looking around to make sure that there were no mourners still lingering on the path from the graveside when she felt a hand on her arm. A completely strange woman was peering up into her face. She seemed to be in the grip of some weird emotion, tearful but blinking and beaming with uncontrollable joy. When Susan looked at her she tucked back her chin like someone going into raptures over a baby. Susan was embarrassed. It was an emotional day but the woman's manner was over-familiar like the Jehovah's Witnesses who came to the door sometimes.

'It's Susan isn't it?' said the stranger in a voice squeezed thin with wonder and delight. 'I knew it must be.'

Another woman, smaller, younger, beakier, came pushing in, gazing up through rain-dashed spectacles.

'It's Cissie and Jane from Barnstaple,' she said.

Both looked triumphant, grinning in expectation of amazement, exclamations, a warm embrace.

Susan stared. She knew she ought to recognise these people, but she couldn't place them at all. She felt quite panicky. The women looked rather common. They had plastic raincoats and frizzy hair beaded with drops of rain. The younger one had an unsuitable red handbag.

'I'm sorry,' she said, stepping back. 'Were you friends of my father?'

'Friends!' they chorused. 'Friends?'

'This is Cissie,' said Jane. 'You know, Cissie Chubb, your Dad's niece. Your cousin. And I'm the daughter, Jane.'

'Oh!' said Cissie, moving in again. 'He was wonderful to us, Uncle Jim. I don't know what we'll ever do without him.'

'No,' said Susan. 'No, I'm sorry, you've made a mistake. My father didn't have any family.'

The two women looked pale and sullen. Susan broke away and hurried off towards the safe, decorous figures of

13

her husband and son. Behind her voices broke into clamour, one shrill, one bewildered and incredulous.

'He must've said. He was always going on to us about you . . .'

'No family? What d'you mean no family? There's us, the Chubbs, Bart, Auntie Vi . . .'

Luckily Sandy, Gail and Duncan had reappeared by this time and were already packed into the back of the McAlisters' Vauxhall, so that Ian was ready to drive away at once.

'I couldn't think what to say,' complained Susan as they turned into the street beyond the cemetery. 'That couldn't be right about one being a niece. I mean Grandad would've said. He wouldn't have had a niece and never said anything about it.'

'I expect they got muddled up,' said Gail easily. 'They must belong to the funeral after ours.'

'But they knew my name. And one of them called Grandad "Uncle Jim".'

Ian was nodding and humming in a way that showed all this was no surprise to him.

'They'd have got the names from the funeral notice in the paper. Easily done. Then it's just a matter of coming along, throwing out a name or two—Susan, Uncle Jim—and the next thing they're invited to the house.'

'But I didn't invite them.'

'No. But thousands would. They rely, you see, on people being confused. It's an old dodge, taking advantage of grief.'

'Oh, God yes!' said Sandy. 'Oldest trick in the book.'

'But whatever for?'

'A good feed, I expect,' said Gail.

14

Sandy frowned. 'Hardly. Planning to go through the coats in the hall most likely. Wouldn't you say so, Dad?'

'Or checking the security arrangements. Laying the ground for a break-in if it looked worthwhile.'

'Oh, good heavens!' cried Susan. 'But really, I mean, they didn't look like burglars.'

Duncan had been sitting quietly between his parents, prodding at a pocket calculator.

'Do burglars kill people?' he asked.

'No, no,' said his mother. 'Of course not, silly.'

Sandy sighed and placed a finger on the bridge of his spectacles as though trying to hold himself in check.

'There is such a thing as armed robbery,' he said patiently. 'Murders do occur from time to time.'

'Are they coming to Granny's house to kill us?'

'No,' said Sandy. 'No. The burglars aren't coming to Granny's house. She sent them away.'

'Perhaps they'll go to another house and kill some other people.'

'That's very unlikely, Duncan. They were just two women who were trying to get invited to the house by using a trick. It's very unlikely that they'd ever use violence.'

'They might be angry now,' said Duncan, starting to snivel. 'They might have guns. They might be coming after us to shoot Granny.'

'Oh, good heavens! Of course they aren't, Dunky. Of course they aren't going to shoot me. What a dreadful idea!'

Gail folded her arms and stared out at the rain.

'I told you we shouldn't bring him. He'll be upset about dying and killing and all that stuff for weeks now.'

Sandy beat his hand up and down, lightly touching his knee in an effort at total calm.

'I've tried to explain it's no use—in fact, it's absolutely counter-productive—you trying to build this protective wall round Duncan . . .'

'But it's just stupid. Dragging him round a graveyard in the rain.'

Duncan's nerve snapped. He threw himself down, squirming over his parents' laps, and started to scream. Gail tried to grab him round the waist and pull him into her arms. Duncan threshed and kicked, catching Sandy a crack full in the face. Sandy's nose began to stream blood. He flung back his head, glasses awry, and scrabbled in his pockets for something to stem the flow. Duncan shrieked in terror and hid his face in his mother's neck.

'Sandy!' shouted Susan. 'Sandy! Pinch your nose! Pinch it!'

'Serve you right, that's what I say. Serve you right,' said Gail loudly, rocking Duncan and glaring at the blood over his shoulder.

The noise swelled and beat against the misted windows until Ian, who had been smiling to himself, began to look exasperated.

Because the McAlisters' house was too small to accommodate all the boys, now that two had families of their own, Sandy, Gail and Duncan had taken rooms in a guesthouse several streets away. It was decided that instead of going straight to Willowdene Drive, Ian would have to take them back to the guesthouse, and leave them to make their own way to the funeral party later on.

'That's if we come,' said Gail. 'Dunky's very upset.'

Sandy was in no condition to argue. His nose had stopped bleeding but his shirt and tie were heavily splashed with blood and would have to be changed before he could join the gathering of mourners.

As it turned out, it was just as well that Duncan was not in the car when Susan and Ian pulled into their driveway. A group of people, clumped under umbrellas, filled the garden path. Colin was there, two or three neighbours, Ian's Edinburgh aunts, and Swampy Marsh, James Phillips's old friend from the British Legion. In their midst, talking animatedly and passing around what looked like photographs, were Cissie and Jane from Barnstaple.

In the end they stole the show. Nobody talked of anything else. When Susan went out to the kitchen to fetch another plate of vol-au-vents or the special devils on horseback Ned had made, somebody was sure to come after her and stand about saying, 'Fancy having all those relatives . . .' or, 'D'you think your mother knew, dear?'

Cissie and Jane sat side by side on the sofa, drinking port and handing round the photos that proved their case: Uncle Jim in a comic hat proposing a toast at Jane's twenty-first; Uncle Jim with Cissie, Cissie's mother, Aunt Annie, Cissie's husband, Bob, and Cissie's brother, Dennis, all standing by an old Wolseley with running boards; Uncle Jim in a garden with young Jane and a terrier pup; Uncle Jim, only last year, standing between Cissie and Jane, hugging their shoulders and beaming at the camera.

'He came to see us regular as clockwork,' said Jane, keeping an eye on Susan's face. 'Always after Easter, then again in August and again before Christmas.'

Susan just turned away and went on handing round Ned's savouries. These seasonal disappearances had been part of her life for as long as she could remember. For years she'd assumed they had something to do with her father's business. When they'd carried on as usual after his retirement, she and Ian had talked the matter over.

'It's probably those British Israelites,' Susan had said. 'You won't ask, will you, Ian? Grandad doesn't like a lot of questions.'

In fact he couldn't endure a single one. Once, at supper, just after James had returned home in a taxi, Duncan had enquired point blank where he'd been. And James, smiling in embarrassment, had quietly laid down his spoon, abandoned his stewed plums and left the house.

Susan smiled until her cheeks ached and she could hardly speak. Her father looked so happy and at ease with these common people in their awful nylon dresses and sandals with ankle straps. She felt like asking why they hadn't come to see him when he was dying.

'Of course we always thought it was funny,' said Cissie, 'the way we never got up to Bristol to meet the family. There was always something. We'd say, "Come on, Uncle Jim, we'll come up for Christmas then." But he'd say, "Oh no, we're going over to Bea's people this year." Or something, you know, always something. So Mum said "He's got his reasons."'

'But we never thought,' put in Jane, 'he'd never told them, I mean you wouldn't, would you?' She looked about defiantly. 'We think he was upset about being farmed out and didn't want to let on about what happened.'

This caused a fresh sensation, questions about James's parents and the Dukes.

'Yes, well, they sent him off,' said Jane. 'That's what my gran always said. Sent him off to Bristol and kept the others. We knew all about it but he wouldn't've wanted anyone else to know.'

Cissie, who had drunk a lot of port by now, began to giggle.

'I was all of a doo-dah, shaking like a leaf. Crying, you know, and laughing. You must've thought we were a right pair. I mean what would you think?'

Everyone was entranced. Mrs Marsh said it was all like the most wonderful soap. Ian's aunts agreed that Susan's family had always fancied themselves a cut above the McAlisters and had very good reasons for not owning to Cissie and Jane.

'Not,' murmured Aunt Essie, 'that they've anything much to pride themselves on in the first place what with that uncle and the grandfather's reputation. That Howard Gale.'

'But you can see she doesn't like it at all. It's brought her down a peg.'

'I daresay that other girl will be very glad she didn't come home for the funeral. The one who went to Cambridge. There's not much Cambridge about the new relations.'

Ned behaved impeccably, skating up to Cissie and Jane to pour more port, whisking out fresh plates of savouries with a bow and a wink. Ned's beautiful wife, Jill, who had a degree in sociology and an interest in oral history, fetched a pad and pencil and settled on the arm of the sofa to get things straight. Colin, equally good-looking, leaned easily over her shoulder.

'So who exactly was your mother?' asked Jill.

'She's the youngest, Annie,' said Cissie. 'Uncle Jim's younger sister. She's a marvel, really. Eighty-nine she is. Then there's Auntie Vi. She's still alive. And there was Charlie but he was killed in the war . . . And Gilbert. He passed on just after.'

'Hold on,' said Colin. 'Who was the eldest?'

'Uncle Jim was the eldest. That was it, you see. He looked out for all the rest of them. Always, Mum said.

19

Whatever it was—any bother, any of them in trouble, or their kids, like me—Uncle Jim'd be there.'

'With his hand in his pocket no doubt,' said Ian under his breath as Susan went past with another tray of nibbles.

Then Colin thought of getting out the earliest of the McAlisters' family albums, the one with pictures of Ian and Susan as children.

'Oh look, Janey!' said Cissie. 'That must be Frank Gale.'

Everyone stopped talking. Jane whispered something. Cissie went red and turned over a page.

'Yes, I think we saw this one. Susan and Louie. Brean 1940.'

'Louie was hoping to get back,' said Susan. 'But her husband died very suddenly. It was a great shock.'

'And so will this be,' muttered Ian, decanting whisky. 'Especially when she gets a sight of the will.'

Susan who had fetched up close to him again was really affronted. She said, 'Oh, Ian!' quite angrily but he simply raised his shoulders and spread his hands in a way that suggested that it wasn't his fault that most of Susan and Louie's inheritance would turn out to have been divided up between Cissie and Jane, Bob and Dennis, Auntie Annie, Bart and Auntie Vi .

'After all we've done,' he said out loud, screwing down the cap on his bottle of Scotch.

Soon after Sandy arrived, Susan went out into the back garden and, although the air was still damp and raw, sat on the bench under the lilac tree, unbuttoned her jacket and eased her heels out of her court shoes. She knew she ought to stay inside and try to keep things going along smoothly but she felt that if she didn't get away for a couple of minutes she'd break down completely. Sandy was in a dreadful temper. His nose was swollen and he'd obviously had a long argument with Gail. Apparently she'd refused point-blank to come with him and had somehow managed to stop him bringing Duncan when, as Susan knew, there was nothing Sandy liked more than showing Duncan off to a room full of people. He always asked him the square roots of numbers and got him to read difficult bits from the *Daily Telegraph*. Sandy was put out too by finding Cissie and Jane sitting on the sofa, and, although Susan had taken him aside to explain everything, insisted on asking a lot of hectoring questions. How did they know about the funeral? If it was true that they'd had a telegram from Grandad's solicitor, could they produce the name and address of the firm? After that Sandy went through all their photographs like a passport inspector, looking suspiciously from them to the pictures and back again. Ned tried, as he always did, to lighten the atmosphere, but now even he was upset because Cissie had got mixed up about who was married to Jill. She'd told Colin he and Jill made a really lovely couple, and the way Jill kept on leaning back against Colin's shoulder you couldn't really blame her. And then for Cissie to go blurting out Frank Gale's name when Grandad had obviously told her that Frank and the McAlisters hadn't been on speaking terms for years!

Everything, thought Susan, had been spoiled. People seemed to have forgotten they were mourners. Even her own grief had lost its clear solid shape, blurred by a mist of confusion and resentment. Staring at the damp ground she told herself that Grandad ought to have let her know about all these relatives so that she could have made proper arrangements.

When she went back into the house she found that everyone had been looking for her. Some people had had to leave without saying goodbye. Others were standing about in their coats by the front door. Colin had offered to drive Cissie and Jane to the station and was helping them gather all their belongings together. They'd got to get back, they said. Jane had to be at work early tomorrow but they'd be down again soon—'You won't get rid of us now!'

Before she left Cissie fished about in her bag and brought out two more photographs, faded sepia studies of James as a young boy with his parents and siblings.

'We've got about four of these,' she said to Susan. 'This one's for you and we thought Louie'd like to have the other.'

THREE

Nobody likes being kept out of a secret, but that, thought Louie, wasn't the real trouble. It was more that she felt now that she'd never known her father, that he'd never been the person she remembered, that it was a stranger who'd whistled through his teeth over the brightly lit blotting paper, spread with spidery wheels from the watches he mended, or come into the house with his air-raid warden's masked torch, saying as she woke in the close smell of the cupboard under the stairs, 'The Bishop's Palace's gone . . . Martins' place's gone . . . St Joseph's is gone.'

Now that his secret was out, she knew more about him than she'd ever known when he was alive and the family still together in Howard Road. But the discovery of what had been hidden changed the significance of what had seemed quite plain. It was as though the eyes in a face had been covered and then the bandage pulled away so that all the features that had seemed familiar suddenly took on an entirely new character as part of a strange, quite unexpected whole.

Thoughts like these ran on and on in Louie's head as she mooned about the house on the wintry morning when the photograph arrived. She couldn't settle to anything. Sometimes part of her mind stood away and watched, noting carefully what she was feeling. This had been happening ever since her early childhood and she often wondered if it meant that her emotions were less deep and real than other people's. Two months ago when she had run out onto the verandah and found George lying dead she had said to herself, 'This is the worst thing that has ever happened to me. This is pure agony and loss.' But that evening she had recorded the moment in her notebook and afterwards used it in a short story called 'The Widow'.

The photograph had come in the morning mail, the first item that Louie pulled out of a package from Susan. It was printed on thick card, peeling apart at the corners, and showed, in various tones of sepia, a thin man with a moustache and mournful eyes standing stiff as a toy soldier behind a straggling family. His wife sat in front of him, one arm cradling a muffled-up baby, the other clasped around the shoulders of a small boy. Three other children, dressed up but untidy and confused-looking, stood in an uneven line, two huddled together and one—the tallest—marooned alone in the centre of the picture. The place, suggested only by an encroaching brown fog, might have been anywhere in the world—Newfoundland, Cyprus, Cawnpore or even beyond the Empire in some remote missionary cantonment, some colony of expatriates, some consulate garden. But when Louie turned the photograph over she found an oval stamp with 'J.T. Burton and Sons—Photographic Studio—Holborn' printed around the edge. Someone had added a date in black copperplate: 17 December, 1898.

It was astounding to find such an object in one of Susan's parcels. She was a faithful but predictable sender of presents. Ever since Louie had emigrated to Tasmania over twenty-four years ago, Susan had been sending her two parcels every year, one at Christmas and another for her birthday in mid June. The packages had always contained a pair of tea-towels or a jaunty apron and a letter full of news about Ian's troubles with his car or his teeth or the management of British Telecom, the amazing successes of the three boys and, in recent years, the still more amazing exploits of Duncan or Ned's adorable little twins. Usually there would be a batch of photographs, quite different from the one Louie was holding in her hand—light, bright, up-to-date shots of Susan and her family walking in Wales, camping in the Lake District, lined up on the church steps for Ned's wedding, clustered around Sandy on the day of his graduation.

Louie collected bits and pieces of Victoriana—prints, fans, chain purses, photographs, oddments of china. The sepia photograph was exactly the kind of thing that she might have picked up for herself in Hobart's Salamanca market on a Saturday morning, but she couldn't for the life of her understand how Susan had discovered this or why, having done so, she should suddenly drop the conviction (which Louie was sure she held) that collecting old, apparently useless objects was queer and unhealthy.

Outwardly Susan seemed almost unchanged. In her own family photographs she always looked much as Louie remembered her—tall, plump, hurrying, anxious, good-hearted and blundering. Everything about Susan flapped —her wavy, shoulder-length hair, her cardigans, shoulder-bags and big, blowing, flowery cotton skirts. As she swept along with her elbows out and her head well in front of her large slapping sandals, she presented such a terrible danger to anything small and easily knocked over that Louie could never understand how Sandy, Colin and Ned had managed to survive into adulthood. She had never meant any harm, of course. As a child she had wept over injured puppies and broken dolls. Sometimes she had tried in a half hearted way to take a look at Louie's albums of pressed flowers or her trays of feathers, pebbles and bits of shrapnel but, when Louie shrieked, 'Don't touch! Don't touch!' so loud that someone else was bound to hear, she had gone heavily and sorrowfully away.

It was easy to misjudge her sister, thought Louie, beginning to feel pleased with her unexpected present. It was Susan, after all, who had been left to cope with their mother's illness and their father's extended old age, with broken hips, memory loss and undertakers. Susan had arranged for nurses to look in each day, picked up prescriptions from the chemist, rushed hot meals on covered plates to their father's flat just four doors up the street, gone daily to hospitals with bundles of fruit and magazines, brought home the dirty laundry and waited about at night in corridors smelling of soup and Dettol; while Louie, always the favourite daughter, whose quick-ness had been the pride of their parents' lives, had sailed away at the age of twenty-eight and never once gone back.

She'd meant to go in April. The telephone had rung at six o'clock in the morning. Still dazed with sleep she'd heard Susan saying Grandad was in hospital.

'Who?'

She could never get used to the way Susan talked about their father, but, of course, she'd never even seen him with his grandchildren, never taken her own son back to meet him and call him 'Grandad'.

'Grandad. Dad. He's asking for you, Louie.'

Shocked reproach, unerringly aimed over the thousands of miles, woke Louie up with a jerk.

She'd meant to go back at once. She'd hurried about conferring with travel agents, making bookings, fussing over how George would manage without her. At long last she was going to get on a plane and fly across half the world to the place she'd left when she was young, gullible and still married to Stuart. Home but no longer home. And then, just two days before she was due to leave when she was standing in the kitchen, washing a lettuce under the tap and looking out at the huge, dark shape of Mount Wellington standing guard over the city, she'd heard the thump, like a chair overturned in a brawl, that was George falling dead just outside their front door.

There were several folded sheets of paper poking out of the envelope that had held the sepia photograph. Louie was just reaching for them and gazing musingly at the lonely-looking boy in the centre of the group when something extraordinary happened. Smoothly, in the twinkling of an eye, the child changed from a stranger to someone unalterably familiar. Louie stared at the soft, meek face. It seemed impossible now that she had failed to recognise, even for a second, her father in early youth. Upstairs, in a purple velvet frame, Louie kept another photograph of the same small boy, a little younger, a little plumper. On the back, under the photographer's stamp—'H.H. Bertoli, Horsefair, Bristol'—Grandma Duke had written: James Edward Phillips, 1896.

Once the child had declared himself, the other figures in the group changed with him. This was no ordinary

27

family because James Edward Phillips had been orphaned long before 1898 and by then was living in Bristol with the Dukes. The thin man, the woman, the other four children were tainted now by a kind of miasma drifting up through time from Grandma Duke with her musty smell of used pennies and her paper bags of sweating liquorice allsorts. Their anonymous, melancholy charm faded away. Their slightly seedy, down-at-heel look, which had seemed at first romantic and Bohemian, began to suggest something dull, cringing and mean. The man and woman must have been hangers-on, acquaintances or relatives of the Dukes—not friends because Grandma Duke had never indulged in friendship. People James had visited or been left with for a time. Though why the couple had placed a nine-year-old outsider from Bristol in the middle of what looked like a family portrait, Louie could not imagine.

When she unfolded the first of the papers from the envelope she found, instead of the expected letter, a photocopy of James Edward Phillips's birth certificate. At first she didn't connect the document with her father because his name had changed. He had begun life as Preston James Edward Phillips. Preston? Louie was startled at how angry and shaken she felt when she realised that, all through the years, her father had kept his real name under his hat. The ARP helmet, the familiar trilby, the old straw boater he wore on the beach at Brean had, each in turn, shrouded the secret knowledge that its owner had been called after a seaport in West Lancashire. Preston Phillips had been born on 16 July 1889 at 40 Waltham Gardens, Hampstead to Kate Maud Phillips, formerly Barker, and John Phillips, who gave his occupation as 'commercial clerk'. Louie couldn't believe her eyes.

Never in all her life had she heard anything of this document and had always accepted that her father, like everyone else, had no idea who his parents might have been. Now all the mystery fell in a dusty heap and Louie, despite the fact that she was over fifty, felt absurdly disappointed.

'Commercial clerk' made her think of Dickens, whose clerks, in her experience, were always poor—Bob Cratchit, scraping along on next to nothing until Scrooge repented of his ways, and Bella Wilfer's father, forced to dine off a single saveloy. But it wasn't the poverty that Louie resented, it was the ordinariness. She found that all her life she'd assumed that her grandparents had been exceptional, the secret source of everything in herself that distinguished her from people like her sister.

The next document Louie found in the envelope did nothing to help matters. It was the record of a marriage, solemnised at the parish church of St Jude's, Chippenham, in the County of Wiltshire on 20 January 1889. The bridegroom, John Phillips, son of George Phillips, horse dealer, was a resident of Lacock. He was twenty-four years old. The bride, Kate Maud Barker, aged twenty-one, gave no rank or profession. She was the daughter of Tobias Henry Barker, brewer, living at the time of her marriage in the parish of St Jude's. The witnesses were Albert William Beddoes and Martha Emily Barker.

Louie found the brewer particularly galling. All the Victorian brewers she'd met in books had been comical if they were poor and vulgar if they were rich. 'Horse dealer' sounded more raffish, suggesting someone who hung around at country fairs and race meetings. For a moment she thought hopefully of Romany speech and exotic blood, but an image of moleskins, bandy legs, a

29

clay pipe, and a shifty eye persisted. All in all she wasn't surprised that her father, who'd been in a quiet way a considerable snob, had chosen to keep silent about his grandfathers. And, of course, there was something else of which he might have been ashamed—his own arrival only six months after his parents' marriage. Unless he had been a premature baby—one of the handful who'd survived all those years ago, swaddled in cotton wool, fed on warm drips of milk and brandy—then his mother, in autumn of 1888, had conceived him out of wedlock.

At last she came to Susan's letter. It began with some references to the little flurry of messages that had passed between them immediately after James's death. Then came a page or two of news about Sandy's move to Wales, Colin's success in setting up the Houston branch of his Datarig consultancy, and Ned's new restaurant at Grantchester. Already Ten to Three was famous for its roast suckling pig and fine almond flummery. 'I expect you're wondering,' wrote Susan finally on page four, 'why I've sent the old photo.' She then gave a rather wandering account of her meeting with Cissie and Jane and their theory that 'Uncle Jim' had never said a word about them because he didn't want people to know he'd been given away. 'But it turns out that all those years he'd been going to see them in Barnstaple, also visiting Violet (the other sister, also still alive). The toddler is Charles (missing in WWI) and the other boy is Gilbert (now deceased). Also enclosed are copies of a few odds and ends we found in Dad's deed-box . . .' The certificates and, less surprisingly, a photograph of Edward VII. James had always been a great admirer of the royal family and, despite his puritan principles, admired the fast living King Edward most of all. Once, scuffling through a desk drawer in search of drawing paper, Louie had come on a photograph of the King in his coronation robes with his crown on his head and his rather protuberant eyes gazing inscrutably into space. In the meticulous copperplate he used in his account books, James had labelled the portrait 'The Peacemaker'.

Louie put down Susan's letter and began wandering about the house, stopping from time to time to stare out of a window at the garden where frost lay on the ground like white sand and bristled from the stems of all the plants. It was one thing to conceal the dead, quite another to conceal a whole living family and secretly keep in touch with them, week after week, year after year, slipping letters under the blotter when your wife and children came near, sneaking out to the letterbox at the top of Howard Road, making up lying stories to explain the visits to Barnstaple or to Violet, wherever she might be.

'Of course,' thought Louie, 'he was secretive about other things as well.' She remembered his surreptitious attendance at meetings of the British Israelites, the sect that believes that the British are God's chosen people, descendants of the lost tribes of Israel. Once he'd shown her the collecting box he kept in a desk drawer. It was made in the shape of the Great Pyramid with a slot in the side and plans of the internal stairs and passages drawn on its skin. If you counted all the steps, he'd told her, you could find out when the world was coming to an end. What had drawn him into that company of senile empire builders? Singled out by his parents for rejection, had he needed a God who made him a chosen son? If so he'd been let down. In the early seventies he'd written to her: 'My faith and belief are such that Divine Power will overrule to prevent us signing the Treaty of Rome.

Sustained by this glorious hope I wish you all a very happy Christmas . . .' But God, having let the British Empire fall, sent no thunderbolt, no fiery angel to prevent His chosen people sinking to the level of mere Europeans.

When she went back to the kitchen to look at the photograph again, Louie found that John and Kate Maud Phillips had taken on the look of figures in a rogues' gallery, staring up with the blank eyes of malefactors who baffle any attempt to find in their faces signs of exceptional depravity. They looked so harmless, but together they had twisted their son's life, made him so wretched that after he had been discarded he could never again speak their names. Not only had they given him away, they had gone on to have one and possibly two more children after getting rid of him or so it seemed. According to Louie's calculations, James had been sent to Bristol at least two and a half years before the photograph had been taken. Kate Phillips must have conceived her baby, Annie, and possibly Charles, the little boy by her chair, after James had been handed over to the Dukes.

As the morning wore on, Louie started to make a spinach pie. Her son Tim and his wife Emma were coming to dinner that night. She wished now that she could put them off. They were difficult company at the best of times, though when George was alive she'd accepted Tim's mind games and Emma's sniping as background shadows. They were something like a wet summer that made her feel more fortunate than ever in the warmth and snugness of her life with George. Now she was exposed to the full force of a contempt she'd never been able to fathom because, although she'd obviously failed as a mother, she couldn't work out quite what had made Tim draw away from her. The trouble had started in earnest when she'd left Stuart, depriving Tim of a father at the age of eight, but this wasn't a simple case of a son taking his father's side against the mother. For years Tim had done everything possible to prove how much he despised all the baggage Stuart had carried with him out of the sixties into the eighties—the guru's cheesecloth tunics, the trips to India, the Dylan records and the whole welter of causes that Tim referred to as 'Land Rights for Gay Whales'.

Emma was Tim's master stroke. By marrying her he had managed to appal both his parents in one hit—Stuart because she came from a family of wealthy right-wing capitalists mixed up with multinationals and implicated in the felling of old-growth forests; Louie because Emma thought the only point of a university education was to get qualified to make enough money to go to the races in the right hat, give poolside parties and drive a Porsche.

Louie began to have doubts about the *spanokopita*. It was bound to be seen as a shot in the war or an edible tract showing sympathy for Stuart's vegetarianism, or preaching frugality and racial tolerance. Emma would eat what her father called 'ethnic tucker' if she'd read about it in *Vogue* or *Harper's Bazaar* but Louie knew that, privately, Emma still thought of garlic prawns, oysters, best steak and crayfish as the only real food for dinner parties.

And what on earth would they talk about? Certainly not the horse dealer, the commercial clerk and the Chippenham brewer. Emma could cope with Stuart who was, after all, a type familiar to her clan for generations— a comic Pommie eccentric, a sort of remittance man distantly related to a baronet—but if her mother-in-law suddenly hurled a horse dealer at her Emma would take it as a spiteful attack on her status. In any case, Louie wanted more time to herself to come to terms with what had happened, to digest the discovery that her father was not the man she remembered and that she herself was changed by what she'd learned.

Always she'd believed that she'd understood her parents completely, that their characters were straightforward and immutable like their household routines and their heavy furniture. Now she had to accept that she'd missed a good deal. And she was no longer simply a younger daughter with one sister and one cousin but part of a weird sprawling tribe of Chubbs and other people whose names she didn't even know. Granddaughter of a commercial clerk and a brewer's daughter who had gone walking out, very probably, in the meadows beyond Chippenham and there, despite the October chill, the impediment of stays, petticoats and combinations, conceived her father.

While she was crumbling feta cheese into a bowl of beaten eggs, Louie began to wonder why a couple who lived in Hampstead should be photographed in Holborn. The obvious answer was that at some point in the nine years after James's birth, they had moved from one to the other. When Louie had last been in London in the fifties, Hampstead had been quite chic, Holborn sooty and impoverished. The late-Victorian terraces which had survived the Blitz were mean and pinched with front doors opening directly on to the street. Had the Phillipses come down in the world? Perhaps in 1896 when they gave away their son, they were already slipping into ruin. John might have lost his place as a clerk. Kate, pregnant perhaps with Charles, might have fallen ill. And Grandma Duke would have given all kinds of assurances: she and Bert would see that James had the best of everything; it was only until things looked up a bit; she'd see to it that he wrote to them every week and came up to see them regular as clockwork.

All at once Louie became sure that the photograph had been Grandma Duke's idea. To chivvy that hangdog family into a studio and sit gloating over their misery was exactly the kind of exercise she would have enjoyed. 'I'll pay every penny out of my own pocket,' she would have said. 'Now, you can't refuse, not after everything.'

'I can't prove it, of course,' thought Louie. 'Not establish it as a fact like me making this pie.'

Yet in a day or two the spinach pie would have disappeared, in a month or two it would have been forgotten. If they ever recalled this evening's dinner, Tim might insist that she'd served some kind of quiche.

'Well, there are some things that can be established,' she said to herself. 'The certificates and the photograph aren't forgeries.'

Pushing aside her bowl and bunch of spinach, she put the three stiff rectangles in a row, then slid them around to make a triangle. She thought of all the thousands of intricate, intertwining strands of cause and effect, feeling and motive that linked the events represented by the three objects.

If she were to go to England and talk to Violet and Annie, track down any descendants of Violet, Charles and Gilbert, hunt through parish registers and search out tombstones in scattered burial grounds, then eventually there would be more photographs and certificates, more definite facts in the story, more points at which all the flickering strands that joined the bits of evidence into a plot would coalesce. If she were to settle down to read more of the major events and movements of the eighteen-nineties she would discover, emerging from the flux of late-Victorian Britain, a series of patterns—a Marxist view of the New Imperialism, a feminist interpretation of reforms in education—all lying, one superimposed on another, over and under, round and across the faint, shifting causal threads of her family's history.

These larger patterns, like the outline of Roman roads that she'd seen from the summits of hills in childhood, could be apprehended only at a distance, but there were, of course, millions of little moments, each one an atom in the strands that linked events, which had been clearly seen for an instant and then forgotten, vanishing as completely as the spinach pie would do. There were also many conditions, many crucial ideas and passions, which had been kept secret even in their own time, or which, like tumours that are never diagnosed, had gone—and would always go—unrecognised.

Tim and Emma arrived rather later than Louie had expected. She knew as soon as she opened the front door that something was wrong. Both looked cheerful and alert. Tim was wearing an opulent overcoat, a suit and his yacht club tie. Emma, swathed in dark blue velvet, had put on diamond earrings. They came in quickly, exclaiming over the frosty night, and immediately looked across the hall into Louie's sitting room.

'Oh. Are we the first to arrive?'

'I thought', said Louie, 'it would be nice with just us. I'm sorry if you got the wrong impression.'

Tim and Emma looked at each other.

'It's all right. It's just we got a babysitter and everything. If you'd just said you could have come to us.'

Emma dumped her evening coat on a hall chair and went and stood in front of the fire. She was dressed in a new after-five number in dark taffeta. An outfit, thought Louie, meant to put a roomful of aging academics in their places. But she wasn't in the mood for war games.

'What a lovely dress,' she said humbly and, while Tim poured their drinks, hurried about fetching savouries and nuts.

'Well this is nice!' said Tim, settling in George's chair, showing his teeth. 'How've you been, mother?'

'How could he?' she thought. 'How could he do that?' But she said quite calmly, 'I'm getting used to things a bit more now. One step at a time. I thought the other day I must start having people around here again. But I'm not quite up to a houseful just yet.'

Emma looked at her suspiciously. She wasn't sure whether Louie was complimenting her and Tim by making them her first dinner guests since George's funeral, or just having a go at her for expecting a party. There was a pause, then Louie asked how Oliver, her grandson, was getting on. This was a fairly safe topic because although they differed on what was important in Oliver's life, they all enjoyed talking about his latest sayings and doings in a way that was impossible outside the family.

'. . . this much taller than Damian Nettleship and he'll be seven next birthday . . .'

'. . . really keen on the boat. He'll be out in his own little Mirror before we know where we are . . .'

'He's really witty. You know those little round segmented things on my big tree? Well he asked me what they were. So I said, "They're fairy footballs, Oliver." He thought that was terribly funny. Then he said, "They're not fairy footballs, Gran. They're baby dinosaur eggs." '

'Yes well. They're all mad on dinosaurs . . .'

At about half-past seven Louie served mushroom soup, followed by the *spanokopita*. Luckily Emma had encountered the dish at a lunch given by Caro Nettleship, but was put out at finding Louie's tasted better.

'Of course Caro says the ones we make here aren't anything like the proper Greek ones. They make all their own filo pastry.'

'And feta cheese. I used to make a kind of feta once when we kept goats. D'you remember Baba, Tim?'

'Not really.'

But he did. He remembered sitting on a low box with his head pushed up against Baba's flank and his father's big warm hands over his own little ones. When they squeezed a teat a jet of milk came squirting out like a strand of taut white wool. It rang against the side of the pail, slipped down over the metal and ran into a spreading pool with the round edge of a dinner plate. He was always with his father in those days. In London and afterwards in Melbourne he'd ridden on his shoulders, high above the packed heads of the marchers, up among the banners, placards and rising waves of singing. And in the communes they'd always worked together, planting out seedlings, looking after the goats, mending bits of machinery—often with other families but hardly ever with his mother who seemed to be always working somewhere else with other women. Sometimes at night he heard them quarrelling, Louie shouting, 'I slave away all day and I never see you. When did we last go anywhere together? All you ever think about is Tim.'

'More salad?'

Emma was talking about their last trip to Sydney, the party her sister had given, the gorgeous coat she'd bought in Double Bay.

'Did you get a chance to see Stuart?'

'Not really. He was rushing off somewhere to fall in front of a bulldozer. Something like that.'

'He doesn't change much does he?'

Tim avoided his mother's eye. This was the party line. 'Daddy's too busy to care about us.' This was what he'd been told ever since Louie had bundled him up and whisked him away to Hobart. He remembered standing in the window of the old house at the top of Forest Road watching for Stuart's car coming up the hill. He used to shut his eyes and count to ten, promising himself that when he looked again the car would be there with its faded psychedelic whorls and his father's big bearded face pushed forward, peering up through the windscreen.

'He's going to work in Sydney,' Louie had said. 'Well, that's no surprise.'

He wondered sometimes now if she had made that happen, persuading Stuart his son didn't want to see him, just as she'd managed to convince the child at the window that his father was too busy with communes and protest marches to bother about visiting Tasmania. He felt himself pulled about by a deep-running grief, a sense of loss, which seemed to have nothing to do with the bulky aging hippie he met sometimes in a vegetarian restaurant in Ultimo. He looked round quite venomously at Louie's crowded whatnots and old-fashioned pictures in gilt frames. Most of these were genre paintings with titles like 'Married for Love'—a young couple with a baby peeping nervously through the gates of a great house—or 'Letters from Home'—girls in white muslin sitting on some tropical balcony reading their mail. The one he loathed most showed a woman sprawled on a beach with one arm flung out: 'Caught by the Tide'.

'What are you going to do with all this stuff, mother?'

Even Emma was caught off balance, despite the fact that she and Tim had had a long talk about making Louie see sense, put all her affairs in order, clear the junk out of her house and cash in on the craze for old heritage places.

'What d'you mean "do with it"? Why should I want to do anything?'

'Won't you want something a bit smaller now? I mean, you don't want a place this size now you're on your own.'

'Don't I? I can't see why not.'

Tim began to talk about maintenance costs, about reduced income and cutbacks. The pension from George's superannuation scheme wasn't going to stretch to renewing the guttering or getting the roof repainted, leave alone putting in a proper heating system. And she'd said herself that Grandpa Phillips had left her next to nothing. She couldn't just go on refusing to think about the future, frittering her money away . . .'

'I don't fritter. What d'you mean?'

Tim waved a hand contemptuously at the whatnots.

'Well, all this kind of thing. I mean, mother, will it appreciate?'

'That isn't why I buy it. Anyway, I earn quite a bit from writing.'

Tim smiled as though they all knew that Louie's claim to be a writer was just a tax dodge.

'The *Hawk in the Rain*'s still selling quite well.' Louie put down her knife and fork. Her hands were starting to shake. Tim was only a few feet away across her mahogany table but she felt the distance between them was quite immense, that it always had been, even when he was quite little and had wriggled out of her grasp to run after Stuart. Still more in Hobart where, however hard she tried to make them into a twosome, he refused to speak, turned away from the treats she arranged and stared dully at her presents.

'It's nice for you to have an interest,' said Emma. 'But what Tim means is you can't just go on drifting like this. You've got to face up to things.'

'But I can't make any big decisions yet. I need to think about what I'm going to do. I feel just now I don't know who I am or where I belong or anything.'

Another word and Louie might have burst into tears. She thought of them groaning together over the scene when they got home to their bright fashionable house with the round quilted bed and the ensuite bathroom. They didn't care tuppence about her. All they were trying to do was lure her into investing more money in Tim's firm.

'I might go back to England.' Louie looked up in time to see Emma turning on Tim in shocked alarm.

'You think you'd like Mrs Thatcher's Britain?'

'I don't know, Tim. I might.'

'It's terribly expensive in London,' said Emma. 'The dollar's terribly low. Caro says the prices are about what you'd expect if dollars were the same as pounds, but, of course, as it is everything costs double.'

'Well that's my problem. I can stay with relatives, of course.' Louie was almost tempted to let loose the horse dealer and the brewer but in the end kept them to herself. To her surprise she heard her voice saying, 'I'm thinking of writing a kind of family history.'

When Emma and Tim had gone Louie sat by the dying fire drinking the last of the whisky. She watched the lamplight beating down on the seat of George's chair, trying to resist the idea that Tim had sat there out of malice. Always after their visitors had gone she and George would settle down together and he'd take any incident or exchange that might have upset her and show it to her from a different angle so that she could slip free of uncharitableness. When she felt scattered or shaken by the different demands people had made, the different images they held, George could draw her back into herself until she felt secure and confident again in her own place.

Now the only comfort lay in the two surprising ideas that had sprung out of her mouth at the dinner table. The prospect of going back to England was too huge to grapple with at the moment. There were so many pros and cons—like losing Oliver—to be faced and considered. But the prospect of writing the story of the horse dealer, the Chippenham brewer, her grandparents and her father attracted and excited her. If she could take the few bones of fact she had and add more to make a passable skeleton, then flesh it out to make something alive, something in which she could believe, then it might be possible to understand what motives had driven her grandparents and her father, to see where she stood in relation to the dead and perhaps even to the living.

FOUR

Until the sudden appearance of Jane and Cissie Chubb, Susan and Louie had always believed that they had only one first cousin—Frank Gale, the only child of their mother's brother, Richard. Louie thought of him as Dear Old Frank. Her early memories of him were lighted by a kind of Edwardian glow, as though they belonged to a golden afternoon before the world changed forever. All through Louie's early childhood Frank had lived with his parents in a large Georgian house on the corner of Sloe Lane in the village of Ollerton about ten miles north of Bristol. His father had been an engineer at Filton Aircraft Works, a huge collection of buildings that straggled along both sides of a section of the Gloucester Road, their walls and roofs painted throughout the war in camouflage patches of green and muddy brown. Louie could remember these buildings much more clearly than she could remember Uncle Richard, who remained in her mind as a tall, dim, vaguely genial presence bending over the bonnet of a two-tone Rover called Jinny. Usually when she visited Sloe Lane in the school holidays, Uncle Richard had already driven off to Filton in the Rover and only Auntie Peggy and Frank were at home.

Beatrice used to take Susan and Louie out to Ollerton on the bus. There was no pavement where they got off. They could see from the bus step straight down into a ditch full of king-cups and meadowsweet.

'Oh that air!' Beatrice would say, throwing back her head and breathing in the scent of the meadowsweet, while Louie, tilting her own head back further still, stared up into a sky which seemed much larger than the sky in town, and was filled with lark song, high, pure and heady as the blue air itself.

Frank and Auntie Peggy used to wait by their front gate across the road. Their house had a beautiful smell—roses, perhaps, lavender furniture polish and something drier and browner like wrinkled apples. There was always more to eat than they had at home—things like raspberries from the garden, cakes made with real eggs from the Buff Orpingtons, braised rabbit and, best of all, loot that Susan and Louie found for themselves when Frank took them for walks—mushrooms, blackberries, watercress and hazelnuts from the spinney behind the parish hall.

Frank was immensely patient. Although he was in his teens he never seemed to mind spending a day amusing his young cousins. In spring he took them to the bluebell wood or helped them catch jam jars of tadpoles from the pond in the orchard. In autumn he joined them in raking up leaves for a bonfire, and all through the long summer days he played French cricket with them or took them on walks to watch hay being cut or the pigs being fed at the top of Sloe Lane. He didn't talk much but he had some funny sayings that made Louie laugh so hard that once, when she was sitting on a five-barred gate, she fell off into the grass. He looked rather comical in the first place with his woolly red hair and clown's smile so that when he started strutting up and down, as he sometimes did, imitating the vicar or showing them how his house-master used to work himself into rages, the two little girls rocked and shrieked with joy.

One day in the summer of 1944 everything changed. Usually a visit to Ollerton was arranged in advance. There were a couple of days of happy anticipation before Susan and Louie went skipping ahead of their mother all the way down to the bus stop in Gloucester Road. Beatrice was always in the best of spirits, looking forward to a deck-chair on the lawn, easy chat and a wander round the garden with Auntie Peggy. But on this particular day they went off unexpectedly, late in the morning. Beatrice rushed the children into their coats and slammed down the street looking so wrought up that neither of them dared to ask a question. There was no Auntie Peggy waiting by the gate, only Frank who went into the house with Beatrice, leaving Susan and Louie to roam around disconsolately by themselves. A doctor arrived, then a policeman on a bicycle, then two men in raincoats, who drew up in a black car. After an hour or so when all the visitors had gone, Frank came out and leaned against an apple tree. He picked up a stick and flicked vaguely at the long grass.

'Is Auntie Peggy ill?' asked Louie.

'Not really,' said Frank. 'She's just upset. It's Dad. He's gone off.'

Susan looked bewildered. At home it was milk that

went off. Louie wanted to giggle. She thought of people sniffing at Uncle Richard suspiciously.

'He's gone off in the car.'

Susan looked more bewildered than ever. She saw that 'gone off' must mean 'gone away' but Uncle Richard was always away in the car. It was his natural state.

'Don't you know where he's gone?' asked Louie.

Frank shook his head. 'Well, they do know,' he said and stopped, looking as though he might burst into tears. 'But he didn't tell Mum or me.'

He put down his head and walked quickly back to the house. Susan and Louie just hung around in the garden. It was a cold grey day and, for once, there seemed to be nothing to do. Eventually their mother came out, looking very flushed and upset, took them into the kitchen and made jam sandwiches which they ate sitting at one end of the kitchen table still wearing their coats.

Back at Howard Road, late in the evening, Louie heard her parents talking in the kitchen.

'I still can't take it in,' said Beatrice. 'I mean Richard was always so reliable. I daren't think what Father's going to say.'

'Throwing away a job like that . . .'

'And what's poor Peggy supposed to do now? She's talking about moving back up to Hull. I mean, as she said, what on earth does he expect her to say to people?'

'She couldn't manage that place on her own.'

Louie lay in the dark cupboard with tears running down her face and wetting the pillow.

'And Frank'll be called up soon.'

Louie was startled into a loud, blundering sob. She hadn't thought of Frank as an ordinary grown-up person who would have to go and fight in the war. She hated the way everything good and beautiful always came to an end.

After that they never went to Ollerton again. Uncle Richard's name was never mentioned. Frank joined the Royal Army Service Corps, and Auntie Peggy sold up and went to live with her parents. After the war, when Frank was up at Oxford, he arrived in Bristol for a brief visit. Later, when he'd settled in London, he took to calling more frequently. His new job in the Ministry of Housing seemed to involve regular trips to the West Country and every time he drove through Bristol he made a dutiful appearance in Howard Road, but Louie, caught up at the time in working for her Higher School Certificate, and love affairs with Bristol Grammar School boys, barely glimpsed him as he came and went.

In 1952 Frank was a guest at Susan's wedding. In some way that Louie had never managed to fathom he quarrelled so bitterly with the bridegroom—actually punching him in the face while Susan was changing into her going-away outfit—that the McAlisters had never spoken to him since. The breach seemed to make Frank shy of all the Phillipses. Even though Louie wrote to him several times from Cambridge, she had trouble persuading him to meet her in London as she passed through on her way home or stopped over for a night when she travelled back to Newnham after a vacation. When she married Stuart, Frank sent her a Royal Doulton tea service that she'd treasured ever since, but he refused to come to the wedding. Perhaps he didn't want to run into the McAlisters, or perhaps he felt that the Phillipses' weddings affected him strangely. It was hard to say. There was a rather unsuccessful weekend in Sussex when Frank came down to see her just before she and Stuart left for Australia. That was the last time Louie and Frank had met, and through all the years that she'd lived in Tasmania she'd heard very little of him. They'd exchanged

Christmas cards and occasional short letters like the one in which Frank announced that he was taking early retirement from the civil service, axed in the course of Mrs Thatcher's onslaught on the public sector, but it wasn't until after James died that he'd written at any length. His letter of condolence was so kind and friendly that Louie had replied at once. Frank had responded with a picture postcard of the church at Ollerton, establishing herself as a regular correspondent.

On the day after Tim and Emma's visit Louie woke up with the sense that something had changed, that the world without George had become a shade less empty than before. Then she remembered her idea of piecing together a story to explain her father's adoption, and began to think over books she might re-read and others she could order from the library to help her build up a picture of life in the eighteen-nineties. Drinking tea in the kitchen as the morning sky lightened behind Mount Wellington, she began to recall stories of her mother's childhood in the Gales' big Victorian house in Clifton. According to Beatrice, James had visited there as a small boy to help Grandpa Duke wind the clocks, and had run up and down the tennis court with her and her brother Richard.

As soon as she thought of Uncle Richard, Louie began to wonder if Frank would be interested in her project. He seemed to be at a rather loose end since leaving the civil service, and might feel inclined to do some detective work, ferreting out more facts about the family who had moved to Beaumont Street. She wrote at once, putting this suggestion, describing Susan's discoveries and enclosing photocopies of the certificates and the sepia photograph.

Frank went at once to St Jude's in Chippenham. Louie had only just begun to frame the opening of her family's story when his first report arrived.

'Imagine the scene. A grey still Saturday afternoon. Low cloud. Nobody about. Probably all watching football somewhere—and, indeed, from time to time, a faint cheer comes eerily from afar. St Jude's in a very bad way. Grilles over the windows. Cracked paint, the colour of dried blood, on the door. Desolate notice board. Everything locked and nailed up. I feel like the man in that Larkin poem who goes into an empty church—"Hatless, I take off/My cycle-clips in awkward reverence" except that I've come in my old Audi and can't get into the building. Graveyard has a broken gate leaning in brambles. Bottles, newspapers, weeds five feet high. Rising from the jungle, a forest of blackened obelisks and brooding angels. Apparently once an affluent sort of parish. Your intrepid private eye, muttering about Ozymandias and needles in haystacks, goes forward, takes two steps, looks to the right. And there it is—your great-grandfather's tomb! "Sacred to the memory of Tobias Henry Barker beloved husband of Minerva Jane who departed this life on 4 December 1894 in his fifty-fifth year. He lived respected as a truly kind and just man and died lamented by all." A simply enormous angel leaning on a sword—sandalled feet, gigantic wings but rather knocked about. And then, among the grass and thistles, another tomb! Very different, very small and plain. "Julia Mary Barker born 3 February 1869, departed this life 22 June 1897. The Lord giveth and the Lord taketh away." Tobias's daughter do you think? A sister to Grandmother Kate? I hunted for more Barkers and found Minerva Jane, died 18 May 1880. A nondescript kind of stone. Went to Lacock to look for Phillipses but couldn't find a thing. All very different here—a spotless church, shaven lawns, ancient tombs of landed gentry. Not a horse dealer in sight. Never fear, I'll track down the parish register next time . . .

'Since I was in Chippenham I thought I'd look up a chap I knew at Oxford, Teddy Gascoigne. Grandfather Gale acted for the Gascoignes for donkey's years and put me in touch with Teddy. Really good man. Lives in a village a few miles south of the town. House a bit run down like the graveyard but pretty grand in the old days. Teddy's grandfather was part of the Prince of Wales's set and had HRH there for shooting parties. Also kept racehorses and yachts which proved his undoing. According to Teddy his grandparents—still in the prime of life and very dashing—were drowned in the Celtic Sea. Their yacht the *Ariadne* just sank like a stone. Not a cloud in the sky, not a breath of wind, but down she went and nobody left to tell the tale but a chef's apprentice who never recovered his wits.

'To resume. Teddy's father is still going strong at 92— luckily left at home with his nannies when his parents went on their cruise. Very helpful. Remembers Old Howard coming to the house to see his aunt on family business. One for the girls, he said. Poor old Grandma. What a life he must have led her. Not that things were very gay at Bathurst Hall after the tragedy. No more balls and shooting parties of course. Old Gascoigne couldn't remember anything about Tobias or Julia Barker. Died when he was an infant. But recalls his father grumbling about the brewery closing down. Swore by Barker's Ale apparently. And he definitely remembers Aunt Elfreda talking about Grandmother Kate. Thinks she took a fancy to her and brought her to the Hall when she was young and single. The oddest thing, though, is that he knew Mr

Duke and your father. They used to come to the house to see to all the clocks. Presumably on Old Howard's recommendation. Or because Aunt Elfreda had known Kate. Or both. Sometimes they brought a man called Bertoli and went on butterfly hunts.

'The Gascoignes were terrifically hospitable. Pressed me to stay the night and took me up to the attic to look through Aunt Elfreda's photos. Trunks of them. Lots of her as a late-Victorian beauty though she turned down all her suitors. Devoted her life to her orphaned nephews and nieces. There are a couple of her with a girl who might be Kate. She looks a bit like the woman in your photocopy but it's too smudgy to tell. Had to come away before we'd looked through everything. Will go back later. More there, I think, than meets the eye . . .'

Although Frank seemed to scent a mystery, there was nothing so very strange in all this. Louie thought of Emma Woodhouse taking up with Harriet Smith. There must have been plenty of upper-class women in the nineteenth century who'd selected some pretty, promising girl from a lower caste to act as a companion and protégé. Someone who could be improved, refined, advanced, shown off. An artistic creation more satisfying than any number of sketches or watercolours, a proof of charitable works more flattering than any Sunday school or missionary society. Only Kate Barker had refused to play the game, running off with her lowborn commercial clerk and getting pregnant. Louie liked her grandmother better for eluding the domineering Elfreda so that the face in the sepia photograph changed again. And yet again when only a few days later Frank's second report arrived.

This time there were copies of the birth certificates of all James's four siblings. Violet, Gilbert and Charles had all been born in Hampstead and Anne Louisa at 46 Beaumont Street, Holborn.

'So I was right,' thought Louie triumphantly. 'They did move house.' But she'd been wrong about the ages of the two little children in the photograph. Charles had been born in 1895, Annie two years later. So instead of ridding themselves of their eldest son and going on to replace him with two other children, John and Kate Phillips had let James go only when Kate was already expecting their last child. Everything seemed to be falling into place. The contrast between Tobias's tomb and Julia's, like the move to Holborn, suggested that the brewer's family had fallen on hard times. With four young children to feed and another on the way they could well have felt desperate enough to let their son go to a couple whose prospects looked so much better than their own.

Frank, it turned out, had paid a visit to Beaumont Street, now part of Islington. 'Very dreary. Probably nine-tenths destroyed in the Blitz. One side taken up by a school, half the other by nasty fiftyish flats. But a few houses from the nineteenth century still standing. Not 46, though the whole street would have been much the same once. Grim, grimy places. Three storeys but very cramped. Backyards probably full of broken bottles. All a far cry from Tobias's pompous angel.'

That afternoon Louie began to write. There was a great deal she didn't know, a great deal even Frank would never find out, but she was eager now to start off with her little stock of facts to see where the trail her characters made would lead.

'Done well for yourself,' said Old George, sucking in his cheeks, laughing in his nose. 'There's always money in brewing.'

His son made no reply. The cottage was even more dank and dirty than it had been in his childhood. There was straw scattered over the floor and the damp smell of horses still permeated everything, though it was years since Old George had given up any real pretence of dealing.

'And they say old Barker's not got long to live. Bad lungs. Consumption in the family.'

At this the younger man got up and walked to the crooked little window that looked out on a square of unkempt garden. He was still carrying his bowler hat, but put it down on the stone embrasure to rub his palms on his trousers as though he had touched something disagreeable.

'I'm not saying your young woman looks chesty.'

When this produced no response, the father got up and made a great business of poking the fire.

'What d'you come here for if you got nothing to say for yourself?'

'I came to tell you I'll be marrying Kate Barker next month.'

'Well you've done that and I've said I'm glad for you.' Old George sat back in his chair.

'You never know, you might come into the business. That'd beat clerking, wouldn't it? Might even be able to do something for your old father.'

'I don't give tuppence for the business,' said the young man hotly. 'I'll make my own way. It's not that I don't care what becomes of you, Father. You know what I mean very well.'

'Course I do,' said the old man, beginning to grin and enjoy himself. 'You just want to get off to Chippenham and play the lord, turning your nose up at where the money comes from just so you've got it to spend.'

'You're not saying I've ever had money from you I hope.'

'Ah, well, so that's what your fine feelings come to, throwing your own father's poverty back in his face.'

For a moment Old George was afraid that he'd gone too far, that John might begin to shout about his mother's death, the misery of his youth, loneliness, hunger and strappings, that he might spring round and overturn the table or even strike his father where he sat. But the moment passed, the young man only said something under his breath and started abruptly for the door. The old one shambled after him, weak and whining, but by the time he got to the doorway, John, his hat on his head, was already at the gate.

'I'll be there at the wedding,' called the father, with a last little glint of malice, but the son, trim, dark-suited and solitary, was almost out of earshot, striding away up the cobbled lane.

❧

Kate's dream began just before her father's death and continued through the months in which the facade of cheerful prosperity that the Chippenham brewer had erected to shelter his family was slowly dismantled. She dreamed that she was walking on a long sandy beach, a little like the one at Weston-super-Mare, except that trees grew down to the sand and there was no sign of human habitation. From far away she saw a hump on the level surface of the beach and began to move towards it. At first she thought it was a sack, then a dead seal, then a bundle of clothes, but as she came nearer she saw the hump was made by the swathed hips of a woman, prone on the sand. She saw the skirt, sodden but still a pale, washed-out blue, wrapped over the thighs, and one bare leg and foot, heavy and white as marble, stretched out towards her. The woman seemed larger than a normal human being, although her clothes and hair, falling free from a loose knot, were dolefully unselfconscious and ordinary. She lay on her side as though asleep and had not long been dead, because when Kate pulled at her bodice sleeve, she flopped over and stared up with wide-open, china-blue eyes. The broad white arm lay quite unmarked at Kate's feet. The fingers with clean, short nails and dryish lines at the joints curled in upon the palm. There was nothing terrible about her except for the sand that clogged her clothes and strings of hair, the abandoned sprawl of her limbs, and the utter vacancy of her gaze.

So vivid was this dream that, at first, Kate feared it as an omen. Although the drowned woman was a stranger, Kate felt sure that soon she would meet her, alive or dead. She was tormented by the idea that she had no way of warning the woman of her fate, or that the warning would come too late. Then it struck her that there was something old-fashioned about the woman's clothes and this, together with the oddity of the tree-fringed beach, made her think that the dream might come from the past; that the drowning, which she never doubted must be real, might have happened years before in some place now changed beyond recognition. This idea comforted her for a time, but in the end seemed only to deepen the mystery, to make the message, which Kate felt was being insistently relayed to her, still harder to decipher.

John, in the early days, accepted Kate's trouble as his own and, like her, never doubted that the drowned woman was living, or had lived, upon the earth, that the beach where she lay was waiting somewhere for them to walk upon. But as time went on and the hard facts of everyday existence became steadily more daunting, John began to fume against the dream. Because it had started to visit Kate not long before the death of his father-in-law, he began to think of it as in some way a cause of that event and of all the disasters that had followed in its train. Gradually the dream became the emblem of everything in the Barkers that he blamed for his predicament—their self-indulgence, their lack of commonsense, their criminal neglect of the real world of duty and responsibility to those who relied on them. At the same time he began to think of the family to which he had allied himself as one that was uncannily unfortunate, dogged by ill-health and ill-luck, singled out by some malicious force as mysterious and inaccessible as the dream itself. What enraged him was that both the force and the dream must always remain impervious to his grievance, his righteous anger at the failure of promises he had never sought to exact but which he had been seduced into accepting until, little by little, he had come to depend upon them absolutely.

∾

'We shall miss Kate,' said Miss Barker, sewing away by the drawing room fire as she always did on winter evenings. 'And I don't like to think of her trying to manage in London on her own with no-one to turn to.'

It was the day after the wedding at St Jude's Church. The festivities were over, the young couple had driven away to take a train to Bournemouth, and the house that they had left behind seemed extraordinarily large and quiet. But Miss Barker's brother, indefatigable in making the best of things, jumped up rubbing his hands.

'They'll do very well,' he said, pacing about as though he had some delightful surprise to reveal, some thrilling secret that would not allow him to sit still. 'Just wait till you see their house, Martha. What a stroke of luck that was! You should have seen their faces that day we first went there. I didn't let on, you see, gave them a tale about having to make a call. And Kate said, "Just look at those roses, John, I do believe they're Gloire de Dijon, my very favourite!" And I said, "Hmm, not such a bad little place, I suppose. I just wonder if it would suit a young couple with the young man starting in the City. Not too far out, d'you think?" And Kate—she knows her father, of course— burst out laughing but John still didn't twig and looked at me as solemn as a judge. So I brought out the key and just said, "There you are. It's yours. Ten-year lease, all settled. What do you think?" Well, they couldn't believe it! Went all over the house, running up and down the stairs like a pair of children. Didn't know what to say to me. Young John he shook my hand and there were tears in his eyes. He was lost for words.'

'So I should think,' said Miss Barker grimly, 'considering where he was dragged up. Did you ever see such a sight as that old father of his yesterday? Coming to the wedding in his moleskins! He did it on purpose to shame us, be sure of that.'

'Now, Martha. He's not such a bad fellow at heart.'

'I don't know, Toby.' Miss Barker put down her sewing and took out a handkerchief. 'Sometimes you try me beyond endurance. There's your eldest daughter, one of the prettiest girls in the place, married to some little pen-pusher without a penny to his name and gipsy blood, and you go on as if you'd won a fortune. Kate could've had anyone she fancied, the highest in the land. There was young Mr Gascoigne head over heels last year. Think of it! Mistress of Bathurst Hall she'd have been in a few years' time! And what does she do? She throws herself away on that Phillips. Phillips! Everyone in Lacock knows that drunken old villain. Horse dealer indeed! Horse thief more like.'

Tobias looked quite amazed. He was a small, sandy man with prominent blue eyes and a high colour that now grew a trifle brighter. He stared at his weeping sister for some seconds, then came and patted her awkwardly on the shoulder.

'This isn't like you, old girl. You're tired, need a change. The wedding's been too much for you, all that work and worry. But don't take it out on young John. The Phillipses have lived in Lacock for donkey's years. They're no more gipsies than we are.'

'A twopenny-ha'penny junior clerk who'll fall into whatever place he can get,' sobbed Martha. 'There's thousands can be got to do his work for seven shillings a week.'

'Now, now, now! He's a good young fellow, you must see that. He's taught himself to keep books all by his own efforts. Bert Beddoes thinks the world of him. And just look at the company! Nothing but a burial club with half-a-dozen agents a few years back and now they're opening an office in London! Insuring anything you want! And they want the boy there! Think of that! I wouldn't be surprised if he goes to the top of the tree. I'd have liked him in the business with me—you know that—but he wouldn't have it. And I admire him for it. He knows what he's after. Independent spirit! You'll see.'

'Yes well,' said Martha, wiping her nose and bundling the handkerchief away. 'I hope you're right. Kate's a dear girl but it isn't as though she'd been brought up to know the value of money. And they'll have to watch the pennies to start off with even if he does make something of himself later on.'

'Oh they'll do very well,' beamed Tobias, jumping up again. 'Don't you worry about that! All they need's a bit of help to start off and I'll see to that.'

'I won't ask what you've done for Kate on top of getting her a house. Some sort of a settlement is only right, but if I know you, Toby, you'll have overdone it, and, since I've started to speak my mind for once, I'd better tell you that you worry me to death, the whole lot of you. Kate's got no idea of money and how she'll get on with servants nobody knows from Adam bleeding her white I can't think. But Julia's forty times worse. Delicate she may be, but even delicate people can give a thought to others once in a while. And you're worse than both girls put together. Presents and parcels! Parties for this, dinners for that! Christmas trees, free beer at the brewery! Trips here, trips there! Off to London, off to Margate, off to Switzerland for Julia's lungs! And the clothes! Those girls have more clothes than the Queen, and nothing but the best, of course. I try to keep things in hand but it's like banging my head on the wall. I order two pound of brisket and in comes a boy with a brace of pheasant that happened to catch your eye. And as for the waste at the wedding, it doesn't bear thinking of. Ever since Minnie died, ever since you asked me to come and keep house for you, I've wondered how the business ever stands it. The way you go on you'd think it was a bottomless pit, but if you run the brewery the way you run everything else it's a black lookout for us all and I'm sure Father would turn in his grave!'

By now Martha had worked herself up into a fresh spate of tears. Out came the handkerchief again. Tobias, surprised into a temper, stamped his foot.

'That's a lot of nonsense! Keep to your concerns, woman, and leave me to mine.'

'It is my concern. If we're all to end up penniless out in the gutter it is my concern. You asked me here to care for the girls. D'you think I want to see them left with nothing? D'you think I want to end up in the workhouse? On top of it all you're a sick man, Toby, though you won't admit it. And what's to become of us all if you drop dead?'

'What tripe! Tripe! Stuff! Absolute tripe! You don't know what you're talking about!'

In his indignation Tobias began to cannon about the room, banging into the furniture. He knocked over an ormolu vase, snatched it up and dashed it among the fire-irons. There was a long silence.

'Well there,' said Martha, 'I've said my piece at last. Not that you'll take any notice.'

She got up and swept the fragments of vase into a shovel. Tobias stood and watched her.

'I'm not ill,' he said at last. 'I got over that weakness I had as a boy and that bit of trouble last winter was nothing much. I'm good for a few years yet.'

Afterwards they embraced rather formally and foolishly, and went downstairs to eat some cold supper together, but nothing was quite the same between them ever after.

∾

The day had been oppressively hot. Some of the guests at the christening party had remarked that there was thunder in the air and, as evening approached, there was a muttering in the darkening sky to the west.

'The wind's getting up,' said Kate. 'It'll bring the fruit down. What a shame!'

Suddenly, without reason, tears came to her eyes and her throat ached. She leaned her forehead against the cool glass of the window and squeezed her lids shut.

'But it all went very well, don't you think?' she asked in a thin voice.

John was sitting on the sofa, unbuttoning his waistcoat. His high collar and dark jacket lay on the cushions beside him. Stripped to his shirt and braces he looked like a young prize-fighter taking his ease in the dusk.

'You're done up,' he said and came and put his arms round Kate's waist, resting his chin on her wreaths of hair. 'Went well? I should say so. I never saw such a spread. Enough to feed the British army.'

'We'd have had enough without what Pa brought. We might have known he'd do something like that.' Overcoming the threat of tears, she laughed and began to recite: 'Ham and pickles, all those preserves, pink sugar biscuits, macaroons, salmon . . .'

'Strawberries and cream.'

'Cheddar, Stilton, and what about that cake?'

'It won't go to waste will it?'

'No, no. I told Cook we'd just have something cold for supper. Eat up the leftovers. You don't mind that, do you? And she and Lily can finish up anything that won't keep.'

Kate sighed and lifted one hand wanderingly to touch her husband's neck. 'Baby was good, wasn't he?'

'Good as gold, and Violet. But it was Jimmy stole the show.'

'True to form,' said Kate a little dryly. 'As far as you're concerned at any rate. He wasn't good all the time though. He got under the table once and started poking out at people's legs and dresses with a fork. Aunt Martha caught him at it and sent him off to Lily with a flea in his ear.'

'I didn't see that.'

'You were too busy with the Beddoeses. I suppose you heard all about the honeymoon.'

John clicked his tongue in exasperation. 'We sha'n't get anything else this side of Christmas. You should've heard that Nutting chap. How they dropped in on Captain This and had

61

a splendid day's fishing with the Honourable Somebody Else. "D'you fish, Phillips?" he says to me and I thought, "I've taken more trout tickling than you'll ever see, my lad, for all your fancy rods and flies." And May just stood there, silly as ever, going, "Yes, Cyril, no, Cyril." Mr and Mrs B were near as bad. "Oh, you are a one, Cyril!" goes old Flo and he looks at her as though she's common as dirt, though she never saw it. You'd think they'd have more sense.'

'You'll have to get on with him somehow, Johnny. May came over and asked us out with them all next Friday. We're going to the St James's to see *The Masqueraders* and there's supper after at the Café Royal.'

'The Café Royal! Oysters at four bob a dozen! That bugger wants to see if we're up to it.'

'It's Mr B's treat. It's a welcome home party for May and Cyril.'

'And I suppose later on we'll be having them here for dinner. And Cyril'll go on like he did today, picking about into everything, poking about. When he isn't blowing his own trumpet that is. D'you know what he said to me? "What a splendid little place you've got here, Phillips! Quite a little rural retreat! Been here six years, have you? Well, well, well! And I suppose the value's gone up no end. So convenient! You'd only need a small staff—three or four servants—in a handy little place like this. Only two have you? Dear me!" I could've shoved his cake down his damned throat.'

'I expect it's just his way. He doesn't mean any harm.'

'Don't you believe it. He'll be coming into the firm as sure as eggs. And he's the chartered accountant, he's the son-in-law, he's the one'll be giving me orders before he's been there five minutes.'

'The rain's coming,' said Kate. 'Just look at that!'

All at once the darkening garden was almost blotted out by

a deluge of roaring water. The flailing apple and cherry trees struggled under the onslaught, the gravel became a mass of prancing fountains. A flash of lightning, jagged as a child's drawing, leaped for an instant somewhere over the trees, there and gone so quickly that the couple at the window were hardly sure if they had really seen it. Then thunder banged overhead like breaking timbers.

'I'd better go up,' said Kate and hurried off to see if the children had woken. She went down the dark hall, looked in on Lily and Cook, drinking tea at the kitchen table, and began to climb through the thrumming gloom to the top of the house. The whole building was quivering under the storm, and at each turn of the stairs the hectic, lolloping sound of water, cascading down past the windows from the roof, sounded over the steady roar of the rain. But Gilbert was still fast asleep in his cradle and, in the nursery next door, Violet's arms were flung out across her pillow, the fingers of one small hand curled in on the palm. The children looked so solid and shining with their curls and round white arms and their mouths like red flowers that Kate felt close to weeping all over again. She quickly settled the covers on each bed and, lifting her heavy skirt in both hands, set off back down the stairs.

As she went down, step by step, the noise of the downpour welled up all around her so that it seemed that she was descending, remote and alone, through some cave that led to the very depths of the sea; that the hallway, when she reached it, was the ocean bed where the noise of wind and waves was muted at last. So it was strange to open the drawing room door and to find that John had lit the gas and was sitting in the brightness, leafing through one of his books on political economy. He often read such things in a hunger for self-improvement that had long ago driven him on beyond double-entry bookkeeping.

'All dead to the world,' said Kate, and when John only nodded and went on brooding over his book, she looked at him more closely to see if he was still angry about Cyril Nutting. She sat on a hassock, close up against his knee, and took his hand.

'It'll be all right, my dearest. It's you helped Mr B get where he is. He knows that. And look at all they've done for us since we came to London—taking us out all the time, inviting us to everything. They're our friends. They're not going to pass you over.'

'That Nutting'd pass me over in a four-wheeler if he didn't think I'd bring in capital. What does he care what I've done or what I am? All he thinks about is what I'm worth. And, speaking of that, what really stuck in my throat was the way he made up to your father.'

'Poor Pa!' said Kate. 'He didn't look too well today, I thought. Aunt Martha said he'd been a bit poorly lately.'

'That Nutting's enough to make anyone feel poorly.'

'I wish we could've put Pa up here. I'd like to keep an eye on him for a bit. I love this place, Johnny, but we could do with more room, you know.'

'Well, we'll have to make do for now. Till I can see my way clear at any rate. If their precious Cyril takes over I might be nothing but a glorified clerk on four quid a week till they put me out to grass.'

'Oh, don't be a silly!' said Kate, beginning to lose patience. 'It's all understood. Mrs B's always saying you're like a son to them. I always thought she had her eye on you for May.'

'Not likely! I was walking out with you when May was still in pinnies. Anyway they've got someone a cut above me now and I'll be playing second fiddle from here on.'

'Ah, well,' said Kate, almost giving up. 'Julia seemed to like him well enough.'

'Wouldn't she just! They'd get on like a house on fire those two. I saw him hanging round her, trying to worm out everything. And she went prattling all our business, you can depend on that: "Oh I never bother my pretty little head with money, but I do know Papa gives my sister a huge allowance because she's married to that low Phillips fellow who hasn't got a penny to bless himself with and was born in a ditch."'

'Oh Johnny, leave it, do. It'll all turn out all right, you know very well.'

John nearly spoke again, but contented himself with tossing his book aside and grimly folding his arms.

'I could wear my new evening cloak on Friday,' said Kate after a few minutes. 'With my blue velvet. Or should I wear that French silk with the ivory flowers?'

'What's it we're going to see?' said John, still grumpy. 'Half those plays Flo's mad about give me the pip.' Then suddenly he laughed. 'I tell you what, the best part of it's always going up the steps with you on my arm. I've seen women done up in diamonds from head to foot go green at the sight of you, and there's not a man in the place tries not to stare.'

This made Kate laugh and blush. They were almost happy again, but that was the night Kate dreamed for the first time of the woman on the beach.

∾

Tobias Barker died on 4 December 1894 at half-past nine in the evening. In the end it was not his weak lungs that killed him but his weak heart which gave out just as he was reaching forward to take a glass of hot negus from his sister's hand.

'You know how I make it up,' said Martha to Kate afterwards. 'Sherry, hot water, sugar, lemon and just a dash of nutmeg. I get them to bring up a tray just before bedtime and make it up myself from the spirit kettle. Your Pa would never touch anything else after his dinner. I always thought it did him a lot of good, and I told him not to disturb himself, that I'd bring him the glass, but he never took a blind bit of notice of anything I said.'

For Kate the most distressing aspect of the affair was that, after a long autumn of travelling up and down to Chippenham and of staying on in her father's house for up to a fortnight whenever he took a turn for the worse, she was back in London on the day of his death. That morning she had written to Aunt Martha, rejoicing that Tobias seemed much improved. 'We are all so happy,' she wrote, 'that Pa will be strong enough to enjoy Christmas.'

As it was, Christmas was a time of gloom. It was not simply that his family mourned the brewer's passing. Even before the funeral, everyone gathered in the big Chippenham house seemed to enter a different dimension in which certainties were all at once uncertain, the messages relayed by objects changed, the character of familiar rooms reversed. Sometimes when Kate was walking about the house she would turn through the wrong doorway and stand astonished at the sight of her own sad face in an unexpected looking-glass.

As Aunt Martha had predicted, her brother had made no provision for his own funeral. John Phillips paid for everything, insisting on a grand cortège, a sumptuous coffin and a monument, topped by a marble angel, fit for a member of parliament, but all this lavishness, so much in Tobias's own style, served only to produce an effect that was both eerie and dispiriting.

The will contained no surprises beyond the number of small legacies for employees, old servants, friends and acquaintances. Generous provision was made for Martha; the remainder of the estate was to be divided between the brewer's two daughters. Although Martha wept at the thought of the family business passing into strange hands, even she agreed that the brewery should be sold.

'And the house,' said Julia. 'Horrid old place! I fancy I shall take a villa on Lake Como.'

Her aunt made no objection. She had a little money of her own from her father and with this and her new legacy would be very comfortably off. She planned to buy a house in Cobham close to the home of her oldest friend, now married to a retired clergyman.

All this was quickly settled, but no sooner had the plans been laid than Mr Finnigan, a partner in the family's firm of solicitors, arrived to disrupt them. The brewery and the house, it seemed, were both heavily mortgaged. Once the properties had been sold the amount remaining to the beneficiaries under the will would not be large. At least, said Mr Finnigan, for the time being. There were other assets— parcels of shares, amounts deposited in various bank accounts, a number of interests in such enterprises as a printing works and a small pottery, even a pair of racehorses in training near Goodwood. The brewer had squirrelled away a remarkable number of nuts, a diverse store of joyful surprises to be whisked out one by one on suitable occasions, but gathering the hoard and settling certain claims against the estate would take time. The matter was a complicated one.

'In the meantime,' said Mr Finnigan, shuffling his papers, embarrassed and apologetic, 'it will hardly be possible to continue the payment of Mrs Phillips's allowance and it would certainly be preferable, simply until things are a little clearer, if some arrangement could be made whereby Miss Barker—indeed both Miss Barker and Miss Julia—might perhaps be provided for without actually drawing further upon the estate at this time.'

Aunt Martha took this remarkably well. She had, she declared, seen it coming all along. She would still go to Cobham, take a cottage and manage well enough on her own small income. She even offered to make a home for Julia, but her niece flew into a temper at the very idea.

'How on earth could she imagine that I'd agree to bury myself in such a place?' said Julia to Kate. 'Can you think of anything more dreadful than being shut up with the Aunt in some poky little hovel? It's been quite bad enough having to endure her here for all these years. And it's no good anyone telling me that it wouldn't be for long, only until Papa's affairs are settled, because a single day in that place would drive me demented. I shall come to you, Kate, just until I can set off for Italy. A winter in London is hardly the best thing for me, I know, but I'm sure I'd manage if you were to move further out. Richmond is perfectly healthy, I believe, and there are some quite suitable houses there.'

'But Julia,' said Kate, 'we can't think of moving until we know what we can afford.'

'Oh, fuss, fuss, fuss! Fuss and nonsense! We can't be expected to know why Papa mortgaged things. Probably it was to buy more shares or something of the kind. It's simply absurd to go on as though he were bankrupt. If there'd been any trouble he'd have said something about it, he'd have done something. He wouldn't just leave us to discover that we're paupers. And can you imagine that he'd give away all that money to the brewery people and the Aunt and heaven knows who else unless there were enough for me to be properly cared for? And I really do think, Kate, that you ought to take account of Papa's wishes. I'm sure he wouldn't like to think of me battling for breath in that ridiculous little box of yours with all those noisy children ruining my nerves all day just because you—or your husband, I should say—have got it into your head that Papa managed somehow to run through the whole of our fortune.'

But John, of course, stood firm. He groaned when Kate put it to him that it was impossible for Julia to live at Cobham, but after that accepted Julia's support as something he must undertake to settle a debt. The cessation of Kate's allowance, though, had suddenly cut the Phillipses' income by three-fifths, so that John was left to keep a family of six, the house in Hampstead and two servants on his own salary of a little over two hundred pounds a year. His employer, Mr Beddoes, quickly saw how the land must lie and offered John a loan.

'Don't you worry,' he said. 'I grew up with Toby Barker. He had the golden touch you know. We've done well enough in our own way, but he had what I'd call a flair for business. You might think he'd overreached himself, then "Hey presto!" he'd pull it off again. If he mortgaged the house it would be because he knew he could double his money somewhere. I'm not surprised he's got the lawyers foxed, but mark my words, when they get it all totted up there'll be enough to buy a dozen houses—half Chippenham I shouldn't wonder. So take five hundred, my boy, just to tide you over.'

John, despite his dislike of relying on the Barker money, believed in his heart of hearts that Mr Beddoes was right, so he took the five hundred pounds, paid the bill for his father-in-law's tomb, made Julia a monthly dress allowance, and settled down to wait.

∾

After many months, simply because it had been repeated so often, Kate's dream began to change. During the day she would often try to picture and scrutinise certain details so that, at night, she sometimes arrived on the beach with the determination to explore her surroundings still strong in her mind. But when she moved towards the dense belt of trees that grew above the sand, she found that a coloured picture of palm trees with huge serrated fronds swam up before her eyes, or that she was confronted by the shiny speckled laurels that had grown in her father's shrubbery at Chippenham. Even while dreaming, Kate knew that there was something irrational in this, but she could never overcome the impediment, never move up among the trees beyond the beach to touch and stare at their mysterious foliage. So the high shadowy greenness that waited always on her left as she walked towards the drowned woman remained indefinite, a presence without a pattern.

When she saw the hump that would prove to be the woman's body, Kate never knew exactly what it was, but after many dreams she knew at least that she wanted very much not to begin the inevitable walk along the shore. She no longer believed that the hump was a sack or a dead seal, but only hoped that it might not be something dreadful; and then, as the months passed, she yearned wistfully after such lost, innocent chances. Confronted inexorably with the heavy body and dead face, she began to feel a terrible sense of bereavement. After gazing at the drowned woman time after time she became so familiar with every detail of her appearance that to see her became much like seeing the corpse of someone known and dear in life. Accordingly when the white arm flopped at Kate's feet and the blue, sightless eyes met her own, she would cry out in appalled recognition and fall on the sand beside the body weeping in an ecstasy of grief. Afterwards she would wake in the dark little bedroom of the crowded house where she and John were dragging along together and find that she was still sobbing and that her husband, in a fury, was stirring and jerking his pillow. Then she would lie quietly in the dark, listening to the plaintive sounds of the night, while the ghostly pain of her dream flowed into the multiple pressing forms of loss that afflicted her daily life. Often in the winter she would lie like that for an hour with the withering cold on her face until, bitterly, she would turn on her side with her back to the turned back in the bed beside her and breathe and breathe, recalling the time of love and pleasure that had been taken from her.

∾

Early in the new year Mr Finnigan wrote asking John to come to Chippenham to look over certain papers. The invitation brought about what was to be the first of many such journeys. In the beginning the excursions always caused a stir of excitement in the Phillips household. Every two weeks or so, all through the late winter and early spring, Kate would go with John to Paddington to see him off. John would mount briskly into the train, turn and let down the window by its broad leather strap, then peer up and down the platform as though among the fog and steam that enveloped the crowds of travellers he might find some answer to the bald little questions that Kate persisted in asking.

'Do you think there'll be any real news this time? Are you sure Mr Finnigan knows what he's about?'

Only when the guard began to blow his whistle and wave his flag would John look straight down at his wife, smile and squeeze her hands. Then he would lean out of the window, waving slowly, until Kate's straight figure and smart little hat were lost to view. But as spring gave way to summer Kate

71

stopped coming to the station. She was pregnant again, listless and often ill. Moreover, she had given up asking questions to which her husband seemed unable to reply.

Despite his anxieties, John always enjoyed the journey to Chippenham. As time went on he came to know very well that what he found at his journey's end was likely to leave him more frustrated and pessimistic than ever, but the steady movement of the train still gave him a sense of energy, of getting somewhere at last. He also liked the feeling of overseeing the country and, as the seasons advanced, of marking its changes. On his first journey in January the fields lay barred with puddles that held the pale light of the sky and the gateways were churned to mud by the hooves of cattle. Here and there he saw patches of white frost under the bare hedgerows, or a tangle of yellow osiers marking the course of a brook, or the black tracery of elms, their crowns clotted with rooks' nests, standing up against a waste of chilly cloud. Now and again a man leading a horse or someone with a dog at his heels walking up a lane would turn and look after the train. Sometimes there were villages—a church spire showing over the shoulder of a hill and threads of smoke going up from cottage chimneys—and John would think of the people there, the shepherds, carters and labourers, many of whom would never travel as far from their homes as the places that ran by while he was still picturing their lives; how boots dried hard by the fire would be pulled on at dawn over chilblains or how, when dinnertime came, the men would crouch in the cold with sacks thrown over their shoulders to eat their hunks of bread and bits of bacon.

Such a life might well have been his own lot had he not set out on a different path and made the most of his chances. As he sat in his warm, softly rocking corner, shielded by glass from the frost and mud, this reflection gave an edge to his pity for those who were trapped and static, feeling the bite of the wind and the freezing touch of iron implements. Yet he was well aware that even the best and wisest of the field workers, had they heard of his rise in the world, would regard it with suspicion, knowing nothing of what it meant to work with books, and looking askance at anyone who enjoyed the gentry's pleasures without being gentry.

'What do they know?' he thought angrily as his mind turned back to the burdens that he bore, the uncertainties of the future, his debts and obligations. All the same, unenviable though his plight might be, he was quite determined that, whatever happened, he would never fall back to a tied cottage and seven and six a week. He would work twenty-four hours a day before Kate came down to hauling water a quarter of a mile or Jimmy and Violet were put to picking up stones in the fields for six shillings a cartload. Not that such things were possible, he thought, for just as the labourers knew nothing of business troubles so his family had no conception at all of life on the land. He saw with a sudden pang of disloyalty that the struggle that had worn down his mother would destroy Kate much more quickly, lost as she was to self-indulgent softness and crazy dreams. There was certainly no going down for him and his family now, but equally surely there might be no going up. For a moment, safe in his train, John felt the vertigo of a man trapped on a cliff face, unable to do anything but cling by his fingernails to shallow, fraying handholds in the rock.

In Chippenham Mr Finnigan made him welcome, bearing him off to luncheon at a nearby chophouse. Afterwards they settled one on each side of a table in the lawyer's office and Finnigan began to explain what progress he had made so far in unravelling Tobias Barker's affairs, from time to time

73

punctuating his discourse by whisking a document from a file at his elbow and passing it over for John to read. Outside a sleety rain had begun to fall, but in the office grate a coal fire burned brightly so that a sense of cosiness developed, made all the stronger by the absorbing nature of the work in which the two young men were engaged.

From the start solicitor and client liked each other and worked together well. Once Finnigan understood that John Phillips could take the facts in quickly and expected no soothing reassurance he lost his nervousness and for the most part spoke briskly and frankly.

'The brewery was in trouble, there's no doubt of that. Mr Barker paid his way in the town but only by raising money from further afield. Up until four or five years ago he'd done very well with his investments. He was quite well known for it, of course, and this, I suppose, encouraged him to embark upon more ambitious schemes of which, I must assure you, this firm had no knowledge at all.'

'This company he bought, the St Albans Brewing Company, that was bankrupt was it?'

'Oh yes. It was simply up for sale for what it would fetch. But Mr Barker raised the wind one way and another, partly with money from Windsor O'Rourke, the financier—you probably know of him—and here he is with a new company coming out for a cool hundred thousand. But here, you see, the Committee of the Stock Exchange complicated matters by refusing to allow the shares to be dealt in.'

Keeping his eyes on his reading, John held out his hand for the next document and the next. The last he studied for some minutes with a look of incredulity.

'But it seems from this that he paid twelve per cent on the ordinary shares after the first year's trading and issued another hundred thousand worth.'

'Indeed, yes. Whether the dividend was paid out of capital I'm afraid we may never know.'

'What about the other directors? Who's this Sir Isaac Henry?'

'A very elderly gentleman. I understand that he died last year at the age of ninety-five.'

'The others must have been blind, deaf and dumb.'

'Certainly so. Since it does seem that Mr Barker, finding the need to travel abroad . . .'

'Put his hand in the till.'

'Thereafter,' said Finnigan, becoming a little flurried, 'he formed another company—the Anglo-Swiss Brewing Company—but its capital issue went flat. There also seems to have been some sense of grievance among some of the shareholders, who found that Mr Barker had contracted to sell to Anglo-Swiss certain properties that he had bought for a considerably lower amount.'

John put his head in his hands. His chief feeling was one of furious anger at having been so thoroughly duped and at how Kate had lavished her love on a father who had utterly deceived her. And how was he to tell her what had happened? Almost as soon as the question came to him, he knew that she would refuse to believe what he said, and for the second time on that bleak January day his love for his wife was blown through by a cold gust of contempt for her insoluble attachment to illusion.

'What about the St Albans Company?' he asked after a moment.

'Yes, well, after the first year's balance sheet had come out he issued debentures to the value of a further hundred thousand which were taken up by the Debenture Corporation.'

'Was the interest paid?'

'I regret to say not in full.'

'He was lucky not to have a receiving order against him.'

'It might have come to that.'

'The shareholders will have to be paid. Will there be enough?'

'I can't possibly say as yet. There may well be enough and to spare.'

'I'm not talking about settling in more shares that never pay a penny piece.'

'I realise that, but there are numerous very substantial assets apparently intact—the pottery shares, for instance, not to mention what we may find in the Paris banks. There are also several blocks of shares in companies such as Western Territories Gold Fields.'

'You know what they call that in the City? Western Terrors.'

'All the same, you shouldn't feel too despondent. It is still entirely possible that every claim on the estate will be met in full and that Mrs Phillips, and Miss Barker, of course, will still receive quite handsome legacies.'

'And do you believe that?'

Finnigan looked unhappily at John, at the papers on his desk and at the rain streaming down the darkening window.

'How can I possibly say? But if you ask me my personal opinion—not a professional view—on balance, yes I believe there will be something. Not perhaps what might have been expected but something reasonably substantial. Some thousands, not forty or fifty but something well worth having. Five, ten, possibly fifteen thousand for each of the principal beneficiaries.'

Heartened a little by this, John went back to London. On the train home he tried to put aside his anger against Kate's father and to lay out all the factors in his situation like a man playing a quiet game of patience. If Finnigan was right about the legacies then, when he looked at things calmly, the future seemed rather brighter than he had feared. He would still have enough to repay the money borrowed from Mr Beddoes and, unless Cyril Nutting came down on him very hard, enough to secure a partnership in the firm. There'd be no moving house for a few years yet but he and Kate would get along pretty well. Julia would take herself off—not to a villa on Lake Como but to some place where she could manage to make ends meet on the little bit of income from her money.

'I'd give something to see her face,' he thought to himself, 'on the day she hears what her precious fortune comes to.'

But if Finnigan was wrong, if his guess proved too optimistic, what then? What if there turned out to be only a few hundred, just enough to repay what he'd borrowed, instead of five, ten or fifteen thousand? There would be a showdown with Nutting and no partnership in the firm. Mr Beddoes would take his part but it wouldn't make any difference. Nutting had grabbed the helm now. He made all the decisions and gave the orders.

'So,' thought John, 'I'd leave Nutting to it and make my own way.'

And why not? There was no real danger of sinking down to labouring for a living. He'd have no trouble getting a place in the City that would pay pretty close to what he was earning now. He'd work hard and do what he ought to have done long ago, get himself properly qualified as an accountant. Later he could try for a senior position in an accountant's office or start up in business on his own, be his own master, beholden to nobody. As for Julia, she couldn't expect to go on sponging off a man battling to support a wife and family on four pounds a week. She'd have to go off to Cobham and make the best of it. Left to themselves, he and Kate would settle how to cut back their expenses—lease somewhere cheaper, perhaps, let one of the servants go—but eventually they'd pull up again to something better. And once Julia had gone, once the child was born and the business of the legacy all finished, Kate would see they needed no great fortune after all but could be happy enough on less than she was used to, at least until he got back on his feet.

After running such thoughts through his mind as the train rushed on through the darkness back to London, John almost smiled. He wasn't wholly convinced. What was dour and bleak in his nature suspected some hidden pitfall, some stroke he could not foresee that a Fate as dour as himself would bring down upon him. But for the moment his mood was lightened. It seemed, he thought, as though for the past hour he had been listening to Kate as she used to be just a little time ago.

∽

All through that spring and summer the estate went on lurching from solvency to insolvency and back again. Finnigan toiled on through a forest of holding companies, nominees and intricate manipulations of paper, and John went regularly to and fro between London and Chippenham watching the grass grow high in the meadows, the hay wains rolling through the lanes in June, the wheat turning gold on the hills and the sheaves set up in stooks across the stubble. At last, on a sunny day in late September, he set out for his final interview in the lawyer's office.

'All done,' Finnigan had telegraphed. 'Can you come down on Monday?'

The countryside on that warm autumn morning seemed glowing with plenty. The cottage gardens were bright with Michaelmas daisies, the fruit trees alight with the rosy sheen of apples and the gold of pears. There were blackberry pickers working in the lanes, a woman gathering mushrooms near a water mill, two men standing among beehives gazing at a giant vegetable marrow. In the pale fields John saw several parties of gleaners, women and children stuffing sacks with the ears left behind by the last of the laden wagons. It was the time of harvest suppers when each farmer killed a couple of sheep and sat the harvesters down to a great feast of roast mutton, pies and home-brewed ale. Afterwards, coming out of the noise and glare into the big, empty, starlit fields, the men would set up a shout so loud that people in the next village would hear it, start up in their beds and shout back.

'Poor buggers,' said John to himself. 'They wouldn't see meat like that more than once in a twelve month.'

He mused on this for a little while and then, coming back to himself, was surprised at how completely he had forgotten his own troubles. It was quite clear by now that Kate and Julia's legacy would be smaller than Finnigan had predicted at the start. It might be as little as two thousand pounds apiece, possibly even less, and although, not so long ago, John had faced such a prospect quite cheerfully, in the past six months a great deal had changed. For one thing there seemed no chance now of getting rid of Julia. In July there had come an urgent message from Aunt Martha's friend, Mrs Burne. Aunt Martha had suffered a stroke and had been taken to the Burnes' house where a nurse had been brought in to help take care of her. Kate, who was close to the time of her confinement, was in no condition to travel so Julia went off to Cobham, with a very bad grace, to see what future provision might be made for Aunt Martha's care. She was back in less than a week reporting that the Aunt had one eye all pulled down and her right side totally paralysed. The Burnes were prepared to keep her with them but wanted help with nursing expenses.

'She won't need the cottage any more,' said Julia, yawning. 'I daresay with no rent to pay, her bit of money will be enough. I don't suppose she'll last a great deal longer.'

Kate was so overwhelmed by this that the doctor ordered her to bed, while John was left to swing between anxiety for his wife and gloomy rage at the realisation that, without Aunt Martha, his hopes of getting rid of Julia were likely to come to nothing. Already he suspected that her legacy would be too small to enable her to set up house on her own. So what was to become of her? She was the bane of his life but he could hardly turn her out to starve in the street. Yet, if she stayed, his whole idea of turning his back on Cyril Nutting, paying his debt, and starting afresh as his own man began to look less hopeful. Kate, as the summer drew on, seemed to be losing her sense along with her strength. All the same, thought John, if he only could have got her away from Julia she would've understood—when the time came—that things had to change. As it was, with Julia always there, carping, demanding, pouring out money like water and making Kate discontented with second-best, the dream of domestic harmony on a shoestring faded away. He began to calculate again what capital he might be able to offer Nutting, how much it would take to buy his way to the income of a partner.

All this was bad enough. What made it worse was that John now had no-one, apart from Finnigan, to whom he could take his troubles. Long ago he'd decided to say nothing to Kate or Julia about the shady side of their father's financial dealings, but he did make several attempts to warn them that their inheritance would turn out to be much less than they were expecting. Julia merely laughed and said that if young Mr Finnigan was bungling the matter, someone more senior ought to take over from him. Kate, on the other hand, looked so white and stricken that John found himself muttering that there was a long way to go yet and things might well look up before the end.

'Well, of course,' Julia would say. 'What did I tell you?'

Her tone suggested a struggle to keep patience with John's absurdities. It drove him nearly frantic. There were times when, if he hadn't left the room, he might have strangled her or beaten both the sisters with his fists. Often, now, he was filled with anger against Kate as well as Julia. Just when he needed her most she had fallen from his side, changing from the companion that he loved to a weak dependant who only added to his growing burdens. In certain moods he blamed her very bitterly for this, fulminating in himself against her feeble spirit, her dream, her attachment to her father and her sister, everything that had risen up between them, blighting their easy converse and mutual trust.

Kate knew nothing about her father's brewing companies, but she suspected that John had discovered rash, over-generous spending which made him anxious and angry. She felt his resentment against her, and it was this more than her heavy body, her dream or the summer heat that made her so ill and weak. Try as she might, she had only to look at John sitting shrugged up and silent in his chair, and the tears went pouring down her face so that all the time her knowledge of the rift between them only served to make it grow wider.

Julia every day made matters worse. Having never lived with the Phillipses before, she imagined that the uneasiness dividing them had existed from the very hour they'd married. She had decided years ago that John was morose and boorish and that her sister was unhappy with him. Everything she saw now proved her right. With some self-satisfaction she made a great parade of lavishing on Kate all the attention that John seemed incapable of giving, and of making demands that Kate seemed too cowed to make for herself. Jimmy, she said, was completely out of hand, running riot, ruining Kate's nerves, and John must discipline him. Kate, she said, needed a holiday, a proper rest, a breath of pure air, and if Switzerland was really out of the question then Bournemouth would have to do and John must write a cheque for their expenses.

All this roused in John a perverse inclination to play the role assigned to him. He fell back into the country speech of his boyhood, slouched, swore, even shied his muddy boots across the room. Julia sighed in disgust, Kate wept, while John, watching his wife from the corner of his eye, told himself she was taking Julia's side, that the Barkers were all tarred with the same brush.

On the eighteenth of August Kate gave birth to a son. He was christened Charles Alfred at a grim little ceremony that took place almost as soon as Kate was allowed to get out of bed. Julia started to arrange an elaborate party but John would have none of it. It was early September and he knew all too well that the time for such extravagance was past. Mr and Mrs Beddoes, who had retired to Maidenhead, came over to Hampstead for the day. Cook and Lily came to the church and afterwards sat stiffly on the drawing room sofa to drink the baby's health with the family. The baby wailed all the afternoon.

∽

Finnigan jumped up the moment John came into the office and hurried to shake his hand. Once they were settled in their chairs he began moving papers about on his desk in a nervous, flurried way.

'The news is not good, I'm afraid,' he said. 'It's particularly unfortunate that Mr Barker instructed us to frame the will so that the amounts bequeathed to what he saw as the minor beneficiaries—and to Miss Martha Barker, of course—are actually specified, with Mrs Phillips and Miss Julia receiving—as he instructed—half each of the residual amount. Had he named a figure in their case, then, of course, in the absence of funds to cover the sum total of the bequests, all the legacies would abate rateably, that is each beneficiary would receive some proportion—a tenth, say—of the money willed to him or to her. As it is we are bound, unfortunately, to abide by what the will actually says. The specified amounts must all be paid first and the remaining monies, however small, divided between Mrs Phillips and Miss Julia, even though it seems probable that the outcome is not what Mr Barker would have intended.'

'You mean the sister ends up with more than the daughters?'

'Well, indeed, yes. Miss Martha Barker's legacy is quite substantial and once that and all the others are paid, the amount remaining is not what we might have hoped. Those creditors, you know, in Cologne. There were more than we anticipated when you were here last.'

He fished a document from one of his piles and handed it to John.

'And Herr Schumann in Berne. That Anglo-Swiss affair. A perfectly well-authenticated claim. And these disbursements, which I do assure you we've done our best to keep to a minimum. But you know yourself the time that's been involved, the cables and travelling and so forth.'

He passed over more papers and went on straightening the collection in front of him.

'So all in all, as you'll see, the grand total in the end is, I'm sorry to say, a mere fourteen.'

John looked up from the columns of figures. He immediately thought, as he'd done over and over again with one estimate after another, 'Five hundred for Beddoes. Can I buy in as a partner with the balance?'

'Nine hundred,' he said aloud with a snort of laughter. 'Nutting'll kick up a fuss.'

'Not hundreds!' cried Finnigan, more agitated than ever. 'No, no, my dear chap, though that would be well below what we hoped at one time, I know. No, you'll see if you look at that last sheet I gave you. It's fourteen pounds. Each, of course. Fourteen pounds for Mrs Phillips and fourteen for Miss Julia.'

~

Cyril Nutting, having taken charge of the St Jude's Friendly Society, was racing the firm along at tremendous speed. The name had been changed to the Imperial Colossus Insurance Company. The London office had been totally refurbished. Cyril had two large desks, a telephone, a lamp with three electric globes, and a figured Axminster carpet.

'Soon,' he would say, drawing finger and thumb through the air to outline the masthead he saw in his mind's eye, 'our name will be a household word in this country. Everyone who is anyone will be with us. Already we have as clients two dukes, six earls and fourteen baronets. Next month we open offices in Manchester and Leeds.'

Every morning, beaming and spruce, he would sweep through the clerks' room and the frosted-glass enclosure full of typewriter girls and install himself in his sanctum. For the first few weeks after his son-in-law's accession to power, Mr Beddoes would come in too, marching with equal purpose to his own rather smaller office behind the typists' room. But after about half-an-hour he often found himself at a loose end, and would stand in his office doorway, pulling at the points of his waistcoat and rising up and down on his toes. Sometimes he would pace about between the clerks' desks, nodding with apparent satisfaction or go hurrying along the corridor to Cyril's office with the air of a man with urgent matters on his mind. These interviews were never very long, and after they were over Mr Beddoes never looked much as though he had agreed with his partner on some new course of action. Instead he would go back to pulling at his waistcoat or sidle, rather crestfallen, into his room. Afterwards, if John knocked on his door and went in to consult him, he would usually be standing by the window studying the decaying hampers and broken chairs scattered about the yard behind the building.

'Leeds?' he would say in a keen, decisive voice, coming quickly to his desk. 'Leeds. Yes, Leeds.'

Then there would be a silence while he rearranged his paperknife and pens. Finally he would say, 'Yes, now I think that's really Cyril's pigeon, John. You'd better speak to him about that.'

As time went on, Mr Beddoes began arriving later in the mornings, then missing a day here and there, until by mid-summer he had almost given up coming to the office altogether. John told himself that he couldn't be blamed for making himself scarce, that Nutting had elbowed him out, but at the same time he nursed an unacknowledged grudge at seeing the last of those on whom he'd relied desert him just at the time when he most needed a friend. In fact, since Mr Beddoes, like Kate, believed so blindly in the man whose tricky dealing was the cause of all his troubles, John had long since decided that there was no comfort to be had from opening his heart to Beddoes. Nor, as it turned out, did the disappearance of his old patron bring on a change in Cyril Nutting's behaviour. John had expected a sudden increase in coldness, constant reminders that he could no longer see himself as a coming man, a partner's protégé, but although he searched almost eagerly for slights, there was nothing much. The Beddoeses, since retiring to Maidenhead, had given up their cheerful round of outings and parties. Cyril and May went about in different company and invitations to the Phillipses had dwindled away. There was no pretence of anything beyond a business relationship between John and Nutting but, given that, the head of the firm remained perfectly, if distantly, polite to his accountant, only slightly raising his eyebrows at the frequency of John's absences in Chippenham.

'I know my work,' thought John. 'I daresay he wants to keep me on. And he's waiting, I suppose, to see how things pan out. The way he's throwing the firm's money about he can't afford to get my back up so long as there's a chance I'll bring in something.'

To all intents and purposes, then, Mr Beddoes's departure made little difference in John's life, and yet he fretted after the free comradely way they'd had of working together and the reassurance he'd taken from the old man's open pride in what he could do and what he'd made of himself.

'Well, there it is,' he told himself. 'I should've known better than think he'd stand by me. He's got himself to think of after all.'

From June to September they never met once, and when the Beddoeses came over to Hampstead for Charles Alfred's christening, they were oddly subdued. They were going on a trip soon, they said. Bert hadn't been too well lately and the doctor thought, and Cyril too, that a bit of sunshine would do him the world of good.

'Some place in Nice,' said Bert dolefully as he and John walked slowly round the garden after tea. 'What d'you think of that?'

John couldn't say. Had Beddoes heard some rumour of Toby Barker's goings-on? Was he clearing out in case the bright future he'd always promised for his young assistant was to come to nothing?

'Nothing grand, mind,' the old man went on. 'Some little place Cyril knows. If we let The Elms we'll hardly be out of pocket, Cyril says.'

He paused, looking vacantly at Kate's wallflowers, and touched them musingly, delicately with his stick.

'Used to call them gillyvors when I was a lad. I've put in more capital, you know. Cyril worked out how much we could manage, went through all I've put away, all the housekeeping accounts down to what Mother spends on a packet of pins. We'll have to be a bit careful from now on, until the dividends come rolling in, that is.'

'That money you lent me,' said John. 'It won't be long now.'

'Oh, don't worry about that, my boy.'

Mr Beddoes stopped short, prodding at a weed in the gravel as though trying to decide how to open a subject he found ticklish.

'Of course he's heard something,' thought John, growing hot as he thought of the way people would carry on once word of his disappointed hopes got about. 'Though I daresay he still thinks his precious Barker'll turn out to be a millionaire in the end.'

As soon as he arrived home after his final interview with Finnigan, John went into the little back room they called the study and wrote a note to Mr Beddoes, asking if he might come out to Maidenhead at the end of the week. He needed a few days to raise all he could towards repaying his debt, but, at the same time, he half hoped that by Saturday the Beddoeses would have left England for Nice. He meant to do what was right, but he needed a breathing space more than at any time in the whole of his life.

As he sealed the envelope he ran over again what Beddoes had said as they walked in the autumn garden. What was it he'd left unsaid? Some exhortation not to listen to malicious rumours or something more?

∽

'I had rather expected,' said Cyril, 'that you would have made it your business to seek an interview with me before this.'

He sat in his captain's chair, filling his well-cut clothes, perfectly barbered and brushed, his hair gleaming in the pale sunlight from the window at his back.

'However,' he continued, raising a hand to cut short any reply, 'I will say no more of that but come straight to the point. I understand from Mr Beddoes that hopes you may have entertained, hopes of investing substantially in the firm, have been disappointed.'

This time John made no attempt to speak. Nutting, after waiting a moment, shook his head very slowly, his fleshy face heavy with disapproval.

'A very shabby business. Not what we care to hear of in the City.'

'I don't know what you've heard,' said John, 'but there's no-one out of pocket.'

'And that, you feel, makes up for sharp practice or fraud if we are to speak perfectly plainly? I'm afraid I must disagree. In any event what you say is not quite true. The firm is out of pocket, Phillips, the firm.'

'The firm?'

'You won't deny, I suppose, that earlier this year you borrowed—simply on the strength of your expectations—the sum of five hundred pounds?'

'Not from the firm. That was a private loan from Mr Beddoes.'

'I think not.' Again Nutting held up a hand for silence. 'You prefer, of course, to put that complexion on it, but my father-in-law, who has placed his affairs entirely in my hands, agrees with me that the debt, in fact, must be seen as one to Imperial Colossus. Now I understand that, although you have taken no steps to declare yourself bankrupt, you attempted on Saturday to settle the matter by paying over three hundred pounds in cash.'

John leaped up and leaned over the desk.

'That's a lie. I told him I'd give him the rest as soon as I could. Ask him.'

'And that was how it was left?'

John stared, threw himself back in his chair and muttered, 'He wouldn't have it. He told me not to worry about the other two hundred. He knew I'd been led up the garden path. He said he was sorry for it.'

'So the matter was to be regarded as settled? The principal, the interest, everything?'

'There was never any question of any interest.'

'You must understand, Phillips, that however much you may have prevailed on my father-in-law's good nature in the past, I simply cannot allow this kind of thing. The matter has to be put on a proper business footing.'

'Prevailed on his good nature? You think I went smarming round him to get out of paying interest? Wheedling and scheming to do him out of his money?'

'Let us just say that my father-in-law, as you must know, is generous to a fault and is not, perhaps, as acute as he once was. His health, as again you must know, is not good. Hence, of course, his virtual retirement. And knowing all this you went, at your own invitation, to his private house and attempted to fob him off . . .'

'No! I never did! I went intending to pay back every penny piece. I told him that. And he'll get his money even though he said he wouldn't take it. But it's between him and me. It's not for you to come sticking your nose in. I'll go out again. I'll tell him he'll get his two hundred and his interest. Anything he says.'

'Oh yes. Well, that all sounds very honourable, no doubt. Except, of course, that you know as well as I do that Mr and Mrs Beddoes are no longer in England, that they left for the south of France two days ago. And during his absence, as I've told you once, all his affairs are entirely in my hands. Everything, including these.'

From under his blotter, Nutting produced two sheets of paper which he placed very deliberately on the far side of the desk so that John could read them. One was an IOU for five hundred pounds which he had insisted on handing to Beddoes back in January, the other a copy of the receipt that Beddoes, by the same token, had written out for him on the supper table at Maidenhead last Saturday.

'It occurs to me to enquire,' said Nutting, looking musingly across at the documents, 'how it is that you were able to raise what is, after all, a considerable sum of money for a man in your position. I hope we shall not find that there has been any further unorthodox dealing, any arrangements, say, between your father-in-law and yourself, any private agreement with Windsor O'Rourke or persons of that ilk to withhold or conceal funds.'

'By God!' said John getting up. 'You say any more and I'll smash your face. If you know so bloody much you'll know I saw to it there's not a penny owing. And you'll know I wouldn't touch Barker's dirty business or O'Rourke's with a ten-foot pole. We've sold everything we could lay hands on, my wife—his daughter—sold her jewels to get that money.

Jewels he'd given her—and then we found that most of 'em were fakes.'

He leaned on the desk again, shaking with rage, pushing his thin dark face into the plump pink one of his tormentor.

'You'll get your money. I'll see to that. And now I'm getting out. I'll never set foot in this damned place again and if you ever come crawling across my path you see if I don't break your bloody neck.'

Nutting withstood this onslaught quite calmly, only leaning back a little in his chair and blinking his pale, round eyes. As John broke away and rushed to the door he said, 'You speak as though you were an entirely free agent.'

'Free of you. Free of this rotten hole.'

'Free only, I think, to make some simple choices,' said Nutting, waving John back to his chair. 'If you leave here now I shall immediately sue you for the recovery of our debt. Two hundred pounds plus some forty-five pounds interest at the comparatively modest rate of twelve per cent. You may, by some means, contrive to raise such a sum. Or, of course, you may choose to declare yourself bankrupt, though I hardly think that thereafter you would be likely to find employment as an accountant. On the other hand, despite your recent outburst and the threat you uttered, I am prepared to allow you to remain in our employment, carrying out your usual duties and putting half your salary towards the repayment of what you owe. It would, I believe, take only three years for you to cover the full amount, after which you would continue to draw your present salary.'

'Three years! On two quid a week!'

'Think it over. Those are not ungenerous terms. You must remember, Phillips, that there are others beside myself who find it more than a little strange that you enjoyed the most cordial relations with your father-in-law and yet never, so you

91

insist, gained even the slightest knowledge of his business affairs. And, of course, where I am prepared to offer you employment—provided, of course, that you apologise for your intemperate language and conduct yourself properly in future—those others may be rather more wary than I of the scandal that is bound to cling to your name. I shall expect to hear your decision in the morning.'

∾

The cab came to a halt in a narrow street running between two busy thoroughfares. John got up without a word, climbed down and held the door open for Kate and Julia. Kate, coming out after him, paused as she stood ducking her head in the cab doorway. She lifted her eyes to the wall of sooty, ochre brick that rose up before her, and remained for some seconds, stooped and peering upwards from under her hat brim at the meagre house front with its three pairs of lifeless, grimy windows. Finally she came down to the pavement and, clutching the folds of her skirt in both hands, went on staring up in total silence.

Julia came out of the cab in a series of jerks, starting back and almost losing her balance. She fetched up breathless and flushed a foot or two from the doorstep of the house and, while John paid off the cabbie, began to mutter rapidly and toss her head.

'What's this?' she said as he turned back to unlock the door. 'What's the meaning of this?'

Kate was looking blankly up the street. A group of grubby children playing hopscotch a little way along on the pavement gave up their game, clustered together and gazed at the newcomers.

'Not here surely?'

Kate looked pale, dazed, uncomprehending, where Julia was all snapping fury, kindling eyes and scarlet cheeks.

'I won't set foot in there,' said Julia, her voice so loud and vehement that two women on the other side of the street turned round to look at her. 'We've been sent to the wrong place. This can't be the house you thought of taking.'

Kate simply looked at John, bewildered and near to tears. She spread out her hands and let them fall again as though she had no hope of understanding his intention.

'Come along, Kate,' said Julia taking her sister's arm. 'We'll walk back this way. We're sure to find a cab before long.'

'Get away from her,' said John roughly. He took his wife's free arm. 'Come on. You need to see it. It's not so bad.'

'Not so bad! It's appalling!' cried Julia, stamping her foot. 'The front door two steps up from the filthy, dirty street! Look at those children! The place is a slum!'

'Shut your mouth. Leave her to me, will you?'

'She's coming with me. We're not going in there.'

'Then stay out. Don't come. Go where you want. I'm sick to death of you always making trouble, carrying on with your bloody airs and graces. You can pack your bags and get out of the house tonight.'

'No, no!' wept Kate, trying to pull away from John. 'You know she's ill. What are you thinking of?'

'Get inside, get inside!'

John clenched his teeth. A small crowd was gathering—grinning women wiping their hands on their aprons, children with spindly legs and dusty boots, a man with a cart full of coal who looked with lively interest from one participant in the fracas to the next.

'Ooo!' screamed a little girl, jumping up and down. 'She's goin' to giv 'im one!'

Even Julia, who was beside herself with passion, realised

that they had to get out of the street and allowed herself to be bundled in through the open door behind her. John slammed it shut and they all stood in the dark passage, breathing heavily. There was a smell of gas, cats and damp. John pushed open a side door and they saw a small room, a rusty grate, bare floorboards, scattered straw.

'Very well. If that's what you want I shall go tonight.'

Julia closed her eyes and leaned back against the wall, one hand clutching theatrically at her bosom.

'You can't mean it,' said Kate. 'I never would've believed you'd treat her so. What on earth can she do? Where can she go?'

'It's none of my affair where she goes. I can't provide for everyone. Not now.'

'Not now,' said Julia faintly, rolling her head against the mouldering plaster. 'Not now you've bungled poor Papa's affairs and let us all be fleeced by Heaven knows who. Or,' she shrilled, coming suddenly back to life, 'filched it all for yourself if the truth be known.'

'You're wrong there. It's not me who's the thief. It was him, your precious father, got over on the windy side of the law.'

'Now we have it! There now, Kate, that's what comes of taking a guttersnipe into the family!'

'How dare you!' sobbed Kate. 'How dare you say such a thing about dear Pa!'

'Ask Nutting. Ask anyone. Why d'you think I'm tied the way I am, stuck in that place with that smirking bugger lording it over me, if it wasn't that what he did's rubbed off on me?'

'I don't know what you mean. It's what Julia says. You've bungled it somehow and now you're trying to put the blame on Pa.'

'Think what you like,' muttered John. 'I made up my mind never to let you know what he'd been up to. I knew you'd never have it even if the thing was staring you in the face. Ah, what's the odds? Just get this into your heads: there's nothing, no money and close on two hundred and fifty quid to be paid off. This is the best I can do for you now and if it doesn't suit, you can clear off out of it.'

Kate rushed to Julia, who had tottered a few steps towards the front door, embraced her and started stroking her cheeks and hair.

'There, there. Of course you shall stay, of course you shall stay.'

The sisters clung together weeping and murmuring. John banged up the uncarpeted stairs, slammed into the back bedroom and stood looking dully out of the window at a jumble of poky backyards, sooty roofs and chimney pots. From below a voice wailed, 'And the children! How can he think of bringing the children here?'

◈

'You'll have to go and see the Aunt,' said Julia. She looked round angrily for somewhere to put the milk jug she was holding. All the flat surfaces in the kitchen were already stacked with objects—sugar casters, pudding basins, frying pans, canisters, shoes, books, pots of jam . . . She pushed her way past a washtub stuffed with bedding to the range and put the jug down in a contemptuous way on the hotplate. There was no danger of it cracking because Kate, so far, had failed to get a fire going in the box between the ovens. Kate thought the flues were blocked with soot, but since Cook and Lily had been dismissed there was nobody to clean them. Nobody, thought Julia, even to make a cup of tea once the fire was burning. The loss of the servants, the way in which she and Kate had been left to struggle with the business of getting everything into the horrid little house in Beaumont Street, with only a carter and his boy to help them, infuriated her even more than the squalor of her new surroundings.

'Tell her it's our money and if she can't understand then tell the solicitors in Cobham it's we who ought to manage her estate.'

'Oh dear,' said Kate, sitting back on her heels. 'I should have gone to see her long ago. But it's been so difficult lately.'

'Well yes, I told you to go as soon as we heard she'd ended up with everything. But the important thing is not to waste any more time. Tell her it's absurd that Papa's wishes should be flouted like this. He never meant her to have half of what we were supposed to get. And now she's taken it all and we're stuck here in this frightful slum.'

To give emphasis to her remarks Julia swept the back of her hand down the front of the costume she had assumed for moving house. Where Kate had simply put an apron over an old blouse and skirt, Julia had devised a weird sort of tunic from dustsheets, pins and string. On her head she wore a pillowcase that ballooned out behind her like a veil. She looked rather like an ill-tempered nun, or, at least, a member of a country house party, dressed up as a nun for charades. This was exactly the impression she wanted to create. The peculiar fancy dress was meant to demonstrate how ludicrous it was that she should be expected to demean herself by labouring like a scullery maid at unpacking cooking utensils.

'I have written,' said Kate, beginning to fish about again in her box of crockery. 'But poor Aunt can't write back, of course, and the Burnes just send such stiff little notes. They say she's getting better but it's hard to know really.'

'Anyway, she hasn't any use for all that money. She can't even get out of the house to spend anything, so why shouldn't we have it? It stands to reason it shouldn't just lie idle when we're in dreadful need. And when she dies she'll leave it to us anyway. Why should we have to wait about when it ought to have come to us in the first place? You'll have to make her see that, Kate. And you must act quickly. Why not go tomorrow? There's nothing to stop you.'

'Tomorrow? How can I? There's all this to see to.' Kate looked quite wildly round the kitchen. Although the best furniture, silver, pictures, dozens of treasures that she'd loved had all been sold, the house was still littered with an astonishing number of boxes, bundles, toys, provisions, tables with their legs in the air, bedsteads leaning drunkenly against walls, and all kinds of strange objects that she couldn't remember ever seeing before. There was a rag rug that Cook might have left behind, a tally iron for crisping bows and gathers, a wicker carpet beater that Lily must have wielded unseen. She had no idea how she was going to find places for everything. And tomorrow the children—all except Charles who was asleep in a basket upstairs—would be brought from Hampstead by the neighbour with whom they were staying the night.

'Well Wednesday or Thursday then. But don't put it off any longer.'

'No. No, I won't. But, Julia, I can't go asking for money straightaway. Not when she's ill and I haven't seen her for so long.'

'You needn't ask exactly. It's bound to come up, isn't it? Either she—if she's capable—or the Burne people are bound to ask how we are. Well, tell her. Tell her what's happened to us. Make her understand and, as I say, if she's too far gone, go to the solicitors and tell them she isn't fit to manage things.'

'But what about the Burnes? We've left them to deal with everything up to now.'

'Oh, the Burnes! I wouldn't trust them an inch. They told me she knew exactly what was going on, but really, you know, I think they just pretend she's making signals, and make out she wants whatever suits them best. I mean it's been very convenient for them, hasn't it, to have her income to spend? I know they've had to hire a nurse and all that, but what's happened to the rest? And now, of course, there are thousands and thousands of pounds at stake. Well, obviously they're hoping to get hold of it, aren't they? Despite the fact that it's really our money. It wouldn't surprise me a bit if they weren't wheedling away to get her to change her will.'

Kate said nothing to this. She was quite shocked because the Burnes, as well as doing everything for Aunt Martha that her family should have done, were, after all, clerical people. She wondered if Julia really believed what she said or whether she was simply driven by a grudge against anyone strong, healthy or long-lived. She hung her head, groping about among the last of the straw in the bottom of her box. To her surprise she came on a shiny brown teapot, as odd and baffling as something in a dream. The whole business of the day, the struggling about in the cramped house among unfamiliar objects, was becoming like a nightmare. In particular there was the sense of having to undertake tasks from which she shrank—not only the visit to Aunt Martha, but the whole ordeal of cleaning the range, making it burn, clearing the kitchen and serving up a hot meal when John came home from his work in the evening. She wanted very much to succeed in all this, to let John see that despite the way he'd slandered her father and threatened Julia, *she* was capable of going on strongly and serenely, of conjuring up mulligatawny soup, boiled ham, potatoes and batter pudding under frightful circumstances without the slightest deviation from proper, good-tempered behaviour.

In the end Kate wrote to the Burnes to ask if it would be convenient to visit Aunt Martha on the following Thursday. She mentioned the move to Beaumont Street, hoping against hope that Aunt Martha would grasp what had happened and do something to help them without further prompting. Although she was fond of her aunt and felt guilty about neglecting her, she couldn't help thinking, rather as Julia did, that it was wrong of Aunt Martha to accept her full legacy and leave her nieces with nothing when it was obvious that Tobias had meant his daughters to be well provided for. And if Aunt Martha was too ill to understand this, why didn't the Burnes or Aunt Martha's lawyer intervene to see that justice was done?

When Kate arrived finally in the Burnes's drawing room she sensed at once that, although Mrs Burne had written to tell her that she might call on Thursday if she wished, her visit was not at all welcome. It occurred to her, as it had done several times before, that Julia must have offended the Burnes when she'd gone down to see Aunt Martha last July. In fact, Julia had behaved abominably. She had sailed into the Burnes's house, peered with distaste at her afflicted aunt and commenced to issue orders, much as though Mr and Mrs Burne, instead of being Aunt Martha's closest friends, were two rather feeble minded servants, hired to look after her. That would have been bad enough but Julia had also made it quite clear that she suspected the Burnes of trying to get their hands on Aunt Martha's money.

'My aunt's income ought to be handled by a lawyer,' she'd said. 'He can see to it that you get enough to pay the nurse and so on, but I want you to keep an account of all expenses. Naturally my sister and I will have to look the figures over from time to time.'

Mrs Burne had replied in her iciest tone that Julia's concern for her aunt was quite admirable but, in the doctor's opinion, Miss Barker was still capable of managing her own affairs.

Confronted with Julia's sister, Mrs Burne, tall and frosty in pearl grey, barely touched Kate's hand with her fingertips while Mr Burne, who had woolly, white whiskers and steel-rimmed spectacles, stared bullishly from the far end of the room and gave the slightest of bows. Beside him, in a chair by the fire, was a bundle of shawls. After a moment, a strange gargling sound came from the bundle and Kate, looking about in alarm, saw a skewed eye glaring at her over a fold of shawl. She hurried forward at once, knelt by the chair, took Aunt Martha's hand and gazed anxiously into her face. Although she was saddened to see her aunt so stricken, she was much less shocked than she'd expected. She'd imagined that there would be much more evidence of sickness—a darkened room, perhaps, a groaning figure among shadowy pillows, at the very least a wheelchair. As it was Aunt Martha, though lop-sided and inarticulate, looked surprisingly like her old self. The frilled collar of a blouse decorated with her favourite cairngorm pin showed between her wrappings. The hand Kate held, the raised veins running from knuckle to wrist, and the mourning ring with its spray of asphodel on a jet shield were all as they'd always been. Years ago, Aunt Martha had told Kate that in the tiny casket under the shield lay a wisp of blond hair, cut from the head of the young man she would have married had he not died, fighting with great gallantry, at Balaclava. Suddenly it seemed to Kate quite natural and right to open her heart to her aunt.

'Oh, Aunt Martha,' she said, clutching the veined hand more tightly. 'I meant to come to you long ago but we've been in such trouble.'

Behind her the Burnes exchanged glances. They knew that

Kate had been pregnant at the time of Aunt Martha's stroke, but they also knew that her confinement had taken place over four months ago. It looked very much as though she had put off visiting Cobham until after her father's affairs had been settled, and had arrived now, hot on the scent of Aunt Martha's legacy.

There was an awkward pause. Eventually Mrs Burne cleared her throat and said, 'The doctor is very pleased with Miss Barker's progress. There's been a marked improvement in the last few weeks.'

'So she can hear me?'

'Of course. She's very well aware of everything that goes on and I do assure you, Mrs Phillips, as shrewd as she ever was.'

At this Aunt Martha jerked her hand out of Kate's grip and made a scrabbling movement on the little table at her side. Mr Burne brought some sheets of paper and a lead pencil. He bent stiffly and, wheezing slightly through his whiskers, arranged them on the table.

'Those should never be moved,' said Mrs Burne severely, as though it was Kate who had taken them away. 'Miss Barker writes quite clearly now with her left hand.' They all watched Aunt Martha as she scratched away with the pencil. Then Mrs Burne picked up the message and, for the first time smiling faintly, handed it to Kate, who, still kneeling on the hearthrug, read the words, 'Selfish spoiled girls.'

Kate flushed. Tears rushed into her eyes. She turned her back on the Burnes, furious that they should go on standing guard through this private family scene. When she had recovered herself a little she looked up again at Aunt Martha, leaning forward to shut out the Burnes as best she could.

'I know how it must seem. I know we're to blame in some ways . . .'

It seemed now impossible to explain what had kept her away or to say, when in part she couldn't understand it herself, why John was so crippled by debt.

'We have to live in *such* a place. The air's so bad for Julia's lungs and Pa, you know, would never have wanted that . . .'

'I think,' interrupted Mrs Burne, 'that if you wish to discuss financial matters, Mrs Phillips, you ought to apply to Miss Barker's solicitors.'

'And I think,' said Kate, getting quickly to her feet, 'that I ought to be allowed to speak to my aunt in private.'

Aunt Martha began to scribble again very fast. Kate got hold of the paper before Mrs Burne could intervene and, although she found part of the message illegible, made out the words 'bed' and 'lie in it'.

'Is it not possible,' boomed Mr Burne suddenly, 'is it not possible, nay probable, that all has transpired according to Mr Barker's wishes?' He gazed at Kate with glinting spectacles, flexing his fleecy jaws. 'Are we to believe that a man of affairs, accustomed to the calculation of profit and loss, had no idea of the extent of his own means? Is it not more probable—nay virtually certain—that it was his intention to reward a lifetime of provident service and at the same time, to lead his daughters, brought up in the lap of luxury, to a more proper apprehension of the value of riches?'

'You know a good deal about my father's will, sir,' said Kate, trembling with emotion, 'but nothing about my father.'

'In any case,' struck in Mrs Burne, 'your husband, Mrs Phillips, has managed to advance himself quite successfully. There are many, many families who would count themselves fortunate if they could enjoy an income such as yours.'

'Two pounds a week!' cried Kate, and regretted it immediately. Why should she be expected to stand arguing about personal matters with these overbearing strangers?

'A hundred pounds a year!' boomed Mr Burne. 'Nay more! How many worthy men, men of god with dedicated wives and abundant families accept far less as ample recompense for all their labours?'

'Then I pity them very much, especially their poor wives and children.'

And with this Kate rushed from the room, nearly colliding with the maid who was bringing in the tea tray. She opened the front door all by herself and ran out into the wintry afternoon, leaving the door swinging on its hinges and the hall curtains swirling in a gust of icy wind.

❧

In the months that followed John put down his head and plodded along like an old horse or a man with a long way to walk on a wet night. Often in his teens he had got a lift with a carter part way to Lacock, and had trudged the rest of the way home through dark and pouring rain with his jacket wringing wet and his boots squelching water at every step. He found there was only one way to get through—set his teeth, try not to feel or think about anything much, and go on plodding, one foot in front of the other, on and on. So now he pushed down his resentment, his galled pride, his frustration at the shipwreck of all his hopes, his confused feelings for his wife, his rage against Julia, and went along from day to day, refusing to think of anything beyond the work he had in hand at a given moment. Every morning he walked from the little house in Holborn to the City, sat all day at his desk, and at night walked home again, often going miles out of his way to pick up extra work from some corner tobacconist who wanted his books audited or some vestryman who was having trouble with his church accounts. Once home, he ate his supper in the kitchen and then went into the front parlour to work until after midnight on the books he had brought back with him. He never complained, hardly seemed to notice what he ate or where he was and barely spoke. For days on end he and Kate would exchange no more than a word or two as they came downstairs before dawn.

She was worn out, nearly as dulled and drained as John himself. She had a fourteen-year-old girl who helped mind the four children for two shillings a week. Julia, with a great deal of martyred sighing, did a little sewing and occasionally made a pot of tea or dusted the parlour. But it was left to Kate to struggle with the full round of household chores, most of which she'd never attempted before. She scrubbed floors, washed windows that grew black with smuts inside a week, raked out ashes, hauled coals up the stairs, trailed round to the butcher's for scrag end of mutton or a couple of pounds of tripe, and wrestled with the ill-conditioned range. Sometimes when John sat down at the supper table, her spirit rebelled and she flew into a frenzy, banging down a spoiled pudding or a pan of blackened potatoes and standing back to see if he would rouse himself at last, look up and see how wretched her life was. But he never did. If what she gave him was completely inedible he'd simply take a bit of bread and cheese from the shelf and go off quietly to the parlour with the plate in his hand.

Only two things seemed to touch him. One was any hint of Kate's dream. When she woke weeping in the night he would turn his back on her in silent fury. The other was his eldest son. All through the week he hardly saw his children. Usually he left the house before they were awake and returned after they had gone to bed, but on Sundays, if the weather was bad, he would sit with them by the range, looking through picture books, telling them stories, covering a sheet of paper with queer little drawings of people and animals while Jimmy sat cuddled on his lap and Violet and Gilbert clambered on the arms of his chair or tumbled over his outstretched legs.

'And here's the old fox that came after the hen and here's the farmer running with his big dog, Tray . . .'

'Oh, look at his tail! Isn't he a funny dog!' shrieked Violet, clutching her father's shoulder and trying to wriggle down from the chair arm to oust Jimmy from his favoured place. But Jimmy eased himself over and twisted round so that Violet was shut out. He tilted his head, rubbing it against John's jaw, so that Violet couldn't even see the drawings.

'Do the farmer's gun, Dad.'

'Can't shoot a fox, Jim.'

'What if it eats up all the farmer's chickens?'

'Don't make no difference. Foxes got to be kept for the gentry's sport. You get put out of your cottage for shooting a fox. The squire and them's got to have foxes to hunt.'

'The squire and them!' muttered Kate, coming in from the scullery. 'Why d'you talk like that? You never used to talk in that rough way! No wonder the child's such a little hobbledehoy.'

Violet, grizzling with frustration, had sidled round to the front of John's chair and was trying again to push her way onto his lap. Quietly Jimmy shoved her away with his boot.

'Jimmy kicked me!' she howled. 'He's naughty! He kicked me.'

'Then he'll go to bed this minute without any dinner!'

'No, no. Get down, Violet, there's a good girl. We'll go out for a bit of a walk won't we, Jim? The rain's nearly stopped.'

'I want to come! I want to go for a walk!'

And Gilbert, taking his thumb out of his mouth, took up Violet's wailing cry, but it was too late. The front door had already slammed.

Walking together, even when they started out with no clear idea of where they were going, was the chief pleasure of the son as well as the father. Years later Jimmy could remember the pride and excitement of walking down Beaumont Street, holding his father's hand and looking sideways at the children he played with on other days. He wanted them to notice how he had been chosen as his father's sole companion before Violet or his mother or any other grown-up person. And always the children stared back, mute and puzzled. It was unusual for a man to go walking with his six-year-old son in that part of London.

Beaumont Street was a frontier where the lowest fringe of the lower middle class mingled with an assortment of working-class families. Some were clinging to respectability, doggedly polishing and scrubbing, dining off boiled potatoes to keep curtains in their windows, turning shirt collars and smearing their menfolk's hats with black ink to hide the rusty patches. Some had given up the struggle and were slipping down into the mire. Others lived as they had always done in a confusion of dirt and noise, while for a few—an ambitious bricklayer, a young plumber and five or six shop assistants—a place of their own with gas and running water represented a step up in the world, a rung on the ladder to a senior position or their own little business, a villa in the suburbs, a proper maidservant with a starched apron, carpets on the floors and double damask on the dining table.

Mrs Lovatt, whose husband had taken to drink and lost his place as a civil service clerk, wiped the leaves of her aspidistra and peered venomously out at the urchins shouting and running past her window. Mrs Gatty cuffed her little boys for muddying their pinafores and playing with the dirty O'Reilly children. Mrs Lovatt sailed past the Gattys with her nose in the air and Mrs Gatty laughed when Mr Lovatt came reeling up the street, roaring and shaking his fist at the smoky sky like a frock-coated Lear. But the Buttons, who kept a lodging house for labouring men, the shock-headed tribe of O'Reillys, and the Figgises who often came to blows on Saturday nights, erupting into the street and chasing each other in and out of the traffic with pokers and frying pans, paid no attention at all to Mrs Lovatt's frostiness or Mrs Gatty's complaints about nits and fleas.

John took some comfort from being among so many who never troubled to keep up appearances. He was set on repaying what he owed, keeping a roof over his family's head and food on the table but as for all the rest of what he'd once had—the piling up of possessions, the smart clothes, the expensive outings, the rubbing shoulders with people like Cyril Nutting—he wondered sometimes why he'd ever bothered to strive for such things. On Sunday evenings in spring, after Jimmy had gone to bed, he took a quiet defiant pleasure in lounging in his open doorway in his shirtsleeves, enjoying a pipe of tobacco and nodding to the men going along to Buttons' or to Mrs O'Reilly, billowing up the street with her hair half down her back. He reflected that if, one day, he were to turn on Julia and give her a black eye or throw her out on the pavement, most of his neighbours would treat the occurrence as nothing remarkable.

Jimmy, too, was at ease in Beaumont Street. He liked having so many children to play with and the way they could run off together away from their mothers, making all the noise they wanted. He liked playing with mud pies and sailing paper boats in the gutters after a storm of rain or doing daring things like shying stones at the cabhorses' legs or ringing the Lovatts' doorbell and running away before anyone could catch him. He enjoyed the smells of gas, coal smoke and horse dung, the breath of the great city that roared and jangled at either end of the street, and the feeling he got when evening came with the lamp-lighter, the aureoles of mist round the streetlamps, a chill in the air and the thought of the warm kitchen waiting. He was often in trouble, of course. His mother would cry out, shake him, sometimes even collapse in tears over the state of his clothes. She couldn't wash at home, she said, because anything hung out to dry in the backyard got covered in smuts, so every bit of laundry cost money. And there was no money for new clothes or boots, and even having boots mended at the cobbler's was expensive. She wept too when he told her about the fight at Buttons' between the big navvy and Harry Button's brother or how he'd gone with Milly O'Reilly to the pawnshop. Aunt Julia swept her skirts aside when he went near, absolutely refused to patch his trousers and said he was turning into a real little monster. She said he had bad blood in him.

Much as he liked his new playground, he always felt exhilarated at leaving it behind as he walked away on a Sunday with his father. Sometimes they merely wandered around the nearby streets, stopping to watch sparrows taking a dust bath or a lascar marching along with a monkey on his shoulder. Sometimes they went as far as Regents Park and strolled round the Botanical Gardens, and on a few special occasions they took a train from Kings Cross right out into the green countryside and flew the kite that they'd flown in the old days on Hampstead Heath.

At first Kate seemed quite pleased by all these expeditions. Molly, the nursemaid, was forever letting Jimmy run off so that Kate lived in a constant fret about street accidents, bad company and mischief. She was glad, she said, to have a bit of peace for a change. The first time Jimmy and his father came home from flying the kite out at Dagenham, they looked so much as they'd done walking down the lane at Hampstead with John carrying the big red kite under his arm, that for a moment their old life flickered back and it seemed that nothing was substantially altered after all. Kate smiled as she made their tea, laid her hand on John's shoulder and that night in bed turned to him more warmly than she'd done at any time since they'd come to Beaumont Street.

∽

One morning in April Kate ran down to the fishmonger's for a few sprats. She didn't like trusting Molly with money and Julia had been up coughing half the night so as usual she had to pull on her hat and hurry out herself. She was still in her work skirt and an old blouse with the sleeves all crinkled from being turned up to the elbow. She was just looking across at Mrs Figgis haggling with the rag and bone man when a large woman, raising her hands theatrically in wonder, stepped out right in front of her. The stranger was very smartly dressed in a walking costume edged with fur and an elaborate hat topped by white plumes like the wings of an angel on a tomb.

'Well I do believe it's Kate Phillips!'

'I went as red as a beetroot,' Kate told Julia afterwards. 'I couldn't think who she was.'

'You remember me, dear,' said the woman, bending forward. 'It's Elizabeth-Jane Duke. Goff I was at school. You must remember me at Briarbrae.'

The name filled Kate with a kind of horror. She could see now that the heavy, simpering face, the long teeth and round, peering eyes with short, light lashes were those of a big, boastful girl she'd once detested. Elizabeth-Jane had won first prize in the Briarbrae embroidery competition. When Kate's traycloth had been handed back with the second-place certificate, she'd found some of the neatly finished threads on the back cut and picked loose.

'Oh my! That horrid Liza-Jane!' the girls had whispered.

'You ought to go to Miss Latimer about it,' said Kate's best friend, little Sarah Palmer.

'I've had such a time running you down and now here you are as large as life!'

It was like another nightmare that Elizabeth-Jane should find her here in Beaumont Street in her shabby clothes with a basket on her arm and her hair all falling down from under an old hat.

'I went all the way to Hampstead,' said Mrs Duke reproachfully, holding out a card. 'That's the address we have on the Old Girls' Association list and I felt sure you'd be careful to keep us up to date. But the lady at Hampstead was really quite obliging and very sorry I'd been sent on a wild goose chase, so she asked me in for tea and we had a nice chat while she looked out the new address. And here we are—Beaumont Street.'

She looked round at the blackened house fronts which seemed more dingy than ever in the spring sunshine, at the carts grinding past, Mrs Figgis standing with arms akimbo and the little mob of street-arabs that had gathered to stare and giggle at her nodding plumes.

'I did wonder if I had the right place. I nearly told the cabbie to wait in case there was another mistake but he was really quite rude so I sent him off, and I was just setting out to find—' she consulted her card 'yes, number forty-six, when I thought, "That's never dear little Kate!" But there you were.'

'What is it you want?' said Kate and then blushed again because the question sounded so brusque, quite as though her manners as well as her appearance were all of a piece with the neighbourhood.

'Ah well now, dear, I'm arranging something very, very thrilling and I'll tell you all about it in a moment. But I do

110

think it would be best if we were to sit down together somewhere and talk it over. I wouldn't intrude for the world but I wonder if we might go back to your house for a little while and find some corner where we can be quiet?'

'I'm afraid you've come at a rather bad time. My sister, Julia's, very ill, you see, Mrs Duke . . .'

'Mrs Duke!' said Kate's tormentor taking her arm and giving it a little shake. 'It was always Elizabeth-Jane at Briarbrae. And you won't mind if I call you Kate, now will you?' Remorselessly Mrs Duke began to steer Kate back up the street towards number forty-six.

'Was Julia at Briarbrae? No, I don't believe she was. I don't recall her at all and I'm sure I would for I never forget anyone I've met. People say my memory's a wonder. But you know I really won't be the least bit of bother. I'm used to dealing with invalids. Poor Mama was a martyr to her nerves. When she had one of her headaches we used to get all the servants to wear felt slippers and they had to put down straw in the carriageway whenever Papa and I went out for a drive.'

'We could go to a tea shop,' said Kate, trying to pull away without actually tugging. She was in despair at the thought of Elizabeth-Jane sailing into her house, staring at the worn linoleum, running her eye over harum-scarum Molly, smiling coldly as Jimmy, caked with dirt, gaped at the plumed hat.

'Now, now!' said Elizabeth-Jane, wagging a gloved finger. 'You're not to make a fuss of me. There's no need for extravagance, Kate, you know. I'm used to the very plainest food. Mama was always very careful about my diet. At home I was never allowed to eat pastries or anything of that sort and at school we simply had to eat what we were given, now didn't we? Oh my! D'you remember the tapioca pudding? No, no. Just a nice cup of tea and some bread and butter and I'll be as happy as a sandboy.'

There was nothing to be done. Elizabeth-Jane walked and talked inexorably on.

'So when Herbert found he had to come up to London on business, I said, "Well, I shall come with you." You see, Kate, there are several besides you that I have to speak to living in London now or nearby. You remember Elsie Dickens? She's married to such a charming man. They have a villa out at Lee in Kent. I wrote to Elsie and on Monday they sent their carriage for me. We had a wonderful day together talking over my plans. And then dear little Sarah Palmer—Mrs West, you know. Her place is on Richmond Hill with such a view. And Alice Oldershaw came to our hotel where we always stay. It's near Grosvenor Square. Nothing grand, dear, but they do try to make you really quite comfortable.'

At the door Kate's worst fears were realised. Jimmy was sitting on the step with his fists in his eyes, bawling his head off, while Violet and Gilbert, both with grubby faces and fingers in their mouths looked on, and Molly, nursing Charles in her arms, jigged uneasily in the doorway.

''E's 'urt 'isself,' said Molly. 'The rag and bone man's 'orse bit 'im.'

Kate thought she'd never been so mortified. She wished the earth would open and swallow her up.

Mrs Duke laughed.

'Oh dear, dear, dear! What a naughty horsie! And what's your name, little man?'

Jimmy shrank back in amazement as the white plumes bore down upon him.

''Is name's Jimmy,' said Molly.

'Well now, Jimmy, big strong boys like you don't make a fuss about a little bite.'

''Tisn't little,' said Jimmy. He pushed up his sleeve and showed her the purple marks. She recoiled in distaste.

'A good wash, I think.'

'Oh, great heaven!' cried Kate. 'Take him, Molly, do, and clean him up. Give Baby to me.'

She led Mrs Duke into the parlour, muttered something about tea and rushed to the kitchen. After quite a long time she came back followed by Molly with a tray of tea things.

'What about their dinner then?' said Molly sullenly. 'Wiv no sprats. There's nuffin' but bread an' drippin'.'

'Just make do as best you can, Molly.'

'Well, what a family you have!' exclaimed Mrs Duke, sipping her tea and glancing round the poky room with its desk and scattered ledgers. 'Four little ones all so close in age!' She waited expectantly with her head on one side, looking very much like a big spruce bird, eyeing a snail, but when Kate offered no tasty confidence she sighed and went on. 'Of course Herbert and I haven't been blessed, though really I'm so busy with my work I'd hardly have the time for a family. And, to be absolutely frank, my doctor feels it's really just as well. I never complain, of course. Everyone thinks I must have perfect health considering all I manage to get done, but between you and me, Kate, there are days when I hardly know how to put one foot in front of the other.'

Mrs Duke helped herself to another slice of bread and butter and sat nibbling thoughtfully. 'I daresay Herbert would have liked a boy—someone to help in the business and train up. And being so much older than I am he worries about me having no-one to care for me later on. I expect Mr Phillips is just the same, dear.'

Kate flushed, since it was very clear that Elizabeth-Jane expected nothing of the kind and was merely trying to goad her into revealing how she'd been dragged down to doing her own shopping in old clothes and living in Beaumont Street.

'Well,' said Mrs Duke after another pause, 'there are some,

I suppose, who just take each day as it comes. Though that won't do at the moment, will it? With next year just around the corner. We all of us have to think ahead for that. I expect you're already caught up in dozens of schemes.'

Kate looked bewildered and shook her head.

'But the Jubilee, dear! You must begin to make plans. You ought to form a committee straightaway. There must surely be at least a few of your neighbours who want to honour their Queen after sixty years. You ought to arrange some sort of commemoration—a horse trough with a suitable inscription, perhaps, and a tea for the poor children. In Bristol I'm laying plans for all sorts of events—a ball and I don't know what. I'm rushed off my feet already. But the bonne bouche, as Mama used to say, is to be my banner. You see, Kate, one of our friends is an alderman and one day he came to me and said, "We need a banner, Mrs Duke, to send to the Queen from our great City of Bristol, a banner to be carried in the Jubilee procession, and only you can design and execute the work." Well, what could I say? I set to work at once on the design— panels, you know, little scenes showing our city's great achievements. And I'm going about finding suitable people to carry out the work. There are orphan girls doing the borders, but I need quite accomplished fingers for the scenes themselves. And you, Kate, as I very well remember, sewed really very creditably at school. Now don't deny it because I remember as if it were yesterday that sweet little traycloth you embroidered for the competition when they gave the prize to me for my funny old doileys. So I want to put you down for the Cabot Tower or perhaps the Suspension Bridge, though that's in the very centre so I fancy I shall have to do that myself.'

'Oh, Elizabeth-Jane, I really couldn't. I never have time for embroidery any more.'

'Now listen to me, dear. All it takes is the will to manage things. I hope you won't mind me mentioning this, Kate, but I really think that if you were to make two or three little changes in your arrangements you'd be really quite amazed at the results.'

'We manage quite well, thank you,' said Kate. She was so angry and mortified that her hands began to shake. She quickly put down her cup, hoping that Elizabeth-Jane wouldn't notice.

'Oh, I'm sure you do, dear. Why, the lady at Hampstead—Mrs Jeffers—said the house there was just as bright and clean as a new pin when she moved in and the garden was a picture. She couldn't understand how you could bear to leave it. But I daresay with hubby working in the City he found the travelling a bother.'

When Kate made no reply to this, Mrs Duke swung back to her previous theme.

'That girl of yours, Kate. Anyone could see she's taking advantage. If she were a servant of mine I'd smarten her up in no time and get her doing twice what she does for you now. And the children, dear. When I was a child, even though I had everything money could buy, I was always taught to help and think of others. Now your Jimmy and even the little girl ought to be learning that they can't always have everything their own way. I'm sure they're old enough to take on simple tasks, lots of little errands and things like that. And I think you'd find that if you were to train them to be obedient you'd have much more time to yourself.'

'It's all very well,' burst out Kate at last, 'to tell people what they ought to do, Elizabeth-Jane . . .'

'Now, now, now! Nobody could ever say of me I don't practise what I preach. One of these days I'll take that little man of yours just for a month or so and show you what can be done. You won't know him when he comes home. Of course, not everyone has my natural gift of authority, but, even so, if you set yourself to make an effort, Kate, I'm sure you'd feel the benefit. Just make up your mind to be really firm. So, now, I'll put you down for the Cabot Tower, shall I?'

∽

For days after Elizabeth-Jane's visit Kate found herself going over and over what had been said, thinking of all the wonderfully crushing retorts she might have made if only they had come to her at the time. In the terrible scene at Cobham she had, at least, managed to speak her mind. Why then, confronted with her old school fellow, had she proved so weak spirited? She grew hot with shame, so violently gripped by the humiliation of having Elizabeth-Jane lording it over her in her own parlour, that she could sweep a whole flight of stairs or finish making a bed without being aware of what she was doing. Suddenly, like a sleepwalker, she would come to herself in the passage or at the bedroom door, quite startled at finding her task had been completed. And sometimes as she gazed dumbly at the staircase or the beds, the hot blood would ebb away out of her face leaving her sick, faint and frightened at the secret force of her feelings.

Over a week or so the sickness and the burning against Elizabeth-Jane became so closely linked that when she woke in the morning, feeling dizzy and nauseous, thoughts of the insolent advice she'd received began at once to go beating round and round her brain. She hung retching over the basin in the scullery stricken by the mortifying hint of truth in what Elizabeth-Jane had said, and as she wiped her face with her apron she began to rail inwardly against Jimmy. She saw him with her visitor's round, cold eye—a dirty, unmannerly, selfish little boy who cared nothing for his mother. He had shamed her so much that her health had broken down.

Much later in the day Kate would sit listlessly by the range and Julia would tell her that John cared for nobody except himself and Jimmy, that he never gave Kate or the other children a thought, that Jimmy wasn't just a naughty little boy, he was a cunning little monster, deliberately playing off his father against his mother and aunt to get his own way in everything. Look at all the work and trouble he made! Look at the way he treated Violet! Look at the nasty lies about them all that he must be pouring out to John when they went off together!

So when, finally, Kate felt a soreness in her breasts and realised that her sickness was caused not by mortification but by a new pregnancy, her horror at the discovery was oddly mixed with resentment against Jimmy as much as against John. It seemed to her that the child was deliberately driving her to breaking point.

Julia had always made such a fuss about her health that even Kate had fallen into the habit of taking her complaints with a pinch of salt, but as the spring wore on it became all too clear that Julia was seriously ill. She was losing weight, her cough was much worse and as she climbed the stairs she put her hand to her throat and gasped for breath. It was, perhaps, because of this that Kate's dream began to change again. Now, when she saw the hump on the beach she was immediately gripped by a terrible fear and began to run through the sand towards it. Although the ground was level and the sand only ankle-deep the running was dreadfully strenuous, as though the air were heavy as water, clogging her clothes and dragging against her limbs. She struggled on, beginning to pant, then, terrified of suffocation, drawing her breath in great shrieking gasps until, by the time she reached the sprawled corpse of the woman, she collapsed and fell with her face in the clammy folds of the blue skirt. And there she would lie, trying to get her breath, her eyes pressed shut against the wet, gritty cloth, while the trees above the beach churned and threshed in black, sibilant uproar.

One evening in early May Jimmy came running in ahead of his father, holding a bunch of cowslips he'd picked in a field. He found his mother sitting at the kitchen table with flushed cheeks while his aunt, looking triumphant and emphatic, sat bolt upright by the range, thrusting her needle in and out of one of Violet's pinnies. When Julia saw him she bundled up her sewing, got up and went out without a word, smiling to herself. For once Jimmy was sorry to see her go because he wanted to tell everyone about the empty blackbird's nest he'd found, with the baby birds all flown, and the old lady with a tabby cat who'd asked him and his father into her cottage, given them a piece of honeycomb and let him lean over her pigsty wall and scratch the pig's back with a stick. He went to give his mother the flowers but she pushed him away and burst into furious tears.

'What's this?' said John, putting down his cap.

'You don't think do you? You never think I might like to go out on a Sunday sometimes, that it might do me good just now to get a bit of a change and a breath of decent air. You never think what it's like for me stuck here in this place day in and day out. I don't know when it was you last took me anywhere. Oh no! It's always the boy!'

Jimmy, who had expected the cowslips to create a different kind of sensation, began to sob, whereupon John made the mistake of bending down to comfort him.

'There you see! He's all you ever think of! I could be lying dead at your feet and you'd never even notice. You'd think with the way I am you'd give me a bit of thought at least. But

118

nothing matters to you just as long as Jimmy gets it all his own way. Well, I tell you, he may be good when he's taken out for treats but all through the week when I'm left to cope with him he's a bad, naughty boy. I'm sick to death of the way he carries on, running wild in the street, tearing his clothes, bringing in mud, getting up to heaven knows what sort of tricks. I've told him again and again he's not to go off with those children from number six but he never takes a blind bit of notice. And what do you do? Just make him forty thousand times worse. Taking him out all the time when he doesn't deserve it! What about poor little Violet? What about Gilbert? What about your wife?'

John said nothing, just stood looking down at Jimmy.

'And what about the fares? There's no money for a bit of ribbon, no money for a proper cut of meat, no money for Julia's tonic. Not a penny to spare, leave alone anything to put by for when I'm laid up and there's another mouth to feed. I stick in this place, I scrimp and scrape all week and for what? Not so you can take me out for half-an-hour, not so I can put on a decent frock and get away from this filthy hole and the work and the dirt. Oh no, it's just so you and Jimmy can go gallivanting off on some wretched train.'

'I thought you'd like the flowers,' said Jimmy dolefully.

'Well, here's what I think of your flowers,' cried Kate, snatching them up and dashing them on the floor. 'There now! You're a bad, bad boy trying to get round me with flowers when you know you've done wicked things. Get up to bed this instant!'

'Now then!' said John roughly, grabbing her arm and giving her a smart shake. 'There's no need for that.'

'Let me go! Look what you've done to me! Look at my hands! Look at my hair! Look at this awful place! And you don't care. It'll kill me like it's killing Julia. I could die with this next one and you wouldn't care.'

'Yes, that'd be right. Julia! I might've guessed she put you up to this.'

'Nobody put me up to it. It's true. Get off! Let go my arm. You've ruined us, you filthy, gipsy brute, you and your nasty, wicked little brat.'

At this John hit Kate hard across the face so that she staggered back and fell heavily to the floor. There was a terrible silence broken only by a child's wailing from upstairs. Kate sat among the limp and scattered cowslips, put her hand to her lip and stared at the blood.

'You'll be sorry for that,' she said.

The idea of humbling herself before Elizabeth-Jane was so horrible to Kate that it began to attract her as the only enormity great enough to mark what John had done to her. If the blow across the face could drive her to that it would never be forgotten, the offence would never be diminished and everyone who knew about it would understand in the end that the wrong she had suffered was so great that it had to change all their lives forever. She was quite sure that if she humbled herself enough, wept, pleaded, confessed what Elizabeth-Jane was longing to hear and then poured on flattery, her old school fellow would be unable to resist her. She would take Jimmy away to Bristol and, if Kate continued to appeal to her in the right way, keep him there for months, perhaps years.

Her only fear was that John would find out where Jimmy had gone and go storming down to Bristol to bring him back. She wanted John to suffer not only from the loss of his son but from the knowledge that his own wicked cruelty to his wife had driven her to send the child away. He must see that it was all his fault, that his obsession with the boy had led him into behaving like a brute. But if he refused to acknowledge that the loss of Jimmy was a fitting punishment for an unforgivable crime, what could she do? If he raged at her, struck her again, even threatened her life, she might give way and tell him that Jimmy had gone to live with the Dukes. And then it occurred to her that she could say that the Dukes would do much more for Jimmy than John could do—that he'd live in a fine house, get proper attention, a good education and grow up to run a business. Then John would understand that he'd failed them all, even the one person he still loved, and Kate's revenge would be perfectly accomplished.

Next day, as John walked along in the sombre crowd hurrying towards the City, it came to him that he was turning out like his father, treating his wife as he'd seen his mother treated. That gesture—the woman touching the back of her hand to her lip and looking down to see the blood—he'd seen it when his mother stood leaning against the cottage wall as he came up to the back gate after school; and again at night, after the shouting stopped, when he crept out of bed to peer down at the dying fire, his father sprawled in a chair and his mother creeping falteringly about, setting the room to rights. The memory pierced him so sharply that he made up his mind at once to try to be kinder and that evening, when he got home, he went straight through to the kitchen to make his peace with Kate. But she shrank from him when he laid his hand on her arm and turned away her head with her face set like flint. And so it went on. Whatever he did to try to make amends, Kate barely spoke to him and never met his look. She went about gripped by her sense of grievance, turning over various plans in her mind. Now that she was calmer, she saw that she would have to move towards her object more cunningly than she'd thought at first. For nearly three weeks she pondered and schemed. Then one morning at breakfast, she said,

121

'My friend, Mrs Duke, wants Jimmy to go and stay with her in Bristol.'

'What! Whatever for?'

'She's taken a fancy to him, I suppose, and she wants to help me, seeing the way I am. Heaven knows I could do with one less to contend with for a bit.'

'Isn't she the woman came bothering you with that sewing? I thought you couldn't stand the sight of her.'

'Well, I like her now. She's very kind to me. When she was here again the other day she saw straightaway I was having trouble with my back. It hasn't been right, well—you know—since that night.'

It flashed upon John that this talk of sending Jimmy away was Kate's way of getting even with him, but he was too hampered by guilt to make much of a fight. He only said in a grumbling way,

'I don't know this Mrs Duke from Adam, or her husband.'

'Well, I've known her for years. You've no need to worry. They're very respectable. Her people were well off and her husband's in a really good way of business. They've got a beautiful house, a big garden, servants. Everything like we used to have in Hampstead.'

John looked morosely at the dresser. He sensed some kind of plot behind all Kate's assurances but could think of no very powerful objection.

'I don't know. What about his schooling?'

'Schooling! You know very well he hasn't set foot in a school since we came here. All he does is run wild.'

This was an awkward point. In Hampstead Jimmy had started to learn his letters at a little school kept by an elderly widow. After the move to Beaumont Street John had taken one look at the National School around the corner and decided Jimmy wasn't to go there. People called the master

122

'Old Skin-'em-Alive' and Molly said he gave the boys what for just to cool his temper.

'I thought you were looking round for some little place like Mrs Culverwell's.'

'There's nothing like that near here, and if there was you know we couldn't afford it. Anyway, Mrs Duke'll do more to help him on than we can.'

John sighed. It was time for him to leave for work. He picked up his hat and stood looking down at it, rubbing absently at a spot on the crown.

'Have you spoken to Jimmy yet?'

'Oh, he'll like it when he gets there,' said Kate quickly. 'It's more what he's used to isn't it? And I'd have thought even if you don't care about me getting a bit of rest you'd be glad for him to get away from this place for a few weeks.'

'How long's it for?'

'Just a few weeks. A month perhaps.'

Kate and Mrs Duke had agreed on a month's trial, although Kate was almost certain that Elizabeth-Jane had already decided to keep Jimmy in Bristol for much longer than that. It seemed to her that her old school mate was feigning caution because she wanted a heavy payment in gratitude and grovelling at every step of the way. This was true, although Mrs Duke was now so set on getting hold of Jimmy that she would have pressed on with the project even if Kate had been less satisfyingly abject. She was quite in love with the idea of moulding a new young spirit, training up a faithful slave to serve her.

After only a few weeks of marriage, Mrs Duke had decided that she wanted no more of Herbert's fumbling embraces, and had banished him to a bedroom at the back of the house. Afterwards, sitting at her dressing table as she brushed her hair and studied her large, pinkish face in the mirror, she had considered what it would mean to be childless. Most people, she knew, would regard her with contempt or pity as barren, inadequate, unfulfilled, but when she thought of the way in which the proud mothers of large families must allow themselves to be used and invaded by their husbands, her own lips curled in contempt. She thought, too, of the degrading shapelessness of pregnancy, the shameful discomforts secretly endured, the awful mysterious agonies of childbirth that destroyed the health of so many delicate women, and shuddered with outrage in all her sleek, carefully tended flesh. All the same, it was unfortunate that her gift of authority should not be given full rein, and troubling that eventually, when Herbert had grown old or passed away, there would be no-one to make sure she was comfortably provided for.

Jimmy, once Mrs Duke fastened her mind on him, presented himself to her as something even better than a son who could be hers without the usual degradation and pain. Because he had no natural claim on her, no familial rights, everything she did for him would demonstrate her generosity. Moreover, with him, she would feel free to use whatever training methods she liked, to experiment, if necessary to be more severe than might have been possible with a boy who had her own blood in him.

As soon as Kate had spoken to John about Jimmy leaving for Bristol, she acted very swiftly. She wrote at once to Elizabeth-Jane, packed Jimmy's sailor suits and nightshirts into a little wooden box, took him along to Paddington station and left him with a guard on the Bristol train. When John put his head into the children's room on Sunday morning, Jimmy's bed in the corner stood smooth and empty.

FIVE

Louie had been writing very fast, scribbling away on notepads until late at night, hurried along by unexpected rushes of emotion shooting up from events buried in the past—like the quarrel in the cabin near Mount Macedon when Stuart had gone blundering into the night and knocked her down. Weird unsuspected passions hidden away under familiar daylight states of feeling. They drove her off the path she was expecting to follow so that 'The Brown Photograph' twisted into a shape she'd never intended.

'It might have been like that,' she thought defensively. Her story took account of most of the facts she held and allowed her to feel she'd reached some understanding of the people whose names she'd given to her characters. But it certainly wasn't a family chronicle. It was more like a novella, though—even if she changed all the names to fictitious ones—hardly something she could send off to her agent.

After only a few days Louie realised that her reasons for starting 'The Brown Photograph' were different from her reasons for going on with it. She looked back at her old self, poised on the brink of the story, with surprise and a faint contempt. At the beginning she had set out to wear in Susan's revelations like a pair of new shoes by spending all her time in them until, in the end, she'd have no need to think about them any more. She'd felt, too, that she had to find a way of forgiving her father for his deceit and the couple in the photograph for handing over their eldest son to somebody as odious as Grandma Duke. But now all that seemed irrelevant. She went on because she had to discover what would happen, following a trail like the children in the fairytale who found their way through the forest by moving from one white pebble to the next. She was trying to get things right by looking through books on Victorian fashion and household crafts. She gathered up memoirs, recipes and maps of nineteenth-century London. She went to the state library and photocopied excerpts from *The Times*, including a long description of Queen Victoria's Jubilee procession which passed through London on 22 June 1897. She was halfway through the account when she realised that this was the date on Julia Barker's tombstone.

She felt as though Fate had suddenly nudged her in the ribs, drawing her attention to some connection between the Jubilee, celebrated with all the pomp of the high noon of Empire, and the death of Tobias Barker's younger daughter. Here was another white stone beckoning in the darkness, another link in the chain of cause and effect that was unwinding little by little towards a dénouement that neither she nor her characters could yet imagine.

Meanwhile, in her own life, it was August—the

southern hemisphere's late winter. The wattles were coming into bloom, acid-yellow and primrose, filling the air with their sweet, powdery scent. From her desk Louie could see them shining in the dark bush on the hills beyond the city like lighted windows. There was one in her back garden with stiff, stemless leaves, sharp as pricked ears. 'The Ovens wattle,' she said to herself, pleased at knowing the tree's name.

Back in her schooldays, Louie had taken quite a pride in being able to name the trees and wildflowers that grew in the countryside around Brean or in the fields near Bath where she used to go for picnics. She'd pressed leaves and flowers between the pages of books and arranged them, carefully labelled, in her album—cowslip, dog violet, bluebell, oak, horse chestnut, elm. But in Tasmania, twenty years ago, she'd felt sad and foreign at not being able to give her son the names of the plants they saw when they went walking in the bush. It had seemed as though she was failing to pass on a title, leaving Tim disinherited in his new country. But gradually, through looking in books and picking up hints from other people, she'd reached the stage where peppermint gums and she-oaks, ti-tree and dolly bush were almost as familiar as the nightshade and primroses of her childhood. 'Look, Tim,' she'd say. 'That's a swamp gum.' But he'd never shown much interest in this landscape tamed and colonised by the naming of its parts.

While she was learning what to call some of the native plants, Louie began to discover more about the history of Tasmania, finding that the network of names laid over the island by white explorers and pioneer settlers constituted a title superimposed on a much older nomenclature, an Aboriginal language spoken by people who had been virtually swept away by the invaders. Here and there fragments of the old tongue—Wayatinah, Koonya, Poatina—showed through the blanket of white men's words, but, for the most part, the names of rivers, mountains and towns made up a map of nineteenth-century British culture. The geologist, Charles Gould, dispatched to search for gold in the western ranges, stamped the terrain with his view of the newly published *On the Origin of Species* by naming three huge peaks in honour of Darwin's opponents—Sedgwick, Owen and Jukes—and three much smaller mountains after Darwin and his allies, Lyell and Huxley. Other placenames commemorated the Empire's religion (Jericho and the Jordan River); its early heroes (Mounts Wellington and Nelson); its statesmen and monarchs (Hobart and George Town); above all its loyalty to the distant homeland (Devonport and New Norfolk, Launceston and Richmond, Exeter, Cambridge and Somerset). Even the native people themselves, where they survived the invaders' guns and diseases, had been renamed. Scrubbed, catechised and dressed in European clothes they'd become Queen Caroline, King Billy, Jackey and—as a tribute to the popularity of Thomas Moore— Lalla Rookh.

It struck Louie that in migrating back into the nineteenth century she was colonising the past in an odd reversal of the way in which the early settlers had colonised the island in which she now lived, letting the old names stand and imposing on them creations born out of her own culture, her own image. And though the path she was following through her ersatz nineteenth-century landscape seemed inevitable, each step determined by the one that had gone before, she knew very well that, all the time, the Phillipses were moving further and further away from the people in the photograph. With every detail she added to their lives, the chances that this accumulation of dreams, quarrels, smells, neighbours, sugar casters and burned potatoes could match any other accumulation of details—any actual set of experiences— steadily diminished. She was changing them all—even her own father—into beings who were acceptable in the enclave of her mind, dressing them according to her own ideas, destroying as surely as a pestilence what had actually existed.

There was one character, of course, about whom she felt no scruples. Even after nearly forty years, Louie could summon up no pity for the old woman she'd last seen propped up in a hospital bed waiting to die. She still felt only aversion, bred into her during the years when Grandma Duke had brooded like a bogeywoman in the upstairs flat. Every memory she had of her was sharp with spite. There was the time, for instance, when James had shown Grandma Duke Louie's school report: 'Mathematics—Very Good; English—Louisa works very well; History—An excellent term's work.' Rubbing one foot up and down the calf of her other leg, almost tying herself in knots in the sly, jubilant expectation of Grandma Duke having to pay her a compliment, Louie had squirmed around in the corner by the piano. She could still see the hand limply holding the report, Grandma Duke's jowl squeezed out in a fat pink roll over the collar of her black dress, the white hair, stained at the roots like a smoker's moustache.

There had been a long silence while Grandma Duke read with her head held back and her mouth slightly open. Then she said, 'Don't they teach them sewing any more?'

James, anxiously bending forward and pointing, suggested sewing might be included in 'Hand-work'.

'Oh yes. "Fair". Dear, dear! Still, they don't make them work like we had to, do they?'

She put down the report and went on with her crochet, never even giving Louie a glance.

Beatrice, when she heard about it, went red with rage. 'Never mind. It's ignorance, that's all.'

Louie could remember her mother glaring round the kitchen, searching for an object as mindless as Grandma Duke, snatching the kettle from the stove and shaking it in Louie's face.

'She's got about as much brain as this kettle!' Bang! went the kettle, down on the unlit gas ring. Beatrice gave it a look of furious contempt. 'Enough to make a cat laugh!'

In a way, though, memories like this gave Grandma Duke a charmed life. There was no filching of her name for some imagined usurper, no journeying along with her into the unknown because her end—the fat hands unfolding the nightdresses, the upended drawers and scattered liquorice—was already in place.

Early in August Frank wrote again, suggesting that Louie might visit him in London. There was plenty of room in his flat in Maida Vale. Together they could go about gleaning all the information she needed for her history. They could call on Aunt Violet, Aunt Annie, Cissie, Jane and the Gascoignes of Bathurst Hall. Or he could do the legwork and she could stay at home in the flat and write. He had a boxful of papers that had belonged to their grandmother, Alice Gale, Old Howard's wife, which he was sure would interest her. It would, he wrote, be wonderful to see her again.

The idea of meeting Violet and Annie began to seem entrancing. They were after all the only survivors of the family who had settled in the cheerless house in Beaumont Street, the only people still alive—so far as Louie knew—who had shared the day-to-day lives of the real Kate and John. Provided their memories were still intact and they were willing to talk about their early lives, they would be able to supply dozens of details which Louie could obtain from no other source. It was as though time in 'The Brown Photograph' had gone rolling on and now, by travelling through space, she could intercept it and move into the world of her own fiction where some of her own characters were still living.

But after a time she began to feel doubtful. She wanted very much to know what had become of her grandparents in their later years and how and when they'd died. Yet, by now, she was so absorbed in the imaginary world she'd created that she was nervous of being challenged by revelations which might destroy it. For the time being, at least, she wanted to believe that 'The Brown Photograph' was about real people in whose company she was moving towards a true discovery. She was also doubtful about the whole idea of going back to England. If she took up Frank's invitation she was bound to come face to face with the question of where she was going to spend the rest of her life—a problem which seemed so huge and complicated that she still shied away from thinking it through.

Sometimes she and George had talked about how they'd travel around the world when George retired. They played endless private games based on books they'd read together.

'Let's go to Venice and look around for that hotel where Hemingway's Colonel used to stay.'

'And what will my Colonel take for breakfast on a fine morning when the cold wind is blowing from the high mountains?'

'Bring me half a hundred Martinis, double and very dry with olives from the dead ground by the canal where the tanks broke through.'

They played the same kind of game about coming across some magical place which both of them would recognise at once as their true home—an abandoned Portuguese fort on a tropical island or a house of weathered brick in chestnut woods.

'It was Fate that led us on to this valley road.'

'Or was it because I was reading the map upside down?'

'Not surprising after that breakfast we had in Venice.'

All the same they'd never thought seriously of giving up the country where they'd met and been happy together. Home was simply where the other lived, the house, the city, the view from the kitchen window which they'd shared over the years with one another. But without George Louie felt like someone who wakes after a long dream in a strange room. Australia in the eighties seemed alien, obsessed with sport and money. Even her closest friends had changed in the weeks since George's death, just as she had changed for them, no longer Louie of Louie-and-George but a woman on her own, a solitary, embarrassingly mournful figure who rejected any comfort they could offer. Perhaps, thought Louie, no comfort could ever be found in a place which she'd known for so long with and through George, so that if she meant to go on living at all she'd have to go back to where she'd started and begin again.

Or was it too late to go back? Places like Ollerton would be so changed she'd feel like a foreigner or a ghost. All the elm trees had died of Dutch elm disease. A motorway, leading to a bridge over the River Severn, ran through the fields where Frank had taken her and Susan to watch the haymakers. If Frank's old house was still standing it would be closed to her, the property of people she'd never met. And her own home in Howard Road would belong to strangers. She was as homeless now in Britain as the tramps who used to come to the back door before the war, asking Beatrice for a drop of meths for their sore feet. Gone too was her safe personal niche in her suburb, her generation, eroded away like a scratch on some windswept cliff. All the elderly neighbours in Howard Road must be long dead: Mrs Morgan who sold saving stamps to help the war effort, old Mr Patterson with his bald red head who strode up and down during air-raids shouting Shakespeare up at the Luftwaffe— 'Blow winds and crack your cheeks.' All Louie's school friends had lost touch with her and vanished into lives of which she knew nothing. And what about the few who remembered her? What would they think when, after staying away when her parents were dying, she turned up a few months after her father's funeral? She knew very well what Ian, Susan's husband, would say. She could hear him already, hinting to Susan that Louie was dissatisfied because James had left most of his money to the daughter who'd looked after him in his old age. 'She's here for what she can get. She's after the furniture, after the clocks, after a hand-out. Keep an eye on that one!'

Nearly all Louie's Hobart friends—most of them migrants, many of them English—had been back to their countries of origin at least once since they'd settled in

Tasmania. People she'd known in her teaching days, other writers, George's university colleagues, went to and fro like swallows for holidays, conferences and family visits. Why hadn't she done the same? In the early days, it was true, she'd been short of money and wary of quarrelling with Stuart about taking Tim out of the country. But after Tim had enrolled in his accountancy course, after she'd found George, she could have arranged a trip to England quite easily. George had often urged her to go and see her father. He'd offered more than once to come with her during a long vacation. But until Susan's phone call last April Louie had always found some excuse for staying put. It was guilt, of course, that had kept her in Tasmania. Guilt at having disappointed her parents by ditching the glittering career they'd expected her to have, marrying a hippie with dangerous opinions and burying herself away in a Sussex commune. And then, when Stuart had entered his Ché Guevara phase and set out to carry the revolution to the Antipodes, she'd deserted her mother and father for ever more, leaving them to grow old and sick and die without ever seeing them again.

Guilt was coming at her now from all sides because George was no longer there to keep it at bay. Except in questions that she'd sealed up from him, secrets stowed in the attics of her mind, George had always shown her what to do—or rather, simply by believing in her, had made it possible for her to find her own way. He had been the great enabler, who helped her go confidently forward making sensible choices. He'd always admired even her smallest achievements. He'd thought her wonderfully good at organising their day-to-day life together so that bit by bit she'd discarded her habit of concentrating obsessively on a few details and become genuinely efficient.

George had reinvented her as superwoman so that she could type up a chapter of a novel before eleven o'clock in the morning, arrange for the plumber to come and fix the shower, plant out a bed of lettuces, take the car to be serviced, whip up a three-course dinner for eight and appear at seven looking surprisingly well groomed to have a drink with George before the first guests arrived. Not so now. Now that George was gone the persona that had fitted her like a protective skin was peeling away, revealing an unwelcome new creature, timid, self-pitying, ungainly, an easy prey to monstrous accusations.

Louie put her head in her hands.

'How absurd! How absurd! I can't refuse to go just because I ought to have gone back years ago.'

SIX

Frank's next report arrived before Louie had decided what to do about his invitation. After his visit to Bathurst Hall, Frank's old university friend, Teddy Gascoigne, had gone back to searching through his Aunt Elfreda's mementoes. Eventually he'd phoned Frank with news of an extraordinary find.

'Masses more photos. Went haring down to look. Will make copies for you as soon as I can though still hoping you'll come and see the originals for yourself. Lots of shooting parties. Some here, some Teddy says at Coombe Bassett, family seat near Barnstaple. A couple with HRH and various cronies, like poor old Christopher Sykes. All with cigars, deer-stalkers, tweed jackets. Gascoignes in full force. Teddy's great-grandparents. Elfreda with shooting stick, brother Henry, lost later on the *Ariadne*, Cousin Grindley from Victoria who took over Coombe Manor. Also, very oddly, several photos of Old Howard sporting huge moustache. NEXT: the pretty young thing

I thought might be Grandmother Kate clearly identified. Kate and Elfreda in ball-gowns—'Miss Barker and Self'. THEN, most intriguing of all a whole stack of photos of YOUR FATHER. Some by himself at various ages. Some with Mr Duke and Bertoli. Some with Elfreda and, again, Old Howard. What do you make of that? Did Elfreda decide to take an interest in James because of her friendship with Kate? Maybe she arranged for him to go to the Dukes. Didn't you tell me Old Howard acted for them? Maybe he handled the whole business. Teddy has more romantic ideas. Thinks James might have been Elfreda's child by some secret tweedy lover. Or possibly Grandmother Kate's by Henry Gascoigne. Annie and Violet may know something about it. Why don't we pay them a visit? Hope you're still thinking about what I said. Do come!'

An undated clipping from the *Barnstaple Courier* was pinned to Frank's letter.

FAREWELL DINNER FOR MR GRINDLEY GASCOIGNE

The impending departure of Mr Grindley Gascoigne for Australia, the land of his birth, has occasioned mixed feelings of sadness and sympathetic enthusiasm in the district in which he and his parents, Mr and Mrs Edward Gascoigne, have become so well known and admired in recent years. As many readers will be aware, Coombe Manor and the accompanying estate have been since time immemorial the property of the Gascoigne family. The property was inherited some years ago by Sir Henry Gascoigne of Bathurst Hall, Wiltshire, who subsequently sold it to his cousin, Mr Grindley Gascoigne, a member of a cadet branch of the family.

Since that time the efforts of father and son, affectionately known as the 'Old Squire' and the 'Young Squire', to improve both the estate and the lot of all those who depend upon them have become an example to every landowner throughout the length and breadth of Britain. Farms which had fallen into other hands have been re-acquired and every agricultural holding put on a sound footing so that they are now among the most productive in the country. Under the experienced eye of Mr Grindley Gascoigne a large stud farm has been established, set fair to yield many famous champions of the Turf. Through the generosity of Mr Edward Gascoigne a new parish hall, model cottages and a number of other amenities have been constructed at Coombe Bassett where the general activity has provided employment for all and sundry, and increased the prosperity of the entire population for many miles around.

Mr Edward Gascoigne has now decided to take up permanent residence at Coombe Bassett and, in consequence, returned recently to Victoria to negotiate the sale of his Australian property. Being impatient to resume the mantle of the 'Old Squire', he has grown weary of the law's delays in the land of the gum tree and the emu, and has requested his son to assume the task of overseeing the completion of this sale. The return of Mr Gascoigne, the elder, is now awaited with an eagerness which is tempered only by the knowledge that, for a time, the 'Young Squire' will be absent in his stead.

At a dinner attended by many local luminaries, a large party gathered on Saturday last at the Crown in Barnstaple to drink the health of the traveller and wish him

God speed. Mr Ernest Bradstock, who has served for many years as butler at Coombe Manor, expressed the sentiments of the assembled company when he raised his glass to his young master, wishing him well in his Australian venture and urging him to return as soon as he conveniently might so that there would be 'Gascoignes for ever more at Coombe Manor'.

There followed a list of dinner guests and a scribbled line in what might have been Elfreda's handwriting: 'Never came back. Married, died in Queensland 1935.'

Louie felt quite bemused by all this: Teddy's seductive theories, the pages about cousin Grindley, who, apart from his Australian connection, seemed to have no real claim on her interest. But the name Gascoigne stirred a faint memory linked in some way with Christmas. In Howard Road one of the annual excitements had been the arrival of dozens of Christmas cards which, after Twelfth Night, Louie and Susan were allowed to cut up. Suddenly she remembered a particularly large card, one of the dull ones with no picture for her scrapbook, nothing but some sort of gold motif on the front.

She'd tried to read the name inside—Elfreda Gas-something—and Beatrice had said, 'Oh, Miss Gascoigne! Lady Muck more like. You'd think she was God Almighty the way people go on.' 'People', it seemed were Grandpa Gale and James, who, now that Louie thought of it, had once remarked that you wouldn't see clocks like Miss Gascoigne's in a day's march. Then Louie remembered the photograph Beatrice had discovered in the attic, and wondered if the third butterfly hunter was the Mr Bertoli mentioned in Frank's letter, released from the cares of his

photographic studio to give Mr Duke a hand with the
Gascoignes' clocks and, afterwards, reap a reward in
butterflies. Perhaps it was he who had taken some of the
photographs of James which Teddy had found at Bathurst
Hall. Or perhaps one of the Gascoignes had been gripped
by a passion for photography and had fastened on the
clockmaker's boy as an interesting new subject.

Next day Emma rang up. She and Tim were off to
Melbourne for the weekend but at the last moment Caro
Nettleship, who'd agreed to look after Oliver, had come
down with flu.

'I'll take him,' said Louie. She was really pleased.
Oliver's visits were few and far between.

'Mum and Dad say you fill my head with nonsense,'
he'd told her once.

Louie went out to buy ingredients for pizzas so that she
and Oliver could cook together, and baked him a tray of
gingerbread men. When he arrived she showed him how
to cut slits in Spanish chestnuts before pushing them into
the ashes of the fire.

'Oliver, I'm thinking of going away for a while to
England. What do you think?'

'Why? Why d'you want to go?'

He was sitting on the floor, watching the chestnuts.
His hair which had been almost white when he was
a toddler gleamed in the firelight like polished black-
wood.

'I want to find out some things about my Grandma and
Grandpa and my Dad. I'm writing a book about them.
About his life when he was a little boy.'

'Did he go to school?'

Oliver was preoccupied with school because he'd started attending fulltime a few months ago.

'Yes. My mum showed me the house once. It wasn't a school any more though. Just a big dark house with a very tangly garden like the Sleeping Beauty's. An old couple ran the school. I don't think they taught the children much but they were quite kind. My dad used to water the old lady's ferns. And they used to have soup, very thick soup.'

'We don't get soup. We take sandwiches to school in our lunchboxes.'

'I don't think Dad had any sandwiches. He didn't live with his own mother and father, you see. He lived with a very nasty woman called Grandma Duke.'

'Was she like a witch? Was she really cruel?'

'She was pretty scary. I don't know exactly what she did. Mum thought she used to lock him up in the cellar.'

'What's a cellar?'

'A dark place under the house where people used to keep coal.'

Oliver picked up the poker and gave the chestnuts a prod. He was trying to picture what it would be like to be locked in a cellar like this other boy. What it would be like to be somebody else who had soup at school and was then shut up in the dark. Grandma Louie often told him stories about creatures who slid out of their own bodies and took on different shapes. Gods who turned into people whenever they wanted. Humans changed into animals or birds, even trees and stars. His favourite stories were about the seal people who looked like everyone else when they took off their skins but when they put them on again changed back to seals. He tried to imagine turning into a seal, everything in his body that was Oliver

142

sucked out like runny jelly and blown into a seal skin so that he could dive down to the bottom of the sea and speed warm and safe far out under icy waves.

Only there was something here, a difference, a baffling problem so immense that it frightened him. What if instead of changing into a seal or a different sort of boy, an Eskimo, say, or an Aborigine out in the desert, he'd been *born* into another shape? Then he'd have a different sort of brain and wouldn't be the Oliver who was learning to ride the bike he'd been given for his birthday and had to go round to the Nettleships all the time to play with dumb Damian. That Oliver wouldn't exist at all anywhere in the world. This idea made him so giddy his legs felt weak, just as they had on the day his father took him to the top of the Bruny Island lighthouse and made him look over the rail at the rocks below.

'I'm glad I'm not that boy.'

Louie looked at him quickly, contrite at having upset him.

'It was all right in the end. He had quite a happy life when he was older. Let's get the chestnuts out.'

After they'd peeled off the flaking black shells and eaten the chestnuts they went into the kitchen to make pizzas for tea. While Oliver was grating cheese he started asking questions about the trip to England. Would Louie go on an aeroplane? Would she come back soon? He had no doubt at all that she would go and when he went home on Sunday night he told his parents Gran was going to England very soon. Within a few days the project developed a magnetic force, drawing Louie towards it much as her characters in 'The Brown Photograph' were carried towards the established facts in their lives, like the gathering in the Holborn photographer's studio—known

143

points through which the threads of their stories were fated to run.

Because she'd taken so long to reply to Frank's invitation Louie decided to ring him up. His voice sounded strange, light, quick, high-pitched with delight when she said she would come to London in September. They talked for longer than Louie had intended, partly because she needed a full description of Bathurst Hall for the next episode of her story.

In the course of the next month Elizabeth-Jane wrote several times to Kate. The letters were filled with sorrowful reproof: 'Our vicar, Mr Chisholm, was really *very* distressed to find that James did not even know his catechism' . . . 'I must say I had not expected our little man's table manners to be good but was rather shocked at the really *slovenly* way in which he ate when he first arrived' . . . 'Having been really thoroughly spoiled James is finding it hard to understand that he must think of others and learn to make himself useful' . . . 'It is a great pity that James, though nearly seven years old, has never been taught to *apply* himself to his lessons. I am afraid it will be quite a long time before he is able to reply to the letters his father keeps writing.'

Kate digested this as best she could, dropped the complaints into the range and told John Mrs Duke was very pleased with Jimmy.

'Where's the letter?' John would say, looking inside the empty envelope.

'Oh, it's there somewhere. They took him to Blaise Castle last Sunday. Next weekend they're going to the seaside.'

John wrote every week to Jimmy, carefully printing the words so that he could read them and filling the margins with drawings of farmers riding to market, Tray eating bones and the farmer's wife running after chickens. Elizabeth-Jane took up the letters in the hall before anyone else saw them, slit them open with her paperknife, ran an eye scornfully over the pages and locked them away in her bureau until she had collected enough to make a little bonfire in the morning room grate.

Late in June, when Jimmy had been in Bristol for just over a month, John announced that he would go down on the train to bring him home.

'Oh, you wouldn't do that!' cried Kate.

'Why not?'

'She can bring him back herself when she comes up to London. If you go down it'll look as though we don't trust her. After all she's done.'

Another week went by.

'Look here,' said John, 'say what you like, I'm going down on Sunday. He was meant to be home two weeks ago. He ought to be here with us, not staying with some stranger all the time.'

'Well you can't. They're going to Weston on Sunday and there's no time now to write and let them know.'

'Then I'll go on Monday.'

'And lose a day's pay? How are we going to manage at the end of the week?'

Jimmy's seventh birthday fell on the sixteenth of July. Sometimes now, when she thought of Elizabeth-Jane teaching Jimmy better table manners or putting him through his catechism, Kate was shaken by a spasm of guilt. And resentment of Elizabeth-Jane's high-handed ways, that she had crushed down so firmly, reared up. She kept telling herself that whatever Elizabeth-Jane said or did, *she* was still Jimmy's mother, until, in the week before the birthday, she decided to demonstrate this by baking him a cake. She decorated it with pink icing, packed it up in a box and sent it down to Bristol. She asked John if he wanted to put a present in the parcel but he shook his head and said he'd send off something himself. Kate stared in surprise, opened her mouth to speak and then turned silently away.

That very afternoon she had come across a box in the

parlour cupboard and, peeping inside, had discovered a toy yacht with a green hull, a hinged mast and two white sails. She'd known at once that John had bought the yacht for Jimmy's birthday and thought he must have hidden it in the cupboard for fear of what she'd say about the expense or the way he favoured Jimmy before everyone else. She'd lifted the toy out of its box, set up the mast and stared at the slick, green paint. The thing seemed to come out of a world far away from Beaumont Street where all was new, spruce and jolly, where neat little children in clean clothes ran between barbered lawns and sunlit lakes, and starched nursemaids walked placidly up and down wheeling beautifully frilled infants in baby carriages. And beyond that world was another where elegant men and women amused themselves on life-size yachts with crisp white sails and hulls as brightly painted as the green one in Kate's hands. She pictured these fashionable people standing on deck, lounging on the taffrail, gazing down to where the reflection of wavelets ran in a net of light on the yacht's flank. And then it seemed that there was a heeling, a staggering, a shrieking as the green hull rose up and up from the water, sliding up like a whale from the sunlit sea, and keeling right over there where the bright tide ran swiftly away to a long pale beach and a mass of trees.

Kate managed to get the toy back into the cupboard but vowed not to touch it again. Thinking of it as something ill-omened, she was glad that soon it would be packed up and sent out of the house. But when she went back to look the next day, it was still on its shelf. Even on the fifteenth, the day before Jimmy's birthday, it was still there, waiting in the cupboard. When she saw this, Kate knew what John was planning to do. He meant to go off tomorrow without saying a word, deliver the present himself and, unless he could be prevented, bring Jimmy home with him in the evening. She

147

called out to Molly that she was going down the street for a minute, pulled on her hat and hurried away at once to the telegraph office.

❧

Mrs Duke was sitting in the morning room by the empty summer fireplace, studying her Bradshaw train timetable. Like the other principal rooms in the house—Mrs Duke's bedroom, the dining room, the parlour—the morning room was handsomely furnished and decorated with an array of ornaments, pictures and silver from her old home in Clifton. The smaller bedrooms and poky apartments known as 'the study' and 'the play room' were very different. They had thin threadbare carpets, cheap deal furniture and skimpy curtains. All Mrs Duke's domestic arrangements were like this—outwardly rather grand, but behind the opulent facade, very meagre.

'All front she is,' said Mrs Beale, the cook, whacking her thigh, wheezing, doubling up at the thought of Mrs Duke's imposing bosom. When she recovered from the joke she would go on contemptuously, ''Er people never 'ad the money she makes out and she ain't got it now neither.'

And it was true that Mrs Duke's father's sugar business had been less prosperous than she liked everyone to think, while her husband's watch and clockmaker's shop in the Horsefair, though a solid concern, brought in too little to support a lavish style of living.

There were only two servants, Mrs Beale, who was old and downtrodden and Mary-Ann, the maid-of-all-work, a big bad-tempered girl with a heavy tread and a slurry Somerset voice. Mrs Duke kept after them all the time, going down to the kitchen, looking through Cook's accounts, exclaiming over the price she'd paid for carrots, ferreting in the cake tins, telling her to put on fewer potatoes, peel the apples more thinly and make the remains of the joint do for supper.

''S all very well for She,' grumbled Mary-Ann.

And it was. Mrs Duke fortified herself with liquorice and Turkish delight and liked to order up little snacks through the day—a few muffins, a couple of soft boiled eggs, tea and cake, a taste of ham and pickles—so that she came to the dinner table quite well fed and sighed when Herbert asked for a second helping of cabbage. James never had a chance to ask for second helpings of anything. He was being trained to finish chewing what was in his mouth before taking another bite. If he failed to do this, Mrs Duke said he was bolting his food and rapped him over the knuckles with one of her heavy silver spoons. However hard he tried he could never manage to finish the little portion served up to him at the start of a meal before Mary-Ann appeared to whisk away the dishes.

While Mrs Duke brooded over her Bradshaw, James sat at a table nearby with a large blotter in front of him. On the blotter was an open copy book with lines of beautifully curved esses, graceful as little swans. Underneath each line of copperplate was a space for James to make his own letters, each of which was supposed to be a perfect image of the one above. He had a bottle of black ink and a pen with a very fine, sharp, steel nib. He was gripping the pen so tightly that the nib bit into the side of his middle finger, making a red ridge. He thought the ridge looked like the weals that came up right across his palm when Aunt Elizabeth-Jane caned him for not polishing her shoes properly or coming to the table with dirty fingernails or, as happened most often, failing to copy his letters neatly enough.

He looked furtively across at her and watched as she reached out her large pale hand. From the box on the table at her side she took a cube of Turkish delight, dusted with fine white sugar. A ray of sunshine, coming from a crack in the gauzy curtains at the window, lay across the patterned carpet and shone like a bar of gold on the far wall. When Aunt Elizabeth-Jane lifted her Turkish delight to her mouth, a flurry of sugar dust drifted into the beam of light. James thought that if he were to stand there by the little table with his tongue out, the dust would settle sweetly on his tongue and he would eat the air.

Very slowly he dipped the pen into the ink, scraped the nib against the bottle lip and started to write. He managed several quite passable esses and was just dipping the pen in the ink again when Aunt Elizabeth-Jane suddenly shut her timetable and tossed it aside. Startled, James dropped a tiny blob of ink on the top of his page. He stared at it appalled and the blot stared back with one bright, little highlight on its blackness, like the eye of a chick. Quietly he pulled out his handkerchief and wiped the eye away, changing it to a smudge that curved up to the edge of the page. Keeping his eyes on Aunt Elizabeth-Jane, he put the handkerchief to his face, as though he wanted to blow his nose, pushed a corner into his mouth and chewed it quickly to make it wet. When he wiped the smudge it almost disappeared although the paper looked a bit grey and had a little wave in it. He thought it might just go unnoticed though, and felt quite relieved until he saw that somehow, in wiping away the blot, he had smudged his row of letters. At home, in Beaumont Street, he had a book full of coloured pictures of ancient gods and heroes, driving chariots or sweeping through the air with cloaks flying out behind them in misty swirls. It seemed to him that his esses, each with its greyish, upswept trail, had taken on the look of the man who went hurtling about in the sun's chariot or the one who fell down in the sea when his wings melted. He wondered how Aunt Elizabeth-Jane would punish him. His heart began to beat against the edge of the table. Perhaps, since it was his birthday, she would just make him stand in the corner for a while and not bring out the cane or, worse still, march him along to the cellar, push him down the steps and lock the door.

At first he hadn't minded being shut in the cellar very much. That first day he'd played for hours under the high slot of cobwebby window that looked out into the path beside the house, and although towards evening he'd begun to feel quite dizzy with hunger, he'd gone on thinking that it was better to be shut up than beaten. But then the light had started to fade. James had never been very frightened of the dark before, but suddenly he was overcome by the terrible fear that everyone had forgotten him, that he would be left down there alone, locked up all night and for days and nights on end until he starved to death. At about this point, when it was so black that he couldn't even see the shape of the window any more, something began to move about behind the strip of wall that hid the coal heap. At first there were just little creaks and rattles that might have been caused by quite a small creature. Then there was a much louder sudden kind of rushing clatter as though a monster like a huge turtle had begun to stir about, sloughing lumps of coal from its back. And then it began to breathe. James sat crouched on a broken box, trying to hold his own breath so that the creature wouldn't hear and find out where he was. He heard the thing pant and sigh, stir sharply again, and he thought it had risen out of the coal and was coming to get him. He started to scream, and screamed and screamed until Mary-Ann came clumping along the passage to let him out.

'Missus says you're to come up now,' she said. ''Ere, what's all this 'ullaballoo? Cook and me 'eard you bawling down in the kitchen. Lucky for you She never 'eard or you'd catch it.'

151

When James tried to tell her about the thing in the coal she seemed to think he was making fun of her and said he was a storyteller.

'Just you try telling She your stories,' she said, 'and see what you get.'

Ever since, whenever he was locked up in the cellar, James had taken to huddling on the top step, as far as he could get from the black opening to the place where the coal was stored. He breathed as quietly as possible, taking shallow sips of air, and all the time straining his ears for the sound of the creature stirring.

'Well now,' said Aunt Elizabeth-Jane. 'How have we been getting on today?'

She came and stood behind James's chair. Her big arm in its white sleeve, her big, clean hand came over his shoulder and the big clean, finger pointed at the smudged page.

'What's this?'

'I'm sorry, Aunt Elizabeth-Jane . . .'

'Sorry!' she cried, smacking him hard on the ear. 'You will be sorry, James, you really will. I suppose you think because it's your birthday today you can idle about, doing anything you want. I don't like that kind of thing, you know. I call that being a very sly little boy, a nasty, dirty, idle, sly little boy. And what happens to nasty, dirty, idle, sly little boys, James?'

'I don't know,' he blubbered.

'They go down in a nasty, dark, dirty place where they can sit and think about how bad they've been. That's what happens to little boys like that.'

Once James was safely locked in the cellar, Mrs Duke considered her next step. According to the telegram that had arrived last night and the Bradshaw she had just consulted, John Phillips would be arriving at Temple Meads in about ten minutes' time. She went to the morning room, picked up the copy book, ink and pen and put them away in her bureau. It had occurred to her that when the maid answered the door, Phillips, or 'the father' as she called him to herself, might explain who he was. Mary-Ann had no love for James. He irritated her because she couldn't make out what he was doing in the house, whether he was supposed to be a servant or part of the Duke family. She resented having to get him up in the mornings and see that he scrubbed his hands after doing the boots. All the same if Mary-Ann found that James's father had come calling at the house, she would certainly tell him about it. Mrs Duke was determined to prevent this. Accordingly, after a period of watching from the front windows, she put on her hat, gathered up scissors and a basket, and went out into the front garden to cut some flowers. She was perfectly calm, strong in her indignation against the meddling father who had no idea how to manage his affairs or bring up his children and no appreciation of what she was doing for his son. She wondered if he would arrive at her house the worse for drink, use foul language, utter threats or try to knock her down as he'd done apparently with his own pregnant wife. She hoped, because of the danger of Mary-Ann's tittle-tattle, that it wouldn't be necessary to send her out to fetch a policeman. On the whole she felt confident that she would be able to subdue the father more successfully than his foolish little wife could do.

At a quarter to twelve a thin, dark man with a box under one arm came pushing at the gate. Mrs Duke straightened in dramatic surprise, a rose poised in her fingers. The father lifted his hat and asked quite civilly if she was Mrs Duke. Having introduced himself, he apologised for arriving unexpectedly.

'I've brought Jimmy a birthday present,' he said, taking the box from under his arm and holding it out rather awkwardly for her to see. 'And since I'm here I thought I'd save you the trouble and take him back with me.'

'Oh my goodness!' cried Mrs Duke. 'You don't mean you've forgotten, Mr Phillips? About the holiday?'

The man stared at her. He seemed quite sober and well behaved, even spiritless, a poor fish. Mrs Duke began to feel angry and humiliated. She felt that Kate had deceived her by erecting this weak creature into an ogre who was bent on wrecking their arrangements for Jimmy's future. All the vexation she had endured, all the subterfuge into which she had been forced, could have been avoided perfectly easily if only Kate had shown an ounce of spirit or if she had been allowed to handle the man herself. As it was, there was nothing for it now but to play out the charade she had devised.

'I did write,' she said, putting her hand to her cheek in consternation. 'You must have got my letter. About the Gales, you know. Mr and Mrs Gale and Beatrice and Richard. The solicitor who was such a friend of ours in Clifton.'

John stood on the tiled path between the rose bushes barely listening. He was aware only that after the long trip and the foolish, pleasurable looking-forward, he was not to see his son. The journey, like everything else that he attempted, had been twisted awry to end in disappointment.

'They asked weeks ago if they could take James down to Devon with them. They go every summer, you see, about this time. Now I did write and ask if you were happy about the arrangement and I'm sure Mrs Phillips said she was. She couldn't have forgotten to mention it, surely.'

The father shrugged in a defeated way. He seemed to have no drive at all. It was so difficult to imagine him knocking his wife down that Mrs Duke began to suspect that Kate had invented the whole story. He muttered something about Kate not knowing about the holiday because she had sent a cake.

'Well yes,' said Mrs Duke, 'but naturally I thought she meant James to have that when he comes home. Cook's put it away for him. Obviously there's been some really dreadful muddle. Do you think my letter could have gone astray perhaps?'

'Perhaps,' said John, though he was beginning to think that Kate must have kept the news about the holiday to herself as she kept nearly all Mrs Duke's letters.

'To think of you coming all this way for nothing!'

For a moment Mrs Duke considered leaving the matter there. It would be easy just to take the box and send this feeble man about his business. He looked so crushed that she doubted that he would see anything odd or unfriendly in her not inviting him into the house or offering him some refreshment after his journey. On the other hand, here was a chance to triumph over her unexpectedly meek enemy. Mrs Duke felt sure that, after a short talk in the morning room, the father could be brought around to her way of thinking. 'Just tea,' she decided. 'Nothing to eat or I'll never get rid of him.'

They went up the steps together and through the open door. Mary-Ann was hanging about in the hall. Mrs Duke gave her a sharp look and sent her off to the kitchen to get the tea.

'When will Jimmy be back?' asked John, putting his box down on the morning room table.

'Oh dear, not for another two weeks I'm afraid, Mr Phillips.'

'Well you've been very good but I think he ought to come back to us after that.'

This was disconcertingly forceful. Mrs Duke lowered her eyes, noticing the father was not so much thin in a weak way as lean and sinewy. His hands, now that she looked more closely, had a kind of nervous strength. She decided to proceed more cautiously.

'Of course, of course. You must miss him dreadfully. He's such a manly little fellow isn't he? You must be very proud of him. Yes, we'll send him off the minute he gets home. Oh, I musn't say that, must I? His home's with you.'

When the tea arrived Mrs Duke poured it out, smiling a little sadly to herself.

'I'm sure he'll be really pleased to get back to London. Once he gets over his little disappointment.'

John said nothing. He was beginning to feel that whatever he did now Jimmy would drift away beyond his reach. He couldn't really picture him in this big house, talking to this big woman whose eyes were pale and round like Cyril Nutting's.

Mrs Duke waited alertly for John to take her bait. When he remained silent she went on.

'It's nothing really. It's just that James has become very attached to the Gale children. And they are little dears, I must say. He asked me if when he comes home they could go for a little holiday with us. "Aunt Elizabeth-Jane," he said— that's what he calls me you see—"if I go away with Richard and Beatrice can they come away with us afterwards?" Well, I couldn't say no, could I? Even though I do have rather a lot of committee work at the moment. So I said, "Well perhaps, James, if your dear Papa and Mama don't mind. Where would you like to go?" And he said, "Weston, please, Aunt Elizabeth-Jane. I do so love the sea!" Ah, yes, he does love the sea. You must have noticed that on your own family holidays, Mr Phillips.'

Did Jimmy love the sea? Certainly he'd enjoyed watching the shipping on the river on a Sunday sometimes. But it seemed strange to John that Jimmy should want to go off to Weston with his new friends instead of coming home. 'He must've changed,' he thought, but, then, everyone changed, everyone drew away, and a child growing up was bound to change more than a woman or a man. He glanced around the richly furnished room. There was no sign of Jimmy living there, but upstairs, no doubt, there would be a large comfortable bedroom that Jimmy had all to himself and probably all sorts of toys and clothes that this woman had bought him.

'Well,' he said. 'I suppose I'd better be getting back. You'll give Jimmy the present, won't you? It's a boat so he can sail it at Weston.'

'Now you're quite sure that you don't mind about that, Mr Phillips?'

They both stood up and John started for the door, but Mrs Duke was struck by a sudden thought.

'While you're here, Mr Phillips,' she said, 'there is just one little matter I'd like to talk over. We're rather worried, my husband and I, about James's education. He's such a clever little fellow. He really does deserve the best and I believe Mrs Phillips was having trouble finding a suitable school in London. Now Beatrice and Richard are starting in September at a splendid little school in Clifton and James has asked, several times in fact, if he might go with them. Just until Christmas, perhaps. Now what do you say?'

'It's not a Free School, I suppose, this place in Clifton?'

'No. No, of course there are fees. But, Mr Phillips, you mustn't think of that! When I saw how poorly dear Mrs Phillips—Kate—was looking I said to her, "Now you must let me take James for a little while. But on one condition! There's not to be a word, not a single word, about terms or expenses or anything of that kind. I absolutely insist. While James is here with us it's our pleasure to provide for him." '

The father fidgeted with his hat. He had, Mrs Duke thought, a bristling, mutinous look as though he might burst out and say he was the one to provide for his own son. She laid her hand urgently on his arm,

'Think of our little man, Mr Phillips! Think how he's set his heart on going to school with dear Richard and Beatrice!'

'I don't know. It couldn't be for long.'

'No, of course, but think about it. Talk it over with dear Kate.'

The father nodded. 'It's good of you, of course,' he said shortly.

When they came out into the hall, Mary-Ann bobbed up again to open the front door but Mrs Duke waved her away and ushered her guest through to the front steps herself. In order to quell any curiosity among the servants, she sighed as she swept back in again.

'Committees! Committees! I really shouldn't have taken on so much!'

~

Usually after hours of crouching at the top of the cellar steps James was so stiff and cold that he could hardly stand up and so hungry that once he'd tried to eat the cuff of his shirt. But on the day that his father travelled down to Bristol, Mary-Ann came rattling the key in the lock and threw open the door after quite a short time. She hurried James off to the scullery and scrubbed at his face and hands with a flannel plastered with carbolic soap. When he was clean enough she marched him upstairs to the parlour where Aunt Elizabeth-Jane ensconced herself in the afternoons. James had a feeling that some critical point had arrived, that something momentous was about to happen. Again he felt his heart fluttering like a bird in a net.

Aunt Elizabeth-Jane was standing by the aspidistra in the bay window looking grave and stern.

'Sit down, James.'

James sat on the edge of a chair and looked at the carpet. Mrs Duke considered him carefully. She too felt that a crucial moment had been reached and that, if she was to shape James as she intended, now was the time to change her strategy.

'Several times,' she said, 'you've asked about going home to your dear Mama and Papa.' James began to tremble. The hope that had almost died in him leapt up.

'Now you know why you were sent here in the first place, don't you?'

'Because I'd been very bad and must learn to be good.'

'That's right. But I'm sorry to say, James, that sometimes when a little boy has been very, very bad his dear Mama and Papa may feel that even if he learns to be better they just don't want him to come home again.'

'My Dad wants me.'

'Papa, James, not Dad. Well, now perhaps he does, but don't you think if he really wanted you to go home he might sometimes write you a letter?'

James said nothing and turned his face away.

'I haven't seen any letters, have you?' said Mrs Duke bending forward and trying to look James in the eye. 'And I did think—well, yes, I really did expect—that he or your dear Mama might send you a present for your birthday. But I haven't seen any parcels. Have you?'

James shrank away still further. Mrs Duke straightened up and said very sorrowfully, 'I'm afraid, James, that if they've decided not to send you anything for your birthday it really does mean that they don't want you any more.'

She waited for some response to this but James made no sound at all.

'Anyway,' said Mrs Duke, 'if they wanted you to go home again they would come here and fetch you, wouldn't they?

And in all this time they haven't been to see you once, have they? Not once.'

She sighed and gazed sadly at the window but all the time she kept watching James's bowed head out of the corner of her eye. She had expected tears, even screams and defiance, a tempest that she could gradually soothe away. But there was nothing, no sound, no movement. It was difficult to tell whether James had been so thoroughly broken down that she could begin now to build him up again in the new form she had long ago envisaged. After a minute she decided to approach him, and knelt down by his chair, folded his shrinking body in her arms and lightly kissed his hair.

'So I think,' she said, 'that you're going to have to stay here and be my little boy and Uncle Herbert's now. And do you know what? I've got something for you. A really beautiful birthday surprise. In a minute we'll go into the dining room and have tea together and you'll see. And after that there's another lovely surprise. A beautiful present from me and Uncle Herbert. It's in the morning room now on the table waiting for you. Oh, James, what can it be? You'll never guess!'

∽

When John got home that night he said not a word about his wasted journey. He simply shut himself up in the parlour with his ledgers as though nothing out of the ordinary had happened. Kate waited, keyed up for a quarrel, running over what she could say to bring matters to a head but scared of making a false move. The evening passed, the next day and the one after that and still nothing was said about Mrs Duke, Jimmy or Bristol. Eventually, late in the week, a letter came from Mrs Duke—not one of the reproving notes privately addressed to Kate but an open, friendly letter to both parents enquiring whether they had discussed her offer to send James to school in Clifton and hinting at the possibility of taking him into Herbert's business later on. She ended by suggesting that, if James was to stay on with her indefinitely, John should perhaps help him to settle in by writing less frequently.

It was clear from the letter that John had seen Mrs Duke so Kate at once charged him with sneaking off to Bristol behind her back, but John swept this aside.

'No,' he said. 'No. I said it couldn't be for long. Give that woman an inch and she takes a mile. He's coming home at Christmas and that's flat.'

'Christmas!' Kate burst out. 'Just when the baby's coming! How am I going to manage? You know very well he went away in the first place because I couldn't cope after you knocked me down. I shouldn't wonder if it's a difficult birth this time after what you did. D'you expect me to get up out of bed with a new baby and three others to cope with and Julia dying on her feet and go running up and down the street after Jimmy? And anyway you know very well the Dukes can do much more for him than you can.'

'He's still my son. Yours too, though no-one'd think it. As for the other, things'll be better once Nutting's been paid off.'

'Oh yes, and how long's that going to be? Another two years at least. And then there's all the bills we're running up. It'll be years and years before we ever get straight. You ought to be grateful somebody wants to give one of the boys a leg up. What can you do to help Jimmy get on? It's not as though you've got a business is it? Not as though you can train him up and leave him to take over when he's older. And there's Mr Duke ready to set Jimmy up for the rest of his life.'

❧

Mrs Duke greatly admired Howard Gale who was, she thought, exactly the kind of man she should have married. She consulted him as often as possible on little points concerning her father's estate, her will, investments and the like. He was such a big, jolly man, so well dressed and gentlemanly, so roguish when he chaffed her, so full of energy and life as he bustled about his office, shouting cheerily for his clerk. Mrs Duke had met Mrs Gale only briefly, although she had seen her several times walking with the two children, Richard and Beatrice, on The Downs. Privately she thought Mrs Gale rather a limp, dowdy-looking woman for such a splendid husband, although, whenever she visited Howard Gale's office, she made a point of enquiring after his wife and family. She kept hoping that one day this politeness might lead to some kind of invitation—to tea, perhaps, or even to one of the Gales' famous tennis parties. After James arrived she dropped hints about his lack of playmates, sighed over his longing for companions of his own age and very nearly suggested that Mrs Gale might care to bring Richard and Beatrice to visit him. But she hesitated on the brink of a definite advance. In her girlhood, her father and old Mr Gale had once served together as wardens of their parish church but, apart from some bowing and murmuring as the congregation scattered after the Sunday morning service, the families had never met socially. The idea that Howard's wife might greet her invitation with chilly amazement sent the blood rushing to Mrs Duke's face and neck. She pictured Howard saying briskly, 'Now why not take the children round to meet young James, my dear? Elizabeth-Jane Duke is a charming woman.' And the contemptible Mrs Gale, dull as lead, replying, 'What? The clockmaker's wife?'

After dwelling on this imaginary insult and brooding over the destiny that had caused her to throw herself away on

Herbert, Mrs Duke began to feel that perhaps it was just as well that Mrs Gale, Richard and Beatrice should keep their distance. They might, after all, unsettle James. The mother, being silly and weak, no doubt pampered her children. The girl in particular had a bold, wilful, precocious look about her.

It was almost true that for a while Mrs Duke had entertained the idea of fostering a friendship with the Gales by sending James to the school where Richard and Beatrice were pupils. But once she considered the bad influence that the Gale children might have, she dismissed the scheme from her mind. And after all, she thought, there was no point in spending a fortune on James's education when, as soon as he was old enough, he would start working fulltime in Herbert's shop. So in the end she sent him to lessons with an elderly couple who lived just around the corner in Woodstock Road, and by insisting that James needed no Latin, Greek or drawing—nothing in fact beyond a grounding in the three Rs—managed to get the usual fee reduced.

To his surprise, James liked his new school. The Ffoulkes were stately old people, both very tall and spare, who looked down on their pupils with a kind of benign perplexity as though puzzled at finding them straying around their house. There were about twenty boys, ranging in age from six to twelve or thirteen. Every morning the smaller children gathered in the dining room with Mrs Ffoulkes while the older boys joined Mr Ffoulkes in the parlour. James's class did sums on slates, so that there was no fear of blots or smudges. Mrs Ffoulkes would sit in her chair, close her eyes and rock slowly backwards and forwards intoning mathematical problems: 'If I were to go to the pastrycook's shop with five shillings and buy six penny buns and four twopenny pies, how much would remain when these purchases had been made?' If the answers written down on the slates were wrong she would grip her chin between thumb and forefinger, brood for several moments and sigh, 'I fear not. I fear not.' Sometimes she read stories from *The Heroes* or Kipling's *The Jungle Book* or conducted spelling bees, again closing her eyes and rocking gently as she enunciated words that James had never heard before—triumphal, radiant, sublime.

After this Mrs Ffoulkes would spend at least half an hour spinning the great yellowish globe on its wooden stand as she pointed out the extent of the British Empire. Her pointer darted from the Channel Islands to Malta, through Egypt to a long litany of African possessions: Ashanti, Basutoland, Bechuanaland, British East Africa . . .

'God,' said Mrs Ffoulkes, 'has chosen the British to be a light to the nations of the world, to bring to them the blessings of Christianity and the benefits of our civilisation. Never forget, boys, that you are British.'

Meanwhile in the parlour the older pupils would begin reading out passages of Virgil which they were supposed to translate, but Mr Ffoulkes, tormented by their false quantities, always broke in and took over the reading himself. He would beat out the rhythm of the lines on the arm of his chair, oblivious to everything but the march of the verse, while the class, getting restive, went from giggling and kicking each other's legs to hurling paper darts, wrestling and tumbling off their chairs. The din, once it reached a certain pitch, could be heard in the dining room. Mrs Ffoulkes would raise a hand for silence, cock her head and then speed away to help her husband restore order.

At dinnertime the maid-of-all-work, addressed by Mr Ffoulkes as 'gentle Hebe', brought in bowls of thick brown soup and platters of bread. After the meal the older boys idled over grammar exercises and most of the younger ones went to Mr Ffoulkes with their Latin primers. Only James and a small plump boy who sucked his thumb stayed with Mrs Ffoulkes in the dining room. These afternoons were very peaceful. Sometimes James and Robin, the thumbsucker, wrote on their slates or chanted multiplication tables but mostly they just pottered about helping Mrs Ffoulkes wind queer, hairy wool or turned over the pages of picture books. Many of these contained portraits of people from remote corners of the globe: savages with wild black eyes and bones in their noses, turbaned Sikhs, Eskimos, and Arabs in white robes. Afterwards when James and Robin went into the conservatory to water the ferns, filling their watering cans from the butt outside the back door, James would think to himself: 'What if I'd been born a savage?'

But this was inconceivable. He was British. One of the chosen, a favourite son of God who looked down from Heaven smiling on him out of the blue sky.

Even when there was no school, James's life was more tolerable now. Mrs Duke was less severe. She whispered little secrets and got James to do her all kinds of little services rather as though he were a handsome page who had taken his queen's fancy. One Saturday at breakfast after he had unfolded her table napkin and passed her the marmalade, she said to her husband,

'Herbert, I want you to take James to the shop today and start showing him what he can do.'

Mr Duke, who was buttering toast, stared in alarm, his knife still in the air. The shop was his refuge, peopled by clocks who, in return for his care, created about him a miniature universe as ordered and musical as the cosmos of the Ptolemaic spheres. Each day he walked round checking his stock, especially the pieces he had kept for years unsold— the carriage clock that was supposed to contain one of the earliest examples of Thomas Mudge's detached lever escapement, the grandfather by H. Deeme of Honiton, the French clock with the handpainted china case. He opened doors, moved hands a fraction, brushed away a speck of dust, applied a drop of oil, then settled himself in the corner next to the safe to start on his repairs. The lamp made a bright circle on the white blotting paper covering his bench. With his eyeglass screwed into his left eye he bent over the ring of light, moving his minute tools among a scatter of tiny springs, screws, wheels and plates. As the moments passed, as he worked away to restore the power of a pocket watch to measure time, he would feel sometimes as though he were seated on a gentle eminence looking out at a world where the mysteries of past, present and future were all being carefully mapped by his steady clocks, some plodding, some tripping, but all, so long as he cared for them properly, delivering the same reassuring account of their journey.

Mr Duke had seen very little of James except at mealtimes. Early and late he was away at the shop and on Sundays, whenever he could escape, he vanished into the countryside to hunt butterflies. He had no clear idea of what his wife wanted with the child. She had said something about an apprenticeship but he hadn't attached much importance to the remark. The boy was very young and he knew that what pleased his wife one day often earned her scorn the next.

'I don't know, my dear,' he said. 'It's not really the place for a child. I mean there are customers' watches there. If a screw were lost . . .'

'James has been trained not to touch things. He'll do what you tell him, Herbert.'

'But I don't know what he could do. There's nothing really. I mean a child of his age . . .'

'He can sweep out the shop, can't he? He can polish the door handles. All kinds of little things.'

'But a boy like that . . . I daresay he has toys. Does he have toys, my dear?'

'James has very little time for play, but he has some toys, certainly. He has a boat. Why do you ask?'

'Some children,' murmured Mr Duke gazing nervously here and there, 'I mean some boys play with magnets.'

He lived in fear of magnets. If one were to come near a clock all its metal parts would freeze at once to a silent immobile block that could never be unfrozen. He felt cold himself at the idea of all his sweetly running, singing charges falling under this terrible icy spell.

'James has no magnets. Have you James?'

James shook his head. He was not sure what a magnet was.

'Well I suppose . . . I suppose I could take him with me on my rounds. I do have some calls to make today.'

'Certainly you could. He can pass you your tools and things like that. Then, later, when you take him on, he'll have some idea of the work.'

At first James was nervous of going to the shop but he soon began to enjoy his Saturdays with Uncle Herbert. They drove off in a gig from the livery stable near the Horsefair, sometimes to churches or other large buildings with clock towers and sometimes to customers' houses. At each church they climbed up winding stairs to a landing of planks where Uncle Herbert tinkered away at the huge, dark cogs behind the great dial looking out from the tower. While James waited for the work to be finished he would stray about, peeping down through windy apertures at the city spread below: the ships in the River Frome, a string of shop blinds curving like a frieze of small light coloured tiles all the way up Park Street; spires and gables and chimneys stretching away to the smoke veiled hills beyond; and, immediately below, a crush of carriages, omnibuses and carts pushing along between pavements which, seen from high above at busy times of the day, looked like two turbulent streams of bobbing hats. He used to squint down at the hats, clutching a bit of broken mortar in his hand and wondering with giddy, secret terror what would happen if he let it go plummeting down into the nearest stream.

When they went to a private home to look over a grandfather clock in need of repair or to regulate all the timepieces in the house, the customer sometimes offered Uncle Herbert a cup of tea and told the maid to bring cake and a glass of lemonade for James. One Saturday afternoon they called at the Gales' house in Clifton.

'I come here every two or three months,' said Uncle Herbert as they walked up the steps to the front door. 'She's a good lady, Mrs Gale. Always sure of a nice tea in this place.'

They were sitting in the drawing room with Mrs Gale, finishing their seed cake, when a little girl with frizzy, ginger hair came and stared at them from the doorway. Behind her with his hands in his pockets came her elder brother, self-conscious in knickerbockers.

'Take James into the garden,' said Mrs Gale. 'Let him see the rabbits.'

Beatrice led him outside and showed him two white rabbits in a hutch. Their names, she said, were Silky and Milky. For a few minutes they pushed lettuce leaves at the rabbits. Then they began to run up and down the tennis court, jumping over the sagging net which Richard patiently raised and lowered according to Beatrice's instructions.

'Are you Mr Duke's little boy?' asked Beatrice after a time.

'No,' said James. 'He's my Uncle Herbert.'

'Where are your father and mother then?'

'I don't know.'

'They're not dead are they?'

James looked at the ground. Richard, very red in the face, muttered something about bad form.

'She's only five,' he said apologetically. 'Bea, you mustn't ask those sorts of questions.'

There was an awkward silence. Beatrice, horribly mortified, turned away and stared at the rabbit hutch. Eventually Richard said to James, 'Would you like a swing?' and led him off between the flower beds to a cedar tree on the lawn below. Beatrice trailed along behind but when they came up to the swing, which hung from one of the cedar's lower branches, she ran forward.

'I can swing myself without being pushed. Shall I show you how?'

They parted on good terms and thereafter played together quite affably whenever Uncle Herbert called at the house. They had been meeting like this for over a year before Mrs Duke discovered that the Gales were among the customers that her husband visited with James on his Saturday rounds. She was much affronted although it was difficult for her to know who to blame. She felt that she had been excluded, insulted, put down and that her decision regarding James and the Gale children—which she had never voiced—had been treated with contempt. At the same time she was scared of putting a stop to the visits in case Mrs Gale should think it odd. Herbert, who was a bad liar, might blurt something out and then Howard Gale would discover that she had objected to her foster son playing with his children. She imagined the change that would come over his manner when she next visited his office—the unsmiling face, the curt greeting, the puzzled but cold expression in his eyes. There was nothing she could do but fold her lips and brood. After a time she convinced herself that there had been a plot against her, engineered principally by Beatrice. She continued to hold this conviction for the rest of her life.

As time went on, James went down to the shop in the Horsefair more and more frequently. Often, when Mrs Duke was busy with her committees, he was allowed to walk down to the Gloucester Road after school, take an omnibus into the centre of the city and spend a couple of hours playing in the musty packing room behind the shop or running a few errands. He never spoke much now, but since Uncle Herbert liked quiet in his shop, they got on very well. When they had a conversation it was usually about food—what they would buy to fill themselves up before going home to their meagre supper.

'What do you fancy tonight, then?' Uncle Herbert would ask, looking around the packing room door. 'Saveloy? Steak and kidney pie?'

'Steak and kidney, please.'

'Yes I think you're right. Chapman's or Marsden's?'

'Chapman's.'

'I daresay you're right again. Better gravy in a Chapman pie. Could you manage a currant bun? Yes? Well just run round to Mr Chapman then and see what he can do for us.'

The pies and buns had to be kept well away from the clocks so they ate them sitting companionably together in the packing room while the gas jet that Uncle Herbert used for melting sealing wax burned over the mantelpiece, and Mr Dickory, his secretive assistant, moved stealthily about in the room above. When the food was finished Uncle Herbert would wipe his moustache with his handkerchief and say, 'Better. Yes, a good deal better. Can't face the world on next to nothing, can we?'

Afterwards he often sent James upstairs to ask Mr Dickory to step down and mind the shop while he went off for half-an-hour with his friend Mr Bertoli who kept the photographer's studio next door. Mr Bertoli, like James, was a person of few words, preferring to communicate his ideas by evocative movements of his arms, eyes and shoulders. People often thought this was because, being a foreigner, he had trouble speaking English, but in fact he was the descendant of a family of court musicians who had come from Genoa to London in the late sixteenth century, and had spoken nothing but English from his birth. Most evenings, at about half-past five, he would come into the watchmaker's shop, jerk his head and raise his eyebrows to indicate that it was time to go over to The Irish Packet for a glass of something. Although James was not included in this invitation, Mr Bertoli was very friendly towards him. He was welcome to visit the photographer's studio whenever he felt like it. Mr Bertoli had shown him how to put his head under the black cloth and insert a plate in the camera, and had allowed him to inspect his magnificent collection of butterflies.

Butterflies accounted in part for Mr Bertoli's friendship with Uncle Herbert. It was with Mr Bertoli that Uncle Herbert drove off on Sundays to woods and fields across the Suspension Bridge or to the green Severn valley out past Filton and Patchway. Soon after he'd started taking James about with him on Saturdays, Uncle Herbert suggested that James might also join him on the occasional Sunday excursion.

'Certainly not,' said Aunt Elizabeth-Jane. 'James must come with me to church. And he has to go to his Bible class after the service. In any case it's time you gave up this jaunting about with that flashy Mr Bertoli. The vicar asked me last week, Herbert, what had become of you.'

But every two or three weeks Aunt Elizabeth-Jane's piety gave way to exhaustion and, declaring that she hadn't the strength to lift her head from the pillow, she would decide to spend her Sunday in bed.

'I'll just slip out for a while and let you rest,' Uncle Herbert would say, fiddling with his hat at the bedroom door. 'I mean, unless there's anything I can do for you, my dear . . .'

'Oh no, there's nothing you can do, Herbert. Go out and enjoy yourself. I'll just lie here until my headache's a little easier. I can't expect you to be interested in what I have to suffer.'

'I thought I might take James with me. To make sure the house is quiet.'

Sometimes Aunt Elizabeth-Jane would object to this proposal, saying she needed James to fetch her eau-de-cologne and bring up cups of tea from the kitchen, but usually, after a good deal of sighing, she would let him go. She was becoming a little bored with James now that he behaved so meekly. Also, once he was out of the house, she could sit up, ring for Mary-Ann and order a dish of lamb chops and a large helping of treacle pudding for lunch.

Bowling along in the gig with the butterfly net that Uncle Herbert had given him propped against his knee, James would feel a rush of excited expectation like the thrill that used to come on him in the old days when he set out on a Sunday from Beaumont Street. He tried never to think about his parents or how they had sent him away or how his father had once pretended to love him, but sometimes the familiar excitement brought the lost past swirling back in a great uncheckable torrent of jumbled fragments—blistered paint on a front door, the sound of steps in a passage, smells of fish, cabbage, paraffin, or coal tar soap. There was Violet hopping on the stairs, Molly nursing Charlie, Gilbert squatting on the rag mat by the stove, skirts sweeping round the kitchen, long black legs stalking the pavement, wheels spinning, Auntie coughing, lamps in the fog, horses looming up and clattering past . . . So James would sit stiffly as Mr Bertoli drove through the still Sunday warmth, trying to fight away the terrible idea that his street, his house, his family were all the time going on just as usual without him.

He was plunged into this kind of daylight nightmare the first time he went with Uncle Herbert and Mr Bertoli to Chippenham, travelling out into the country on a train just as he'd done with his father in his other life. But so much was new and mysterious that soon the nightmare receded. Mr Bertoli, gaily dressed for holiday in a loosely fitting suit, boater and flowered cravat, flashed his gold filled teeth and burst into song.

> Drink to me only with thine eyes
> And I'll not ask for wine . . .

Uncle Herbert beamed and nodded his head in time to the tune, more elated than James had ever seen him. This particular day he and Mr Bertoli had both shut up shop to combine work with pleasure. Old Lady Gascoigne had sent for him to look over her late husband's clocks, preferring him over all the clockmakers in Bath or Chippenham. Mr Gale had told her Duke of the Horsefair, Bristol was the Best in the West.

'Though I daresay it was Mrs Gale put in a word for me to Mr Gale,' said Uncle Herbert. 'Best in the West! Can you beat that?'

At Chippenham station a dogcart was waiting to take them to the Hall.

'Pretty quiet we are now with Sir Henry away,' said the driver. 'You should 'a' seen the place at Christmas time. Horses! Don't you tell me about horses.'

After a time he turned into a great gateway surmounted

by a coat of arms and drove up an avenue shaded by oak trees until suddenly they burst out into the sunshine and went wheeling round to pull up at the door of the largest house James had ever seen. They all took off their hats and, much subdued, trailed away after a huge striding man in a frock coat. Across a great hall they went and on through a maze of passages to a little room where a table was laid ready for a meal.

Uncle Herbert, Mr Bertoli and James stood close together on the hearthrug, speaking in whispers until a maid appeared at the door to ask if they'd take soup.

'You're to sit down there,' she said and vanished to fetch what she called the puray de poys.

'What is it?' whispered James when the soup had been served.

'Tastes like pea soup. Bit of all right.'

The soup was followed by ham with pickles and lettuce, gooseberry tart and cream, bread and cheese, ale and ginger beer.

'My word!' said Uncle Herbert. 'They look after you here! Still, can't face the world on next to nothing, can we?'

'As you say, sir,' said Mr Bertoli.

When they had finished eating they gathered by the window and began to talk about the species of butterfly they might find in this new territory after Uncle Herbert had attended to the Hall clocks. Mr Bertoli was a good deal more knowledgeable about this than Uncle Herbert. In fact, Lepidoptera was the only subject on which he was prepared to speak at length, enunciating the Latin names as though he relished their taste. Uncle Herbert's interest lay much more in the business of preserving and mounting. James, who was still new to butterfly hunting, said nothing and Uncle Herbert, glancing at him several times, got the idea that he might be unhappy about killing such beautiful creatures. He laid his hand on James's arm and said,

'They're not long-lived, you know. I mean there's some live only a few weeks. Even the Brimstone . . .' He paused, waiting deferentially for Mr Bertoli to explain further.

'Gonepteryx rhamni,' said Mr Bertoli. 'Longest lived of all British butterflies. Emerges in July. Hibernates in yellowing ivy leaves matching in colour the underside of the wings. Some hibernated individuals still on the wing in July of the following year.

'But most won't last the winter. A touch of frost and they're all gone. It'd be a shame to let them go to waste.'

James thought of the cases ranged around the rooms behind Mr Bertoli's studio: blue butterflies set out like lines of brooches, with tiny insects whose wings were no bigger than his own thumbnail at the top, and bolder, white-fringed creatures at the bottom; wings patterned like quilts and the windows of churches in segments of red and blue, green and gold; markings like staring eyes or the feathers of birds; delicate antennae, cylindrical bodies whose dryness he could feel in his skin, and hind wings that tapered to fine, black, hairlike points. He thought too of the jigging Cabbage Whites that flew above the plants in Mrs Ffoulkes's garden and the brighter insects that he and Robin sometimes chased when they were sent to fill their watering cans. He found it hard to think of the dead butterflies and the live ones as the same creatures.

'I should like to catch one in my net,' he said.

Uncle Herbert and Mr Bertoli laughed, relieved that James had no qualms about the coming hunt.

There were a great many clocks in Bathurst Hall. For hours Uncle Herbert hurried from room to room with a footman to show him the way and Mr Bertoli clumping along behind with a stepladder. Some of the time James watched Uncle

Herbert clambering up to inspect a clock mounted on a huge marble mantel, but mostly he just strayed about wondering at the paintings on the walls, the glittering chandeliers hanging from the ceilings, the cabinets filled with china figurines, crystal, coral and the eggs of exotic birds. Some of the rooms at the side of the house had French windows opening onto a terrace, so James stole outside to lean over the stone balustrade and watch a family of peacocks strutting about in the rose garden below.

He was taking a last look at the peacocks when he heard footsteps on the paving behind him and, turning around, saw a tall lady in a blue dress standing only a few feet away. He stared at her in alarm, afraid that he might have done something wrong, but she smiled at him quite pleasantly and said, 'Now you must be James Phillips. Mr Gale has told us all about you.'

Then, stooping down, she looked into his face.

'You have your mother's eyes, James. Is she well, your mama?'

'I don't know, Ma'am.'

'Don't know! Doesn't she come to see you or write you letters?'

'No.'

'Well!' said the lady. 'Well! Poor child!'

She stood up again and smoothed back James's hair with her long fingers. 'But then, what else would one expect? Faithless! Not a word, not a sign have I had in all these years. Not since before you were born, little James.'

James thought the lady was about to burst into tears but she recovered herself and said more calmly, 'I'm afraid it's rather dull for you here just now. Next time you come perhaps my nephews and nieces will be at home.'

James was surprised that anyone should think this was a dull day.

'I'm going after butterflies when Uncle Herbert's finished with the clocks. Mr Bertoli's coming too.'

'Mr Bertoli?'

'He's our friend. He takes photographs.'

'Of butterflies?'

'No. Ladies and gentlemen and little children and babies.'

'Has he ever taken a photograph of you?'

James shook his head.

'Perhaps he should. My brother has several cameras. I think I'd like a picture of you, James.'

Just then Uncle Herbert and Mr Bertoli came out onto the terrace. The lady, who turned out to be Miss Elfreda Gascoigne, immediately pressed Mr Bertoli to photograph James for her on the following morning before the party from Bristol set off for home.

'Taken a real fancy,' said Uncle Herbert when Miss Gascoigne had gone away. 'Can you beat that?'

A little later, after Uncle Herbert had delivered a report on the clocks to old Lady Gascoigne, the three butterfly hunters made their way through the Hall garden towards a stretch of woodland where James might be able to catch a few specimens of the Speckled Wood. Beyond the trees rose the grass slopes of a hill known as Updown. Just the place, said Mr Bertoli, for a Marbled White. This butterfly, he explained, had black and white patterning like a draughtboard but about twenty-five years ago a pure black specimen had been found. It was Mr Bertoli's ambition to discover and take another pure black.

'Not,' he added, 'that I'd say no to the white as was taken in the year 1843.'

Meantime, as they came into the shade of the wood, James ran forward after humbler prey. The place was very silent, filled with dappled, golden light that spilled across the winding path and the bramble thickets growing between the trees. High up a number of brownish butterflies flickered through sun and shadow, far beyond the reach of James's net. He ran on, hoping that Mr Bertoli and Uncle Herbert wouldn't hurry after him. He wanted very much to catch a butterfly by himself, to make it his own, something he could carry with him in his pocket and bring out to hold in his hand when he was alone. He went as fast as he could, getting hot, breathless and more and more wrought up as every butterfly he saw fluttered away at his approach. He realised that he would have to risk being overtaken because, unless he slowed down and crept forward quietly, he would never catch anything. He stole around a bend in the path and looked about. At first he could see no flying insects at all apart from a few blowflies buzzing around some overripe blackberries, and then, on a stone beside the path, something he had taken for a shadow suddenly flexed its wings. It was a black butterfly. James took three quick steps and brought down his net. The butterfly fluttered up and began to struggle. James knelt down and stared at it. Through the mesh he could see its tiny, clubbed antennae and parts of the wings, soft as black feathers, making frantic, pulsating movements. He still wanted the butterfly for himself but he couldn't see how to get it out of the net without letting it escape, and the more he thought of it the more certain he became that this must be the rare specimen Mr Bertoli had set his heart on catching. He began to tingle with excitement. How amazed Uncle Herbert and Mr Bertoli would be and how they would admire him for catching such a prize! So he got up, left the net on the rock and ran back the way he had come, shouting, 'Uncle Herbert! Mr Bertoli! Come and see what I've caught.'

'Black?' said Uncle Herbert. 'Well I'm blessed! You're quite sure it's black?'

Mr Bertoli had been holding the killing jar up to the light, looking carefully at a Clouded Yellow that he'd netted a few minutes before. When he heard the words 'black butterfly' he raised his eyebrows.

'Not the Marbled White is it? Agte galathea?'

To James's dismay he roared with laughter at his own suggestion. All the same, he seemed quite anxious to take a look at James's catch and led the way along the path so fast that even Uncle Herbert had to trot to keep up.

'I don't know,' panted Uncle Herbert, 'what it could be. I mean, there aren't a lot of blacks . . .'

'As you say, sir,' said Mr Bertoli, thrusting brambles aside as he ploughed along.

'It couldn't be a Black Hairstreak . . .?'

'Too far south.'

Mr Bertoli was a big heavy man but his hands were surprisingly deft. He quickly extracted the butterfly from the net and popped it into the killing jar. They all stared at the dying insect. James could see at once from Mr Bertoli's expression that it wasn't, after all, the Marbled White. It wasn't even, now that he looked more closely, a true black— more a chocolate brown. At first he was tremendously disappointed but then he began to think that if there was nothing special about the butterfly he might be allowed to keep it. Uncle Herbert said, 'I daresay it looked black—black as your hat—from a distance . . .'

'Hipparchia hyperanthus. The Ringlet.'

'Can I keep it?' said James.

'You caught it fair and square, young fella-me-lad,' said Mr Bertoli.

Uncle Herbert, thinking of his wife's complaints about his own collection housed in the dismal room she called 'the study', seemed for a moment nonplussed.

'We could fit you up a case in the packing room at the shop,' he said, brightening. 'Yes. You'd be right as ninepence there.'

'But can I touch it?'

'Touch it?'

'Can I keep it with me, please, and hold it?'

'I don't know about that. I mean it ought to be properly mounted.'

But Mr Bertoli, for once, took a different view. Uncle Herbert deferred to his friend's opinion and the butterfly was tipped into James's hand. It lay in his palm as lightly as thistledown. He could see now that the dark brown wings were decorated with ringed eye spots. Because he'd been so full of the idea of a pure black butterfly he'd failed to notice them, and yet the creature was the same—absolutely the same—as the one that had perched on the rock by the path only a few minutes earlier. It was still complete in every minute detail of its body, legs, antennae and wings. Only now it made no effort to escape. It was no longer frightened and with its fear had gone its power to struggle or fly away. It moved now only when James flicked it to and fro. It had become a thing, like a beautiful leaf or feather, an empty shell.

All the way back to the Hall James held the Ringlet lightly enclosed in his hand. He decided that when they got home he'd smuggle it up to his bedroom and put it in a secret place. Under the mattress, perhaps, or under a corner of the rug. While he was making this plan, Mr Bertoli and Uncle Herbert had a discussion about Clouded Yellows and the Gascoignes' remarkable collection of clocks.

'You wouldn't see better,' said Uncle Herbert, 'in a day's march.'

Eventually, as they drew closer to the Hall, the talk turned to other subjects. Uncle Herbert remarked that the Tuesday after next was his wife's birthday. He couldn't, he said, for the life of him think what present to get her. Mr Bertoli, with some eye swivelling and shrugging, suggested that Miss Gascoigne might not be the only one who'd be pleased to have a photographic portrait of James.

Uncle Herbert was very taken with this idea. Next day he watched closely as Mr Bertoli set up one of Sir Henry's cameras and Miss Gascoigne directed James to stand with one arm leaning on the curved end of a chaise-longue. On the train home he suddenly remarked, 'Those velvet frames are a bit of all right. What d'you say to a purple velvet, James?'

The gift was a great success. Aunt Elizabeth-Jane expressed approval and even asked for more prints of the photograph. She felt that the image it presented did her credit. Fattened by Mrs Ffoulkes's soup and Mr Chapman's pies and buns, James appeared well nourished. He also looked quiet, attentive and gratifyingly eager to please. Aunt Elizabeth-Jane decided to send a copy to James's parents to demonstrate the triumph of natural authority over even the most ill-trained and spoiled of children.

∾

The banner displaying the glories of the City of Bristol had begun to cause difficulties. The orphan girls did their part. Elsie Dickens obediently completed two panels and Kate Phillips managed a presentable representation of the Cabot Tower, but the other embroiderers failed to keep promises, misinterpreted their instructions and even, in some cases, challenged Mrs Duke's authority. Mrs West wrote icily from Richmond denying any undertaking to complete a depiction of the Guildhall, and Alice Oldershaw turned in a poorly executed Suspension Bridge instead of the Corn Street

Exchange she had been asked to contribute. Then the alderman who had first mentioned the banner to Mrs Duke began to shillyshally. Nothing, he explained, had been definitely decided. He had never meant to give Mrs Duke the idea that she was to take charge of the work. If the Council finally endorsed the making of a banner, he thought that the wife of the Jubilee Committee's chairman might expect to direct the enterprise. In any case, he'd heard it said that the procession was to be all soldiers and people from the colonies, with no British cities, bar London, represented. Mrs Duke flung the completed panels from her in a rage and vowed that even if the City Fathers came crawling to her on bended knees she wouldn't raise a finger nor put in a single stitch to help them.

There were similar setbacks in her committee work—broken promises, resentment of her authority, backbiting and muddle.

'It's always the same, of course,' she said to Herbert. 'Petty spite. Squabbling. Self-important little people jealous of the few who can really organise things. Well, I shall leave them to it. If they think they know best, I'll simply leave them to blunder on by themselves, and then we'll see. Oh yes, then we'll see what a dreadful fiasco they make of everything! Of course I'd have left before except that I can't bear to see our whole city made a laughing stock. But what can I do? These people who've pushed themselves into power—by bribery very often I shouldn't wonder because they certainly haven't a scrap of ability—they won't listen. I've told them over and over again what ought to be done but, of course, they think they know best. So I shall resign, Herbert, resign from the Ball Committee and absolutely everything. But every cloud, as they say, has a silver lining and now that I'm not needed here any more—or so some people think—we can go up to London in June and see the Jubilee for ourselves.'

182

Over the question of whether James should go with them Mrs Duke became troubled by uncharacteristic indecision. On the one hand she was enchanted by the prospect of showing off the triumphantly reformed James of her birthday photograph to his parents. She imagined herself seated again in the Phillipses' dowdy little parlour while James arranged her footstool, passed round the teacups, and then retired quietly to his post behind her chair. The Phillipses, shamed into realising their own inadequacy as parents, would pour out admiration and gratitude, hang on her every word and gaze in humble amazement at the miracle she had wrought. On the other hand, Mrs Duke was uneasy about the kind of conversation that might ensue. Even if she never left James alone with his family for one minute, it was possible that the father might ask him some questions about holidays in Devon or at Weston, about letters or birthday presents or going to school with Richard and Beatrice Gale. The father might mention coming down to Bristol last July. There was also the question of expense, the cost of an extra hotel room for instance, and the fact that even an obedient child was bound to be a worry and a nuisance in a large crowd which could, at any moment, swallow him up. And yet she could hardly put off taking James to visit his family indefinitely. Already Kate seemed puzzled at the length of time that had passed since Mrs Duke had last travelled up to London.

In the end, to her surprise, it was James who settled the matter.

'Now, James,' she said to him one day. 'I know someone who might—just might because it's not settled yet—be going to London next summer to see the Jubilee procession with our own dear Queen riding in her carriage and thousands of soldiers and horses and kings and queens from all over the world, and I don't know what!'

To her surprise James just hung his head as he sometimes did and said nothing.

'And,' she went on, 'that someone might be going to see somebody else as well—his dear Mama and Papa and all his dear little brothers and sisters . . .'

'No,' said James.

'What did you say?'

'No. I won't. I won't go.'

And James got up and ran out of the room. Mrs Duke was aghast, once again torn two ways. Her first impulse was to send after James, have him dragged back and forced into submission but when she paused to think for a moment she realised that his rebellion was a proof of his altered loyalty. She was, in fact, to be congratulated on having brought him to a point where, of his own volition, he rejected his family and tacitly declared himself all hers. And in doing this, of course, she removed the danger of those awkward questions that might have been broached in Beaumont Street. Mrs Duke smiled to herself at the thought of explaining the matter to Kate.

'I must say I was surprised, dear. I did expect that he'd be quite excited at the idea of seeing you all again and meeting the new, dear little baby. But he just said 'No'. Just like that— 'No!' And when you think about it I suppose it is quite natural, because, after all, he has become very attached to me. Of course, I could insist, dear, and he always does what I tell him. He really seems to put all his little heart into trying to please me, in fact. But I don't think it would be wise to force him, and not really very comfortable for you and Mr Phillips, knowing all the time he didn't really want to see you.'

It was particularly gratifying that James hadn't allowed even the bait of the procession, the thousands of soldiers and horses, the kings and queens to lure him back to Beaumont

Street. Eventually, of course, in a year or so they would have to make the visit, but by then the Phillipses' memory of past events would be growing uncertain, or could at least be made to seem so.

'Oh no, Mr Phillips, you must have misunderstood. We didn't go on holiday to Weston that year—it was the next one . . .'

It might be pleasant, thought Mrs Duke, to insist on a family photograph taken at some studio nearby. Ever generous, she would pay for it out of her own pocket—a lasting image of James, all hers, overcoming his revulsion in obedience to her wishes, and the Phillipses, well aware of how he felt about them, grouped around him.

SEVEN

Once Louie had decided to go to England she went about the arrangements quite briskly. She let her house for three months to a penologist who was writing a book on Governor Arthur's convict system. She packed up her treasures and stowed them away in George's study, organised her finances and overhauled her winter wardrobe. But she couldn't make up her mind about Susan. Eventually Susan would have to be told about the visit, and at some stage Louie would have to go to Bristol to see her. The trouble was that, because of the feud between Frank and the McAlisters, Susan was bound to take offence at Louie's decision to stay with Frank. Worse still, Louie was going to Frank first instead of rushing straight down to Bristol. It was easy to imagine Susan in outraged tears: 'After all, I am your only sister!'

The best plan, Louie thought, was to get Susan interested in 'The Brown Photograph'. If she could be convinced that Louie's quest for information was really important then she was much more likely to understand why her sister had to spend time in London working with Frank. Susan had to be given a mission of her own, and although Louie would have preferred to open negotiations with Violet and Annie for herself, in the end she wrote to Susan explaining that she was writing a family history and needed to know everything the two old aunts could tell her. She made out a list of questions. What did they know about the Gascoignes of Bathurst Hall, especially Elfreda Gascoigne? Had they met Grandfather Gale? What had become of their parents? Where were their graves?

'Louie wants me to go and see the old aunts,' said Susan. 'Something about some family story she's writing. Oh dear, I've been meaning for ages to contact the poor old things. Ever since Cissie gave me the addresses.'

Ian gave his crisp newspaper a shake and said in his humming way. 'And now Louie wants it, it must be done.'

Susan sighed. Ian was in a nasty mood again, when for weeks he'd been quite cheerful. Her father's will had improved his temper no end. James had left a good deal more than anyone had expected and although Annie, Violet, and various other relatives were all to receive bequests—as well as Louie, of course—the size of the McAlisters' share still made Susan blink when she thought about it. Although the matter hadn't been wound up yet, the solicitors had already advanced them the difference between what they'd been able to get for their Vauxhall and the price of a new Peugeot.

'We could go down in the car and see Aunt Violet,' said Susan. She thought it would be a good move to remind Ian of the Peugeot, but he only jerked his paper again and said in an incredulous kind of way, 'How old are they?'

'I don't know, exactly, but Aunt Violet must be over ninety. Grandad was ninety-six wasn't he?'

'And what exactly does sister Louie want with these antiquities? She's very family minded all of a sudden.'

'She just wants to know, well, anything about the family they can remember really. About Grandad and their mother and all that.'

'Probably blind,' said Ian, smiling for the first time. 'Or senile. They couldn't tell you much. Not at that age.'

'Well, Grandad wasn't senile. Goodness me, the day he passed on he did the *Post* crossword. Every bit of it.'

'I daresay. But old women! Once they get to eighty the brain goes.'

Despite what Ian said, Susan wrote that morning to Aunt Violet, explaining how she'd met Cissie and Jane and suggesting that she and Ian might come down to Devon one day for a visit. About a week later the telephone rang, and, to Susan's horror, when she answered it, she heard the heavy breathing that people always talked about. She said in a sharp, panicky voice, 'Who's there?'

'Is that Jim's girl?'

'Oh. Yes, yes. This is Susan.'

'That's right. You want to come down, do you?'

'Is that Aunt Violet?'

'That's right. You want to come down and see me?'

'Oh, yes. We'd love to. We've got the address. When would you like us to come?'

'Doesn't matter to me. If you can't make anyone hear I'll be down with the bees.'

Aunt Violet rang off then. Ian was at work, turning over the papers on his desk and relishing the sensation he was going to cause when he announced his early retirement. So Susan, who was excited and wanted to tell somebody about the call, rang up Jill and Ned at Ten to Three in Grantchester. Jill told her to be sure to get everything Aunt Violet said on tape. Susan started to say that she and Ian didn't own a tape recorder but remembered there was no reason now why she couldn't go out and buy one whenever she felt like it.

'You go down the lane past the church,' said the woman with the labrador. 'You can't miss the house. And she's always there of course. Old Mrs Stringer. Quite a character.'

She smiled and nodded, bending down to talk to Susan through the car window and glancing round at the Peugeot's blue suede upholstery.

'She's very independent. No meals-on-wheels for her. You know her well, do you?'

Susan was rather flummoxed. 'Not really,' she said. 'It was my father who knew her. He passed away not so long ago, so we thought, perhaps, we ought to come . . .'

Ian gave a little sigh, turned away and started drumming his fingers on the steering wheel.

'Ah,' said the woman, 'she'll like that. She doesn't have a lot of visitors. Well, just the son really. Come far, have you?'

'From Bristol.'

'From Bristol! Oh yes, I believe she said she had friends in Bristol. Actually, my husband's sister used to live in Henleaze. D'you know Henleaze at all?'

'Thank you,' said Ian. 'The lane by the church.'

He smiled blandly and drove off.

'Oh, Ian!' said Susan. 'That was a bit abrupt wasn't it?'

'Ha! I know her type. She'd've kept us there till she'd ferreted out every last thing about us.' He bent forward and peered at a No Through Road notice. 'It must be up here.'

The lane was unsealed and looked muddy.

'I hope,' said Ian, thinking of the high polish on the car, 'sister Louie realises the trouble she's put us to.'

It was no use arguing. Susan murmured to the window, 'It's not just Louie . . .' and peered out at the trees up ahead.

'D'you think that's it?' she said. She sounded doubtful. She'd expected thatch, mullioned windows, beehives nestling among roses and hollyhocks, but the only house in the lane was a spanking new, red brick bungalow with a red tiled roof and filmy white curtains at every window. A gravel path, running between patchy squares of lawn, led to the front door. The place had an unused, unoccupied air.

'There's nowhere else,' said Ian. He seemed pleased that the expedition might turn out to be a wild goose chase. He began to back the car onto the grass verge, making rather a business of the manoeuvre as though he wanted to prove all over again what difficulties Louie was causing. Once the Peugeot was positioned to his satisfaction he gave the glovebox a tap.

'Don't forget your tape recorder, will you?'

Susan fished it out, getting rather flustered and tangling the cord.

'I hope she won't mind about this. It's just Jill's so keen on her oral history.'

'Oral history! Yes, I can see there's a good deal of history being made here. Really in the thick of things!

191

Though, of course, Dear Old Auntie could very well think she's Joan of Arc or Florence Nightingale!'

They went up the path, knocked and waited. The house remained silent and they could see no sign of movement through the panel of pebbled glass in the door.

'She did say if she wasn't about she'd be with her bees.'

Ian looked around and spread his hands, showing the total absence of bees, but just then a very old woman with a widow's hump and a kind of white stocking cap on her head came limping rapidly round the corner of the bungalow.

'Hoo!' she said, out of breath. 'What d'you want then? Honey?'

'No, no. Not honey.' Susan stepped forward, wondering if she ought to try an embrace. 'I'm Susan, Aunt Violet.'

'Eh? Oh you're the one that wrote. Jim's girl. This your husband is it? Oh yes. What's that jumper then? Wool? Don't go near my bees in that, will you? Bees don't like dark colours and they don't like stuff from animals.'

She turned round and started back the way she'd come.

The McAlisters had to hurry to keep Aunt Violet in view. Just inside the back door there was a sheet of green plastic protecting the figured carpet in the hall. Aunt Violet looked closely at her visitors' shoes.

'Got clean feet have you? I take mine off when I go in, but you needn't bother if you haven't been in the dirt. I been out with the bees, you see.'

She bundled into the kitchen, seized an electric kettle and filled it at the sink. In the middle of the room stood a table with a green laminex top, and six chromium plated chairs with vinyl backs and seats in matching green. The McAlisters sat down at the table. The kitchen was small, neat and dazzlingly clean.

'There's a cake in that tin,' said Aunt Violet. 'D'you want cake? Bart brings them over for me.'

'That'd be lovely,' said Susan. 'Shall I get a plate?'

'You sit there. I'll do it. We'll have tea out here if you want cake. I'd take you in the front but I don't want crumbs on that carpet.'

'Is Bart your son?' asked Susan. 'He must be my cousin. It's strange isn't it we haven't met in all these years?'

'I don't know about strange,' said Aunt Violet dealing out cups and saucers at high speed. 'D'you want milk? Sugar? We were all of us sent off after Mother went—ended up all in different places. So we all went our different ways as we got older.'

'But I thought . . . Cissie and Jane—you know Cissie, Aunt Annie's daughter—said Dad was the only one who was adopted.'

'Well that's right in a way,' said Aunt Violet, sitting down at the head of the table. 'He was sent off to these people Mother knew, oh, years before she went. Duke their name was. He was all right, old Mr Duke, but she was a real tartar.'

Susan had put the tape recorder on the table. Ian now laid his hand on it and said in a way that he hoped would stop Aunt Violet in her tracks, 'My wife wants to record all this.'

Aunt Violet looked immensely pleased. She glanced coyly from Ian to Susan.

'Well that's something. Bart's got one of them but he's never wanted me on a record. You can plug it in over there by the kettle.'

They sat at the table for over an hour before tidying away the tea things and going through to the front parlour to study Aunt Violet's collection of family photographs.

As the interview went on, Susan tried to bring in Louie's questions and Ian created diversions by coughing, asking for the lavatory and announcing that he needed to stretch his legs. Afterwards Jill edited out most of these interruptions, so that when Louie eventually heard Aunt Violet's story, it went like this:

Mother and Father were pretty well off at one time. They used to live somewhere in Hampstead. I was born there but the only home I remember was in Holborn in London. We moved there to Beaumont Street when I was very young. Mother still had some lovely things though— beautiful china, knives with pearl handles, silk dresses she kept packed up in a trunk and real jewels, rings with diamonds, gold chains and I don't know what. But it all went, sold off bit by bit I s'pose to keep us going. Father had some job in the City but it couldnt've brought in much.

He was pretty stiff necked was Father. Stand up to anyone, wouldn't be beholden to any man. Not that it did a bit of good in the end. Still, we got on all right for a time. Never went hungry, made our own fun not like they are today with their discos and the television. We used to get round the fire of an evening—Mother, Father, Mother's young sister, all of us children. Father had a fiddle he used to play and we all used to sing. Sometimes we'd have a bit of a dance, jigging round the table. Father used to get a jug of beer from the public house. He liked his beer did Father, too much if the truth were known. After Mother went he couldn't let it alone and he just went down and down.

Life wasn't all fun though. We had to work hard in those days to make ends meet. London's not like the country where you can have a pig and bees and grow a bit in the garden. Everything had to be bought and paid for. Mother used to say to me, 'Run up to the grocer's and get half-a-pound of tea. Tell them I'll pay next week.' The grocer's wife was all right—she'd let me have it—but if I struck the grocer he'd say, 'You'll pay next week? Then tell your mother she can have the tea next week.' Everyone standing round thought that was a real joke. I used to wish the floor'd open and swallow me up, so after a bit I used to look in through the shop door and if I couldn't see the grocer's wife I'd go home and tell Mother we couldn't have the tea or whatever it was.

Hoo! It was a dirty place. London was all soot then. Everything was done with coal, you see, all the cooking, heating, water for the wash, everything. A couple of years ago Bart took me up to London in his car and I couldn't believe it. All the buildings white as snow and the trees in the parks all green! When Mother was there we used to scrub all the time—wash the windows, scrub the step, scrub out the passage and the kitchen, and next day they'd all be black again.

Visitors? Father didn't hold with visitors. We kept ourselves to ourselves pretty much. There was that painter chap Annie went to used to look in now and again. And that other one. You'd know him, that Howard Gale. Ended up your grandfather didn't he? I remember him in our kitchen just after they had the Jubilee celebrations when Mother's sister dropped down dead. Mother had this pot of dye on the stove so she could put us in mourning, dye our clothes, and the stink of dye was all through the house. Then in comes that Gale with this great big bunch of roses, all pink, and the smell of the flowers was all mixed up with this smell of the black dye.

A bad day it was for the lot of us when he came grinning round with his stinking roses. Yes, well I'm not saying any more. You speak to Annie if you want to know any more about Howard Gale.

There were five children in our family. Jim, your father, was the eldest one. I don't know exactly what went on, I was only very young at the time, but I think this Mrs Duke that knew Mother offered to give him a bit of a holiday down in Bristol and it just went on from there. Mr Duke wanted to take him into the business. Clocks it was, but you'd know that. He did well for himself in the finish but he had a hard time growing up. That Mrs Duke had him trained like a little dog. I stayed there for a bit after Mother went but I couldn't stand it. I wouldn't knuckle under, you see. I was like that when I was young even when I was in service. I got the sack when I was twelve and the housekeeper at this big place near Lacock said to me, 'If you go on like this you'll end in the workhouse.' Well, that gave me a fright I can tell you, so I watched my step a bit more after that.

I never saw a lot of Jim after I left the Dukes but we kept in touch. A couple of times he helped me out when I was in trouble, like when my husband joined up in 1914. You were supposed to get a separation allowance but a lot of the time after the man joined up the wife and children were left to starve for months before they saw a penny. I was living with my husband's mother then over in Suffolk. I walked for miles seeing this one and that one, trying to get a bit of help. I wasn't much of a hand at writing so I got the parson to write to the Government for me but it didn't do any good so I got word to Jim. He saw us right until our money came. He helped Bart out too, did Jim, when Bart was starting up with the combine harvester. He never said much but he was a good brother. Lately I didn't hear from him a lot, just a card at Christmas. I didn't know he'd gone till I heard from the lawyers. It was a shock, I can tell you. They didn't let me know till about a month after he went. I just sat here where I am now when I heard about it. I must've sat here for hours. Then I did what my old mother-in-law used to do when someone went. I walked down the garden and told the bees and put some bits of black crepe I had on the hives. She always said if you didn't do that the bees'd die too. It's funny that, when dark colours upset them.

The one Jim did most for was Gilbert. That was the middle brother. Even when he was little he was always in trouble. He was very good-looking, Gilbert, he took after Mother. She was a real beauty. She had what they used to call a 'rose-petal complexion' and hair—oh, beautiful hair—real auburn. People used to spoil Gilbert because of his looks. Perhaps that's why he turned out the way he did. First off after Mother went he was sent off down to Father's people in Lacock with Charlie and me. Anything was good enough for us. It was different with Jim and Annie. Nothing but the best for them though whoever it was arranged things never got the measure of Old Ma Duke. Never knew what a life she led poor Jim. I s'pose the lot of them thought he was in clover when all the time she treated him like dirt.

Anyway, Gilbert never did a proper day's work in his life. Always catching on to someone, poking his nose in their business, wheedling money out of people. It was self, self, self with Gilbert. He was worse than Annie if the truth were known and that's saying something. He came to see us just after the first war when we'd moved back down this way. Wanted money, of course, though

I hadn't set eyes on him for years and years. Just a couple of cards from France was all I got from Gilbert all through the war. 'You can't stop here,' I said. I wouldn't have it. My husband, Harry, was a good man but soft as butter. I knew very well Gilbert'd get money out of him soon as my back was turned and times were hard enough without that. So I sent him off with a flea in his ear and we never heard another thing about him for months on end. Then Jim told me he was gone. In the hospital up in Chippenham. Bad lungs he said, from the mustard gas on the Somme. But I said to Jim, 'What if it wasn't gas finished him off? What if he went poking his nose in somewhere a bit too far? Tried it on with the wrong sort?' Chippenham! What did he think he was doing up there?

My youngest brother was Charlie. Poor little Charlie! He never had much of a life. Our old grandfather sent him out to work when he was about twelve on one of the farms. They did that in those days—got you out to work as quick as they could. Charlie looked after this farmer's cows for three bob a week I think it was. Then he went up working on a farm in Yorkshire. They were short up there because all the farm workers were going into the mills. Then he joined up when he was nineteen and got killed nearly straightaway in the Dardanelles. Jim said he was on sentry duty. Charlie stuck up his head and the Turks shot him.

Last in our family was Annie. I can't say much about her because I haven't had anything to do with her for donkey's years. She was only little when Mother went. These people who took her came down to Coombe Bassett and lived in a place the Gascoignes got done up. Plenty of money, of course. Always had everything she wanted, Annie did. But she was just like Gilbert—take,

take, take and never a word of thanks at the end of it. Of course she got into trouble straight off. Took up with that fancy man of hers before she was twenty. Never mind what he'd brought us to already. Never mind he was old enough to be her father. Jim and me tried to put a stop to it but she wouldn't listen. I even said she could come and live with me after I got married but she turned up her nose at that. Got this house in Barnstaple, with a motor car and I don't know what and went flaunting round the place like Lady Muck. Called herself Annie Anjoulème. I ask you! But she slipped up in the end. Got herself in the family way with that Dennis and married the first who was fool enough to take her. Married that gawk Jack Quant, used to be a footman at the Manor. Daft great good-for-nothing. All he ever thought about was fooling round with a lot of conjuring tricks, pulling eggs out of people's ears. And the boy's ten times worse. Daft as a brush. Though you can't wonder. Annie never took a blind bit of notice of him or that girl she had, that Cissie. Left them with Old Ma Quant half the time and went on running round doing just as she liked. I don't know how she got on after that. Jim knew I didn't want to talk about her so he never said. But I know she's still alive in a home somewhere. I thought of writing when Jim went but I don't know what I'd say if I saw her, so what's the use?

So that's the lot except for me. I was happy enough till Mother went. That was a terrible thing. I came down to Bristol with her to see Jim. I'd've been nine or ten at the time. We were supposed to be going on this holiday. Mother went on ahead for some reason to Coombe Manor. We were taking a place somewhere near there. I never knew why she went on alone like that. Perhaps she wanted to give the house an airing. I never saw her again. The next thing we heard . . . oh dear, it still upsets me after all these years. When we got to Coombe Bassett they were all out looking for her, all the men. There was this big chap who kept saying, 'We mustn't give up hope,' but it was no good. She was gone.

'Excuse me, Aunt Violet,' said Susan. 'I don't want to up-set you but I don't understand. I mean, what happened? Was there an accident?'

'Could've been. Or not. But we never saw her again. Never once.'

'But wasn't there a funeral? Was she buried, your mother, in this Coombe place?'

'Funeral? We never went to any funeral. Never told us a thing. There's plenty of stories, of course. Jim swallowed some of 'em, but I never did. I've got my own ideas but I don't say.'

Well, I stayed on with the Dukes for a few months, but Old Ma Duke couldn't stand me. I used to stick out my tongue at her when she told me off. She chased me round the place with the boiler stick And didn't she give me what for when she got me cornered! But it only made me worse, so she sent me back up to Father and I tried to keep house for him. I couldn't've been more than ten. I did the wash and everything, cooked the dinner. But I don't think Father liked to see me taking Mother's place. I used to dish up the dinner and he'd just sit there at the table with one hand over his face—like this—and push me off with the other. 'Let me be,' he'd say. 'Let me be,

200

girl.' One night he fell down the stairs. Oh, I was frightened! He made such a noise I thought the house was coming down. I ran out of the kitchen and there he was, stretched out on the floor. I thought he was gone for sure and let out such a scream all the neighbours came running. But he came round all right in the end. He had to go into hospital though, poor Father, so I went off to Lacock for a bit. I went to school down there with Gilbert and Charlie. Then one day the parson came and said I was to finish at school and go into service, looking after this old woman in the village. She was blind, you see, and her son that was living with her got married. They paid me sevenpence a week out of Parish Relief for that. Then I went to this place near Lacock but I didn't last long there. That gave me a bit of a shake-up. I was scared I wouldn't get another place but I did in the end, with Miss Gascoigne over at Bathurst Hall near Chippenham.

What's that? The Gascoignes? My father couldn't bear to hear the name but I can't see they did wrong. Miss Gascoigne used to be a bit flighty as a girl they say but she changed out of sight the day she lost her brother. Young Sir Henry that was, and his wife as well, went down in that yacht of theirs. Very religious she was all the time I knew her. Always wore black, never married, gave up her life to rearing the brother's children. Mind you, she wouldn't stand for any nonsense. Wanted everything just so but you can't blame her for that. And she did what she could for Jim. Took an interest, kept an eye on him when he was young. Then the cousin, Mr Grindley, the one took over the Manor from Sir Henry was a bit on the wild side but there wasn't any real badness in him. It wasn't him brought trouble and shame on the lot of us.

Anyway, I toed the line, I can tell you, at Bathurst Hall. Oh, it was hard but I knew it was that or starve. My grandfather said to me, 'Don't you come back to Lacock again telling us you've lost your place. We'll show you the door next time.' And he meant it, I knew. I don't know how I stuck it, looking back. I was there seven years. I started in the kitchen, then housemaid then parlourmaid. They never gave you a minute to yourself. She was after us all the time, the housekeeper was. Girls these days they wouldn't put up with it but we didn't have any choice, it was that or nothing. My husband came to the Hall as a gardener's boy. They used to wear collars and ties in the garden and green baize aprons. Fancy that! You wouldn't see it now. And every day they brought fresh flowers up to the house, roses, lilies, lupins, all kinds of flowers, different every day they had to be. Harry used to get a note to me sometimes in the flowers. We courted like that for years, Harry and me, a word here, a note there. There wasn't any other way, you see. Then Harry heard of a place with a cottage for a married couple over near Exeter. He came up to the Hall bold as brass in his green apron, came in where we were having tea with the butler, Mr Cripps, at the head of the table and he said, 'Good morning, all. I've come to ask Violet there if she'll be my wife.' Just fancy! It took some nerve, Harry doing that. Well, the housekeeper—Mrs Jay she was—went red as fire. 'You sly thing!' she said to me. 'You sly thing! How long's this been going on, then?' She felt I'd put one over her, you see.

Well, we came down to Devon until the war broke out and Harry joined up. I went over to Suffolk, then, like I told you, to Harry's mother. After the war Harry wanted to start out on his own with a market garden. We liked it down this way so we got a bit of land near Williton where Bart is now. He worked hard, Harry. Every blessed minute he could he was out in that garden. He built it up from nothing all by himself, really, though I used to give him a hand whenever I could. Bart was born over there. He's been on that place all his life, Bart has. We were there all through the last war, though we gave up doing flowers then. We used to grow all sorts of cut flowers before and take them over to Taunton to sell. But it was all vegetables through the war. 'Dig for Victory!' they said. They let Bart stay and do a lot of the work. It was what they called a reserve occupation, growing food.

Harry got very ill after the war. He was up and down to Taunton and Bristol having operations, but they didn't do any good. I went up to see him one time in the Bristol Infirmary and I hadn't been home ten minutes when they rang up to say he'd gone in the afternoon. I wish I'd kept him at home, now. I'd've been there then when he went. But you're not to know, are you? I used to think they were always right, the doctors. But I haven't had much to do with them since Harry went.

Bart got married not long after that. She's all right, I s'pose. She means well but she's too slack in the house for me to put up with. I've always dusted every single day like I was taught to. They don't bother with that nowadays. Half of them leave their beds when they get up and get back in the muddle when they go to sleep—never make the bed from one year's end to the next. I've never seen anything like it. All black their mops are. Just swish them round and leave a mark on the wall, a black line all round where they're supposed to've washed the floor. It's all machines now, of course, so half the girls never learn how to do things. Just throw everything in the washing machine, never soap the collars first or anything. I can't put up with it. I said to Bart, 'You live as you like but don't ask me to stay and watch her making the place a pigsty.' So I went to live in Williton on my own, then back near Bridgewater—that's where I started the bees— then a couple of years ago I got this place. I like it here. One thing about the modern places—so long as they're solid—there's no cracks and crannies for the dirt. You always know it's clean, a place like this.'

EIGHT

A line of black heads with large ears and long necks stood out against the movie screen. They belonged to the young surfies who all the afternoon had flopped about the plane in T-shirts and shorts, drinking tinnies and tumbling against each other as casually as if they'd been horsing around back home at the beach.

Louie watched them, half amused, half exasperated. They'd almost certainly never been to Britain before but seemed to treat the journey like some sort of sports outing; whereas she, who had spent over half her life in England, was what her mother used to call 'a mass of nerves'. Perhaps this wasn't so surprising. The surfies, after all, had each other. In London they'd probably head straight for the Australian ghetto in Earls Court, settle in a share house with a horde of youths exactly like themselves, and go in packs to watch the cricket or drink in the Ozzie pubs, so that nothing strange or unexpected would ever touch them.

Louie, on the other hand, was alone. Longing for George, which, ever since she'd set out for the airport, she'd kept in check, rose up and seized her. All through their years together Louie had managed the house but on outings and holidays George had always taken charge. Every expedition—even just a film and dinner out somewhere—had turned into a treat under George's hand. He had a kind of floundering charm—a mixture of apparent ineptitude and radiant goodwill—that made even the most bloody-minded people practically fall over themselves to get him the best seats in a theatre or the best table in a restaurant. Holidays became adventures with strangers they met on trains offering to drive them to retreats in places like the Blue Mountains or lend them fishing boats. And all these people had smiled at Louie as though they saw her through George's eyes and wanted to make her happy. But now, if she were to press a buzzer or go blundering about in search of something to drink, nobody she disturbed would feel like smiling. They'd wake up to mutter and glare, putting her down as a captious aging woman with a grudge against anyone less solitary than herself.

Louie began to wonder why on earth she had ever been induced to leave home. Nothing terrible had happened. By now she wasn't particularly afraid that the plane would lose a wing over the Mediterranean or burst into flames on landing, but the grim side of her nature, determined not to lose face entirely, was busily flinging up every minor worry, every small, buried fear it could discover. There was the arrival at Heathrow, for instance. She had no idea how she was going to locate her baggage and get it through customs by herself. She was sorry now that she'd told Frank not to come to the airport to meet her. When she'd telephoned to confirm their arrangements he'd volunteered to drive out to Heathrow but because the plane was scheduled to arrive at six in the morning she'd felt guilty about making him get up in the small hours, and had said she could manage very well on her own. But even if she could, what then? The whole idea of staying with Frank might be a mistake.

She'd loved Frank when they were both very young. His voice on the phone and his recent letters suggested he was still Dear Old Frank, kind, patient and amusing. Reassuringly, he read Larkin and Keats. All the same, it was nearly forty years since the morning of his father's disappearance and from that day to this she'd learned next to nothing about his life. The Royal Army Service Corps. Oxford, reading some sort of history. Some job in the Civil Service. Redundancy. Years in the same Maida Vale flat. An old Audi. No wife. No talk of marriage. That was about the sum total of Louie's knowledge. She had no idea what Frank did with his spare time when he wasn't wandering around Chippenham graveyards. She knew nothing about his friends or lovers or even if there were— or had ever been—such people. She knew nothing about what the years had done to him. He could very well have become the sort of aging bachelor who bites his lip in agony when somebody uses the wrong cooking knife to cut up meat—if he ate meat. He could be a vegetarian who'd expect her to live on grains and leaves. Or he could be weirdly absentminded or have some addiction like greyhound racing or poker machines. Maybe he lived in an absolute tip with a rumbling geyser spitting out tepid, rusty water, a black-throated lavatory, rats in the basement. He might live in a tower block where gangs raced along concrete walkways snatching handbags.

She would know soon enough. It seemed odd that in a few days, unless things were so unbearable that she had to flee, Frank's flat, his stairs, cupboards and carpets would be so familiar that she'd no longer notice them as she went to and fro opening his doors, turning on his taps, snapping on his lights, handling his books and plates and tea-towels. What would she be thinking about? The book, of course, and all the web of family mysteries which encircled it.

It was a relief to turn back to 'The Brown Photograph'. All around her dimly lit shapes, swaddled in blankets, drifted on through the night in a wash of deep breathing. Only Louie and the surfies, sitting up watching their movie, were too wide awake to sleep, but now, instead of feeling lonely and bereft, she eased back in her seat, glad of a chance to return to some of the puzzles in Violet's account of her family's history.

As soon as Susan's tape of the interview with Violet had arrived Louie had started playing it over and over. She couldn't picture the John Phillips she had created playing the fiddle for a singsong in his kitchen but she was pleased that a good deal of Violet's narrative accorded quite well with her own imaginings. At the same time, parts of the tape were baffling, making existing mysteries deeper and creating new ones. Why did Violet see James and Annie as somehow different from herself, Gilbert and Charlie? Was it just that these two were special favourites who'd ended up in foster homes which, despite all James's early misery, gave them a much better start in life than anything the old horse dealer could provide? There seemed to be more to it than that, a hint of some secret patron ('Whoever it was arranged things') who took a benevolent interest in the first and last of the Phillips family and supplied them with money. James had been hardworking and methodical but, now that Louie thought of it, it seemed queer that the little shop in the Horsefair had provided him with enough cash to keep his own family in comfort when all the time he was dishing out substantial sums to Gilbert, Violet and Bart, and building up the unexpectedly large amount he'd left in his will. Annie, too, with her motor car and her house in Barnstaple had been very well provided for.

Both were linked with the Gascoignes—James through his visits to Bathurst Hall and the photographs taken there, Annie through her adoption by the anonymous painter who had carried her off to live in the house done up by the Gascoignes on Cousin Grindley's estate. James was also linked with Howard Gale, solicitor to both the Dukes and the Gascoignes, a customer of Mr Duke, and ultimately, of course, James's father-in-law. Was there some similar connection with Annie? She was only a baby when Howard burst into the kitchen in Beaumont Street carrying his bouquet of pink roses. But who was the lover she'd taken before she was twenty? ('Never mind what he'd brought us to already. Never mind he was old enough to be her father.') Could this have been Howard, whom Violet seemed to blame for all the Phillipses' misfortunes?

That would be startling enough, but was there some other great scandalous secret at the heart of the maze? Was there substance, after all, in Teddy Gascoigne's high-romantic theory? Had pretty Kate Barker, invited up to the hall by Miss Gascoigne, become pregnant with James by the ill-fated Sir Henry or dashing cousin Grindley from Australia? Was that why John Phillips hated the Gascoignes? And had this highborn lover tracked Kate down years later to rekindle the affair and father Annie?

Was this the secret Gilbert had gone to Chippenham to unearth, only to find, perhaps, that the Gascoignes didn't take kindly to threats of blackmail? A man with weak lungs might very well die of pneumonia after being pitched into a duckpond by a couple of brawny retainers from the Hall. And what about Howard Gale? Was he the Gascoignes' emissary, the useful man of business who, despite the resistance of John Phillips and, possibly, Kate as well, tried to ensure that the progeny of his noble client were suitably looked after? And had he, later, undertaken another mission, appearing with his pink bouquet to lure Kate back to her lover? Had he succeeded in the end in inveigling her into Gascoigne territory under the pretext of giving her and all her children a holiday? Had he played a part in whatever became of her in Devon? Kate's disappearance was the greatest mystery of all. Her family had never seen her again after she left for the holiday house, but there seemed to be no evidence of her death. Had she simply abandoned her children and vanished to emerge in Edinburgh, Paris or Baden-Baden as the mistress of Sir Henry or Grindley Gascoigne?

It was tempting to give oneself up to this kind of fantasy but there were simpler explanations. Miss Gascoigne, because of a passionate friendship with Kate, may have taken such an interest in James that she had made some kind of provision for him in her will. Annie's wealth could have come from her adoptive parents, who could easily have acquired their money in some ordinary way, and, later, from her elderly lover. Howard Gale, one black day, might have set out to seduce Kate on his own behalf, drawn her away from her home with talk of a holiday, and somehow brought about her death, hushing it up so that even her children never discovered the truth.

Louie had no trouble believing this of her grandfather. Looking back she was still outraged at the blind awe with which her mother had regarded him. When Beatrice heard her father was coming to tea she always flew into a frenzy, rubbing up the silver teapot, rattling through her cake tins, hurrying up and down from sitting room to kitchen with her arms going like pistons and her cheeks blazing. This was partly because she knew Old Liza-Jane would get wind of the visit and come sneaking down in the middle of tea to tap on the sitting room door. 'Oh, Mr Gale! I'd no idea you were here. Don't let me interrupt . . .' And Grandfather Gale would jump up, clearly relieved to have somebody other than Beatrice and her children to talk to. He'd press Old Liza-Jane to sit by the fire and take a slice of cherry cake. Beatrice would always bang about more than ever after that, though if her father looked at her directly or asked her a question she would squirm and blush like a schoolgirl. She seemed to regard him with an odd mixture of jealous adoration and scorn. Whenever she heard him mentioned she would say, 'Oh, *Fa*ther', coming down heavily on the first syllable in a way that suggested he was a law unto himself and there was nothing a reasonable person could do about his goings-on; though at other times she held him up as a protective god who would be enraged by whatever had offended her.

But Louie had always disliked her grandfather and his great mausoleum of a house with its dark brown smell of cigars and cork mats. Even when she was very young she'd sulked and complained when she and Susan were summoned to afternoon tea or one of Old Howard's tennis parties. She didn't like the way he patted her bottom and squeezed her thighs with his creased old face pressed close to hers. His eyes, which seemed as blue as cornflowers from a distance, had a queer metallic look, like bits of stained enamel jewellery. There were pale cloudy rings round the irises and red veins netting the whites like tiny road maps.

He pestered Susan more than Louie because she was softer, plumper and more tractable. One day when they were all having lunch in his cavernous dining room he said to Susan, who was in her early teens, 'Well, Susie, I s'pose you've got a boyfriend nowadays. Hey? Some strapping young fellow-me-lad?' When Susan blushed and hung her head he leaned closer. 'Don't do anything naughty will you, Susie? Though it's not so much what you do, it's more what he gets up to, isn't it?' And he flicked with one of his blunt fingers at the place in her blouse where a nipple might have been. Susan stared at her blouse buttons for a moment and then burst into tears. Old Howard, who liked girls to be giggly and submissive, was very put out. 'Oh dear! Oh dear!' he said very loudly, looking about for something on which to vent his annoyance. He fixed on the soup which he claimed was nothing but dishwater, rang for the maid and had it carried back to Cook.

Nobody knew how in the late forties he still managed to find servants. 'Oh *Father*!' said Beatrice when someone remarked that you didn't often see a uniformed parlour-maid any more. He must have paid his maid, cook and gardener a small fortune to stay on and put up with his bad temper, making him as comfortable as he'd always expected to be. At any rate, in his final years he managed to run through most of his money. According to rumours Louie picked up later, a good deal of it had been squandered on fast women. Or on one woman in particular: perhaps a much younger woman, living in Barnstaple, who was prepared to put up with the squeezing, patting blunt-fingered old hands and the bloodshot eyes under the scrubby white eyebrows, provided she was well paid for her tolerance.

When Old Howard died his children were left to find that the big house in Clifton was as heavily mortgaged as Tobias Barker's properties and there was next to nothing left for them to inherit. Or so Louie had surmised in later years, remembering how Beatrice's colour had risen when she'd asked her mother if the family would have to move into the house with the tennis court and the cedar tree in the garden.

'You can't keep up a place like that nowadays. It costs a fortune.'

'But Grandfather did.'

'Oh, *F*ather!' And Beatrice had turned away, slamming a pot or kettle onto the stove, as she often did when her feelings were running high.

And what had James made of all this? If, like Violet, he harboured a grudge against Old Howard—as well he might if Howard had seduced both his mother and sister—then he never made his feelings plain. Presumably, he said nothing at all to Beatrice about her father's philandering and, as far as Louie knew, never made any attempt to stop his two young daughters visiting the house in Clifton and handing round the sandwiches at his tennis parties.

Even a few weeks ago Louie would have condemned James for this but now she could recognise that he had belonged to a time and place in which it was believed that children were sexually null and paedophiles simply didn't exist. Through her dual search—the one in the outer world that had revealed James's generosity to Violet and

213

his other relatives, and the second one that drew her on through the world of 'The Brown Photograph'—she had come much closer to her father. In trying to recreate the child he had once been she had touched a spring which seemed to open up his secretive adult mind in a way she had never known before. As this happened she realised with surprise that back in the days of Howard Road, under all the surface concerns of daily life, she had felt for her father a plain and solid love and, even more surprisingly, had gone on loving him, so that her desertion of him seemed somehow less terrible. In betraying him she had betrayed herself because she was bound to him, and so had suffered an inevitable punishment, a grief and guilt which seemed now like a natural atonement.

Yet, she couldn't feel this about the wrong she now acknowledged she had done to Tim and Stuart. Because they were still alive, she would have to do much more than deal with her own conscience. She had made a first step towards expiation by unearthing the awful business of the boat and making herself look at a version of what she had done in the fictional actions of Kate and Liza-Jane.

About two weeks before Tim's eleventh birthday a parcel had been delivered to Louie's house in Hobart. A large square box, wrapped in brown paper, posted in London where Stuart was spending part of his study leave. It was summer, school holiday time, but Tim had gone with a friend to the Olympic pool so Louie was alone in the house. She put the parcel on the kitchen table and sat and looked at it, thinking about how Stuart always came between her and Tim, making him restless, stirring him up just when he seemed to be accepting that he couldn't go and live with his father in Sydney. 'He's hardly ever there anyway,' she'd said to Tim, though she had to admit now that if Stuart had thought he had any chance of having his son with him, he would have postponed his overseas travels.

Eventually she took a knife from the dresser drawer and cut through the brown paper and the shiny red wrapping underneath. After that there was no going back because she had no way of explaining to Tim why she'd attacked his parcel. So she opened the box and found among a nest of wadded newspaper a toy yacht just like the one she'd made Kate take out of the cupboard in Beaumont Street and Old Liza-Jane claim as her own present to James. After that Louie had acted very quickly, frightened that Tim might come home at any moment. She'd gathered up the box, the wrappings and the boat, rushed them into the backyard and burned them in the besser-block incinerator. The hull took a long time to burn away so she fed the fire with torn-up grocery cartons. She thought as she stirred the ashes and watched the green paint blister and blacken that if ever any questions were asked it would be easy to pretend the parcel had been lost in the post.

Tim said nothing at all when it seemed that Stuart had forgotten his birthday.

'Nothing from Dad,' said Louie. 'Oh, well, he's busy, I expect, in London.'

Could she ever confess all this to Tim? Would anything be gained by such a confession or would it simply make his hostility more implacable than ever? Though that, Louie told herself, was not really the point. She had done all she could to separate Tim and Stuart. So, in expiation, she ought to do all she could not to bring Tim closer to herself but to repair his bond with his father. And having done that perhaps she should leave them alone, give up Tasmania, give up Oliver and settle in Britain. Here was

215

another reason for making this visit a form of reconnaissance, a prelude to a final return. Just so long as it was final. The trap into which Louie had seen any number of migrants fall was perpetual indecision which left them swinging between the old country and the new, always discontented, always homesick for the one that wasn't there.

She tried to imagine herself settled in a flat in London, so busy with theatres, exhibitions and parties that she never gave a thought to Tasmania's wild west coast, its Georgian houses set in green gardens, its high country of lakes and snow, its orchards, farms and quiet reflective bays filled with black swans, ibises and oyster catchers. She pictured herself walking with Oliver over a sloping paddock above the sea, holding his hand, staring at the ground which had become somehow transparent so that she could see, far below, a network of secret bonds, interlinking rivers of affection, blood and money which twisted away in all directions and sometimes burst to the surface in startling fountains.

The pictures became more vivid. Now Oliver pulled at her hand. He wanted to go to the beach, so they clambered down a low cliff and set off along the stretch of sand. Across the bay interlocking lines of hills ran across the horizon, some flat and grey, some brushed with fawn or green and patched with dark trees. Closer in, a headland like a black, basking crocodile rested its snout on the water and at the end of the beach a dense huddle of gums pressed down the slope to a fringe of rocks and pale driftwood. The sea stretched blue and twinkling under a band of elaborately sculpted cloud, clear-edged, with bluish shadows like a woodland under snow. Oliver pointed to a dark bundle lying near the water. He skipped about excitedly, calling out over his shoulder that it might be a sack of treasure. Then he started off running with his yellow towel fluttering out behind him while Louie, feeling more and more anxious, began to trot in his wake. Oliver stopped, turned back, came rushing full pelt towards her, shouting and waving his arms. Louie came to a halt. She seemed to remember that the dark shape was something appalling but felt that her memory was incomplete or mistaken in some way as though the object belonged to another time and place.

'Its a seal!' shrieked Oliver. 'Come and see!'

When they came up to it the seal stared at them. This was no ordinary creature. They both knew that under the velvet pelt a beautiful woman, like the fisherman's wife in the story, was dreaming of her first home in the ocean's depths. Scornfully the seal turned away and began to waddle on its curved flippers towards the water.

Oliver watched anxiously. 'Is it sick? Will it be able to swim?'

Without looking back the seal splashed through the shallows and began to oar itself along with its dark pointing head above the waves.

Someone gave Louie a nudge. All the people around her were awake now. Most of them had got rid of their blankets and some already had breakfast trays. Light lay on their hair and sleeves, flashed from coffeepots and cutlery. Louie got unsteadily to her feet and joined the queue pressing towards the washroom at the rear of the aeroplane. In the open space between the last row of seats and the washroom door two Arabs were bending in prayer on their outspread mats. Beyond the windows of the aeroplane Louie glimpsed a vast desert landscape, utterly empty and unmarked, pale and smooth as flesh in the first rays of the sun.

NINE

Frank's back garden was like a deep cool well—a little courtyard enclosed by creeper-covered walls and beds of shrubs. The centre where Louie was sitting under a golden ash tree was paved with stone slabs, still damp with morning dew. It was the kind of place that in winter turns to a dark roofless cellar, and where in wet weather snails multiply, but in the warmth of late September it seemed to Louie a perfect spot to sit while the huge city, spreading out all around her under the bright sky, roared incessantly on like a train in a deep tunnel. She felt surprisingly well and elated. Frank was still Dear Old Frank but even kinder than he'd been at seventeen. He'd appeared at Heathrow after all, brought her quickly home and installed her in a bedroom overlooking a street lined with plane trees, Mercedes-Benzes and BMWs. The cars, parked nose-to-tail along the kerb, belonged, Frank said, to popstars and Arab families from Kuwait and Saudi Arabia.

Louie had slept for ten hours, woken up for a bath (in a bathroom with a good supply of hot water), eaten an omelette and gone back to sleep until the following morning. Over breakfast she and Frank began to talk. They talked on all day while Louie slowly unpacked, while Frank cooked lunch, while they sat together through the afternoon under the golden ash in the court-yard. They told each other about the way they had lived for the past forty years though, so far, the exchange had been rather one-sided with Louie pouring out the story of her marriage to Stuart, the divorce, her relationship with Tim, how she'd come to write her first two novels, her years with George, his death, what the writing of 'The Brown Photograph' had come to mean to her. At inter-vals in this spate of revelation Frank had volunteered brief accounts of his time in the RASC and the Ministry of Housing. He'd also admitted to writing poetry, climbing mountains and working in a Brixton youth club. At the moment he was in the kitchen putting their elevenses on a tray. It was understood that when he came out and sat with Louie he was going to say more about himself. The prospect of closer and closer intimacy, of being able to ask any question, confide every feeling to another person created an addictive excitement. 'It's rather like waiting for a lover,' thought Louie, although she had always been quite selective in what she told her lovers, even George.

When Frank appeared in the doorway she saw that he'd put a flattish cardboard box on the tray next to the mugs. He sat down opposite her, poured her coffee and said, 'Did you ever hear much about your other grandmother, Granny Gale?'

'No. Not a lot. A few stories about how vague she was. Something about a tennis cake meant to have green icing turning out pink. And one about putting her glasses in a rabbit hutch instead of lettuce. Why? Can you remember her?'

'Not really. I was only about five when she died. But she seems to have been quite interesting. My parents— Mother really—kept some of her papers. Letters she wrote to Dad when he was away at the war and lots to this friend she had, Cynthia Campion. Pretty intense sort of friendship, really. Anyway Cynthia seems to have kept every word Granny Gale ever sent her.'

'And when she died the letters went back to Granny?'

'I s'pose so. Something like that. There are poems too. Terribly melancholy. Lots of French translations. But the great thing's the journal. It suddenly struck me, if you want to write about the Diamond Jubilee, this is what you need. She went up to London, you see. All of them went— Grandfather, your mother, my father. They had seats in a stand outside the United University Club in Pall Mall. Watched the whole procession from start to finish. It's all there.' Frank patted the box. 'She got it all down. She was terribly shaken though by something that happened that night. They were driving back from looking at the illuminations through this crowded street. And what d'you think? She looked out of the window and saw a young woman. Pale as death, she says. And just then the girl keeled right over dead as a doornail. Fell down right before her eyes.'

Louie was astonished, all at once convinced that Alice Gale had witnessed the death of Julia Barker.

'I know that would have been a terrific coincidence, but I don't think coincidence—or what we call coinci- dence—is as rare as we pretend. You go to Melbourne, meet someone from Hobart walking down Swanston Street and everyone says "How amazing!" But for every

221

person you recognise there must be dozens, connected to you in some way in the past or future, relatives or friends of your family or people you know, that you *can't* recognise. They must go past all the time—millions of coincidences we never discover.'

Frank considered this, then laughed in his sudden way as though he liked what Louie had said.

'Actually you know the young chap opposite? Vertical white hair. Studs and black leather. Owns the green Mercedes. You might have noticed him. He's in a band called the Fruitbats. Well it turns out he comes from Ollerton. His parents had the pub at one time.'

'There you are! And back in the days when the population was smaller, one person in London, say, would've had some sort of dealings with a much bigger percentage of the whole number than they do now. There must be thousands of people who are friends or lovers or business partners without ever knowing that their ancestors had some kind of connection. It's quite possible, for instance, that your father's great-grandfather and mine fought together in the Napoleonic wars or sold each other cows. If we knew about it we'd call it a coincidence, though really it wouldn't be anything unusual.'

'All right,' said Frank, laughing again. 'Dear Louie!'

'People complain about coincidence in novels. They say it's unrealistic but it's only the discovery of the way we're all linked up that's fairly rare. What Dickens does is remind us that we're all tied up together, how what we do inevitably affects other people, how a society isn't simply a collection of individuals but a community of lives.'

Louie stopped. It seemed that every conversation she had with Frank ended with him nodding and pottering about while she went on talking more and more volubly.

'Anyway,' she said. 'That's enough about that. It's your turn today.'

'I don't know. Not much has happened with me, really.'

'Well, just for a start—I hope you don't mind me asking about this—did you see your father again? You know, after that day at Ollerton?'

'Oh yes,' said Frank, looking surprised. 'He wrote. After a bit I went to see him. Him and Norman. In High Wycombe.'

'In High Wycombe? Why on earth did he go to High Wycombe?'

'Oh well, Norman's uncle or somebody left him this shop there. They started a bicycle business. Sales and repairs. Norman was a pastrycook by trade but he was a handy sort of chap. Could turn his hand to anything really. They did very well because of petrol rationing. After the war they started turning out their own racing bike. The Nordic. That was their little joke. And Dad patented some sort of five-speed gear.'

'A five-speed gear?'

'Didn't Sue ever tell you any of this?'

'Sue?'

'Do stop echoing, darling. She must've said something, surely. Or the hideous Ian.'

'No. Never.'

'But you must have heard about Norman.'

'I haven't. Never.'

'But why d'you think Dad left then?'

'I don't know. I've never known. Actually, I've always thought he must have had an affair . . .'

'Well, of course he did!'

'But who with?'

'With Norman.'

223

'What?'

'You mean no-one's ever told you, Louie? I'm amazed. I thought Ian never missed a chance for a bit of snide moralising.'

Louie just gaped. She was flabbergasted. Then, as she began to recover from the shock, she asked herself how much her family could have known. It seemed impossible that back in the forties her parents and sister could have grappled with the idea that one of their own was tarred with the same brush as Oscar Wilde and Lord Montague of Beaulieu. And—if they had ever known—never given any sign of their unimaginable shock. And Auntie Peggy, how had she coped? Or Uncle Richard, himself, driving to and fro between Filton and Ollerton in the two-tone Rover struggling with the realisation that his pleasant, pretty wife at home in Sloe Lane—though he might still love her in a way—was dust and ashes compared with Norman, whoever Norman, the chap handy with bicycles, might have been? Or Frank, who had stood in the orchard flicking the grass with a stick and afterwards had vanished into the war?

'It was a nasty business,' said Frank. 'Someone started blackmailing him. That was the trouble back then. Gays were always seen as a security risk. Weren't allowed to work on anything secret. Not that Dad was doing anything very hush-hush. Routine stuff really.'

'Is that why he left?'

'Well partly. Also, of course, he felt he was living a lie with Mother. So he resigned and just cleared out straightaway.'

'Did you know this at the time? Did everyone know?'

'It was odd, really. They did and they didn't. The Filton people kept dropping dark hints about "the man, Judd".

My mother, for instance, must have realised. But she never spoke about it. There was a kind of polite pretence that Norman was a Svengali-figure who lured Dad away to design bikes for him. I was a bit confused. I knew he wasn't getting on with Mother. Anyway he told me that. But I didn't really get the picture until I was up at Oxford. I used to go and stay with them. They lived over the shop for quite a time. I used to sleep on a camp bed in the workshop. Later they bought a house. Wonderful garden. A bit like Ollerton really.'

'But Susan knew?'

'Well I told Sue, of course. She'd never suspected anything. But I think your mother did. Anyway she wouldn't have anything to do with Dad. She wouldn't even see him when she was ill.'

'Before she died you mean?'

'Yes. He went up to Bristol but it was no use. Uncle Jim came out of the ward and told him to go. He tried to insist. He thought it was just your father who wanted to keep him away, but she—your mother—wrote on a bit of paper: "No. No brother".'

'Oh Frank, I'd no idea.'

'I didn't see her either. Couldn't really. Sue didn't want me there, obviously.'

'Not obviously. I've never understood all that either.'

'It's pretty straightforward really. Sue told Ian about Dad. He kept on making stupid, ugly remarks. Then that day at her wedding I felt I'd got nothing to lose. Thought I might as well let rip and give him a thump. Too much to drink, of course. I don't know. I don't understand how I could've forgotten what she'd feel. I wrecked her wedding day. I made things totally impossible. Absolutely impossible. I haven't seen her once since.'

'Susan?'

'Susan. I don't s'pose anyone now except you knows what we meant to each other. And I haven't changed, Louie. You're meant to get over these things aren't you? But I didn't. I still think about her every day. I still love her just as much. I've had women friends, of course, over the years. A few affairs. But nothing like that. It's quite funny really. You wouldn't think I was the sort of chap for a grand passion, would you?'

Louie felt her face going stiff. She knew she must be glaring at Frank like a basilisk. She had never been more outraged. She couldn't believe that her heavy, stupid, boring sister had inspired such love in a sensitive, intelligent man like Frank. And how could he have fallen in love with Susan when she was there to be loved instead?

'You are pulling my leg, aren't you?'

It was Frank's turn to look amazed. He stared at Louie with his round blue eyes. His hairline had receded, leaving an aureole of reddish-grey frizz over the back half of his scalp. He put up one hand and clutched at his hair as he sometimes did when he was very bewildered. How could she not have known? Why did she think he kept calling at Howard Road after he came down from Oxford?

'We were engaged for God's sake. Well briefly. I know that was supposed to be a secret but . . . good heavens! You were living under the same roof, Louie.'

'It never ever, ever crossed my mind.'

'You sound like your mother. I don't know why she was quite so shocked about it. Dead set against it from the start. And your father. I never quite understood. I know I'm not up to much but I'd've done everything I could to make her happy. I had a decent sort of job. It was partly the first cousin business, of course. And they knew I still saw Dad. Maybe they felt that accepting me as Sue's husband meant taking him back into the fold. He and Norman would've come to the wedding. They might've had to eat Norman's sausage rolls.'

'Well I can see they wouldn't have relished that. But, Frank, don't you think they might've seen you weren't suited? I mean, I just can't imagine you with Susan. Frank, she's so *thick*.'

'Oh, I know she's not clever. Not like you. When you were little you always cottoned on twice as fast as she did, even though she's—what?—three years older. She used to stand there in her Wellingtons looking sad. That's how it started, I suppose. I always wanted to give her a hug and tell her it didn't matter if she didn't get the joke or couldn't play the game or whatever. I wanted to make things right for her. And if I did—when she was happy—she used to light up. Beautiful. That amazing smile as though you'd given her the earth. I felt she knew she'd always be safe with me.'

'And she left you for Ian? She's even thicker than I thought.'

'Oh, she was under a terrible lot of pressure. Uncle Jim kept saying the Lord had forbidden first cousins to marry and Auntie Bea used to go red and thump about. The odd thing is I think they were quite fond of me. But they kept on telling Sue that if we married the family would fall apart. And you know what Sue's like. Family's everything. And she can't bear scenes. I think she began to feel I wasn't safe after all. I was a threat. And once she finally got the point about Dad and Norman . . . I don't know . . . she may've felt I'd turn out the same. Like father, like son. "Why don't you marry that nice young McAlister instead?" they said. So she did.'

'Oh, Frank, I'd no idea. I'm so sorry. But I still think . . . well, I simply can't believe you'd have been happy. Your poetry, for instance. D'you know what she said when I sent her a copy of *A Magpie in the Rain*? That she didn't know how I'd had the patience to write such a long book, the printers had done a wonderful job and the garden on the cover was really lovely. You couldn't have stood thirty years of that, could you?'

Frank laughed. 'She was scared, I expect, of saying anything about the actual book. She would be. She'd be afraid she'd misunderstood it. "Louie's the brainy one." That's what she used to say. How is she by the way? I wrote to her when Uncle Jim died. About the time I wrote to you. But no reply. I didn't really expect one, I suppose.'

'She's fine. Just the same as usual. The boys are doing well. And Ian's just bought a Peugeot.'

'Ah. I hope he lets her drive it. She gets awfully flustered but once she settles down she loves driving. Just thought I'd ask. Mum used to give me the news but since she died I don't hear much.'

Louie said nothing. She was wondering whether Frank's kindness to her, his interest in 'The Brown Photograph' and the Phillipses' family history, even his idea that she should come to London, were all prompted by his extraordinary passion for Susan. Was he using her to get news, and hoping, perhaps, that through Louie he'd manage at long last to meet his beloved again? Even as she formed this idea she recognised its meanness. Whatever Frank thought or hoped regarding Susan he was still her friend, his affection was still real.

'Look,' he said. 'We ought to get on, oughtn't we? Would you like me to see what I can find in the library on the Diamond Jubilee? And you have a look at Granny Gale's journal.'

'I will. I'm looking forward to it. But I'd quite like to go out for a bit. I want to check the route of the Jubilee procession. St James's Street, Trafalgar Square, the Strand—you know.'

'I'll come with you.'

'No. Please don't worry. You can't give up all your day to me. I'll be back by tea-time.'

How strange it was, thought Louie, that they were talking as though nothing had happened when neither would ever again see the other in the way that had seemed inevitable and true twenty minutes ago. From now on, Frank would think of her as less perceptive than he'd imagined, as someone whose innocence or self-absorption had left her on the edge of the events that had shaped his life; while for her Frank was so vastly altered that, for the moment, he seemed like several different people who refused to coalesce into one personality. Walking down to the tube station through the gentrified terraces of tall houses—like the one where Frank lived in his ground-floor flat—Louie felt as though the old life in Howard Road had become an alien country from which Frank and Susan survived as migrants into the present. They were half familiar figures weirdly transformed to lovers and overshadowed by Uncle Richard's fantastic passion for Norman Judd. As she walked along she wondered in a distracted way what had become of the families that had lived in these streets in the days of peeling stucco and graffiti—'Ban the Bomb!', 'Get out of Suez.' All her internal maps of London—of everywhere she'd once known in England—would have to be revised, but for the moment her mind kept swinging back to her girlhood, a past whose population had been more drastically changed than any of the places of her youth.

She tried as hard as she could to remember signs or scenes she'd glimpsed as she rushed in and out of the house, pausing only to check her pageboy hair in the hall-mirror. Susan had cried a lot in the early fifties. Sometimes when Louie wanted to get into the bathroom she'd heard Susan snuffling inside. Once when she was going past Susan's bedroom door, she'd seen her sitting hunched up on the edge of the bed. Susan was wearing a crochet-work top that Louie secretly despised. It was mauve, a colour Susan loved, along with baby blue, while Louie liked to dress in hot pink, emerald green and, above all, black. Susan's fleecy hair, blonde on the surface, darker underneath, had been spread out over the mauve crochet in thick strands. Her face was buried in a handkerchief and when she looked up Louie saw that her eyes and nose were red and swollen. She looked, Louie thought, like a defenceless, bewildered pig. Louie asked what the trouble was and Susan sobbed out some story about her job at Boots, the chemist, and somebody getting angry because she'd made a mistake over a prescription. To Louie, high on existentialism and Ezra Pound, the whole thing sounded so pathetically silly that she'd never for a moment questioned it. How astonished, entranced and envious she'd have been if she'd known about the secret engagement and her parents' terror of the looming cloud of scandal gathered over High Wycombe. It wasn't, after all, so very surprising that even Susan had managed to keep quiet. They must have shivered in their shoes at the thought of Louie, who yearned for high drama in her life, plunging into the fray, shouting the unmentionable, carrying on at the top of her voice about 'the love that dare not speak its name', slamming doors, rushing out to tell her friends about Norman, and exhorting Susan to elope at once with Frank. Later scenes, like the one when Louie tried to insist on wearing black as Susan's bridesmaid, would have been as nothing to the havoc she'd have wrought at seventeen if she'd known then all that Frank, more than thirty years later, had at last revealed.

TEN

Next day Louie settled under the ash tree with her set of photocopied pages from *The Times* for Wednesday, 23 June 1897.

THE DIAMOND JUBILEE
CELEBRATION IN LONDON
THE QUEEN'S PROCESSION

That great day of national and Imperial rejoicing upon which the hopes of all have been fixed for many weeks and months has come and gone with triumphant success. It had been anticipated eagerly, but not without anxiety, in all parts of her Majesty's dominions. There was reason for some anxiety on account of the strain which participation in a prolonged and splendid pageant must place upon the gracious lady and matchless Queen who was at once the centre and the cause of the ceremonial

. . . Deeply sympathetic as the Queen has ever shown herself in the joys and sorrows of her subjects, the storm of acclamation through which she passed yesterday must have laid upon her nerves the strain which is produced by even the most welcome excitement. It is matter for heartfelt congratulation that she endured it remarkably well. Then there was anxiety upon the question whether the sun would follow his usual custom. He has shone always heretofore on occasions devoted to Royal progresses in which the Queen has taken part. But this was an unprecedented day. The Empire had met to celebrate in Imperial fashion the 60th year of a reign unprecedented for its length, its glory, its prosperity, and, let it be added, its goodness. Rain would have marred the splendour of the military pageant, which had been made military not because the glories of the Victorian era have been entirely or even principally military, but because soldiery make a brave show. The early morning was cloudy and still, and those of doubting tendency trembled. But there was something touching in the confidence of a sturdy constable who announced that it would surely be fine 'because she is such a good Queen.' And fine it was. Very shortly before the Queen's carriage became visible within the courtyard of Buckingham Palace the clouds grew thinner and less ominous towards the west and north; before she was out in St James's Park there was occasion to quote the glorious line— 'Quadrijugis invectus equis Sol aureus exit'; and the rest of the morning and the afternoon were permeated with the spirit of happy sunshine . . . To the framework of the moving picture no accessory was wanting. The decorations along a great part of the route were certainly more lavish and in better taste than they had ever been before. The stands, which men had feared to see half occupied by reason of the prodigious prices which their owners hoped to extract, were well filled. Their occupants, especially the ladies and the children, added colour and freshness to a scene already brilliant. In a word, it is no exaggeration to say that from beginning to end this unique celebration was perfect in itself and admirable in its surroundings. It may be summed up by saying that the Queen and Empress of a great kingdom and of a huge Empire, preceded first by a procession representing the political and military strength of dominion, colonies and dependencies, and then by a military and Royal procession of unparalleled grandeur, has successfuly made an unexampled progress through the greatest city of the world, between enthusiastic crowds of her subjects, and before visitors from all quarters of the earth . . . The pageant as a whole was of wonderful splendour and variety, and not to be matched by any of which history holds the record.

There followed seven pages of detail: the start from Buckingham Palace, where Field-Marshal Lord Roberts, carrying his baton and mounted on a beautiful grey charger, led out the first procession shortly after nine o'clock; the procession in Piccadilly, St James's Street, Pall Mall, Trafalgar Square, the Strand and Fleet Street; the thanksgiving service at St Paul's; the return to the Palace by way of the Mansion House, London Bridge, South-wark, the Borough and Whitehall; the illuminations—gas lamps and electric lights—which, as darkness fell, blazed out across the city in thousands of different multicoloured devices; the Jubilee Bonfires; Mr Gladstone on the Queen's reign; celebrations in the country; the Jubilee throughout the empire . . .

Louie looked through it all and began to make notes, then decided to read Granny Gale's account before she went any further. Inside Frank's box were at least twenty exercise books, tightly packed in batches, and several packets of letters. Louie opened the first book and found pages of poems, mostly translations from Musset, Victor Hugo, Arnault, Lecomte de Lisle, mostly about lost love, lost innocence, lost faith. Every so often she came on an original piece: 'Circe's Lament', 'A Night in Spring', 'If One Should Come'. It was all steeped in weary, fin-de-siècle melancholy and at first seemed rather tedious, though the discovery that Beatrice, who hardly ever opened a book, should have had a mother who translated French and composed verse of any sort was, to say the least, surprising.

> *If my cruel Fate some hours with thee*
> *Hath granted, they are gone. Beyond I glimpse*
> *The engulfing waters of my lone despair . . .*

Alice Gale, wife of a prosperous solicitor, with two teenage children and a solid, affluent home in Clifton, had produced this rendering of Autine Deschamps in June 1909. It had been a busy month. Eleven other poems carried the same date. Although Louie had already brought this maternal grandmother into 'The Brown Photograph' and given her a line about the rabbits to whom she'd tried to feed her glasses, she'd never thought much about her life. Alice had died before the Second

World War and left no trace of her existence in the house where Old Howard lived out his last years.

Poor Alice Gale couldn't have had much in common with her husband and children, all so large and vigorous, keen on games, hearty and practical—though Richard, of course, couldn't have been quite like that, after all, and might have suffered as keenly as his mother's poets from frustrated passion. Louie thought of her, an Impressionist's woman of hazy blue and gold, sitting at her window with her exercise book open before her, her cheek resting on her hand, yellow flowers in a vase nearby, and, beyond the rhododendrons in the garden below, bounding, white-clad figures crying 'Fault!' and 'Deuce!'.

> *Would that across the main as swallows fly*
> *I might flee far from love's abiding grief.*

As she went on reading, Louie began to find that the dominant theme in both the translations and Alice's own compositions was escape, a longing to be something, someone, somewhere else. Even states of mind or dreams were envisioned as far-off places in which the speaker yearned in vain to find a refuge from pain.

> *Fling wide the Gates of Dream whose mystic key*
> *Is held alone by those who hear the song*
> *Of sirens chanting by the wine-dark sea!*
> *But ah! Alas! We may not tarry long!*

or:

Land that is lost to me!
Dream I shall never hold!
Now doth the spring unfold
Love that could never be!

Was it all a literary exercise or a fashionable pose? Or was Alice brooding over real sorrows—the fading of love in her marriage, the loss of some gentle poetic youth in the eighteen-eighties?

Louie untied a bundle of letters. The top one was addressed to 'My darling Dickie'—Uncle Richard, who, with Auntie Peggy, must have rescued the box of papers when his mother's belongings were cleared out of the Clifton house after her death. Beatrice, although she warred with Grandma Duke over relics from James's past, was usually a great clear-outer who liked nothing better than making bonfires of the 'old rubbish' she found in cupboards and drawers.

As well as a few letters to her son, written when he was away on holidays and later at Oxford, there were over fifty letters from Alice to her friend, Cynthia Campion, who had lived near the Gales in Perceval Road, Clifton. They came in bursts over thirty-five years, starting in 1894 when Cynthia visited Scotland, and breaking out again whenever the two women were parted for more than a few days.

In 1896 Alice wrote from a holiday house in Devon to say that she had been reading Victor Hugo on the beach and, on a trip to Exeter, had picked up a copy of Walter Pater's *Renaissance* for one-and-threepence. Louie hurried on, hoping that Alice had written to her friend during the Diamond Jubilee visit to London, but, perhaps because Cynthia had gone up to see the procession for herself, there was nothing until the late autumn of 1897. Alice, apparently, had not been well and had gone with her children to recuperate in Bournemouth. Louie found the first Bournemouth letter baffling. As well as being physically ill—her weight had dropped to seven stone, four pounds, she had 'terrible headaches' and 'a bronchial tendency'—Alice wrote as though some secret shadow had fallen across her life: *How I long for the steady reliable love that is not subject to alterations of doubt and distrust, but which keeps one warm quietly without extremes of any kind . . . I am very near the edge of a precipice . . . A high pressure of feeling, long-continued, is ruinous to both body and soul . . . I try to deaden the one big aching with all sorts of little interests . . . I felt I must get out today despite the terrific gales that blow till they make you feel deaf and silly, so I put on Mary's big mackintosh and walked to the station . . . Mary* [apparently a cousin] *keeps the children amused. She understands that though I love them dearly my nerves are at breaking point . . .*

Two days later, Alice wrote again to Cynthia, addressing her, as always, as *'Dearest old girl': Let all that go into the past, now, the present is different and the last few months have set life on a different footing for us altogether. I must face this and can do it here, so remote from all <u>that</u>, no-one knowing of it, no reminders constantly cropping up—not that I forget . . . But when I come home I don't know how it will be. H. wants us to go on together, as you know, pretending nothing has changed . . . It's the awful blank that lies ahead, after the vividness and joy of the past years, that simply kills me. I know there's much to be glad of and thankful for and I'll see them all in time when I get more used to the loneliness, but no-one on earth will ever know how much there is to miss.*

And again after another three days: *I have a strange sense of unreality . . . but it's better to be moving about again, the long lying still and thinking in Bristol was torture . . . I hope to arrive at the condition of mind you speak of. If all goes well after the return I know I shall. If I could foresee that it would eventually be all right, I could turn my thoughts completely to the joy of what has been—yet it is hard to say <u>completely</u> when one knows it is yet in existence but closed to me, I think, forever . . .*

There was nothing more until over two years later, when Alice was again with Cousin Mary in Bournemouth: *Dearest old girl, I have been so distraught for the last two days that although I thought of you and how worried you would be when you found me gone without a word, I could hardly string half a sentence together. I am calmer now but can't write much just yet . . . I had to leave on Thursday night. It was simply impossible for me to stay in the house or even in the same city as H. You can guess part of it. You know better than anyone how I schooled myself to bear the weight of sorrow and, for the children's sake, to go on calmly. You know the agony I went through when H. swore that all <u>that</u> was over—and I dared not believe him. But hope did come. Blindly I began to think our love might knit together more strongly than before. Well, I have been deceived and that is all I can think of even though I know he is in pain. <u>She</u> is lost to him—actually dead, I think, in some way for which H. blames himself. On Thursday night he was quite broken down, hardly knowing what he said and not caring at all that I should find there had been months and probably years of absolute deception. It will be desperately difficult to know how to take things up. I can't face coming home. I can't write to H. and must get used to the complete separation which must eventually come . . .*

But the crisis passed. After 1900 Alice's letters from Bournemouth and other holiday destinations became again concerned with day-to-day activities: *I have been to a lecture by Mary's curate on 'Have Animals Souls?' for my share of dissipation. I believe they have at least the same—something which for want of a better name we call soul, that we have ourselves . . . I have been reading* Westward Ho! *and Shelley's translation of Euripides which I found very dull . . . Poor R. has a dreadful cold . . . Today I sat in the little upstairs sitting room with the French windows wide open to the sound of the sea . . . R. and B. are utterly delighted at the prospect of an expedition in the Undine, the yacht belonging to Mary's friends, the Stokeses . . . Are you writing at all? I felt as if I might do something in that way yesterday, but it came to nothing.*

Shortly after the outbreak of the First World War, Cynthia left Bristol, to nurse convalescent wounded at a hospital in Surrey. Richard was in France, a second lieutenant in the Royal Engineers. Alice wrote at least once a week to her friend, reporting on his doings and fretting over his safety: *I must tell you that I got my letter this morning, quite a long one considering the little time there evidently is to write in. Also my first one had not come to hand then, even by the 12th, though it should have been there by the 8th. Isn't it rotten?... No news from R. for two weeks. I shake from head to foot whenever I hear B. going to the door . . . B. is immensely busy with her concert parties, raising funds to supply extra comforts for the troops. She is fretting rather over the Phillips boy (adoptive son of our dear old Mr Duke, the clockmaker) though I can't help hoping she will see in the end that an engagement wouldn't be altogether suitable (H. for reasons I fail to understand thinks otherwise) . . . R. is doing a grand job, travelling about from post to post so that letters have been written at the expense of sleep . . . H. has taken to going* *away again at every opportunity. For myself I no longer care, but that he should be so wrapped up in all <u>that</u> when R. is every minute in danger makes me sick with disgust . . . R. is working in the most appalling conditions constructing roads of planks and boards through mud with thousands of shell-holes filled to the brim with muddy water. Despite all the engineers can do many men are drowned . . . I've had two letters from France and am frightfully shaken up. R. was wounded at the Battle of Polygon Wood on September 26th and although he can at least manage to write I am desperately worried over what he has <u>not</u> told us. He has shrapnel in both legs but won't say how bad it is . . . Dearest old girl, I pray that by the time R. is well again the war may at last be over . . . You will hardly believe that even though R. is home at last—very weak and only able to walk a very little each day still on crutches—H. continues to take himself off whenever it suits him. I wonder at these times how long I can endure it—this life of absolute coldness and mutual contempt . . . B. tells me that young James Phillips is still in Mesopotamia. He has had a terrible time, living at one stage on a single cup of flour a day . . .*

Once the war was over and Cynthia back in Perceval Road, the correspondence came to an end and, apart from a few postcards, revived only in the late nineteen-twenties when Alice went to stay for a few weeks in Lyme Regis. By this time Cynthia had apparently become a demanding friend, jealous, captious and intent on establishing herself at last as the central figure in Alice's emotional life.

Why, wrote Alice, *do I always do the wrong thing by you, my dearest? If I write regularly I am wrong, if I write cheerfully you think I am not telling you things, if I write sadly it makes you unhappy. <u>What</u> shall I do? . . . On Saturday R. motored down to see me with Peggy and darling little Frank. He is such* *a dear little fellow, so sunny and affectionate . . . Dear old kid, of course I am glad of your love and remember the absolute loyalty you have always shown over all these years . . . Dear, <u>why</u> do you love me so much when I never give out to the same extent as I receive? . . . Just now I feel quite drained. The old trouble has flared up again so I have to spend the next few days in bed. I haven't even the energy to read and feel eaten up with boredom . . . B. and J. were here last week with little Susan— a very <u>slow</u> baby not at all like R's Frank though B. is naturally fond of her. J. is still very silent though I suppose he and B. are happy enough . . . I must come home soon. The sea air is doing me no good this time. The headaches and sleeplessness are worse here, I think, though it is some relief to be away from the eternal indifference and humiliation, the being made to feel one is a burden . . . My dearest, of course you know you make all the difference to me and I shall be enormously glad to see you . . .*

Under the last letter was a card with a black border— the announcement of Alice's funeral in February 1933. Louie stared at it in horror. It was as though someone whose voice had been speaking in her ear had suddenly dropped dead.

Finally she came to the journals, the last set of exercise books in the box, one for each year from 1893 to 1900. In a way they were disappointing. During these years Alice had apparently used poems and letters to express her feelings and kept her journals for carefully polished essays on topics ranging from 'Verlaine and Baudelaire' to 'A Walk on Durdham Downs'. It was as though she had hoped that one day, when her poetry was famous, someone would find the journals and publish them. *This morning,* she wrote, *on opening my copy of* Fleurs du Mal *I began to reflect upon the qualities that Baudelaire's poetry has in common with that of Verlaine . . .* And: *In all Bristol there is no vista more picturesque than that which meets the eye at the Sea Walls as one stands high above the Avon Gorge after strolling over the Downs . . .* The description of the Diamond Jubilee celebrations began in much the same vein. Part of it—the section dealing with the decoration of the streets and buildings along the route of the Royal procession— had been written on the evening of 21 June 1897 after Alice had returned from a tour of inspection: *We stood for a time at the point where Pall Mall runs into Trafalgar-square. To the right, all up Pall Mall, immense streaks and splotches of vivid colour—red, yellow and blue predominating—met the dazzled eye of the observer. Flags and bannerettes innumerable fluttered in the breeze from windows and housetops. St Martin's Church, lined to the roof with decorated galleries, raised its stately spire above the great square, dubbed by Sir Robert Peel 'the finest site in Europe'. And wonderfully fine it is as everyone must admit who has viewed it from a height on its northern side and gazed down the open vista of Whitehall and Parliament-street. Statues and buildings, each marking some stirring chapter out of our national history, were all around with the colossal figure of Nelson looming up on his lofty Corinthian column in the foreground. We obtained only a back view of the hero of the Nile and Trafalgar but were compensated by the sight of the flocks of pigeons, who lent a delightful touch of nature to the scene as they wheeled and cooed about the hero's head, oblivious of anything strange in the splendid spectacle spread below them.*

Alice and her family were staying with their 'kind friends, the Burtons' in St John's Wood. Bright and early on the morning of Tuesday 22 June, the whole party drove in the Burtons' carriage to the seats reserved for them in the stand outside the United Universities Club. *The scene,* wrote Alice, *was filled with animation and colour as vehicles of every description filled the roadway, mixed with an* immense throng of pedestrians eagerly searching for favourable positions on the pavements. Shortly before 9 o'clock, by which time the road was largely clear, a party of military pensioners, some in civilian dress and some in the scarlet uniform of Chelsea Hospital, passed slowly by, many leaning on crutches or sticks, all wearing clusters of medals on their breasts. At the sight of these warriors, battered and scarred in the service of Queen and country, the crowd raised a great cheer. Then came the soldiers commanded to line this portion of the route, each battalion earning hearty cheers as they moved into position behind the police who were already stationed at the kerb on each side of the way.

This historic part of the route was decked in crimson, gold and purple—a vivid vesture indeed—relieved by the softer, more aesthetic hues of natural flowers and evergreens, but it was not the decorations—splendid though they were—that gave peculiar distinction to the street in which we were fortunate enough to have places. It was rather the varied assemblage of men eminent in the Church, in literature, science, art, medicine, in all branches of naval, military, and civil services, and in politics, who thronged the pavilions erected in front of the numerous clubs and public institutions.

Time passed swiftly, so much was there to see and comment upon both in the adjacent stands and in the street itself where the masses, crowded a dozen deep on the sidewalks, presented an astonishingly various and animated spectacle. Before one expected it the magnificent pageant of the day began to unfold before us. The colonial procession, led by the band of the Royal Horse Guards and preceded by a storm of cheering, came bursting out of St James's-street. First came the Canadians, riding stoutly along and followed by their Premier in a landau drawn by four horses with splendidly dressed postillions; then troops from New South Wales with graceful felt hats, brown boots and serviceable

245

bandoliers; Victorian mounted troops in slouch hats with puggarees; New Zealanders, including the picturesque Maories with mystical black and white feathers in their hats; the Premiers of New Zealand and Queensland in another landau; the Queensland Mounted Rifles in buff uniforms with scarlet facings; the Cape Mounted Rifles. And so it went on—a veritable torrent of colour and sound, men, horses and carriages—Zaptichs from Cyprus in dark blue uniforms with red sashes and fezes; wiry, khaki-clad natives from Borneo, one of whom is said to have taken thirteen heads in his less civilised days!; swarthy bands of infantry from Trinidad and Ceylon; detachments from Hong Kong and the Straits Settlements—a wonderfully picturesque demonstration of the varied races who are members of the Empire, passing before us to the rousing strains of the National Anthem and 'God Bless the Prince of Wales' mingled with the vociferous acclamation of the crowd.

But all this—magnificent and stirring as it was—served only as an introduction to the dazzling spectacle that was to come. After a short interval the commanding form of Captain Ames, astride his immense steed, announced the approach of the Royal procession. For an hour and a half it swept past, stately, magnificent, picturesque—dragoons, hussars, lancers, batteries of guns, some pulled by sturdy blue-jackets; a throng of equerries and aides-de-camp, amongst whom Lord Charles Beresford was greeted with cries of 'Charlie!' and 'Good old Condor!'; officers from the Prussian Dragoons and the Imperial Service troops in strange rich uniforms; bands on horseback; glittering cuirasses and helmets; flashing swords, nodding plumes of white, black and red; waving pennants like flocks of dancing, gaily coloured butterflies; prancing horses richly caparisoned; soldierly forms splendidly clad in scarlet and gold. Then came a line of dress landaus bearing foreign envoys—the Papal Nuncio and the representative of the Emperor of China, complete with fan, riding together!—followed by eleven carriages filled with ladies of the Royal household and prettily dressed children who bowed quite charmingly to right and left. Then a brilliant cavalcade of English and foreign princes, riding three abreast, clad in a dazzling array of uniforms and glittering orders; the Queen's Indian escort followed by Lord Wolseley; and finally the central figure of the entire pageant, the Queen herself. Her Majesty was dressed in black silk embroidered with silver and a black lace bonnet trimmed with diamonds and a wreath of white flowers. Opposite her sat the Princess of Wales wearing mauve satin trimmed with lace and spangles, and the Princess Christian. The carriage was drawn by cream horses, gorgeous in new harness and ridden by postillions, with red-coated footmen running at their sides and the Duke of Connaught, the Prince of Wales and the Duke of Cambridge—the last two glorious in scarlet—riding as escort. What a waving of flags and handkerchiefs there was, as though the whole crowd were a frantically twinkling sea! What shouting, singing and cheering as a perfect tempest of patriotic affection seized the hearts of every subject, high and low! There were tears in every eye at the sight of the tiny gallant figure who commands with her frail strength such a vast Empire and is served by such countless thousands of gallant men, all of whom would cast down their gold and scarlet in the dust, give up their jewelled orders and lofty titles, yea, thankfully lay down even life itself if by so doing they could save their beloved Sovereign a moment's pain and bring but a fleeting smile to her pale lips.

When the Standard and the large squadrons of horse had passed by on their way to the service at St Paul's there was a great stirring in the crowd. Some, who had camped all night in the streets in order to secure the best vantage points from which to view the procession, were all for making their way home to rest. Others, who had brought baskets of provisions, began to share out the good things, while a great many were seized with the hope of viewing the procession all over again and began to press towards Whitehall and the Mall. Our party had risen with the dawn; our little ones were growing heavy-eyed. The sun which had shone so brightly on the procession began to induce tantalising thoughts of a shady corner and a cold collation. There had been much talk amongst us of viewing the illuminations in the city at nightfall, but we now began to understand that if we were to enjoy this spectacle, the afternoon must be devoted to refreshment and rest. With one accord we decided to journey back to St John's Wood, there to savour what we had already seen and make ready for what was yet to come.

It seemed that Alice, on returning to the Burtons' house, had cut short her afternoon nap in order to write out her impressions of the pageant she had witnessed in the morning. Perhaps she had meant to spend part of the following day describing the illuminations that she went out to see in the evening, but, as things turned out, it wasn't until a week later, when she was back in Clifton again, that she felt able to write something about what happened to her that night.

We drove out in the evening to see the illuminations. Mr Burton, realising how tired we would be after walking through the City, gave orders that the carriage should wait for us in a street behind the Strand. The display in Fleet-street was very fine—the columns of Child's Bank lined with opal, amber and pale blue lights, the letters 'VR' and the dates '1837' and '1897' blazing out there and on many other buildings. Very fine effects were obtained by using decorations such as gold and green palm branches intermingled with the lights. I made notes of it all as we walked on and on up Ludgate-hill to St Paul's where the dome, illuminated by search lights stood out in bold relief with its golden cross shining against the night sky. Dear H. was amused by my jottings but understood, I think, why I wanted to make a detailed record of the whole occasion—something to keep like a precious photograph to remind me always of this special day which seemed to mark not only the glorious culmination of the Queen's reign and the triumph of the Empire but, in a more personal way, a celebration of my own great happiness with my darling husband and beautiful children over the past ten years. Yet because of what occurred later in the night there is no doubt I shall remember every instant whether I write it down or not, and as I look now at my notes—Messrs Bensons' windows outlined in green and ruby lamps; over the clock a crystal medallion surmounted by a cut crystal crown, Royal arms and 'VR' on either side and so on and so forth—I can't help feeling somehow ashamed that all of us should have gone straying about exclaiming in a quite childish way over coloured glass and baubles when all the time the shadow of Death stood so near. It was like the story by Edgar Allen Poe of 'The Mask of the Red Death' where the people go on in their heartless gaiety, revelling in the vanity of vanities, while all the time a terrible pestilence rages close at hand.

We went back to the carriage sometime after midnight. The streets were very crowded, all kinds of vehicles jostling together in the roadway and hundreds of pedestrians moving to and fro. We had not gone far and were coming along from Chancery Lane towards Oxford Street when the road became absolutely blocked and our carriage came to a standstill. While we were waiting we looked out, idly enough, at the decorations and lights and at the people pressing along close beside our windows on the left-hand side. I remember staring up at several huge arc lamps, enveloped in yellow silk, which served to illuminate portraits of the Queen and other members of the Royal family. Then my eye was caught by a kind of eddy in the crowd and I saw two people—a man in

249

a cap and a youngish woman with a pale, intent face—supporting, almost dragging, another woman. All three were quite respectably dressed, but I thought at first the woman in the middle must be drunk, and looked away, as one does, embarrassed and rather disgusted. Then there was a thump as the woman lurched forward and thrust the man back against our carriage door as they were all staggering past. Her hat—a straw boater—was all askew, knocked over one eye, and her hair was coming down over her neck and shoulders. Just inches from my face she threw back her head and stared straight at me—such a wild, terrible look, burning black eyes in a face as white as chalk. Her mouth fell open and she slipped down, like someone drowning, with the others still clinging on to her arms and trying to pull her up. And then, suddenly, blood gushed from her mouth in a great stream and ran down her chin, spilled all over her blouse. I gave a scream and H. jumped up at once. He was sitting opposite me and must have seen it all, just as I did. It all happened in just a few seconds. Then everything was confusion, with dear H. out on the pavement, trying to help lift the poor woman who went on staring up straight at me with that fixed, dreadful blank gaze that has only one meaning. And Mr Burton was struggling to get out of the carriage to help H., and H. was holding the arm of the other woman and pushing back the crowd that came pressing round to see what was going on. And all I could do was shriek, 'Close her eyes! Close her eyes! Cover her face!', so that poor Mrs Burton, who might have done something to help the others, had all her work cut out attending to me with her smelling-salts. Then Mr Burton came back and said H. would stay until a doctor could be found, see the poor people safely home, and come on later to St John's Wood. And in a moment the mass of carriages, cabs and so on began to move again and we went off, almost as though nothing had happened. But Mr Burton admitted that, as I feared, the dark-eyed woman was probably beyond human aid. He also said that she had been ill a long time but insisted so violently on going out to view the illuminations that her relatives were forced to let her have her way.

H. was away until dawn. When he came he confirmed our worst fears. The woman's brother or brother-in-law (the young man) had gone in search of one of the St John Ambulance contingents who had been patrolling the streets all day. They made it plain that nothing could be done. The woman was quite dead, though H., who is wonderfully kind, had stayed on to help the bereaved couple with all those arrangements which, at such times, place such a strain on nerves already taxed by the shock of a sudden loss. I wish with all my heart this had not happened. H., I think, is even more disturbed by it than I am. He is oddly silent and seems to feel a need to be alone. It was a sad, ill-omened ending to our great day, a terrible reminder of the transience of human happiness and the hollowness of pomp.

~ *The Brown Photograph* ~
III

In the late spring of 1897, Cyril Nutting sent spies into the offices of his chief competitors to discover how they meant to decorate their buildings on the great day of the Diamond Jubilee procession, and what plans they had for illuminated displays once darkness fell. He found that the West End branch of the Royal Insurance Company was to be covered right up to the second floor with vertical stripes of pink and white material, box pleated, while the first-floor balconies were to be hung with dark blue plush with a valance of gold. On this dark blue ground on the face of the balcony overlooking Piccadilly there would be an inscription in burnished copper: 'Thou art alone the Queen of earthly Queens.'

'And on the St James's Street side?' asked Nutting, busily taking notes from his informant's account.

'A similar sentiment in Hindustani.'

'Hindustani? It's we who are the Imperial company.'

'They're having trouble, though, fashioning the signs in copper. They're talking of having recourse to yellow cloth.'

'A cat's breakfast, in fact. Anything more?'

'Pink geraniums and banners.'

'Very well. And at night?'

'Ah! They're very cock-a-hoop about their Lombard Street display. A huge crystal star in three parts, all turning in opposite directions.'

'Indeed! Well, we shall see who comes off best in the end. We, after all, are on the Royal route. Any news of the National Temperance?'

'Entirely electric—red, white and blue lamps. A "VR", I think, and shields.'

'Hardly very original. Anything further?'

'Guardian Assurance are all electric. Commercial Union have a crystal medallion and crown, "VR" and arborescent dates, "1837—1897". London Lancashire, and Union Insurance much the same. New York Mutual are making a splash—heart-shaped devices in amber hanging from the arches over the windows, an American eagle and the motto "Prosperity to 'The Mutual Life' of Queen and Nation".'

'And what about Atlas?'

'A crystal medallion and crown again, but also an illuminated figure of Atlas with "World-Wide Empire" round the border.'

'World-Wide Empire! We'll see about that. Oh yes, Imperial Colossus will give them something to think about.'

Meanwhile Nutting himself fell into deep thought. He was determined that his company's new offices in Cheapside should be the most spectacularly decorated in all London. A towering, illuminated representation of the Colossus at Rhodes would form the keystone of the display, but there were certain difficulties in the project. The figure had to be virtually naked but at the same time entirely tasteful. A fig leaf, even if coloured red, white and blue, was out of the question. A crystal crown or shield would only draw attention to what the delicately minded would wish to ignore. A flagpole, complete with Union Jack, springing from between the colossal thighs, might induce unwelcome suggestions about the nature of the Imperial achievement, while to place a 'VR' over the offensive area could well amount to lése-majesté.

In the end, Nutting realised that in this, as in much else, the answer lay in a large, bold conception—a long scroll, for instance, sweeping from one end of the roof to the other and passing through the Colossus's hands in a great loop that covered him from knee to navel. The scroll could bear a line of verse or the three words, 'Imperial—Colossal—Achievement'. Or the Colossus could hold in his arms a sheaf of flags, or a vast horn of plenty.

'No,' thought Nutting, 'no. Not a horn.'

❧

John had no patience with the business, the coming and going of designers and mechanics, the confusion and muddle as carpenters swarmed around the steps and windows, and clambered over the roof of Imperial Colossus. He looked sourly at the tiers of seats going up in front of the lower part of the building; the bolts of red, white and blue cloth with gold edging which were to be draped over the stands; the golden trees—pine, palm and oak—attached to the facade between the windows of the upper storeys. Nutting was particularly pleased with the notion of the trees, which, like most of the display, he had designed himself.

'The Canadian pine, you see, the tropical palm,' he would explain to his admiring cronies, 'indicating the huge extent of Imperial power. And, of course, our sturdy English oak, the heart of it all. At night they'll be illuminated by red, white and blue bulbs, creating a very natural pleasing effect as though there were fruit or flowers among the branches. And of course, the patriotic colour scheme, along with the Royal gold, runs through the whole. My idea, you see, is that the red, white and blue represents military might while the gold, as well as standing for royalty, represents the life-blood of commerce—the twin pillars of the Empire you might say. And that's where we come in—Imperial Colossus—the emperor of insurance companies sustaining the Empire.'

He was more guarded about what was going forward on the roof where the crowning glory of the decorative scheme was being prepared. At first all that could be seen was a framework of struts—a high oblong fence with a flat tower in the centre. Then, a few days before 22 June, a long swathe of canvas, painted with curling waves and studded with golden ships, made its appearance. It ran the full length of the roof, sweeping up in the middle to run through the massive hands of a gilded Colossus, fully forty feet high, who now stood forth, magnificent but modestly girdled, to astonish the City.

Nutting, approaching the Imperial Colossus building each morning, kept his eyes lowered then raised them suddenly to recapture the effect of the brilliant surprise he had created. Always there was a crowd on the opposite pavement, gathered to marvel and point at his creation.

'Wait,' he thought, 'until they see it illuminated.'

He longed for the moment when his finger would press down the control switches, when his trees, jewelled with coloured lights, and his ships, outlined in red, white and blue, would leap into dazzling life, while his superb Colossus, illuminated from head to toe, would spring forth from the darkness like a pillar of living flame.

'Great hulking thing,' grumbled John when Julia, who had heard talk of the Cheapside wonder, asked him about it. 'Must have cost a fortune.'

He stopped short. He wouldn't complain, especially to Julia who complained enough for all of them put together.

'Well I shall see for myself on Tuesday.'

She sat upright at the table, looking over Kate's head at the dresser and waiting for her sister to object. It was very hot in the kitchen because of the range so that Julia looked more feverish than ever with hectic cheeks and beads of sweat on her top lip. She'd been in bed all day but had suddenly got up at about seven o'clock and come bursting into the kitchen, dressed in her best skirt and blouse. Kate had just finished putting the children to bed and was laying the table for supper in the soft, summer evening light.

'You know you're not well enough,' she said as she was expected to. 'You don't want to go out in all those crowds.'

She went to and fro, setting out cold mutton, beetroot and pickles. She made the tea at the range and put the pot on the table.

'I don't care about the procession,' said Julia in a high, excited voice. 'I don't care about it at all. It'd be dreadfully hot and dusty in that stand and I don't suppose John took the trouble to get us good seats. But I do want to see the illuminations.'

She waved away the plate Kate offered her.

'Just tea. I can't eat anything. Just tea.'

'Won't you go in the stand?' said John to Kate.

She shook her head.

'I told Mrs Gatty she could have our places. She said she'd take Violet and Bertie if we wanted. Mr Gatty'll go, of course, with the boys.'

'I pity the poor devils lugging guns along if this heat keeps up,' said John. 'And standing to attention hours on end done up like dogs' dinners. They'll be dropping like flies.'

'Still, most people will enjoy themselves.'

'I certainly shall,' said Julia. 'The illuminations should be really quite remarkable.'

Kate sighed and kept her eyes on her plate. She didn't know what to do. Julia was terribly ill—the doctor said she might not last the year—and although, in the end, she'd brought herself to write to Aunt Martha pleading for money to get her sister away to a place with better air, all that had resulted was five pounds and a cold lecturing letter from the Burnes.

'You're not up to it, now are you? You know how walking tires you out.'

'I'd have thought that just for once we could take a cab. Can't we order one? Book one tomorrow?'

'It's not that. You'd have to walk when we got into the City. I don't suppose a cab could get along through the crowds.'

'Well I'm sure I could manage. At least, if John, for once, would help us. I'm sure I'd manage well enough if I had some support. I want to see the Colossus.'

Julia's eyes filled with tears and her voice quavered like a child's.

'It's not much to ask,' said Kate in the end, giving John a look. 'You'll come with us in the evening then, will you?'

John shrugged and muttered something.

'All right, I'll get Molly in to mind the children. They'll all be asleep anyway. It's not dark till late.'

Nobody spoke for a few minutes. The street was quiet and upstairs even Baby Annie was sleeping so that the only sounds in the kitchen were the chink of knives and forks and the little stuttering noises of cups on saucers.

'How far should we take the cab, d'you think?' asked Kate at length.

'Just to the City. You can see that Colossus thing and if it's lights you want there's plenty there. The Mansion House'll have 'em and the Bank and all the big firms.'

'I want to see Piccadilly and St James's Street. That's where the best display of all is going to be. The Princess of Wales has promised to press the switch.'

'You can't walk all the way back from there to Cheapside,'

said Kate but Julia looked so cast down that she relented again. 'Well, perhaps as far as the Strand. Then we'll come back past St Paul's and get the cab to wait somewhere near.'

∾

On Tuesday evening as they drove away from Beaumont Street towards Clerkenwell Road, they passed the sooty little parish church of St Barnabas. Kate had taken to going there sometimes on a Sunday although John refused to go near the place and Julia scorned its impoverished vicar and motley congregation.

'Kate,' said Julia suddenly. 'I want you to make sure I'm buried in Chippenham.'

'What?' said Kate, looking startled. 'Oh, now, don't talk like that, dear. You oughtn't to be dwelling on such things.'

'I'm not a child or a fool. I know very well I haven't much longer, and I want you to promise you'll do as I ask. I want to be buried in Chippenham. I couldn't bear it if I thought I'd be buried in a place like this. I want to be with Papa. I don't care that we don't live in Chippenham any more. People know us there. We're still respected and everyone knows what sort we really are.'

Kate looked around in a worried way at John but he was sitting hunched up in his corner, thinking grimly of the inscription they'd chosen for the tomb of the man who'd deceived and ruined them all.

As they came towards the Strand the crowds grew more and more dense. There were family parties, hundreds of couples wandering arm in arm, and groups of young men shouting and throwing confetti. The noise was terrific—a deafening medley of cheers, droning snatches of loyal songs and ragged, blaring music. Everywhere people were blowing on trumpets and pipes—even combs and paper—and swaggering along in parody of bands they'd seen in the Royal procession. Eventually the cab came into a quiet side street and drew to a halt. As they climbed down onto the pavement they could see at the end of the lane the glow of many-coloured lamps flickering through a haze of dust, and the dim, shifting silhouettes of the throng pressing down the Strand. Julia seemed quite stunned by the bustle and noise.

'Come on, then,' said John, taking her arm, but she drew back.

'No, no! We can't go that way. It's too dusty. Look at it! I shan't be able to breathe. We'll go the other way into Oxford Street.'

'You'll never manage to walk back,' said Kate, but she couldn't see what else she could suggest so they turned around and started making their way northward behind the Law Courts. They got along well at first but as they were passing Lincoln's Inn they met a large crowd heading for the Strand and had to swing into single file with John shouldering their way and Julia, supported by Kate, clinging on behind him. When the crowd had gone by Julia collapsed onto a low wall and started to cough while the others stood over her, watching her hat and shoulders jerking up and down as she gasped and retched into her handkerchief.

'We'll never get back to St Paul's in time,' said Kate to John. 'You told the cabman we'd be there at half-past, didn't you? What if he doesn't wait? We'll never get another cab in this jam and she can't walk home.'

'I suppose I could carry her at a pinch.'

'Oh, no! No!' panted Julia, getting up from her seat. 'I won't have that. We'll go on. We haven't seen a thing yet.'

Because it was well away from the route of the procession, the part of Oxford Street into which they eventually emerged

259

was much less lavishly decorated than the thoroughfares through which the Queen had driven earlier in the day. Beyond the corner of Tottenham Court Road they caught a glimpse of Heath's, the hatters, covered to the roofline in lamps and flowers, and an art furnishing house with illuminated parapets, but when Julia tried to move in that direction, Kate and John pulled her back and tried to steer her up New Oxford Street towards the City.

'There's nothing up here,' she wailed. 'I want to go back . . .'

She began to struggle, broke into a fresh fit of coughing and, snatching her hands away from the Phillipses, clutched at her throat. The crowd, though thinner than in the Strand or the western stretch of Oxford Street, was still pretty dense. By now, a line of vehicles, carrying some of the sightseers home, had appeared in the roadway. It moved mostly at a snail's pace, but every so often it surged forward, pushing aside the masses of pedestrians and forcing them in waves onto the pavements. Caught up in one of these sideways rushes, Julia was carried away from Kate and John and jolted to and fro. Her hat slipped over her eyes, her hair fell in loops over her shoulders and she began to scream, feeling blindly round for her protectors. By the time they got hold of her again John was in a black rage and Kate close to tears.

'Where are we going? Where are you taking me?'

'It's all right, dear,' said Kate, trying to rearrange Julia's hat with her free hand.

'Just don't let go again. We'll go on now and see the Colossus. Oh, and do look there at Pears and Co!'

She pointed up at a line of gigantic braziers and then, wheedling her sister along, started exclaiming over a building close by where four enormous portraits—the Queen, the

Prince and Princess of Wales and the Duke of York—were illuminated by a set of lamps enveloped in yellow silk.

Julia gaped and threw back her head. At last she seemed to be moving tractably towards the City and taking in the sights she'd come to see. Kate even began to think that they might get to St Paul's in time, at least, to ask the cabbie to wait a little longer while they went on to have a look at Cheapside and the Mansion House. Then Julia made a strange gargling sound, and seemed to slip and half fall, wrenching Kate's arm so sharply that she nearly toppled over. She could never quite remember what happened next. She knew there was a carriage in the road close by with blurred faces peering out, and that when Julia fell she tried to get her up, frightened that she might get trampled underfoot by the crowd. And then there was a presence near her, an arm in beautiful, smooth cloth, that had nothing to do with her life or family, lifting and holding Julia. She could remember the shock of seeing something dark spilled all over Julia's blouse. She thought what a shame it was and how upset Julia would be at having her best clothes spoiled. Then there was a hand on her arm, a strong arm around her shoulders shielding her and forcing back the people trying to press in behind her. Looking down she saw a large glove on her sleeve, a yellow, stitched glove that was utterly strange to her, grasping her yellow sleeve. Everything pale was changed to yellow in the light of the arc lamps illuminating the line of royal portraits.

There was a smell of soap and cigars, clean and strong, a smell into which she could sink and rest in safety. And a face with a light moustache and blue eyes—such kind, steady eyes—looking into her own. Someone was screaming, 'Cover her face! Close her eyes!' John, very thin and black, was kneeling on the pavement. Kate couldn't see what was happening to Julia. A policeman and several women, bending down with their backs to her, had come between her and her sister.

'Oh! I must go to her!' she sobbed out to the stranger who was holding her arm. 'What was that on her blouse? It was blood! I think it was blood!'

'Please don't distress yourself,' said Howard Gale and, still gripping her arm, he leaned away and spoke to another man, grave like himself and elegantly dressed, who might have been his friend. John looked across at her and lifted his hand in a gesture that might have meant almost anything. More policemen came, pushing back the crowd, moving people along. One of them went off at a run, the men spoke together again for a moment, and then a door slammed and the vehicles in the road began to move.

'Everything is being attended to,' said Howard. 'An ambulance will be here in just a moment and your husband will stay and do all that's necessary. I think you should let me take you home, if I may.'

Kate gazed at him in astonishment, starting to sob again.

'I can't leave my sister. She's had an attack. She's ill.'

Howard was stooping over, still looking into Kate's face. He thought her astonishingly beautiful with her wide eyes gazing up so appealingly and her bright hair, curling and falling, shining copper in the weird golden light of the lamps. For a moment he felt as though his spirit had left his body and was hovering over the scene in the street, looking down with ironic amazement at the sight of his ordinary, decent, prosperous existence invaded by the totally unforeseen. Kate's bewilderment, her terror, the drama of the sudden death of her sister came on him like the exotic, alluring music of a flamenco song that he'd heard once long ago strolling in the streets of Madrid—a rush of heat from a life full of passions and mysteries that he'd never known. All his life there had been only one way to behave and he'd gone along dealing honestly, keeping his word, using his strength and prudence—as he was doing now—to help the unfortunate, loving his wife, in a cheerful, rallying fashion, caring for his children, looking after his money and enjoying good fellowship, jokes, games and fun. At times the glimpse of another way of living—a reckless, dishonourable course—came palely before him in papers relating to bankruptcies, adulteries, even criminal assaults, and sometimes some wretched wastrel or faithless husband would sit opposite him in his office and he would think to himself disgustedly, 'What a cad the fellow is!' And in all this time he had never once wondered how it would be to cut loose, to do something wild, to plunge into an adventure. Not even as a young man because the ordinary way, the decent way provided plenty of change and fun: predictable scrapes at Oxford, jolly girls, sailing, tennis and dancing.

He had no idea where he was going, moving along in the dreamlike golden light with the beautiful stranger pressed to his side. He knew only that what had seemed alien and shameful was suddenly close and filled with a heady promise he had never dreamed of before.

'But I must go back!' cried Kate, struggling to get away.

'No, I beg you. There's really nothing you can do. Please let me take you away from here.'

'Oh! You can't mean . . .'

He looked at her then so sadly and compassionately that she knew quite certainly that Julia must be dead, plucked out of the world like a tree that has always formed part of the outline of a garden and in the twinkling of an eye is snapped off in the wind, leaving only a space. She began to weep hysterically while Howard guided her along and people in the crowd turned round to stare.

'Oh I should never, never have let her come out, but she was so set on it. And I thought, she has so few pleasures. But I knew, I knew it would be too much.'

'You mustn't blame yourself. I'm sure you did right.'

Kate looked up quite sharply, aware all at once in the midst of her grief and shock that the man beside her admired her extremely and was gazing at her with an expression she hadn't seen since the days when she used to walk up the steps at a theatre in her blue velvet evening dress or her embroidered French silk. For a second she felt outraged; then, even though she was a married woman with five children and her sister had just dropped dead in the street, her vanity began to smile at finding that she could still evoke admiration in such a well-dressed, handsome, gentlemanly person.

'Oh,' she said, 'do you really think so?'

'Of course. From the little I saw, I'd say this was bound to happen very soon. Your sister might have collapsed tonight even if she'd stayed at home. The disappointment of missing her treat could have brought it on. I think you were very wise and kind to act as you did and I'm sure, I'm very sure that your sister would think that.'

How well he spoke, thought Kate, how providential that he should have come to her aid when otherwise, since John had simply gone off without a word, she would have been left to manage quite alone with nobody to comfort her or help her through the crowd. Then it struck her that all the passers-by, seeing the stranger's arm about her waist and his head bent so attentively towards her, must take them for lovers or married people, and she felt a little flash of pride and pleasure at being lifted up out of her own life to be seen as the consort of this masterful, good-looking man. But this thought made her alarmed at her own badness. Lately, ever since Jimmy had announced that he didn't want to see her or his father or any of the family, she had begun to think of herself as bad. Secretly she'd wept over the wrong she'd done in driving Jimmy to take such a step, and had even spoken to John about why Jimmy had turned against them. They'd agreed that Mrs Duke might have withheld John's letters and done other things to make Jimmy think they didn't want him to come home. For a time they had got on quite well as together they damned Mrs Duke, but all the time, of course, Kate could see that John blamed her for what had happened. And although this made her feel even more guilty, eventually it began to sharpen up her old resentment against John. It was he, after all, who had driven her to send Jimmy away in the first place and it was he who kept her slaving away in Beaumont Street, never showing a particle of the concern so evident in the eyes of her chivalrous escort.

Howard, meanwhile, was wondering what on earth was to be done. Having leaped from the Burtons' carriage, abandoning his family and friends, to take charge of this pale, beautiful creature, he had to find some way of looking after her, of making her as safe and comfortable as possible. He had said he would take her home but unless she lived close by this was easier said than done. There were no cabs to be had and she was obviously in no condition to walk very far—or so he told himself, because the feebler Kate was, the more necessary his presence became. He thought of taking her to a hotel, somewhere with spacious public rooms, comfortable chairs, few guests and windows opening on the summer night. He would get her to rest and order brandy. They would talk, sitting close together. He would take her hand and tell her not to worry about arrangements for her sister's funeral or, indeed, anything at all. He would see to it. He would see to everything, although, even as he framed the words in his mind, he recognised that the husband, the thin dark fellow who had, by now, gone off to the hospital with his sister-in-law's body, might expect to take a hand in the proceedings.

He was frowning to himself over this when Kate said something in his ear about a cab waiting near St Paul's.

'Though I don't expect it would wait, do you? Not all this time?'

But it was worth a try, so they went forward more briskly, moving on towards Ludgate Hill where he'd walked earlier in the evening with Alice, who, true to form, had wanted to keep scribbling in her notebook even when they were out enjoying themselves; or, at least, he thought, supposedly enjoying themselves because, in fact, one display of lights had begun to look very like another after a time and, since there was nothing to do except walk and stare, the whole thing had become rather a bore. But now he was very far from bored. He felt as though he was on the verge of some immense expedition, about to plunge into a new element.

Kate told him that she lived in Holborn. He didn't know Holborn well at all. Beaumont Street? He wondered suddenly if she might be badly off, and amazed himself by becoming more excited than ever at the thought of her being in need. He would help her in some way, change her life . . .

'I should have gone to the hospital,' she said. 'She mustn't just be left there. She'll have to be brought home, won't she?'

'I'm sure the hospital people will tell your husband what to do. I expect they'll put him in touch with an undertaker. And of course tomorrow, if I can be of any service . . .'

'You're very kind.'

'Anything at all, regarding the funeral arrangements or anything of that nature. I'm here on holiday, you see. Up for the Jubilee like half the world. So tomorrow I'm really at a loose end.'

This, of course wasn't true at all. There was supposed to be another outing with the Burtons and the children, a picnic by the Serpentine, a visit to Madame Tussaud's and a theatre with supper afterwards in the evening. It was all arranged and he had quite been looking forward to being the life and soul of the party, bustling the others about and making the children laugh. But they could still go, he thought hastily. It wasn't as though he was robbing them of their pleasure, and Alice would understand his wish to help a bereaved family. Indeed, she would admire him for it. This reflection made him ashamed for a moment, then irritable because Alice always made such a song and dance about ordinary things, weeping and quoting that morbid French stuff she was so fond of at the oddest moments.

Kate had begun to talk about her sister having a premonition that something dreadful was about to happen. Apparently, this very evening, she had expressed a wish to be buried in Chippenham.

'Chippenham?' said Howard. 'Do you come from there?'

'Well, we used to live there when my father was alive. At least, my sister did but I moved to London when I married.'

'I know Chippenham quite well. I go there sometimes on business. Perhaps, since I know the town, you'd allow me to arrange lodgings for you . . .'

They talked this over for a little while, with Kate demurring in a rather embarrassed way because, despite John's firm having begun as a Burial Society, they had made no provision at all for Julia's funeral and she was frightened at the thought of what it would cost to get the coffin and all the family to Chippenham. Eventually Howard said something about how easy it would be for him to break his journey in the town on the way back to Bristol. Kate started and said,

'You mean you live in Bristol? My little boy is there, staying with a friend—well, with a person I knew at school.'

It came out then that Mrs Duke was one of Howard's clients and Kate, stopping still in her amazement, cried, 'Oh you're Mr Gale! How astonishing! You're the Gascoignes' solicitor! Miss Gascoigne often spoke of you. And you're Beatrice and Richard's father! Jimmy's school friends!'

She knew, of course, that a good deal of what Mrs Duke had said about Jimmy's friendship with the Gale children was a pack of lies—the story of the holiday, for instance, that had been used to stop John bringing Jimmy back to London—but she did believe her son was going to school with Beatrice and Richard and was fond of them.

Howard was thunderstruck. It dawned on him that this woman who had erupted into his life had once been the Miss Barker whose unfortunate marriage had thrown Elfreda Gascoigne into a frenzy, although, later, when he'd mentioned that her friend's son had come to live in Bristol with his clients, the Dukes, nothing would do but that the boy should be brought to Chippenham. 'I shall do something for him,' said Elfreda Gascoigne, throwing back her dark head. 'I at least know the meaning of friendship. Mr Duke shall bring him to see to the clocks.'

What Kate meant by saying that James went to his children's school, he had no idea since his daughter went to one school and his son to another, but he was very eager to make the most of any bond with Kate, so he accepted without a quibble what he saw as some kind of misunderstanding.

They looked at each other incredulously. How extraordinary that there should be these ties between them! Both felt that there was something fateful in the coincidence, that Destiny had contrived that they should meet. At once everything changed. Even the way they were walking along the street became quite different. They moved forward more quickly, talking quite volubly together, and when one was pushed a little behind the other by people who passed them, they craned their necks, keeping their eyes locked, one still speaking, the other anxious not to miss a word.

The cab that John had ordered had gone, of course, long ago. But by now the crowds were beginning to disperse so that soon there would be other cabs to be had on the streets. They walked on past St Paul's into Cheapside where the Colossus, towering up against the sky, was still drawing a sizeable throng of admirers. Since framing his original design, Cyril Nutting had discovered that his electricians could devise a way of flicking lights on and off to create an illusion of movement. So the line of golden ships were all sailing rather jerkily along their river and up through the hands of the Colossus while the crowd in the street below looked on quite spellbound.

'Oh Julia did so want to see that!' said Kate. She stopped and began to sob again, horrified at how easily she had put aside thoughts of her sister's death. After a moment she explained to Howard that John was employed by Imperial Colossus and had told Julia all about its illuminations. Howard immediately looked up at the golden giant with a more critical eye. It struck him as absurd that each ship, as it finished its voyage, suddenly vanished in darkness as though it had dropped like a stone to the bottom of the river or sailed off the edge of the earth.

'Not much of an advertisement for British commerce!' he thought to himself. 'Though I suppose it shows the wisdom of full insurance.' He would have liked to point this out to Kate but decided that under the circumstances it might be rather indelicate to start making jokes.

When Kate had recovered herself a little they went on, supposedly looking for a cab, but so intent once more on their conversation that they had made their way all along

269

Aldersgate Street and crossed Clerkenwell Road before they realised where they were. By then they were so close to Beaumont Street that it seemed pointless not to walk the rest of the distance.

∾

When they came to the house everything was silent and dark. Molly had gone to bed upstairs with the children, leaving no light except for the gas burning low in the kitchen. As they fumbled their way down the passage from the front door, the realisation that Julia was dead came over Kate like a wave of cold black water. She could hardly believe that only a few hours before she, John and Julia had set out from this place together and that now her sister was gone from the house forever. She pushed open the kitchen door and looked round at the table and chairs standing mild and forlorn in the half light, at the place where Julia used to sit by the range, at the plates and cups on the dresser that Julia had handled daily, not considering them at all and never dreaming when she went off to see the illuminations that she'd never touch these ordinary things again.

Kate sank down on the nearest chair and covered her face with her hands, so overcome that for a moment she forgot that Howard was with her. She looked up startled when he put his hand on her shoulder and stared as though she'd never seen him before. He'd turned up the gas and in the brighter light looked so tall and broad, so glossy and groomed, that the little kitchen seemed to shrink and become more dingy than ever. She was suddenly pettily ashamed of it and mortified that Howard should see how she had to live.

He, for his part, was surprised to see that Kate was older than she'd looked in the street, with faint silvery lines across her forehead. Her hand, lying on the bare wooden table, looked rough and discoloured against her white cuff. But, instead of dismaying him, these discoveries seemed to make Kate even more appealing, like the broken wing of a finch he'd once picked up and taken home and healed and made his own. Her house, as she feared, shocked him. As they'd walked through the streets she'd talked about her girlhood, which seemed to have been affluent, and had hinted at coming down in the world, but nothing she'd said had prepared him for a place as miserable and poky as this. He felt quite outraged, and at once began to fume against Kate's husband for expecting a woman like her to live in such a hole. He decided that the thin, dark fellow was a thoughtless, heartless fool and probably a drunkard. No wonder Elfreda Gascoigne had been enraged by this marriage.

Eventually Kate got to her feet and put on a kettle for tea. It struck Howard that she must do nearly all her own work and he felt quite angry that his own wife should lead such a comparatively pampered existence, sitting about all day with her books and taking her servants for granted. He watched Kate moving to and fro, entranced all over again by the light on her hair, and told himself soberly that he must think what was to be done, bring his knowledge and skill in monetary affairs to bear on Kate's circumstances, and yet proceed very cautiously in case she took fright or offence and drew away from him.

When the tea had been made and they were settled at the table, Kate began to talk about Julia again. She had fixed on the idea of bringing her sister's body back to Beaumont Street. She spoke of how, in Chippenham and the villages round about, the dead were always laid out, washed and dressed in good clothes by the women of the family. She seemed distressed that, when her father died, Aunt Martha and Mrs Cotton, the midwife who had brought Kate and Julia into the world, had attended to the body before she herself could arrive from London. On the day of his funeral he'd lain on his bed with closed eyes and smooth hair, pale hands folded on the dark cloth of his coat, while a host of people crowded into the house to pay their respects. At last the coffin was brought to the door in the hearse, carried upstairs and placed on chairs by the bed. The undertaker and his people had lifted Tobias into the coffin and then looked around at the family to see if they were ready for the lid to be put on. Was there anyone else who might wish to say farewell? No other relatives? Nobody waiting downstairs? When they shook their heads, the lid of the coffin was screwed down. The screws, Kate remembered, were silver like the coffin handles.

'She shouldn't have gone to the hospital,' Kate said. 'She has to come here.'

'Nowadays, you know, in cities especially, things aren't always done in the old way. It makes a difference, too, if your sister's to be buried in Chippenham.' Howard paused, shifted in his chair and cleared his throat. 'Please don't think me impertinent but I wonder, now, if I might ask—since I hope you'll let me make some of the arrangements—if any provision was made for the funeral?'

Kate flushed and turned her head away. 'You'll think us very improvident. We meant to do something, of course, but things have been so difficult . . .'

'Your sister might have made some private arrangement, private insurance . . .'

'I'm sure she didn't. I'm sure I'd have known if she had.'

'Perhaps she put something by, saved something since she was so anxious about the burial.'

'No, no. I know she didn't.'

272

'One can't be entirely sure.'

Howard pulled out all the money he had in his inner pocket, folded it and pressed it into Kate's hand, putting his own large hand over hers and squeezing hard. It gave him an immense thrill, a joy at taking this step into Kate's life so that, despite himself, he smiled in her face.

She tried to snatch her hand away but he held on, alarmed now that he'd allowed an impulse to spoil everything. He bent forward and said earnestly, 'You must take it for her, for your sister. This is my pleasure and privilege to help realise her last, dearest wish. And it might have been found—something she'd saved, as I'm sure she would have done if she'd been able.'

'But I can't. It's too much. Why should you do this?'

There was a rattle at the front door, a step in the passage. Howard gave Kate's hand, still holding the money, a meaningful push, and, before she could think further, she had tucked the banknotes into her sleeve.

❧

Once out in the street and walking alone in the direction of St John's Wood, Howard was seized by an astonishment similar to that which had come upon Kate when she arrived back at her starting point in Beaumont Street and realised the change that had come about since she, John and Julia had left the house earlier in the evening. Everything, on the surface, seemed quite normal again. Here he was returning to his friends' home, his wife and children, his ordinary, pleasant existence quite as though nothing very extraordinary had happened and yet, incredibly, his whole life had changed. For a moment fear of scandal, loyalty to his family, placid attachment to untroubled routines, all rose up to draw him back to his familiar path, but they might have been so much mist. All his vigour and love of action were galloping him off in a totally different direction. He stripped off his gloves and beat them against his thigh, striding faster and faster along the streets. He was trembling with excitement but furiously vexed because, in giving way to the pleasure of thrusting his money into Kate's hand, he had managed to lock himself out of the funeral. The husband could do it all now. The role of solicitous benefactor that would have kept him close to Kate had been tossed away in one throw. And yet he would still go back tomorrow. Even with no pretext he must go back. Would she be at home? Would she be expecting him?

There had been no chance to exchange even a word once the husband had arrived, sitting down at the table and expecting her to minister to his needs as though it were he and not she who needed comfort and care. Did she understand that they must meet again? Did the husband suspect anything? Would he believe the tale about the sister having put money by?

And what of the future? he thought, slowing his pace. They must meet when she came to Bristol to see her son. But how, and where, and what would he say to his wife? And how would he go on with Alice now when he saw that he'd never really loved her and felt a positive resentment against her for trapping him into a marriage that had never suited him and from now on would be nothing but abject servitude to convention? He would get away, come up to London whenever he could. Would Kate agree? She felt something for him he was sure, but would she go so far? He pictured her in his bed, under his hands, naked and soft, and he began to shake more violently than ever. He must be cautious, go forward one step at a time so as not to alarm her. Not that he wanted to entrap her. No, no, no! He wanted above all else to give her a better life, to care for her, to give her just a little of all the good things Alice accepted with such blind, indolent smugness. Would he break free, carry her off? Leave Bristol? Leave England? Part of him leaped at the prospect, but too much stood in the way. She had other children besides the boy in Bristol. He hadn't managed to ascertain how many but there were at least two. She would never leave them and he, too, had children and all sorts of ties: profession, friends, property, a place in society. If he tossed them away, everyone would suffer. He couldn't leave his son and little Bea without a father. He had duties and responsibilities that could never be set aside.

Cooling, he bit his lip. It was, of course, absurd that he should lose his head like this over a woman of whom he knew next to nothing, someone he'd met only a few hours ago. Poor Alsey! She tried so hard to please and make him comfortable. But, then, for all her poetry, how little she understood about strong feeling. Certainly she'd never inspired any in him. He'd married her more out of pity than anything else because she'd been so set on it and had been there, adoring and ready to serve him, at the point when he'd begun to feel the need for a wife. But she wasn't the right mate for a man like him—too lackadaisical, dull and bookish— always fussing over his health and his clothes but never really sharing his pleasures, never enjoying a good game or a joke or a party, just sitting about in the shade with her nose in a book making everyone feel awkward. And although she tried so hard to please, as often as not she made a nonsense of everything, like the time she'd ordered a pink cake for the tennis party and then couldn't see at all why they'd all laughed at the idea of a cake, meant to look like a tennis court, being pink. Whereas Kate—ah, she was altogether different! You could see just by looking at her how she'd throw herself into work or games or pleasure. And again his mind leaped away towards the woman who had just come into his life and began quite frantically running through every detail he could visualise or remember.

I mustn't call too early, he thought. Perhaps at about eleven.

∽

Kate had learned a good deal about telling lies in the past year. She saw at once that John would never believe Julia had denied herself all kinds of little luxuries in order to save money to pay for her funeral. So Kate pretended instead that the telegram she'd sent Aunt Martha, announcing Julia's death, had brought on a fit of remorse and prompted her aunt at last to loosen her purse strings.

'She's sorry now,' said Kate. 'I expect she wishes she'd helped Julia get away from London. If she'd done something earlier she might have saved her.'

At least, with the money to hand, it was easy enough to arrange matters in Chippenham. As Howard had feared, John, with the help of Mr Finnigan, did all that was necessary. When Kate murmured that Mr Gale had offered to do what he could, John only stared and shrugged.

'He's not coming here again is he?'

'He thought he might look in. He wanted to help us, knowing Jimmy, you see.'

'Well, there's no need. I'll go down early tomorrow. You follow on with the children and we'll have the funeral on Friday. They'll dock my pay but we'll keep something back from what you've got there to make up for it.'

'There's a lot to think of. I'll have to get mourning for Violet and the boys. And, John, shall I send a wire to Liza-Jane? Jimmy should come.'

'Don't suppose she'll bring him or he'll want to see us.'

'He ought to come.'

'Ought. Well "ought's" one thing. What goes on is another.'

Kate was in a fever, uncertain whether Howard would call at the house, fearful of missing him if she went out, but full of self-accusation at finding that her mind ran more on a man she'd just met than on her sister's death. In the end, instead of taking the children along the street to get fitted out by a seamstress who lived six doors down, she sent Molly out to buy a packet of black dye, boiled it up in a large pot and pushed Violet's best dress down into the mixture with a wooden spoon.

Violet clambered on to a chair. She gaped in amazement at her frills wallowing in greyish scum and let out a shriek.

'It's all dirty! My dress is getting dirty!'

Gilbert and Charles, who was nearly two by now, started trying to climb onto the chair.

'Dirty, dirty!' crowed Charles.

Kate, who was about to go upstairs to look out boxes for tomorrow's journey, rushed back to pull the children away from the boiling pot. Molly came clumping in with Annie in her arms and ran forward to help. Violet had got hold of the wooden spoon and was trying to fish her steaming dress out of the dye.

'Leave it alone!' cried Kate.

Because she was in mourning she was wearing the stylish black dress that she'd had made for her father's funeral two-and-a-half years ago. Her hair was carefully dressed and before breakfast she'd rubbed away at the stains on her hands with pumice stone.

'You're got up nice, missus,' Molly had said.

But now, as she wrestled to get the spoon away from Violet, dollops of dye splashed her clean apron and spattered

277

her face. A stream ran down on the floor where Gilbert promptly dropped on all fours to dabble his hands in the puddles. When he looked at his grey palms he seemed disappointed at finding them so pale and, turning on Charles, tried to rub the dye off on his hair and pinafore.

'Dirty, dirty!' sobbed Charles, looking sadly at his streaky front.

'Ha, ha! You're a little chimney sweep! You're a little chimney sweep!'

'Stop that, you Bertie,' snapped Molly. She didn't care for Gilbert at the best of times so when he poked out his tongue at her she lost her temper and whacked him across the head with her free hand.

Violet, who was used to clothes being boiled to get them white, not black, decided everyone had gone mad and began to scream in terrified desperation. Gilbert screamed more loudly still because Molly had hit him quite hard and he wanted his mother to be angry with her. Charles and Annie, appalled by the din, opened their mouths and joined in.

Howard came to the front door, found it half open and heard from the kitchen such a dreadful shrieking that he thought the house must be on fire. He dashed down the passage, flung open the kitchen door and, seeing the room filled with swirling steam, thought for a wild moment that it must be smoke. He stared at the figures near the range, the black puddles on the floor. Had something burst into flames and been doused with water? Kate gazed at him with utter astonishment, too stricken even to lift her hand to the smudges on her face. The children, hiccupping and shivering from their screaming bout, gaped up at the huge, glossy-looking man who had erupted into their kitchen. He was carrying an enormous bouquet of pink roses. Violet could smell their perfume even through the dark, acid stink of the boiling dye and the old kitchen smells of paraffin, dishcloths and cabbage. But the beautiful colour reminded her of her ruined dress which had ended up draped over the lip of the dye pot, still dripping blackish water over the hissing range. She scrambled off her chair, ran away upstairs and crept under the coverlet on her bed.

Lying in the hot darkness she listened for footsteps on the stairs, for her mother coming to find her, but for hours she heard nothing except occasional thumps and rattles from the kitchen below or a burst of voices with Bertie chanting something and Molly shouting. Sometimes it seemed as though it might be late evening and everything as usual, night coming on and the boys asleep in their truckle beds, but when she pushed down the coverlet and saw bright morning sun on the opposite wall, shining hotly on the picture of a little boy and a dog that Aunt Julia had framed, she knew that everything was changed and horrible. Her mother had spoiled the dress she had always been so careful to keep clean and had shouted at her, and she herself had been naughty and rude and run away from the visitor without saying 'How do you do?' And then Violet thought of how Aunt Julia had gone to Jesus in the nighttime, like Mrs Gatty's baby, Eva, and Reggie, the boy in the story her mother had read to her, who lay with his little white face on his pillow murmuring 'Before morning!' until he woke up in Heaven with God and for him the morning broke on the golden shore. But Aunt Julia hadn't found Jesus in her bed but had gone to him somewhere else so that her bed in the room next door looked neat and straight as it always did in the daytime on the days when Aunt Julia got up. As she was thinking about this, it struck Violet that Aunt Julia wouldn't need her bed or her bedroom any more now that she was in Heaven and that, perhaps, she would be allowed to have them instead. She would turn the key in the lock, as Aunt Julia had often done, and however much Bertie screamed she wouldn't let him in.

❧

'I don't know what you must think,' said Kate. She looked down at her hands, still faintly grey on the backs and black around the cuticles, although she had scrubbed them as hard as she could in the scullery. She wondered what Molly had thought when she'd thrown off her apron, rushed away to wash her face and hands, caught up her hat and, without even stopping to run upstairs for her gloves, left the house with Howard.

'I must go back soon. We have to go down to Chippenham tomorrow and I still have to see to the children's clothes.'

'I think, perhaps, you should abandon the dyeing operation,' said Howard. He poured a little more sauterne into her glass and looked around with satisfaction, trying to imagine how Kate must see the room in which they were eating luncheon—the thick carpets, the mirrors and chandeliers, the hurrying waiters, the tables of fashionably dressed patrons, the silver and glass glinting through an opulent haze of cigar smoke.

'I haven't been to a place like this for years,' she said as though she had read his mind. 'But I shouldn't have come, you know. There's so much to be done and it does seem wrong. Poor Julia! How heartless to be sitting here eating meringues! You must think I don't feel for her at all.'

'On the contrary. I know, I really do know how intensely you feel everything. I wanted you to come here because of that, because I could see that unless someone saw to it that you gave a little thought to yourself, you'd forget to eat, perhaps allow your grief to affect your health. It's very clear how sensitive you are.'

'I don't know. Sometimes I think I'm really quite hard-hearted.'

'You! Impossible!'

'But you hardly know me. We only met last night.'

'Of course, but just occasionally—it might be only once in a lifetime—one meets someone who is so sympathetic, so absolutely attuned to one's own nature that all the usual business of getting to know the character of an acquaintance is simply unnecessary. One knows all in a flash. Don't you agree? Don't you, perhaps, feel something of this, I mean, regarding myself?'

'Oh,' said Kate, blushing and looking away, 'I know you are very kind and generous and, yes, I do feel that—well, I suppose that I could always trust you absolutely. I know Elfreda did.'

'Ah,' said Howard, taking her hand. 'Trust is everything. I shall never forget what you've said. And you'll see you're perfectly right. I shall never fail you. Never.'

'But after today we may not meet again.'

Howard looked down at his plate. For the first time in this conversation he felt nervous of saying too much too soon. He sliced deliberately at his cheese and bit into a Bath Oliver biscuit. Finally he said, as lightly as he could, 'Oh, I think we shall. Don't you?'

'But I hardly ever go anywhere. I'm always at home with the children.'

'You wouldn't object to me visiting you sometimes when I come to London? I come quite often, you know, on business and so on. In fact, I shall be back again in a couple of weeks. You wouldn't object to me calling to see how you are—I mean, just to enquire if the funeral went off smoothly?'

'I'm afraid my husband might think it strange.'

'Then, perhaps, since I am—I will be—anxious to know

281

you came through all this trouble, we could meet just for a little while somewhere? Here, for example. Just for an hour or so.'

'Well I suppose so. You're so kind. I don't suppose there'd be any harm in that, would there?'

'Harm?' exclaimed Howard, tremendously elated. 'My dear, what harm could there possibly be? Two friends having a meal together simply because I'd like to know all is well!'

'I must go,' said Kate. 'Oh dear! Do you think it would be all right if the children just wore black armbands?'

'Of course! Perfect! And now, may I write to you to let you know when I'll be here next?'

'I suppose so. Yes.'

'You don't mind if I write to Beaumont Street?'

'Well, perhaps it would be best if you sent the letter to the Holborn Post Office.'

She flushed and looked down, and Howard thought, Ah! She understands! She knows and doesn't draw back!

Alice Gale was sitting upstairs in the little room she called her study. She had intended it to be very simple and plain, a cell for contemplation, serious reading and artistic experiment, but over the years it had become extremely cluttered. The Morris wallpaper was almost entirely covered with framed photographs—her parents and sisters, her wedding, her children, above all her husband who appeared, high-collared and clear-eyed, in a number of formal studies and, here and there, more casually posed in holiday garb, leaning on the wheel of a dogcart in Devon or standing among the heather on a Scottish moor. There were also half-a-dozen water-colours, mainly by Alice's friend, Cynthia Campion; some copies of Pre-Raphaelite works; and—rather daringly—a collection of Beardsley prints from *The Yellow Book*.

The furniture had accumulated in much the same way. Alice had meant to have nothing apart from her rosewood desk, a chair, a bookshelf and an easel, but soon she had felt the need for a sofa, several little tea tables, a Japanese screen, an armchair where a visitor might sit, and a larger table to carry the overflow of books, papers, vases of flowers and oddments that gathered on every level surface in the room.

Sitting at her desk in the window she saw nothing of all this. She was staring out at the cedar tree beyond the tennis court almost paralysed with misery. She could hardly believe that Howard had spoken to her as he'd done at breakfast time and searched and searched in herself for what it was that made him so angry and strange. Like someone who hardly dares confront a beloved face for fear it might be drawn with pain, she began to look back into the past, running over what Howard had said at various times: the day when she'd criticised one of his Oxford friends, the famous occasion of the muddle over the tennis-party cake or the evening—just over two weeks ago—when he'd teased her about the notes she kept taking as they went about the London streets looking at the Jubilee illuminations.

'Look here, Alsey, this place has four VRs, not three like the last one. You've got that down I hope.'

Nearly always it had seemed kind enough, affectionate, even admiring.

'What's this? Ibsen? What a little brainbox you are, Alsey!'

It had never occurred to her—or at least only for a split second once or twice—that there was anything sharp or despising in what Howard said. And for a week after their return from London he'd said very little. Both of them had been very deeply shocked by the death of the young woman

283

who'd dropped to the ground by their carriage door as they were driving back to the Burtons after the long, glorious day of the Jubilee procession. The incident had come like a terrible reminder of the transience of glory, the hollowness of pomp, casting a shadow over all their holiday pleasure. Or so Alice had felt, although she was a little surprised and then rather alarmed that Howard, who was usually so sensible and practical about such things, should remain silent and downcast even when her own spirits had begun to revive. Howard, of course, with the generosity she so loved in him, had gone off to help the dead girl's family and Alice had begun to wonder if something about their circumstances had upset him. Mr Burton had said the young woman was consumptive. It could be that the whole family was afflicted and that Howard had found himself plunged into the middle of a dreadful tragedy in which everyone was dying or doomed like the Brontës.

Last Friday evening, just over a week after the Gales had arrived back in Clifton, Alice had come in from the garden with some lilies for the drawing room and found Howard standing at the window. He looked so dejected, standing alone in the twilight, that she went up to him very quietly and laid her hand on his arm.

'Dearest,' she said, 'what is it? Are you still thinking about that poor girl? Is it something to do with her family?'

'Why d'you say that? What on earth gave you that idea?'

'I don't know,' said Alice, beginning to stammer and blink her shortsighted eyes. 'I thought, perhaps, you seem so troubled, dearest. I thought, perhaps, those people had upset you in some way . . .'

'Upset me? I'm not upset. What on earth makes you think I'm upset?'

'You seem so quiet and sad.'

'What nonsense! I was simply thinking. I suppose I'm

allowed to think from time to time. I never complain about you sitting upstairs thinking about your poetry or whatever it is.'

And he drew his arm away and went out of the room, saying something about letters he had to write. It was a small thing, that drawing away, but it seemed to Alice that for the first time since they had met eleven years ago, Howard found her touch irksome or offensive. And then the next day and the one after that he was strangely irritable. Everything she did was wrong. If arrangements weren't just so she was neglecting him. On the Saturday night for instance he was angry because she had forgotten to see that his dress clothes were sponged and pressed for some law dinner. But when she flew about, saying she'd do it herself at once he accused her of making a fuss, of always making a drama out of nothing.

It was the same on Monday night. It was a hot day and Alice ordered a light dinner of clear soup, lobster salad and strawberries and cream. Howard came home late after the children had gone to bed. The two of them sat down to dine alone in the cool dining room with the windows open on the garden and the scent of Alice's mignonette and night stocks in the air.

'What's this?' asked Howard, spooning up his soup and letting it pour back into his plate.

'It's clear soup, dearest.'

'Clear! It's coloured water. I've been working all day, Alice. Surely when I come home I'm entitled to a proper meal.'

'I'll ask Cook to get you something else,' said Alice, jumping up in a flurry.

'You can't go bothering Cook now. It's all right. I'll make do. Just sit down. There's no need to make such a fuss about it.'

Alice took off her glasses and put them beside her plate. Her eyes filled with tears which she struggled to hold back as they drank the offending soup. Beyond the centrepiece of white roses Howard appeared as a broad greyish blur with highlights glinting on his smooth, fair hair. Eventually he said,

'I'm sorry, Alsey. I'm an old bear. It's just that a chap gets hungry after a day's work. I'm not one of your poets living on moonshine, you know.'

And it had seemed that, after all, everything might be all right again until, on Wednesday morning, Howard said casually,

'Oh, by the way, I have to run up to London tomorrow.'

This might have meant nothing in another man or in different circumstances but Alice was astonished. The Gales never went to London more than once or twice a year and they had only just come home from their last visit. Nearly all Howard's clients lived in Bristol or on small estates in nearby counties, so that professional business rarely took him further than Chippenham or Bridgewater. And when, for example, old Mrs Morland, who had gone to live with her daughter in Twickenham, insisted that he hurry to her bedside to change her will, Howard had come galloping into the house and shouted up the stairs.

'Alsey, are you there? Pack your best bib and tucker. We're going up to London on the four-fifteen!'

She couldn't remember when Howard had last set out on such an excursion without her, so that when he said, 'I have to run up to London tomorrow,' she assumed—or insisted on believing despite a small, cold doubt—that he meant her to go with him.

'Oh good gracious! Oh Howard, I wish you'd told me before. D'you want the children to come?'

'The children? No, no. It's purely a business trip.'

Howard fiddled with his letters, glancing over one and folding it again.

'I'll be back on Friday, Saturday at the latest.'

Alice drew in her breath and then let it all out in a rush.

'But you do want me to come with you?'

'I told you, it's purely a business trip. I won't have time for gallivanting. And, after all, you had nearly a week there in June.'

It was true then. And he hadn't even said he wished that he could take her with him. After a moment she asked as steadily as she could, 'Will you stay with the Burtons?'

'Oh no, I shouldn't think so. I'll put up near the City somewhere—some hotel.'

'The Criterion is very good.'

'Yes, I may stay there. Or I may find somewhere else. I really can't say at the moment.'

'Dearest, I hope there's nothing wrong.'

'Of course not. Why should there be?'

'It's just that you usually tell me why you have to go away.'

'Oh, good God! Well, if you must know I have to deal with the sale of some property. A client's property. It's a very delicate matter. I really can't discuss it any further.'

Alice said nothing. Howard picked up his letters and shuffled them together, louring at the envelopes. Eventually he burst out,

'It really is quite extraordinary that you should expect me to go tattling about a client's affairs over the breakfast table. It's a private matter. That should be enough for you. I don't know why it is you always have to go prying into what doesn't concern you.'

'Prying!' cried Alice, cut to the quick. 'How can you say such a thing? You've always told me things of your own free will.'

'I've never betrayed a client's confidence. Is that what you're suggesting? That I come home here and tattle about

287

my clients so that you can run across to Cynthia Campion and spread scandal all over Clifton?'

'I never have! I never would!'

'Because I've never given you the chance. It's absolutely preposterous to suggest I've been in the habit of discussing clients' private business with you.'

'You told me about Mrs Morland and the inquest on Colonel Masters . . .'

'That was absolutely different! Can't you understand that? I don't know, you don't seem able to grasp the simplest thing these days. You're at me always, questioning and cross-questioning, but nothing I say seems to make the slightest impression.'

'I don't know what you mean. I don't cross-question you. Howard, I'm your wife!'

'There's no need to remind me of that.'

With this, Howard got up and went banging out of the room. Alice sat on at the table hardly able to move until Elsie came in to clear the breakfast dishes.

'Are you all right, mum?' asked Elsie.

'Oh, yes. Yes,' said Alice. She thought of Desdemona, berated by her husband for reasons quite beyond her understanding—*Faith, half asleep*. She felt dazed herself, lethargic and somehow dishevelled. She put up her hands to her hair, which was dark and heavy, always slipping down in lopsided loops.

On the stairs she paused, thinking she might go across to Cynthia, the only person in the world to whom she could turn for comfort. But her friend had never liked Howard very much so that it seemed disloyal to run to her with tales of his cruelty. And whatever he might think—so unfairly, so unjustly—they very rarely talked about personalities. Instead they discussed their reading and writing, Cynthia's pictures

(Alice had decided she herself had no talent for painting), and general issues like the nature of truth and beauty. When they talked about love it was usually in a quite abstract way. Yet Alice knew that, in the end, she would have to tell Cynthia something about what had happened. It would be impossible to appear absolutely carefree under the scrutiny which Cynthia would turn on her face.

'Dear old girl, you're very pale today. What is it, dear one? I've never seen you so white.'

Then Cynthia would insist on wrapping her in shawls, fetching tea, and stand about frowning, wanting to call the doctor, until Alice, unable to keep back her tears, would let the whole business come spilling out. The prospect filled her with shame. It seemed to give substance to Howard's awful charges.

Still staring at the cedar tree, the black depths between its spreading fans, the dense shadow on the lawn beneath its branches, Alice folded her hands across her forehead. She felt quite feverish and her head had begun to throb. She wondered, almost with relief, if she might be sickening for something which would provide an unequivocal reason for her changed looks and her longing to creep off and hide in a darkened room. Howard had gone away to his office without saying another word to her, after that last dreadful comment. Tonight he would come home and she would have to confront him, with the words still working in her mind. Though, perhaps, she thought, if one turned them about a little they didn't mean—as it had seemed—that having her as his wife was a hardship, only that he resented being reminded of his duty to her when he had always been such a good and loving husband. Ah, how easily any difference was overcome when there was loving goodwill on each side, how hard it became to settle anything when that goodwill had withered away.

'Not withered away!' she thought in terror. 'It's simply that something has happened to worry him, something I ought to see or sense for myself.'

It struck her then that she must have got everything mixed up and back to front, that because she had been so oppressed by the death of the young woman she had leaped to the conclusion that it was this that was troubling Howard, when, in fact, his mind had been fixed on something quite different—the property he had to sell, for instance, or stocks and shares.

Suddenly everything seemed to fall into place. If Howard, himself or his firm, had financial difficulties that he'd heard of first when they were staying at the Burtons—and there had been letters forwarded from Bristol—then that would explain why he'd suddenly gone off on some business matter instead of coming to Madame Tussaud's. This was the cause of his silence and his irritability when she pressed him for the reason for his second visit to London. There must be some dreadful debt, some failed investment that was forcing Howard to raise money where he could. Naturally, he wanted to spare her the anxiety he was feeling. How infuriating it must have been when first she imagined he was brooding over the dead girl, and then later, wanted to go with him to London! Alice almost laughed with relief. Perhaps soon they would be poor. Perhaps, the firm would fail and the house would have to be sold. They might have to move to a little country cottage like the one they took for holidays in Devon where the children could run wild in the woods and fields and she and Howard could wander along the seashore hand in hand. What need did they have of wealth when they had each other? She pulled a notebook towards her and began to write, pausing sometimes and crossing out a word or phrase:

Oh, not for us the golden prizes of the busy world,
The chink of coin, the fervid hastening crowd!
My gold is laid up where your hair lies curled.
I see you standing tall, Apollo-browed
Wrapt in the sun's last ray. You take my hand
And tell me that my price excels by far
The cost of rubies. This plain golden band
You placed upon my finger when my star
First led me to your arms is all the wealth
That you and I will ever seek to gain.
Come, dearest! See! The stars with gentle stealth
Have laid out all their treasure and the main
Gives back their light! What need of pelf
Have we whose love is free of any stain?

Alice thought this so beautiful that she began to weep again. Should she go now and lay it on Howard's desk? She hesitated. Perhaps not. She would keep it as a surprise for him when he came home from London.

Kate woke in mid afternoon and lay in the strange hotel room listening to the rumble and clatter of traffic in the street below. The window curtains were drawn but the shaded room was stiflingly hot, filled with the sour smell of semen and sweat, and the languorous perfume of the roses on the washstand. Howard had arrived at the restaurant carrying a bouquet even larger than the one he'd brought to Beaumont Street on the day after Julia's death, and afterwards Kate had carried it through the streets like a bride, bending her head as though to drink in the flowers' scent when they entered the hotel. Once in the room, the bouquet had given her something to do—thrusting it into a jug, fanning out the roses—so that she'd been able to avoid the difficulty of returning Howard's look until he'd finished drawing the curtains and come to take her in his arms.

He was still asleep. She turned her head and gazed at him, laid out huge and strong beside her, this man who was not her husband, whose sweat clung to her thigh as she pushed herself up in the bed. His watch with its heavy gold chain lay on a cabinet at her elbow. When she reached out and lifted it up, afraid that she might be late getting back to Beaumont Street in time to cook the supper and make everything seem ordinary again before John came home, she was startled to see that it was only three o'clock. They had been in the room no more than an hour and a half. The doze into which she'd fallen after their long lovemaking could only have lasted for ten or fifteen minutes.

She was surprised, too, to find that the thought of John failed to make her guilty or ashamed. She felt nothing but a breathless excitement at being party to a secret he would never share, and a wondering contempt at his inability to understand that what he and she had accepted as the only way to make love was, after all, quite different from what had happened here with Howard.

'I've no shame,' she thought and, in order to test this idea, began to think rather fearfully about Howard's wife. He'd said that Alice was a good deal older than he was, always ailing and quite wrapped up in interests of her own—modern pictures and foreign plays and books. She seemed, Kate found, no more than a hostile circumstance or—like everyone else who would never see into this room where she lay with Howard—a grey ghost moving about on the circumference of a charmed circle, ignorant of what life could really be.

Propping herself on one arm, Kate looked down at her lover's face—the thick, straight hair falling across his forehead, the solid, shining planes of hard flesh, red where the sun had caught him. She watched the blond hairs of his moustache stirring over his lips and square white teeth, his wiry eyebrows, the sweat on his blunt nose. One arm was flung over the sheet, frosted with hairs, ruddy and freckled where he'd rolled up his sleeves for tennis, but above the elbow as white as the spread of his chest and naked shoulders. Very softly she touched one of his nipples and lifted his hand, staring at the fingers that had caressed her so deftly and then tightened on her thighs to force her down on his member. She could hardly breathe when she remembered how he had overmastered her, huge, heavy and strong. He seemed, even in his sleep, more vigorous, more full of sap than anyone she had ever seen before. It was absurd to ask herself if she loved him. She was entranced by him and, since he had chosen her, unable to do anything but bend in a delicious swoon to his will.

When he woke he stared up at her with his bright blue eyes. He looked as though he thought he must be dreaming, then smiled and reached out his hand to touch her breast.

'I wish he'd seen me when I was younger,' thought Kate. Even after she'd suckled Jimmy and Violet, her breasts had still been firm, but now, after three more children, they hung down, soft and weak like little, pale purses. She hadn't been able to feed Annie for long. Her milk had dried up and they'd had to put the child on the bottle. If she'd had milk still in her breasts, Kate would have taken her lover's head in her arms and let her nipple slide into his mouth. The very thought made her thighs slacken again and she dropped her head on his chest, stifling him with the loose masses of her hair.

∾

After Kate returned to her family for the night, Howard found himself at a loose end. He was tremendously keyed up, delirious with pleasure and desperate to go on enjoying himself in some huge celebration. He would have loved to take Kate to a great, cheerful party where he could laugh and drink and dance amid throngs of people. Left to himself, he began to feel edgy and sullen. He thought of going to the Empire, but couldn't fancy an outing on his own. His closest friend in London was George Burton, but if he spent the evening with the Burtons, Alice would certainly hear about it and discover that his time in London hadn't been as full as he'd pretended. In any case, he wasn't in a mood for domesticity. He had no intention of boasting about his conquest but he wanted to be with people to whom he could drop a hint, who would clap him on the shoulder and order up champagne.

For an hour he walked by the Serpentine, growing more fretful by the minute. He was elated, of course, at the way in which Kate had succumbed to his advances and the thought of their lovemaking left him quite dizzy. He had never suspected that a woman's body could yield such delight. When he pictured her face looking up at him from the pillow and imagined again how he'd driven into her softness he almost groaned with longing. But what—now that the thing had come to a head so quickly—was to be done now? Were they both to go on for months, perhaps for years, meeting just now and then for an hour or two? Was he expected to spend his life plotting and scheming for a few furtive meetings, each time tamely letting her go back to her wretched husband?

As on the night of his first meeting with Kate he began to think about making a break for it. Frowning, prodding at the pathway with his stick, he tried to recollect what he knew of Sydney or Toronto and to calculate the cost of a double divorce. He wasn't, after all, short of money. His father had done well in shipping and his uncle, who had been the senior partner in the firm of solicitors he'd joined after coming down from Oxford, had helped him to manage his inheritance, putting him on to one good thing after another. Together uncle and nephew had gone on cheerfully building up the family's fortune until, at the age of twenty-four, Howard had announced his engagement to Alice.

'She hasn't got a bean,' said Uncle Rupert.

'But she's a good little thing,' said Howard. 'And it's a very old family.'

'Thin blood. Thin everything.'

At least, thought Howard, as he wandered on towards Lancaster Gate, nobody could say he'd been ungenerous to Alice, and if he left her he'd do the decent thing, see her well provided for. Nobody would be able to accuse him of meanness. But people would say other things about him and it was this—the loss of face, respect, position—more than anything else that overmastered his impulse to rush headlong into new adventure. Glumly he thought of the Irishman, Parnell, whose career had been totally ruined seven years ago when O'Shea sued for divorce. He'd died less than a year later, a broken man. How they'd hounded the fellow! The Irish had thrown mud at him and hung shifts out of their windows to show their contempt. The Queen had called him a man of very bad character devoid of all sense of honour. If the news of his own divorce spread through Bristol, his older clients would condemn him in similar terms. At the moment he was liked and respected all through the West Country, virtually every door was open to him, he could rub shoulders with whom he pleased. He had titled people as clients and one or two of them—Sir Henry Gascoigne for instance—had invited him to their houses for a weekend's shooting. An earl had urged him to stand for parliament. If he fled to the colonies he would never be able to go back to Bristol. The practice he'd nursed so carefully since his uncle's death would fall in ruins. He'd be cut dead, shut out and scorned as lower than a beggar in the street. He snorted to himself, thinking what hypocrites they were, that half of them kept women on the sly. The great sin was not to kick over the traces but to get found out. All the same, even while he fretted and fumed, he felt his fear of public opinion shift and settle at the back of his mind like a massive weight sinking to the bed of the sea. It anchored him far more securely than concern for his children. He was fond of Bea, but Richard was a very stiff little sober-sides, polite, willing, but somehow aloof, not the jolly little comrade a man wanted as a son; he was his mother's boy.

As Howard walked on, away from Hyde Park, he fell back into idly picturing life in the colonies. He imagined a white house, an impossibly blue sky, native servants bowing as he rode in through wide open gates, and Kate in a filmy, light coloured dress waiting among tropical trees. But it was all rather like gazing out to sea from a boat securely moored in a safe harbour. When he started to realise this, glimpsing out of the corner of an inner eye his settled aversion to scandal, he bridled and told himself all over again that he and Kate couldn't go on as they were. Something would have to be done. And so, eventually, when he looked about and found that he had walked some way along the Edgeware Road, he remembered all at once that Grindley Gascoigne lived in one of the streets running off to the right.

Grindley, who was a distant cousin of the Gascoignes of Bathurst Hall, had grown up in Australia. He had been in Howard's year at Oxford where he'd proved himself a cheerful companion with a taste for fast living and enough money to indulge his tastes. He had gone home to manage a family sheep station but had found apparently that life among the sheep was too slow. About four years ago he had written to Howard announcing that he was back in England and had taken a house near St John's Wood. Thereafter they had met occasionally at Bathurst Hall and last year, during one of the Gales' infrequent visits to London, Howard had introduced Grindley to Alice. The evening had not gone well. Grindley had insisted on talking about nothing but racehorses all through a long uncomfortable dinner.

'Oh dearest, he's dreadful!' said Alice afterwards. 'I can't believe he was at Oxford. He's such a typical colonial. You don't really think he'll come and stay with us in Clifton, do you?'

Howard had felt it only civil to offer Grindley hospitality if he happened to visit the West Country. That Alice should challenge his judgement in this seemed to him outrageous.

'You're a dark horse, Alsey. I didn't know you knew all about Oxford chaps and colonials.'

'Oh! I didn't mean . . .'

'Actually, I think he's quite a decent fellow. He may not spout poetry or that sort of thing but he knows a lot about breeding. If he comes to Clifton, you won't make him feel unwelcome, will you?'

Alice had been suitably chastened, even waking in the night with the horrible idea that Howard had been hinting at something ill-bred in her reluctance to receive Grindley as a guest. But if he came, she thought in panic, of course I'd make him welcome. I wouldn't dream . . . Howard couldn't think . . .

Sometimes Howard made jokes about Alice's breeding because her father had been very distantly related to the Earl of Shaftsbury while his own uncle and father had risen from rather humble origins, but in the end she convinced herself that he had been referring to bloodlines in horses, not courtesy in people, and drifted off to sleep again quite peacefully.

As it turned out, Grindley had never come to the house in Clifton, but just a few months ago he had dropped in at Howard's office on his way to look at a promising colt in Taunton. They had drunk a good deal of claret with their steak and kidney pie at luncheon and parted affably, with Grindley urging Howard to look him up when he was next in London. Now, as he began to walk more briskly along the Edgeware Road, feeling the heat of the day beat out at him from the walls of the buildings he passed, it seemed to Howard that the Australian was just the fellow to suit his present mood—jovial, easygoing and very much a man of the world. Even more importantly, he would know all about the chances of getting a berth in a suitable firm of Melbourne solicitors, where to look in Victoria for land, what it might cost to build a house or engage a cook or buy a decent horse. To talk to Grindley as though he really meant to emigrate, to jot down names and figures in his pocket book, was just what Howard needed to satisfy the sense that he ought to be doing something to break out of the tormenting situation into which he had fallen so quickly. Later, when he relayed all the information to Kate, she'd see he was not a man to let the grass grow under his feet, though she'd never agree, of course, to simply up sticks and leave England forever.

A few more paces brought Howard to the corner of the street in which Grindley lived. It was evening now and he began to worry about the propriety of calling uninvited at such an odd time. He was always punctilious about social niceties in his dealings with men of his own or a higher class. But he reminded himself that Grindley, as an Australian, was more casual than most, crossed the street, climbed the steps to Grindley's front door and rang the bell.

ELEVEN

Louie had arranged to go down to Bristol to see Susan after ten days in London.

'I hope she's not upset about you staying with me,' said Frank.

'I decided not to mention it. At least not yet. I just said I was staying with friends. I'll let her know I've seen you, though, and tell her what a lot you've done for me.'

'I don't suppose it'll do much good.'

'It's absurd this feud dragging on and on. I'm going to talk some sense into her.'

Frank looked nervous at this and began fiddling with his hair.

'And now,' said Louie, 'we'd better do something about this letter. I'll ring Sue and tell her I can't get down to Bristol before Friday. And we'd better ring Annie's hotel.'

The letter had arrived in the morning mail. After her interview with Violet, Susan had seemed reluctant to follow it up with an expedition to Annie's Eveningtide Home. So Louie had written to Annie, explaining that she'd be in London soon and was going down to Bristol shortly afterwards. Could she and Susan drive down to Barnstaple to visit her? But Annie had other ideas. A letter arrived announcing that she was coming up to London for a few weeks' holiday. If Louie wanted to meet her she was welcome to join her for tea at the Elberton Hotel in St John's Wood on Thursday at four o'clock.

'I'll ask if you can come too.'

'Wouldn't miss it for worlds.'

Frank picked up the letter and looked at it again.

'Very good paper. Embossed address. Smells of money to me.'

'But the lover old enough to be her father must have died years ago. She can't be all that well off now she's lost him. I think the notepaper's one of her little vanities. Something to keep up appearances and remind her of the good old days.'

'What about this secret patron you were talking about?'

Louie brushed this aside. She knew exactly how Aunt Annie would look—sparse, frizzled hair dyed black, heavy pancake makeup coagulating in her wrinkles, vivid lipstick, long scarlet nails, high-heeled sandals, a pant-suit, possibly a relic of the sixties with flares and a psychedelic pattern ('I do like a bit of colour, dear'), and lots of jangling bracelets on arms whose skin hung down in sad, limp valances from the bones. The eyes would be very dark and bright, the voice furred by cigarettes and whisky. There might be a cigarette holder. There would certainly be a bottle in a dark corner of a cupboard.

'And the Elberton Hotel's rather seedy, patronised by aging theatrical people. Her room's piled with old albums and newspapers. The springs have gone in the sofa and it's covered in cat hairs.'

'But she doesn't live there, darling. Anyway, the Elberton's in Gladstone Gardens. Not the place for sagging springs at all.'

'Well, the Elberton's missed out on being gentrified. I think the proprietress must be an old friend who keeps a room for Annie in the basement. For tea she'll give us broken biscuits and afterwards a tot of something stronger.'

'Lucky it's within walking distance.'

Gladstone Gardens was longer and quieter than the street where Frank lived. There were fewer cars at the kerbside and the houses looked more at ease with their new paint and windowboxes of pelargoniums and lobelia. Instead of being divided into flats most were opulent family homes or small private hotels like the Elberton.

As soon as she started up the steps of the hotel Louie's image of Bohemian decay began to dissolve. The dark blue paint on the front door, the brass knocker, the urns of flowers on the top step, were all glossed with a sheen which suggested Harrod's walnut cake rather than broken biscuits.

When they rang the bell the door flew open to reveal a young woman with frizzy hair and glasses. She stared at Louie and Frank for a moment then dashed forward and seized Louie's hand.

'Mum!' she shouted. 'Mum! It's Louie and Frank Gale!'

'Oh, we were going to ring but what with all the upset we never did. I'm Jane Chubb, from Barnstaple. Mum's your cousin Cissie—you know, Sue must've told you about the funeral and everything. Gran said you were coming round but we've been that upset we never thought to do anything about it . . .'

Cissie appeared at the door, even more distracted than

her daughter. Aunt Annie, it emerged, had had one of her turns. Cissie and Jane had been summoned from Barnstaple and had come up to London last night.

They all moved into the hall in a huddle. Louie caught sight of an antique mirror, discreetly gleaming doors, a huge vase of jutting blue delphiniums. They passed through the shadows of branches flickering across a panel of etched glass in a window at the back of the house, and filed into a room marked 'Private' with a kitchenette and tiled bench at one end.

'We'll show you her room after,' said Jane. 'But we'll come in here for now.'

Cissie sat down and began to dab at her eyes. 'We've just come back from the hospital. She's all right. Perky as ever really, but it's still an upset. And we couldn't just up and leave could we? We had a lot to see to.'

Jane began to make tea, setting out cups on the kitchen bench.

'This is the housekeeper's room. She's gone up to see Gran for a bit so we're holding the fort. There's not much going on in the afternoon though. Not today anyway. Just a couple of Arab blokes coming in later.'

Gradually everyone settled down. Cissie and Jane exclaimed over meeting Louie at last: 'You're the image of Uncle Jim. Sue'd be more like your mum . . .'

Then they had a good laugh over the shock they'd given Susan and her family by turning up at Uncle Jim's funeral. 'You should've seen their faces . . .!'

'And now you're writing a book about it all!'

'Well, just for my own satisfaction. I don't think it'll ever be published.'

'Sue said she got a tape of Auntie Vi. Mind you, Gran'd tell you you couldn't believe a word.'

'Perhaps when she's better she'll be able to put me straight then.'

'I don't know,' said Cissie. 'She's pretty close, Mum is. Never told us that much.'

'We know a bit, though. What was it you were after?'

'I wondered how well she—and you—knew our grandfather, Frank's and mine, Howard Gale. Violet seems to absolutely loathe him. She thinks he brought shame on the family.'

Cissie and Jane looked startled, uncertain. This wasn't what they'd expected. They glanced at each other and Jane shrugged, offended at being excluded right at the start. Howard Gale had died years before she was born and she'd never heard much about him.

'Well, he used to come down to this place where we lived when I was a girl,' said Cissie. 'He was a lawyer to the people who had the big house there before the estate was all broken up. Mum knew him pretty well. He used to drop in to see her quite a bit.'

Louie felt triumphant, convinced now that Howard was the lover old enough to be Annie's father, that after losing Kate at the turn of the century he'd consoled himself with her daughter in later life.

'D'you think he was a really special friend?'

Cissie stared and let out a giggle. 'Oh no! Nothing like that. Not on your life. He had other fish to fry.' Her voice dropped. Jane leaned forward, grinning at the scent of scandal.

'He was on for years with this Millie Morris. They met up at the Manor when she was a housemaid there back in the First War, but she had the pub by the time I came along. Everyone knew about Millie and her fancy man. Went on for years. He was no spring chicken when

I knew him and neither was she if it comes to that, though she was a good bit younger.'

Frank, who had heard Louie's theory, looked quizzical. Louie refused to meet his eye.

'Don't suppose his family knew a thing,' said Jane with relish.

'We knew there was someone or I wouldn't have asked.' Louie sounded so affronted that Cissie writhed in her chair and began gabbling away about Aunt Annie.

'*She* had a special friend,' broke in Jane, pleased and sly. 'This old bloke who adopted her when his wife was still alive. The one she went to after they lost their mum. This artist bloke, St Clair. Kept him on a string till the day he died. She never said, of course, but Granny Quant knew, didn't she, Mum? And Auntie Vi. She couldn't stand him. She always said it was him started her dad on his drinking. And Uncle Jim said too. It upset him no end.'

Cissie, who cried often, dabbed at her eyes. 'It was hard on Dad. My gran I lived with, Granny Quant, couldn't make out why he ever married her in the first place. She used to go off with this chap—Uncle Pen we called him—abroad and that. Never cared a bit what anyone thought.'

'She wouldn't've given Grandad the time of day if it hadn't been for the money. All he was was a footman and a gardener. But when he won the pools it was a different story. Still, he put one over her there, didn't he, Mum?'

'That was a crazy thing, a terrible thing,' mourned Cissie. 'Doesn't bear thinking about when you think how poor old Gran had to scrimp and save.'

'They still go on about it down there. About Mad Jack Quant and his money. You go down there you'll see. There's this tea place, Mad Jack's Hideaway. D'you know what he did? Well, one time when she'd just come back from swanning around somewhere with this Pen St Clair he took the whole lot out of the bank in fivers. Those big notes they used to have. And he took her up to this big hill round the back of the Manor—Giant's Tump— and he burned the lot in front of her. It was blowing a gale and half of it blew away. There was people going along the beach and round the fields for weeks after and fivers hanging up like hankies drying out in the cottages.'

'Mind you,' said Cissie, wiping her nose, 'she never went short even after that. That St Clair had plenty I s'pose. No, it was us suffered for it. I don't know what we'd've done without Uncle Jim. He always saw us right. She never gave us a penny-piece if she could help it. She didn't like my Bob, of course. That was part of it.'

'Mean as dirt and stuck up with it.'

'She was clever, though. Give her a pound and she'd make it two before you could turn round.'

'But she turned up her nose at just about everyone. And she's worse than ever now isn't she, Mum? Treats us like dirt.'

'The more we do the more we might.'

Louie and Frank sat close together, quite bewildered at the storm of resentment lashing at them across the teacups.

Jane reached out and took a photograph in a silver frame from the bookcase beside her. 'Look! There she is! Looks nice as pie doesn't she?'

The little woman in the photograph smiled up at them. She was quite unlike the Annie Louie had imagined— beautifully coiffured, elegantly dressed, even in old age as graceful as a slender little finch. The eyes, appealingly dark and bright, were the only feature Louie had got

305

right. Though when she looked more closely they made her think of birds with stabbing beaks.

'There's just one more thing. I don't suppose you know what became of her mother.'

Cissie and Jane shook their heads.

'She was funny about that. Auntie Vi always said they lost her in some accident down at the Manor, back when young Mr Gascoigne had the place, but *she* just laughed. She always goes on like that. "That's for me to know and you to find out," she says. Then she'll go on in French or some language and get sarky because we don't know what she's saying.'

On the way out Cissie opened one of the doors in the hall. She led the way into a long shadowy room filled with button-backed sofas and small white and gold tables laden with photographs, lamps and bowls of flowers. There were more pictures on the walls, mostly photographs of various members of the royal family: Prince Andrew and his new bride; the Prince and Princess of Wales; the Queen and Princess Margaret as small girls playing with corgis; George V and Queen Mary; Edward VII and the unfailingly beautiful Queen Alexandra. Louie was disconcerted. She associated royal-watching with women like Cissie rather than people of wealth and taste who spoke French and consorted with artists.

Cissie pulled back a brocade curtain and watched Louie and Frank straying about. The room, unlike a normal hotel room, was filled with Aunt Annie's personal possessions. The photographs on the tables were nearly all of various men, though most of them might have been the same person at various stages of his life. The high-collared, intense young man leaning towards the camera like a matinée idol might well have changed into the older figure with a beard like Joseph Conrad's, or the one with silver hair, posed in an olive grove. On the mantelpiece there was a family group, a handsome Edwardian couple with a young girl in a frilly hat. This, thought Louie, must be Pen St Clair, his wife and little Annie. And if that was so, then it was Pen who gazed out from other frames scattered about the room.

Frank, who had joined Louie on the hearthrug, was admiring a carriage clock which stood among the clustered photographs.

'Uncle Jim gave Mum that last time he came,' said Cissie from behind her curtain.

'Did he come here to see her a lot?'

'Quite a bit.'

And all at once there he was, on the same table as a youthful Pen, James Edward Phillips, looking pleasant and untroubled, sitting up prosperously in his best suit and the hornrimmed glasses which, when Louie was a child, he always put on for photographs, meetings and church services. He looked out unblinking at his daughter, one elbow propped on the arm of his chair so that his coat was drawn back to show his waistcoat with its loops of gold watch chain and the guinea coin he wore with his fobs like a talisman. He seemed perfectly at home in the strange garden in which he sat and in the elegance of his sister's hotel apartment where he had come in secret to take an accustomed place.

Yet Louie found it almost impossible to reconcile Annie's apparently easy acceptance of wealth and what it could buy with her own sense of her family in or out of the 'The Brown Photograph'. It seemed incredible that the child photographed with the St Clairs could have been the baby Molly carried about in Beaumont Street, or that Violet or poor young Charlie, who had looked after cows for three shillings a week, or even James himself should have had this sister who took her ease on these velvet sofas with her old feet in beautiful Italian shoes resting on the white and gold carpet.

'I don't understand,' said Louie at last. 'Was this room always reserved for her?'

'You could say that. She owns the place doesn't she?'

'But I thought she lived in an old people's home!'

'So she does now and again. In this special unit she's got. That's all hers as well.'

'But it's us keeps the place running.'

Out on the steps by the front door Jane burst out again. 'She's worth a mint but we wouldn't be surprised if we never see a penny of it. She's just as likely to leave it all to a dogs' home or some arty lot, isn't she, Mum? Just to spite us.'

Frank and Louie walked home in the quiet evening under the plane trees whose leaves were collecting in brown rustling drifts on the pavements.

'Should we go and see Annie in hospital d'you think?'

Frank, for all his usual kindness, made a face.

'Not really called for is it? And you're going to Bristol tomorrow.'

'She sounds just horrible doesn't she? And you can't pretend those two are making it up.'

Cissie and Jane were living proof of their story. If Annie had given them a share in all the advantages she'd had in such abundance—money, education, travel, love—they would have been different people. The thought oppressed Louie so much that she almost wept. Frank took her arm and tried to cheer her up by drawing her back into their private game of detection in which treachery, hurt and hatred lost their sting and became just pieces of a puzzle, blank harmless shapes they could shuffle around to make patterns.

'More and more I think Teddy's right, you know. Your father's tied up with Bathurst Hall and we know Annie was mixed up with Coombe Manor. You remember Violet talking about a neighbour, an artist who visited the Phillipses in Holborn? He must have been this St Clair. He and his wife couldn't've been too flush if they lived in Beaumont Street. Then all of a sudden they take on Annie and they're well off. And there's Old Howard again, hanging around keeping an eye on the child, maybe making reports and dishing out the allowance.'

'So you're all for the highborn lover? You think he fathered my father and then started up the affair again and got Kate pregnant with Annie?'

Not long ago this idea would have enchanted Louie. It was just the kind of solution to the mystery of James's birth she had yearned for since the days when she'd crept up into the attic in Howard Road to turn the key of his box. But now 'The Brown Photograph' had developed its own momentum. There was no place in it for an affair between Kate and Henry or Grindley Gascoigne.

'Actually,' said Frank, giving her arm a little shake. 'I've got an idea about the highborn lover. Couldn't believe it at first but everything points that way.'

Louie smiled. Frank was so good to her, trying so hard to get her interest and lift her out of her depression. She was very lucky to have him. In his own way he was like George—generous, concerned, a loving friend interested in everything she thought or did—so that within days he had come to serve as a crutch, supporting her until she could find a way of walking by herself. Though that, thought Louie, wasn't quite the analogy she wanted. If losing George had been like losing part of her own body, Frank was more than a useful wooden prop. The two relationships were closer than that. It wasn't as though one had been intensely passionate while the other was just a bland companionship. Years ago when Louie and George first met and he was still married to Joyce, their longing for each other had driven them into fierce lunch-hour couplings in the back of George's station wagon, but for a long time before his death this physical desire had been leaching quietly away. For Louie at least. When George had begun to have trouble getting an erection she had taken his penis gently in her mouth, nibbling and licking until it stiffened.

'Quick! Quick!' he'd say, but when the stiffness left him too soon he buried his face in her breast and wept. 'I'm sorry, darling, I'm sorry, I'm sorry'.

'It doesn't matter,' she told him, trying to look into his face so that he could see she was telling the truth. She felt they had known a season of sex as good as it could be and now another time had come. She still felt this and knew quite certainly she would never take another lover because that would undo the reality of what she had sworn to George. It was all right. She didn't mind about being celibate because she had enjoyed what she felt was the very best in its time. Now was the season of gentler feeling, of friendship. Walking along under the trees, arm in arm with Frank, she felt her heart suddenly expand as though a force which she had kept pent up and enclosed in George had spilled outwards.

All at once tears began to stream down Louie's face. Frank was quite frightened. He put his jacket around her shoulders, held her close and hurried her home. When they were safely indoors he switched on his heater, arranged her in a nest of cushions on the couch and rushed about making tea.

'I think I'd rather have a scotch.'

Frank looked relieved. This was more like the Louie he knew. He poured two large whiskies and began rattling about in the kitchen, heating up a casserole for their supper. They ate at the kitchen table and then sat drinking coffee. Louie could see Frank's arm and shoulder, a segment of his frizzy head and her own pale hands clasped round her mug reflected in the black panes of the French windows that led out into the courtyard. She looked at the papers and oddments pushed back to make a space for their plates.

Frank was quite an orderly person but he liked working at the kitchen table and, in any case, had given up his desk in the living room to Louie. There were bills on a spike, three or four copies of the *New Statesman*, several flyers from the youth club where he went to help out from time to time, a blue bowl of oranges, looseleaf folders with red vinyl covers, a china mug bristling with pens and pencils. If someone had been sitting in the darkness under the golden ash or had come to the windows, peering in through the panes' fragmented images what would they have made of the scene before them? How would they have connected the people at the table with the litter of coloured objects under the light?

TWELVE

Early next morning Frank went off to see his optometrist about a new pair of reading glasses. Louie wasn't leaving for Bristol until the afternoon so she sat at her desk after breakfast, turning over papers and brooding over Annie's treatment of her children. She wondered what had become of Cissie's brother, Dennis, 'daft as a brush', as mad as Mad Jack Quant. At about half-past nine the telephone rang and when she answered it Susan said, 'Louie? Is that you?'

'Oh, yes, Sue. How are you?'

'Well, not too good, really. I mean I'm not ill or anything—but oh, Louie, I'm afraid we're going to have to put you off for a bit. I'm awfully sorry. Something really terrible's happened. Absolutely terrible.'

'Oh, dear Sue! What is it? Is it one of the boys?'

'Yes, it's Ned and Colin.'

'Both? Not both? But I thought Colin was in Houston.'

'No,' said Susan, beginning to sob. 'He's in New York.'

'Did Ned go over to see him?'

'What? No, no. He wanted to go. He wanted to go after them, but we managed to stop him.'

'I don't understand. What's happened exactly?'

'It's Jill. She's run off with Colin. Ned's absolutely heartbroken. He always looked up to Colin. More than Sandy, but I told him I don't really blame Colin. It's Jill. She's just turned his head. He doesn't know what he's doing. And the twins are just devastated. We were up— I was up—all night. Two o'clock, half-past three, five. They can't understand. They just cry and cry. I get one settled and the other one starts. Ian's just beside himself. And what on earth is Sandy going to say? He doesn't even know yet. He's gone to a conference in Oslo and Gail says he won't be back for a week. I'm just dreading telling him. He'll be absolutely furious. I don't know what we can do, I really don't. Ned's closed down Ten to Three but he's got to go back. He'll go bankrupt. I said to Ian we could help him, but it's thousands, Louie. Thousands and thousands. I blame Jill. They never should've borrowed all that. They could've started with just a few tables. Ian said he thought they'd got in too deep. But Jill had to have everything new—freezers and mixers and everything. And linen tablecloths. And serviettes. I mean, what about the laundry? And how's he going to manage now? Jill did the books and half the cooking. It's just awful. And we'll never be the same again. We'll never see Colin now. He couldn't face Ned. Ned'll kill him, though, I said, it's not his fault. She must've got round him. He was always so open and honest. He's too good-hearted really. But she'll turn him against us. I've written to his New York office, Datarig. But we haven't heard a word. I suppose he's too ashamed. D'you think Ian should go over? Or should I go? We can't just do nothing.'

'I'm terribly sorry, Sue. Look, has Ned seen a solicitor yet? I think that's the first thing.'

'He's gone to see someone this morning. Ian took him on the way to work. It's not as though Ian's retired yet, you see. He's got to get some sleep or he can't get up in the morning. So last night he went into Colin's old room and I had the twins. They were in with Ned but he's so upset he can't really cope. But I don't know. I couldn't manage for long. They just scream and scream. Jill spoiled them, I think, with this demand feeding. Josh throws the most awful temper tantrums. It's not his fault, I know. They're the most lovely little boys, both of them. They just can't understand where their Mummy's gone. I can't believe she could leave them just like that, her only children. I always thought she had a cold side. Ian said she was too extravagant right at the start and that's it, you see. She saw Colin making all that money, photos of the house and the Porsche and everything. Apparently she was making up to him months, years ago, even before he went to America. And then he stayed with them last Christmas and again after he came here for Grandad's funeral. Ned thought there was something funny about it and I said to Ian after the funeral she seemed to be trying to flirt with Colin all the time. With the Chubbs there and everyone. Cissie thought Colin was Ned. I mean she thought Jill was married to Colin.'

'Is there anything I can do? Or Frank? I'm sure Frank would help too if you'd let him.'

'I don't know about that. We don't have anything to do with Frank. I don't think Ian would want Frank getting involved.'

'Still he's awfully good at lots of things. Perhaps he could help Ned get the restaurant back on its feet.'

At this Susan began to moan and sob so Louie started off on another tack.

'If someone went to New York—you, say, or Ian— d'you think Colin would listen to reason?'

'I don't know. We don't even know where they're staying, really. Jill just told Ned in this letter she left she was joining Colin in New York. But they'll go to Houston, I suppose. I mean that's where he lives. He can't just throw up everything for Jill. Not his business and everything.'

'Have you tried phoning Houston?'

'Ned did, but they said Colin was away.'

'Look, wouldn't it be best if Ned went back to his restaurant? Even if he decides to sell up he ought to try to keep it going in the meantime, don't you think?'

'But he can't manage without Jill!'

'I know that. Someone else will have to help out. That's what I meant about Frank. And I'm sure the twins'll be much better back in their own home.'

'But who'd look after them?'

'Maybe you could go to Grantchester for a bit.'

'What? With Frank?'

'I don't see why not. He's a terrific cook and terribly kind—just like he always was. And he's still devoted to you.'

'Frank is? To me?'

'Yes, he told me.'

'No, you've got it wrong. He's had a grudge against us for years and years.'

'He hasn't, Sue—well not against you, anyway. He'd love to see you again.'

'But Ian would be furious.'

'Oh dear, well that settles that then.'

'I couldn't leave him on his own anyway. I mean, how could he manage working all day with no-one here to cook an evening meal or anything?'

'Plenty of people do. He isn't totally helpless is he?'

'Perhaps you could go to Grantchester.'

'I'm no good with babies. And they don't know me from a bar of soap. They know you, you're their granny. I tell you what, I'll come down to Bristol and share the cooking with Ian if you like.'

'Oh, Louie. I don't know. I don't think Ian would like any of this.'

'Still. Think about it. The offer's there if you want it.'

Afterwards Louie walked around the flat moaning at the thought of what she'd done. 'What am I trying to do? Wreck a marriage that's lasted thirty years? I must be off my head. And supposing she did settle down with Frank, how do I know it wouldn't be a disaster? She'd probably be racked by guilt. All the boys'd turn on her. Everyone she knows'd be horrified and she'd end up blaming Frank for the whole catastrophe. I've no right to meddle. If Frank wanted her to know how he felt he could have told her himself years ago. Now if I tell him what I've done he'll probably never speak to me again. Why should he want to leave everything he's got in London and go running off to Grantchester to work in some ghastly pretentious restaurant with two shrieking babies and wet Ned? And why on earth did I offer to cook for Ian? He loathes me and I loathe him. We'll probably end up murdering each other.'

When Louie heard Frank's key in the door she jumped up and nearly ran to hide in the bathroom. He came in looking mild and rather shabby in his old raincoat, weighed down by plastic bags of shopping. He'd bought some Australian wine in Louie's honour and a wedge of Brie, which he thought they could have at lunchtime.

Louie watched him unpacking at the kitchen table, looking at the labels as he lifted things out of the bags and sorting his purchases into groups.

'Sue rang up,' she said. 'I gave her this number but I just said it was my friend's where I was staying.'

She went on to tell him her visit to Bristol had been postponed and sketched out the story of Ned, Colin and Jill. He looked so grave and sad that she felt abashed. Her own reaction—treating the affair as a soap opera that needed a new twist at the end—seemed shallow and heartless.

'How awful for her,' he said. 'All she ever thought about was the family. Keeping it together.'

'Frank, she thought you had a grudge against her. I told her you hadn't. I hope you don't mind.'

'Me? A grudge? Against her?' Frank was so astonished that he sank down on one of the kitchen chairs and stared at Louie with his mouth half open.

For the first time, it struck Louie that he was quite handsome in his way. He had very thick curly eyelashes that gave his eyes a childlike, starry look.

'I suppose because she married Ian. And Ian, of course, would think that. He always attributes horrible motives to people.'

'But I never even dreamed . . . I never blamed her. I never thought for a minute . . .'

'It's pretty obvious really. Anyway I told her you hadn't. And I said I was sure you'd want to help. You know, if there was anything you could do.'

'Of course. Of course.'

Frank got up and began to roam about the kitchen, still in his raincoat with his hands in the pockets. 'I'd do anything, of course. But in this kind of thing . . . I mean what is there? That's what's so awful.'

'Sue might go back to Grantchester with Ned to help look after the twins. I said I could keep the home fires burning in Bristol while she's away.'

'You mean look after Ian? You?'

'Well I thought I could teach him to boil his own eggs. And I am due to go to Bristol. But Ned'll need someone to help him in the restaurant.'

Frank nodded. There was a long pause. Then he said, 'You weren't thinking of me?'

Louie went bright red. 'Well, you are a terrific cook.'

'What? I've never worked in a restaurant in my life. I wouldn't have the faintest idea. Did you suggest this to Sue?'

'Well Ned's very short of money, you see, and Jill used to do half the cooking and he can't really afford to employ someone just yet and you're so good at counselling you'd help Ned get things in perspective.'

'And Sue'd be there as well? And you'd have Ian pinned down in Bristol?'

Louie stared at the shopping spread over the table—the slice of cheese, the green riesling bottle, a bag of coffee beans, a jar of honey, broccoli, apples, a red oblong box containing a tube of toothpaste. Frank came and sat down and tried to look her in the eye. The difference, she thought, between real characters and fictional ones is that real ones catch on. They see how you're planning to manipulate them.

'Louie, I'm sure you mean well but d'you really think I'd try to start that up again? Now? After all these years?

319

What on earth are you thinking of? She'd be appalled. With good reason. She'd really write me off then, wouldn't she?'

'I just thought you could be friends.'

Frank took no notice of this. 'Sue's been happily married for thirty years. Mother of three boys. D'you think she's going to chuck all that? For me? D'you think I'd ask her to?'

'No, no, no. I'm sorry. I'm sorry. Forget it. Do please.'

'Anyway Sue wouldn't even go to Grantchester if she thought I'd be there.'

'Now she knows you don't hate her she would.'

'How could I ever hate her? All right. If she really thought that, I'm glad you said something. I am. I really am. But as for this restaurant business . . .'

All the same, Frank apparently went on thinking about the whole crisis all that day. He seemed distracted and every so often—as they sat over their cheese and wine at lunchtime, in the evening while they were watching the TV news—he'd suddenly say, 'Maybe Jill's going to find she's done the wrong thing. Bound to miss the twins,' or, 'Even if Jill came back things couldn't ever be quite the same could they? Poor old Sue.' Or, 'She said she'd go to Grantchester. You suggested I go. What did she say then?'

At about ten o'clock Susan telephoned again. This time Frank took the call. He said 'Oh, Sue. Yes I'm very well . . . Louie told me . . . I'm so sorry.'

He clutched his hair and shuffled up and down with his back to Louie, who crept about picking up coffee mugs and then scuttled into the kitchen as though her life depended on doing the washing up. It was nearly fifteen minutes before Frank appeared at the door and said Sue wanted to speak to her.

'Louie? I spoke to Frank. I didn't realise you were staying with him. Louie? Are you there? His voice sounds just the same.'

'So what's happening now?'

'Oh well, Cissie and Jane arrived this afternoon. Not long after I phoned you. I'd no idea they were coming. Aunt Annie's much better today so they thought they'd go back to Barnstaple. You saw them, didn't you? You know about all that. Well, the twinnies were worn out after last night so they'd gone back to sleep. And then Cissie and Jane came ringing at the door just as I was trying to get things a bit straight. I've asked them before to let us know when they're coming to Bristol but actually it's all turned out quite well. I mean for the moment. Ned's going back to Grantchester tomorrow and Cissie and Jane are going too. They've got someone filling in for them at this home where they work, so there's nothing to stop them really. Ian thinks it might pan out quite well. For now anyway, at least until we hear from America. So Ian and I'll just stay on here.'

'Would you like me to come?'

'I was going to say. It's all right now. We'll have room again after tomorrow. Actually, Frank offered to drive you down. But I don't know. I'd like to see him but it might upset Ian. On top of everything else just now.'

'I can get the train.'

'It was nice of Frank, though, wasn't it? I wish now I'd written back when he got in touch after Grandad died. I should've written really . . .'

Frank gave Louie a copy of George Moore's *Esther Waters* to read on the train.

'There's lots in it about nineteenth-century racing,' he said. 'Bit earlier than the nineties, but it might help you with Grindley Gascoigne.'

They embraced on the platform at Paddington, both rather surprised and embarrassed at how moved they were at the parting. Settling into her seat on the train, Louie felt confused, weak and tearful. Frank was her only true friend in a country that felt all the more alien for having once been so familiar. Long ago in her student days every term had ended with taking the train home from this same station, only then it had smelled of smoke and the huge, black engines had hissed and snorted behind their towering breastplates. She remembered humping her case along the corridors of heavy cream and chocolate carriages, looking through the glass panels in the compartment doors and then, when she found a seat, sitting in a row of three or four people facing another row. Always there were sepia photographs of holiday resorts below the luggage racks—something to look at to avoid staring straight at the other passengers. And the seats had always been upholstered in the same bristly material with the same pattern. It bothered Louie that she couldn't quite remember the background colour—fawn? grey?—or how the small black dots or lines of the pattern had been arranged. Everything now seemed lighter and brighter but at the same time rather shoddy. The aura of solid Victorian comfort had disappeared. People were herded together in long carriages with central aisles. They roamed around, glancing without much interest at the flying landscape, utterly changed from the one that Louie had remembered when she described John's journey to Chippenham. There were many more buildings—neat centres of sunrise industry, villages swollen with scores of commuters' houses, so that the countryside, which looked strangely barbered after the Tasmanian bush, seemed like an artificial backdrop carefully rolled out to please the tourists. It was even worse than she'd imagined. The loss of the elm trees had changed everything. The fields had lost their shady secrecy, the villages were laid open to each other, the bare hills glittered with marching pylons. It was hard to know why all this made her so furiously miserable. Perhaps, since she had gone away, she'd been deceived into imagining that the past, the world of childhood, would remain unchanged, waiting far away across the sea for her return. But that world had disappeared as completely as the child she'd once been. It existed only in her own imperfect, wishful memory. And Bristol, she thought, will be worse.

A man seated opposite her on the other side of the laminated table was reading a newspaper. She caught sight of something about a memorial to those who had fallen in the Falklands war and thought of Frank's rage aginst Mrs Thatcher, whipping up the crowds to sing 'Land of Hope and Glory' to distract them from the dismantling of the welfare state, the rich getting richer and the poor getting poorer. 'How would you feel,' he'd asked her, 'if you'd marched as a young boy in one of the twenties hunger marches, fought in the Second World War, seen the welfare state set up—health care for everyone at last, children properly fed, even the chance of a university education—and now this?'

'I'd feel despairing,' she'd said, but Frank had been unhappy with the answer. Perhaps he thought she despaired too easily. He certainly thought this about her characters in 'The Brown Photograph'. He'd faithfully read all she'd written, but, as he laid aside the last sheet of the fair copy she'd given him, had looked sadly out at his golden ash tree. When she pressed him he'd said eventually that everyone seemed to give up too easily. They didn't care enough to survive. John, for instance. Surely he would have struggled harder to keep his son if he'd really loved him. But John, as Louie had invented him, gave up because he thought it was inevitable that he should lose his best beloved. He felt that his life was controlled by a dark Fate, but, in fact, if he'd believed otherwise things might have been different. Had she brought that out clearly enough? Or was everyone in the novel presented as deprived of choice because, looking back at them through time, she knew the milestones all of them had to pass? And yet, when she looked to the future, she truly believed that, even if Nemesis had sketched in a skeletal map of events, she was still the author of her own story, the one who would supply the connections, reactions and, in the end, the significance of her life.

THIRTEEN

Susan was waiting on the platform at Temple Meads. Louie spotted her at once and sat watching her for several minutes as the train drew to a halt, the doors were opened, and the passengers gathered their baggage to start edging into the aisle. She looked exactly as Louie had expected, like a photograph of the young Susan that Louie had touched up herself, adding ash grey to the hair, weathering to the cheeks and deep straight wrinkles, like Beatrice's, to the forehead. Even the clothes—the cotton skirt, cardigan and sandals—were as she'd imagined they would be. And the expression, the anxious searching as people began to spill out of the train, the craning and struggling as the crowd pushed forward—all of it was a replica of the picture Louie had conjured up when she'd looked ahead to this return to Temple Meads—the station where, years ago, the Phillipses had come to catch their train whenever they went to Blue Anchor or Minehead instead of Brean for a holiday. Louie and Susan had waited on this platform, holding their tin buckets and red metal spades while James and Beatrice had hurried about making sure the big family trunk was safely stowed in the luggage van. Trunk? Had they really used a trunk only forty-five years ago? Yes, there was no doubt about it. Louie could remember kneeling on the bedroom floor in the guesthouse at Blue Anchor while Beatrice lifted out ironed shirts in wads, balanced on her free arm, and striped pyjamas and woollen bathing costumes that soaked up water and clung to the skin, clammy and freezing after dips in the icy sea.

She began to feel ashamed of herself, sitting there letting Susan struggle for a sight of her long-lost sister. She banged on the window and waved but typically Susan went on watching the door, giving panicky little jumps when anyone got in her way, so Louie collected her belongings and slipped into the line of passengers moving out onto the platform. Susan took a few moments to recognise Louie, who smiled and waved. Then she started battling her way forward, flourishing a bunch of chrysanthemums and calling out as though Louie hadn't made any sign at all and was bent on rushing off in the opposite direction. When they finally came face to face Susan threw her arms round her sister, nearly pulling her off her feet and kissed her wetly on the ear. As they broke apart Louie saw that tears were pouring down Susan's face. She was overcome by the whole mass of feeling that pinned the two of them back into their old roles—pity, fondness, contempt, irritation, guilt—everything that marked her out as the clever, cold-hearted one and Susan as the blundering creature who loved and suffered, blind, stupid and loyal to the bitter end. And yet of course, thought Louie, weeping a few tears of her own, I've loved people and suffered for it and she gave up Frank for Ian . . . Still, Susan had been the one who'd looked after their parents and had never once uttered a word of complaint.

'You look wonderful,' said Susan. 'You've hardly changed at all.'

She rushed Louie into the Peugeot, hugely excited, all trace of her former resentment and worry lost in the thrill of the meeting. They shot off on a quick tour of the city centre: Neptune's statue, the Cathedral, the unicorns prancing on the roof of the Council House, the University Tower—'D'you remember we went to see Alfred the gorilla in the Museum?'—the Victoria Rooms, site of dancing displays and annual prize-givings . . . Everything looked oddly clean and highly coloured. The last relics of the Blitz, pits like weedy quarries fenced with corrugated iron, had vanished and the derelict warehouses along the river had given way to cafés, boutiques and a museum set up in honour of Isembard Kingdom Brunel's iron ship, the *Great Britain*. There was no time to feel anything in particular, only a queer sense of detachment from all the people walking the pavements or going in and out of the shops in Whiteladies Road, an urge to run up to one of them and explain that after twenty-five years the city wore a face that those who had gone on living there would never see. This reminded Louie of going for a walk to the park at the top of Howard Road after she'd been in bed with chickenpox. The outside world, closed off for over a month, had seemed hugely wide and bright in the blustery wind.

'She hasn't been outside the door for five weeks,' Beatrice had told a neighbour and the woman had looked curiously at spindly little Louie, wondering, perhaps, how someone who had been shut away for so long would see the low garden walls, all set with the stubs of railings taken to make munitions, and the hurrying white clouds in the March sky.

As they sped across the Downs, Louie, returning to here and now, asked how things were going in Grant-chester. Susan shook her head like someone attacked by gadflies.

'Oh, it's not working out, Lou. We had a call from Ned yesterday morning. He was absolutely beside himself. You see, we knew Jane worked in the kitchen at this old people's home, but I don't suppose she'd ever been in a place like Ten to Three. She did the most awful things. You wouldn't believe it. She got hold of this beautiful sirloin Ned had there and overcooked it and then she sliced it up in this awful pasty gravy. She went out and got all these packet things, Ned said. He didn't realise. I mean I use packet soups and things myself sometimes but you can't in a place like that. Not even for custard. And she was going to serve up this packet mashed potato. Ned nearly had a fit. He had a good talk with her, he said, and he thought she understood but then he just went down to the wine cellar and when he came back she'd boiled the smoked salmon.'

'Boiled it?'

'Yes, this beautiful piece he'd had sent down from Scotland. Ned couldn't believe his eyes. He's usually so patient, you know, and absolutely lovely with everyone but that, he said, was just the last straw. He really hit the roof. I don't know what he said exactly but I think he swore at her. And Jane will argue. She said it wasn't healthy to serve raw fish. I think he threw something. Well, he did actually. He threw a bottle of claret.'

'At Jane?'

'Well, not exactly at her. More at the floor, I think. Anyway they left—Cissie, too, of course—and went straight back to Barnstaple. But I expect they'll be up here again before long. I don't really know what I can say to them. I mean, I know Ned shouldn't've lost his temper but when you think what a piece of salmon like that must cost . . .'

'What did he do with it?'

'He said he was going to make it into a mousse. But it's not the same is it?'

Louie began to laugh. Susan looked startled, then aggrieved, but in the end she gave a little giggle.

'I suppose there is a funny side to it. Anyway, it's turned out for the best. Jill's mother's come back from the Costa Brava and she's gone over there today and Ned ran into this friend of his from the college of hospitality who's going to give him a hand, so he should be all right for a while.'

Louie sighed and wiped her eyes.

'Oh dear, oh dear,' she said.

'And we've had a letter from Colin. He says—and I daresay it's true really—Ned and Jill hadn't been getting on for a long time. Well, I never thought they were suited. Ned's very creative, you see, and artistic but Jill's not imaginative at all. Actually, I think, she rather held Ned back. Before they had the twins he wanted to go and do a course at this place in Switzerland but she put a stop to it. He was upset about her going off, of course, but I think that was just the shock, really, and not knowing what to do about the restaurant and everything. In time he'll probably feel he's better off without her. She'll come over once or twice a year to see the twins, Col says, but

Ned won't mind that. And Col's quite different from Ned. She won't get the better of Col. I mean he wouldn't have done so well with Datarig if he couldn't stand up to people, would he?'

Louie listened in bewilderment. All this seemed such a far cry from the lament Susan had poured into the telephone less than a week ago. It was as though she had been labouring night and day, like an oyster in its shell, pouring smoothness over the intrusive grit that was one son running away with another son's wife, until its sharpness had been nearly covered up. Soon everything would be seen as having happened for the best. Perhaps what Susan said was a pearl of wisdom. Perhaps this was what wise families always did—made the best of things, insisted that disasters were blessings in disguise. After all, if James hadn't been sent away to Bristol he would never have met Beatrice, and Susan and Louie would never have been born. But it was hard to see how the death of nineteen-year-old Charlie could be construed as anything but waste, or the loss of Kate anything short of a blighting catastrophe. And nobody in 'The Brown Photograph' was compensated for what they lost. But then her novel, like every piece of fiction, was a lie because it would have an ending. It would stop short instead of moving on to this new time when she was sitting in her sister's car, looking out at the Downs where she'd taken riding lessons on a fat brown pony called Jessie; this moment when, to her considerable surprise, she felt such a rush of affection for Susan that she touched her arm and said,

'I'm really happy to see you, Sue.'

Susan was so startled that she swung right round and made the car swerve. She gave a little shriek, 'Oh, what am I doing? Well, yes, I mean it's lovely to have you here.' And she smiled in the way that Frank had described when he was trying to explain why he had fallen in love with her.

Susan had cooked a special dinner in Louie's honour—mushroom soup, a chicken casserole and pineapple sponge pudding. The mahogany table that had belonged to Grandpa Gale was laid in the dining room with pink napkins folded in waterlily shapes. Louie would have liked to settle down with her sister, drink tea and go on talking, but as soon as Susan opened her front door she began to hurry around, worried about getting the vegetables on to cook before Ian came home. She rushed Louie's case up the stairs, flung open cupboards and drawers, pointed out the bathroom and dashed away to the kitchen.

Louie poked about her bedroom, identifying oddments from Howard Road: a bedside table with a drawer in which she'd hidden her Ponds lipsticks when she was thirteen; a paperweight with a picture of Stonehenge pasted under a glass dome. She rummaged in the cardboard boxes stowed in the bottom of the wardrobe—Colin's school exercise books, lifesaving certificates, a rolled photograph of tiers of schoolboys with masters sitting in a row at the front. Otherwise the room seemed quite impersonal. It struck Louie as odd that its occupant had grown up to found Datarig, drive a Porsche, and run off with his brother's wife.

She touched up her makeup at the dressing table mirror, with the old sensation of watching herself like a monkey in a tree. In Bristol virtually everything she saw or did carried in its train some memory so that immediately she remembered the guilt she'd felt at eight years old when the monkey had sat coolly on its branch the night after their neighbour, Miss Wesley's house had been flattened by an aerial torpedo. 'Now,' she'd told herself, 'I'm feeling how queer it is that only a week ago old Liza-Jane was drinking a cup of tea by Miss Wesley's fire and neither of them knew that soon the room would be all rubble and Miss Wesley would be dead.' And then she'd thought how cold and cruel she must be to let half her mind look down like that on what she felt about poor Miss Wesley being blown to smithereens.

She wondered what to wear for Susan's dinner. A skirt was probably expected but if she overdressed Ian would start smirking and raising his eyebrows—unless he'd changed for the better over the years. Louie was feeling unusually benign, anxious to please, ready to try to find affection for anyone, but the thought of Ian nipped her good intentions like a frost. She remembered Professor Godbole in *A Passage to India,* unable to extend love beyond the wasp to encompass the stone it clung to.

Eventually, as the evening was cool, she put on a long sleeved, dark blue, jersey dress. Downstairs, she found Susan in the sitting room, arranging sherry glasses on a tray.

'Oh you do look smart, Lou,' she said. 'Now sit there and I'll get us a drink.' But before she could fetch the decanter Ian arrived looking greyer and leaner than the snide young bridegroom of thirty years ago, but as tight-lipped and fanatically neat as ever.

'And how are things Down Under?'

He seemed amused, as though Louie's emigration had been some kind of comic eccentricity. And now, predictably, she had come back. He refused to show surprise or enthusiasm and went on about his daily rituals—going upstairs to wash and change his suit for immaculate slacks, a viyella shirt and buttoned-up cardigan. Then he sat in his armchair by the sitting room window where every evening he read the *Daily Telegraph*.

'Ah, the sherry decanter,' he said as Susan filled the glasses. He sounded as though it made a poor substitute for his newspaper. He put on his goldrimmed spectacles and folded the *Telegraph* slowly before laying it on the arm of his chair.

'So you're retiring soon, Ian.'

He pursed his lips as though there must be something slighting in the remark.

'Oh, yes,' broke in Susan. 'At the end of the year. We thought we might go on a cruise. We've never been abroad really. I mean, you know, it was a bit difficult with Grandad and everything.'

Ian smiled, gratified that this might make Louie feel guilty and irresponsible.

'Why don't you come to Tasmania?'

'I doubt if we could rise to that.'

'What? Yes, we could, Ian. I'm sure we could. I think it's a lovely idea.' Susan beamed at Louie. 'Wouldn't that be a thrill! We could meet Emma and Oliver and everything.'

'I've got plenty of room. You could stay as long as you liked.'

The offer changed the entire evening. Before she made it Louie had been wondering what on earth the three of them could talk about over dinner. There were so many topics that might offend either Ian or Susan: anything connected with Frank, especially his engagement to Susan or Uncle Richard's elopement with Norman Judd couldn't be discussed in Ian's presence; the visit to the Elberton, made without reference to Susan, was rather

333

touchy; the McAlister boys—apart from Sandy—were hardly subjects for a celebration. On top of all that, Louie couldn't face talking much about George, and knew very well that whenever her parents were mentioned Ian would make a point of reminding her that the McAlisters had done everything for them in their old age while she had done nothing.

'What a minefield,' she thought to herself. 'I suppose it was always like this—not being able to talk to each other. No wonder I missed so much.'

But once the idea of the McAlisters coming to Hobart had been broached, suddenly there was a great deal to be said. Louie could talk about Tasmania without seeming self-centred or boring and, as they talked, she felt that, in time, she and Susan would be able to move on to the questions they'd never been able to bring into the open before. Ian kept a suspicious silence over the soup but, since he couldn't find much to say against the proposed visit, once the casserole arrived, even he began to show a condescending interest. Louie had no idea how she was going to put up with him for weeks on end in Hobart, but for the moment she was too elated to think much about the difficulties she might be making for herself.

At half-past ten Ian went, as he always did, to check the locks on the windows and doors before going to bed. To Louie's disappointment Susan accepted this as putting an end to the evening and started making Horlicks in the kitchen.

'We'll need an early start,' she said. 'I thought you might like to go over to Howard Road tomorrow and we could go up to the school. Anyway, I thought we'd just look around Bristol tomorrow. Then the next day we could take a picnic up into the Cotswolds and I've booked us in at a nice little place in Lyme Regis for the weekend after next.'

There were other plans—day trips to Bath and Exeter, another weekend at Blue Anchor, lunch with the people across the road . . .

'When am I going to get any writing done?' wondered Louie peeping out between her bedroom curtains at the silent, lamplit pavements of Willowdene Drive. It was only ten to eleven but nearly all the neat semi-detached houses were in darkness. She sighed, sat down at the desk where Colin had done his homework, and began scribbling away as she'd often done in her teens when everyone else in the house had gone to sleep and her window was the only lighted one in Howard Road.

Grindley Gascoigne's racing career had begun with the purchase of a chestnut colt called Firefly. One summer, not long after his return to England, he went to spend a few weeks with some distant cousins at Bathurst Hall, near Chippenham. The whole household ate, drank and breathed racing all day long. Everything revolved around the stables. Nobody talked of anything but weights, trials, old steeple-chasing triumphs and the secret hope that Blackbird would carry off the Steward's Cup at Goodwood. Every morning at dawn Grindley went with his cousin Henry to watch the gallops. They scuffed their boots on the turf, cursing the dryness of the ground. Then the weather turned colder and the rain came down in blustery showers, softening the earth, relieving fears for the horses' delicate legs.

One raw, misty morning high on the hill behind the Hall, Grindley turned around to speak to Henry and found he was alone. He stood quite still, straining his ears, wondering how he'd managed to get separated from his cousin. He could hear voices far away in the mist and the faint drumming of hooves. He shifted uneasily, trying to guess from which side the horses were approaching. The beat of hooves grew louder, the vapour all around him seemed filled with sound. Then suddenly they were upon him. He leaped back as the colt burst out of the mist, two lengths ahead of his stable-mates, surging past in a blast of heat and power. Grindley ended up sprawled on the wet grass not two yards from the flashing palisade of striding legs. A clod of earth sailed slowly through the air and within seconds all the horses had vanished. Grindley sat up, listening to the hammering of their hooves dying away in the valley below. Then he climbed to his feet, brushed himself down and started back towards the house in a kind of trance as though he had fallen in love or seen a vision.

The Bathurst Hall Gascoignes were rather put out when Grindley made them an offer for Firefly. They pointed out that the colt had been carrying under six stone that morning. They tried to persuade him that Golden Rain and Conquistador were better prospects. But Grindley stuck to his guns, scraped up five thousand guineas and went back to London convinced that next year Firefly would win the Derby for him.

On the great day he saw his horse race into the lead at Tottenham Corner as the crowd began to shout 'What price Firefly?' But it was only a flash in the pan. The 100 to 1 chance, Kilkenny Lad, came up on the rails and Firefly dropped back to finish ninth.

Grindley, pale and clammy with sweat, blundered away into the crowd. He had staked almost everything he could raise on Firefly. Usually he was a wary, meticulous gambler. He studied form, tracks, weights and jockeys. He worked at knowing his tipsters, kept his ears open and grinned in contempt at superstition and sentiment, but his belief in Firefly had overpowered him like a fever, growing in intensity as rapidly as his longing to come out of the blue—a colonial, young and barely known—to snatch the greatest prize of the English turf.

After wandering about for half an hour he sat on the grass among the picnic parties, took a long drag from his hip flask and began to think about Murrimbah, his father's sheep station in Victoria's Western District. He pictured the manager's house, where he had boarded while he learned how to run the property—the sun blazing down on the iron roof, the windowpanes black with blowflies, the greasy mutton dished up at every meal. He thought of the featureless brown plains stretching away as far as the eye could see under the hard blue sky, and Sunday drives to the little church his father had built on the outskirts of the distant township. Then he got up and went to speak to his trainer, Tom Ratho. He brushed aside all Ratho was boiling to say about Firefly's failure and asked instead about a different horse, a useful plater called Lucinda, who was due to run in about an hour's time.

'I don't think she can be beaten,' said Ratho, which, to do him justice, was more than he'd ever claimed for Firefly.

So Grindley went off, borrowed all he could from every crony or acquaintance he could find, put five hundred pounds on Lucinda and ended the day with his debts paid and more in his pocket than Firefly's win would have brought him. The story, as it spread, gave him a name for daring and luck—not the prestige of the owner of a winner of the Derby, but a reputation that changed the colour of his colonialism so that people saw him more as a card than an outsider. If Firefly had won, some, at least, would have looked at him askance as a cocky upstart. As it was the racing world liked him for refusing to admit defeat when he was down. Everyone sought his company, laughed admiringly at his nerve and asked him what he fancied for the City and Suburban.

It wasn't often, then, that he dined at home. Occasionally he'd play host to a group of cronies, but usually, at about the time Howard Gale was approaching his front door, Grindley would be setting out for a convivial evening at someone else's dinner table or club. But, as luck would have it, on that particular evening he had decided to dine alone and turn in early. He was planning to get up at crack of dawn on the following day and travel down to Sussex to look at a property that he was thinking of buying.

When Howard was announced he was half pleased and half sorry. He thought his visitor might expect to be taken on a round of London's fleshpots which would put paid to any hope of catching the early train to Brighton in the morning. But when it turned out that Howard was quite happy to share a quiet dinner and simply wanted some advice over the brandy and cigars afterwards, Grindley began to feel that his friend's unexpected visit was a bit of good luck. He was easily bored by his own company. Now, although the evening would be short, it wouldn't be dull. It wasn't as though Howard had brought his wife, whom Grindley didn't much like. Her prim silences made him self-conscious. She reminded him of the churchy spinsters his mother befriended in Melbourne.

Over dinner, Grindley told the story of a particularly good day he'd had at Goodwood recently. He'd backed a stylish filly named Runaway at 50 to 1. Then, not long before the race, his commission agent had told him, 'I can get you twenty-fives to another monkey if you want it. There's just time.' The monkey had been produced. Runaway had scrambled home by a neck amidst roars of excitement, and Grindley had driven back to London convinced that he could now afford a place in the country.

'What I'd really like, of course,' he said, 'is something like the Gascoignes' place. You remember old Henry, don't you, at Exeter? No? Well he's a rattling good sort and his guvnor's one of the best. One of the best of the old gentlemen jocks. They've got these top-hole stables near Chippenham. Blackbird's one of their horses. And they do all their own training. Bring on their own little stablelads and everything. But I s'pose it can't last, can it, that kind of thing? Not with the kind of people you get in racing these days. You've got to have a professional trainer. And even the Gascoignes'll have to stop using their own jocks before long. Still, I wouldn't mind a place where I could do a bit of breeding.'

After a time it struck Grindley that Howard wasn't responding to all this as eagerly as he might have done. He said, 'This business you wanted to talk over later on. You aren't in any trouble are you, old boy?'

The meal was almost finished. Howard waited until the servant had carried away the empty dishes. Then he gave a sigh and said, 'You've met my wife.' Grindley was baffled. He couldn't understand why Howard should think of consulting him on anything concerning plain and dismal Alice.

'I hope she's not ill.'

'Oh no, no.'

There was a silence in which Howard began to relish his friend's curiosity and the sensation he would create as Grindley drew his story out of him.

'How did she strike you?'

Grindley was embarrassed and rather shocked. He had no idea how to respond. All he could think of was that Alice must have done something frightful and that he was being asked if he had noticed ominous signs.

'She was very quiet. I couldn't say, old man.'

'I made a terrible mistake there. We have nothing, absolutely nothing in common.'

'No, well. I did rather think . . . Well, you know, that she wasn't quite . . .'

'To be perfectly frank, my marriage is a living hell. You're a wise fellow to have kept clear of all that.'

'Never really appealed, old boy. Not that I'm averse to the ladies. But I love 'em and leave 'em, you know.' This sounded rather heartless under the circumstances so Grindley

340

tried to elaborate. 'I mean, I might go on with one for quite a long time. As a matter of fact I've got a little girl now I've had for nearly a year. But that's more my style—dancers and so on. I just set 'em up somewhere where I can drop in from time to time. Then if there's any trouble I just clear off.'

'I'm thinking of leaving Alice.'

'Oh steady on, old boy. It hasn't come to that has it?'

'I can't stand it much more. I tell you, she's driving me to desperation.'

'But surely . . . I mean won't there be the devil of a row? With you being in the law and all that? Couldn't you just put a good face on it? After all you can always find a bit of consolation somewhere else.'

'I already have.'

'Ah!'

'In fact, I've fallen head over heels.'

'The devil you have!'

'I'm thinking of making a break for it. If she'll agree I want to take her to Australia. That's why I've come to you.'

Grindley was appalled. He hurried Howard out of the dining room, settled him in a chair in his den and poured him a brandy.

'I thought,' said Howard, 'that you might give me a few tips about Melbourne.'

'Now steady on,' said Grindley again. He was thoroughly upset. His own chancy way of life depended, after all, on a degree of certainty, on bookies paying up and good horses running true to form. 'This isn't like you, old boy. You don't want to go running off to Melbourne.'

'We could make a fresh start.'

'But not in Melbourne! It's not your style at all. Believe me, old boy, I know. It's full of people like my guv'nor. You know, churchy, down on a bit of fun.'

'I thought it was pretty free and easy with all the new money.'

'But they're not your sort either. Oh no! You don't want to throw up everything you've got here and go chasing off to Melbourne. Why don't you set your girl up in a little place of her own somewhere in Bristol? Or out in the country? Get her a little cottage in Devon or Somerset?'

'But I've got clients all through the West Country.'

'So much the better! Gives you an alibi, old boy. Look here, I tell you what. This place I'm looking at tomorrow might not be quite what I've got in mind. And the price is a bit steep. I was thinking if this falls through I might take a look at Coombe Bassett.'

'In Devon?'

'That's where my people come from. At least, they did. My great-grandfather was one of the younger sons and the Chippenham Gascoignes've got it now. But they're having trouble keeping it up. They've been selling off the farms on the estate and now the manor house is going up for sale. So I thought, if the price was right, I might make an offer. My guv'nor doesn't think too much of me. Can't see why I wouldn't stick to sheep farming. Wouldn't he just sit up if I came up out of the blue as squire of Coombe Bassett! Kept the old place for the Gascoignes! He'd pretty soon change his tune then, wouldn't he?'

'I suppose he might.'

'You can bet your life he would. But the point is, old boy, there are plenty of nice little cottages and so on there. I went down and had a look around that time I bought Scallywag. He's come on well by the way. There's the home farm and a lodge and quite a decent house they call the Old Forge. Now if you were to set up your girl down there you could pop down whenever you felt like it. And if anyone wanted to know what you were up to, all you'd have to say is you were spending a couple of days with me.'

'You're a good fellow. But what about this property in Sussex? You can't change course in a thing like that just to suit me.'

'It might suit both of us. That's what I'm saying. Look here, when are you going back to Bristol? How would it be if I came with you and went on to Devon from there? I could send a wire tomorrow to tell them I'm coming.'

'You mustn't do anything hasty on my account.'

'Don't you worry about that. I'll go through the place with a fine-tooth comb. But the more I think of my guv'nor's face when he hears I'm lord of the manor the keener I get. How about we go down on Saturday?'

Kate had quite lost touch with Sarah Palmer who had been her best friend at Briarbrae. When the Phillipses were living in Hampstead she had exchanged several visits with Sarah, married now to a Mr West with a large house on Richmond Hill. But the move to Beaumont Street had put an end to these meetings because Kate felt ashamed to ask anyone from her old life to the dingy little house in Holborn. For months she had been afraid that Sarah, like Mrs Duke, might track her down, but so far her old friend had not appeared.

On the Thursday after Howard arrived back in London, Kate served up John's supper and sat down opposite him. Julia's death had changed the shape of the family, shaking it into the old pattern of father, mother and children. Suddenly John and Kate were brought face to face as though they were meeting again after a long separation. Secretly they studied each other, looking for the person who had once meant

343

happiness, although neither now expected to find any trace of what had seemed so clear and close a few years ago. Kate was so absorbed by her passion for Howard that she could hardly believe she had ever been in love with John. She watched him out of the corner of her eye, trying to fathom what she had seen in him. He looked so dour and black, so lean and uncouth, like the gipsy Julia had always said he was. He never made a joke or paid her a compliment. He shaved in the scullery, leaving grey froth spiked with little black hairs in the basin. His boots smelt when he stuck them by the range to dry out. She felt ashamed, not of being unfaithful to him, but of ever letting him get around her in the first place. She couldn't understand what had possessed her.

John, for his part, felt nothing much beyond self-contempt. He knew that Kate and Mrs Duke had hatched some kind of plot to keep Jimmy in Bristol but he still believed his little son had turned away from him of his own free will. He didn't blame him or Kate or even Mrs Duke. He simply felt now that he had been a fool to set any store at all by human loyalty or affection. His love for Kate, what she had seemed to feel for him, the bond between himself and Jimmy, were all nothing but eyewash. A man was a fool to get taken in by soft words and smiles. And now he was trapped. Even though Julia had gone, things between himself and Kate would never change. Even when his debt was paid off nothing would get any better. He would just go on toiling along, getting up each day, pushing food into his mouth, moving to and fro, sleeping his exhausted sleep and then starting all over again until he dropped.

'I met Sarah West in the street the other day,' said Kate in a high, bright voice. She felt all the time as though she were in a fever. Her hands shook. The blood beat in her cheeks. 'She asked me to go over to Richmond to see her on Friday. I think she's in some kind of trouble.'

344

John kept his eyes on his plate, chewing stolidly. He shrugged very slightly as though he didn't care one way or the other. If Kate had known, he wouldn't have reacted very differently if she'd told him the truth—that she'd taken a lover and was planning to spend the night with him at his hotel. He would just have thought Howard Gale was a fool for sticking his head in a noose when he had no call to.

'Molly says she'll look after the children and cook the supper. I'll put everything out for her before I go. Sarah wondered, you see, if I could stay the night. Otherwise I'd have to turn around and come back as soon as I got there.'

John shrugged again.

'You don't mind?'

'Why should I mind?'

'Well, I don't usually stay away like that. I haven't spent a night away since we came here.'

'You go if you want to.'

'Well then, I will. I'll come back on Saturday.'

Kate felt rather nettled. She'd expected more opposition, more suspicious questions.

'He doesn't care for me at all,' she thought. 'Well, one day I might go off for good. We'll see how he likes that.'

On Friday night in the intervals between their lovemaking, Kate and Howard talked about the future. Without knowing how it had come about, both accepted that eventually Kate would leave her husband and go with the four children still living at home to some place where she and Howard could be together. Constructing this golden idyll was becoming an all-absorbing game. The two of them worked happily side by side, piling up stories and dreams like children making a secret refuge hidden away from the loud world.

'I thought first,' said Howard, 'that we might go out to Australia.'

Kate was astonished and thrilled. All the way to Australia! She snuggled into her pillow like Violet or little Charlie when she sat down to read the children a story at bedtime.

'What would we do in Australia?'

'Oh we'd have a house somewhere near Melbourne. A little farm, perhaps, with orchards and a few cattle and horses.'

'Would we have a carriage?'

'Of course, and we'd ride a great deal together. Would you like that?'

'Oh I should, my love! You'd have a great, strong chestnut horse.'

'And you'd have a beautiful white mare.'

'And all the children could have ponies.'

'But now, my darling, I've got another plan . . .'

Howard went on to explain all about Grindley Gascoigne's interest in the manor house at Coombe Bassett and how, if she were to move into the Old Forge, he would come down to see her every week. The country all around was quite beautiful, he said. He and his family had often gone to that part of Devon for their summer holidays. Together, he and Kate would ride through the country lanes, picnic on the seashore, swim naked in some secret cove . . .

❧

'Oh Alice, dear old girl, it's splendid.'

Cynthia put down the poem reverently on the tea table. She smiled at her friend who looked, she thought, rather pale and strained today. The sonnet, though wonderfully fine, seemed to hint at secret trouble. Could it be that Howard Gale had made some disastrous error, that the wife who loved him so selflessly was about to be dragged down into poverty? A terrible suspicion shot like an arrow through Cynthia's heart. Was Alice trying to warn her, to prepare her for the awful news that the house across the road would have to be sold, that Alice herself would soon be leaving Clifton?

'But is there really some trouble about money?'

Alice glanced up. Cynthia was leaning earnestly over the table, small, square, intently gazing. Alice longed to lay her head on Cynthia's broad bosom, bury her face in the crisp whiteness of her friend's blouse and weep out all her sorrows. But she was terrified of being disloyal to Howard. Perhaps it had been wrong to show the poem she'd written for him to a third person. And yet if her suspicions proved well founded, if she and Cynthia were forced to part, surely her friend, who had always been so devoted, had a right to know what lay ahead?

'Howard hasn't been himself lately,' she said in a low voice. 'And he's never gone to London without me before. I'm afraid he may have some financial trouble. I think he's trying to spare me the worry of it.'

Cynthia thought, 'And as a result she's nearly worried to death,' but aloud she said, 'He hasn't actually mentioned money though? Not asked you to economise or anything?'

Alice shook her head, looking down, close to tears.

'Well, then, dear old kid,' cried Cynthia, bouncing up and coming to put her arm round Alice's shoulders. 'It might not be that at all. He might have a difficult client or a sore throat. Anyone can feel a bit off colour.'

At this Alice gave way and began to sob.

'But he's been so strange. I've never known him like this.

Never. Never. And when he left he barely said a word. He wouldn't even look at me. Oh, Cynthia!'

'There! There! Dear old girl! He doesn't understand how you feel things!'

'I only want to help. I wouldn't complain. I'd never reproach him or anything like that. I know he's always done his best for me and the children. I wouldn't hold it against him if something's happened. I wouldn't mind if we had to be poor. I really mean what I say in the sonnet. I really do. I wouldn't mind anything so long as he doesn't stop loving me.'

Cynthia stroked Alice's hair and murmured soothingly, but at the same time she said to herself, 'That great brute! How dare he make her so miserable with his wretched nonsense!' She looked out scowlingly over Alice's shoulder. She doubted very much that the root of the trouble was financial because Howard seemed to her a man who would be very careful not to jeopardise his own comfort. She thought it much more likely that, being too coarse-grained to appreciate his wife's sensitive nature and intellectual interests, he was feeling jealous or bored and making her suffer for it.

'He doesn't understand how you take things to heart,' she said again.

Eventually Alice wiped her eyes and began languidly preparing to go home. Howard was coming back to Bristol in the evening and she wanted to be sure Cook had understood that dinner would be early.

'No, no, I must go,' she said, picking up her poem and staring at it. 'D'you think I should put this on his desk?'

'I hope he realises how lucky he is.'

'It's I who've been lucky. He's been so good, so kind. All these years.'

'Dear old girl, no more than you deserve.'

'He seems so distant now. So taken up with worry.'

'It may not be anything really serious. Dearest one, try not to fret too much.'

When she had spoken to Cook, Alice crept upstairs and opened the door of Howard's study. She thought how neat and manly it looked, compared with her own untidy little den—the books ranged in rows in their glassfronted cases, the mahogany desk cleared of everything but the blotter with its stamped brass cover, Howard's heavy glass inkwells and a squared-off batch of documents with red seals. She ran her fingers along the back of his leather armchair and watched the sunshine, filtered through the trees outside the window, winking in dazzling slivers over the desk. She put down her poem on the blotter and looked at it. Then she began to think that Cynthia might be right, that Howard's trouble might have nothing to do with money after all. If this was the case he might find the sonnet baffling, even infuriating. So she picked it up again and tiptoed away.

Howard was quite cheerful when he arrived home. He would have been even more elated if he could have persuaded Grindley to spend Sunday in Clifton before travelling on to Devon because his friend would have given him a good reason for avoiding Alice. But Grindley didn't much relish the idea of minding his ps and qs at Alice's dinner table and had arranged to spend the day looking around Coombe Bassett on his own before meeting his distant cousin on Monday morning. So when Alice heard Howard's voice in the hall and came flying out to meet him he had to confront her as best he could.

'Did things turn out as you hoped, dearest?' she asked, clasping her hands and gazing up into his face.

'Oh yes. Not too bad.'

And Howard turned away, making rather a business of telling Elsie, the maid, to be careful with some papers packed in his bag. They had to be kept in order and put away in his study.

It was still early evening. From the drawing room Howard caught sight of Bea and Richard playing in the garden and dashed out to join them. He chased Bea through the rhododendrons, growling horribly, and went on in tearing spirits, playing lions and tigers until after the children's bedtime. Alice went to and fro between the kitchen and the French doors opening onto the garden, desperately anxious that dinner, which would begin with a thick, hearty soup, might be spoiled, but nervous of annoying Howard by cutting short his game. Elsie complained that Master Richard was getting overheated which he wasn't supposed to do when he was getting over a nasty, summer cold, and Cook began to grumble over her stove.

At last Howard and Alice settled down together at the dinner table, neither knowing what to say to the other. At length Alice plucked up the courage to ask if Howard had found time in London to look in on the Burtons.

'No, no. I was rushed off my feet.'

Howard brooded for a few minutes then he said, 'But I did run into Grindley Gascoigne. He's done very well for himself lately. He's thinking of buying a property in Somerset as a matter of fact. A business venture.'

'Oh, I'm glad he's done so well.'

'Very well actually. As a matter of fact we may be acting for him a good deal before long.'

'The firm you mean, dearest?'

'Yes. With all his business concerns you see. Investments and so forth.'

'Are you pleased about it, Howard?'

'Pleased? Well of course. It's very good for the firm. There's quite a lot of work involved though. I'd have to go down to Somerset fairly regularly.'

'You do already, don't you?'

'Oh I don't mean once a month or so. I'd have to go down every week. For a time at least.'

Alice nearly burst out, 'But he can't expect that! When you have so many other clients to attend to!' But she bit back the words thinking Howard might tell her, quite justly, that she knew nothing about the matter.

The rest of the evening passed off quietly. On Sunday morning the whole family went to church, strolling through the leafy streets among all the neighbouring families, Alice and Howard bowing and smiling like everybody else. Then at about two o'clock Howard went off to play tennis with a friend he'd fallen in with after the service.

In the heat of the afternoon while the children were resting, Alice lay on the sofa in her den, worried all over again that Howard was concealing some trouble from her. Although he seemed so much more affable than he'd been before he'd gone back to London, she sensed something forced and hectic in his cheerfulness. He seemed reluctant to be alone with her or to meet her eye. The mention of Grindley Gascoigne had made her uneasy because, so far as she knew, the only business that interested him was horseracing. She began to be frightened that Howard, having lost a lot of money, was planning to join Grindley in some gambling project. Perhaps he had convinced himself that, with Grindley's help, he could recoup all his losses by backing horses. That would account for both his wild spirits and his reluctance to meet her look. As she mulled all this over, Alice began to feel, yet again, that she had to prove to Howard that money mattered little compared to love, that she was truly his 'for richer or poorer', and that there was no need for him to throw himself into desperate schemes in order to keep up appearances or go on paying for luxuries which she and the children could easily forgo. So, in the quiet Sunday heat, she crept through the creaking house, stole into Howard's study and, once again, laid her poem on his desk.

He found it in the evening. After dinner, after an hour or so of sitting over newspapers in the drawing room, Alice had said, 'I think I'll go on up, dearest'. And had waited to see if he would say that he, too, was ready for bed. But Howard, scanning a page, had told her that he wanted to finish off a few letters before turning in.

Upstairs, huddled under the covers, Alice listened for the sound of Howard's study door opening and closing. She heard him moving about, a muffled bumping as he pulled out his chair and sat down at his desk. Now he would be turning on the lamp. Now he would see the oblong of pale cream paper placed in the centre of his blotter cover. Now he would be picking it up and looking at it, surprised and rather puzzled. Now he was reading,

> *Oh, not for us the golden prizes of the busy world,*
> *The chink of coin, the fervid hastening crowd!*

She could hardly breathe. Her heart beat so violently she had to press her hands hard against her ribs to calm it. She waited for the click of his door catch, quick footfalls on the landing, his voice in her ear, 'Oh, Alsey! Dear old girl! My own true love!' But she heard nothing—for hour after hour nothing but the faint stirring of the night wind and the minute whisper of plants stretching their roots under the earth in the garden beneath her window.

∽

What was she getting at? Free at last of everyone, hurrying to his desk to write to Kate, Howard found the sonnet like a bar nailed across his private pathway to Paradise. How dare Alice come stealing into his study, spying, hinting, reproaching? He felt almost mad with fury. What claptrap! 'Apollo-browed'! What insipid, maundering rot! 'My price excels by far/The cost of rubies'! If she only knew how he utterly loathed and despised her—hanging about him pale and limp, weighing him down with her clammy hands, blinking eyes and lank hair. Calming down a touch, he began to be fearful that someone or something had given him away and that Alice, instead of coming out with it in an open, honest fashion, was trying to prick his conscience with this stuff about her wedding ring and love free of any stain. But how on earth could she have found him out? It was all just nasty, jealous suspicion, fuelled no doubt by the mischief-making Cynthia Campion. He glared down at the sonnet in outrage. What was all this twaddle about being short of cash? He had always been the soul of generosity. Nothing, nothing had ever been denied her and here she was going on as though he'd forced her to go about in rags. 'Oh, not for us the golden prizes of the busy world . . .' For years he'd sweated and slaved to give her everything she asked—clothes, carriages, servants, everything a woman could possibly want. And instead of thanks, here she was telling him none of that was worth a straw. Let her try living in Beaumont Street for a bit! She'd pretty soon change her tune if she had to put up with that.

The curtains hadn't been drawn. Howard stared at his reflection in the dark glass of the window, the outline of his hulking shoulders, the gleam of his hair. It was sickening to think that he'd toiled all these years for a woman who had no appreciation at all of what he'd done for her, whereas

Kate—so beautiful, so full of life—valued even his smallest gift as something precious.

He put one of his hands over the poem, drew in his fingers, crushed the paper in his fist and threw the crumpled ball into the wastepaper basket. Then he opened the blotter, took a sheet of clean paper from a drawer, dipped his pen in the ink-well and began the letter he had come to his study to write:

> *My own darling girl,*
>
> *Here I am back in my study in Clifton with everything around me much as usual but all the time I am thinking of you, my angel, picturing your face, your glorious hair, your tender breast which I long to kiss again and again. It seems like a month since we parted although it's not yet two days. I don't know how I shall get through the time before we meet again. I only wish I could come to London again this week but, failing that, look forward to next Thursday. Your idea of a meeting place part way between Bristol and London was an inspiration. I can be in Reading by eleven on Thursday morning and will meet your train . . .*

This was absurd. The meeting in Reading was all arranged. There was no need to go over it all again. Alice's wretched poem had spoiled his mood so that he couldn't open his heart to Kate in the way he had intended. He screwed up the letter, threw it away, took a fresh sheet of paper and started again. This time things went better. He began to write rapidly, sometimes smiling to himself, sometimes sighing as he thought of Kate drinking in the words that he was writing, alone in his darkened house where everyone else was asleep.

In the morning, Alice sat at the breakfast table watching

Howard devour a pair of kippers. His worries, however severe they might be, had not affected his appetite. He ate briskly, announced he had an early start and went off with never a single word about the poem. Alice was dumbfounded. She couldn't understand what could have happened. Had Howard been so preoccupied last night that he'd barely glanced at the sonnet? Perhaps he had put it aside, meaning to read it later. Perhaps he had put a pile of papers on top of it and missed it altogether. Could a breeze have blown it onto the floor? Or had Elsie put it away inside the blotter or in one of the desk drawers?

She had to investigate. As soon as Howard had left the house she hurried up to his study. Everything looked exactly as it had done yesterday afternoon before she had placed the poem on the blotter. There was no sign at all of the sheet of cream paper with its rectangle of spiky, black writing. Gently Alice lifted the pile of legal documents and looked under-neath. She opened the blotter and riffled through the sheets of blotting paper. Then, glancing down, she noticed three or four crumpled balls in the wastepaper basket. One was cream in colour. She dropped on her knees, stretched out her hand and, in touching one of the other screwed-up sheets, saw some words written across the base of a stiff point, poking up like a pricked ear: 'My own darling . . .'

At once Alice saw what had happened. Howard had read her poem and had tried to respond by writing her a note, a letter, some sort of matching tribute—perhaps even a poem of his own. She laughed, touched and thrilled. But, of course, the words wouldn't come. He hadn't been able to express all the feelings her sonnet had roused in him so that, man-like, he'd lost his temper and screwed up the lot. She took up the letter, pulled it apart and spread it out. She read the first sentence smiling tremulously as she slowly got to her feet.

Then she felt as though her blood had turned to ice. She thought stupidly, 'What does he mean? We shall see each other tonight,' but even as she thought that, before she read on to the part about the assignation in Reading, she knew that the darling girl was somebody else. Not her. Some other woman. Howard, her husband, her Apollo-browed beloved, loved somebody else.

Elsie heard the thud, like a chair overturned in a brawl, while she was clearing the breakfast table. She called out from the bottom of the stairs, 'Are you all right, mum?' and, when there was no reply, ran up and started opening all the doors leading off the landing. There was no sign of Alice in any of the bedrooms, in her den or anywhere that Elsie expected to find her. Finally, because there was nowhere left to look, she peeped into the master's study. She gave a fearful shriek that brought Cook and Matthews, the man-of-all-work, running into the hall. They were starting up the stairs when Elsie came rushing along the landing, screaming that the missus was killed.

'There's blood all over the floor! Under her head! Blood! Blood all over!'

'Go for the doctor, Ted,' said Mrs Galloway, the cook, and ran off to the kitchen for a jug of water and a bundle of tea-towels.

'Stop that caterwauling, Elsie, and give me a hand.'

Together they turned Alice over and saw that, in falling, she'd gashed her forehead on the sharp edge of the back of Howard's chair. Mrs Galloway put a towel under her head, washed the wound and bound it up as best she could. Then they carried Alice into her bedroom, laid her on her bed and covered her with a quilt.

'Shall I go for Miss Campion?' said Elsie.

'Can't hurt. And we'd better get word to the master.'

'We could telephone him.'

'You can. I wouldn't touch that thing.'

'She must have fainted. Whatever brought it on, d'you think? And what was she doing in there in the master's study?'

'How do I know? Get on, do, and fetch Miss Campion.'

Cynthia came rushing over and took charge at once. She made sure that Mrs Galloway had staunched the blood from Alice's wound, waited by her bedside until the doctor arrived and telephoned Howard's office. A clerk told her Howard had gone to visit a client and wasn't expected back for an hour or two.

'Try to get a message to him,' said Cynthia. 'Mrs Gale has had a serious accident.'

On the way back to Alice's bedroom she paused by the door of Howard's study. She went over to the desk to see where Alice had fallen and noticed a crumpled page lying on the floor under the desk. This struck her as odd in such a neat room. She picked the paper up and, as she explained to Alice afterwards, couldn't avoid seeing what was written. Everything was immediately clear to her. She folded up the letter and put it in her pocket. Then, trembling with indignation, she marched back to the bedroom where Dr Jeeves had just finished bandaging Alice's head.

'She's coming round,' he said in a low voice. 'It's a nasty wound but only superficial fortunately. With rest and care she should recover fairly soon.'

'I think you should know, doctor, that Mrs Gale has had a terrible shock. That's why she fainted in the first place.'

'Oh, I see,' said the old doctor looking agitated.

'And as you know,' said Cynthia severely, 'Mrs Gale is very delicate. What do you suppose a shock like that might do to her?'

'Well, I don't know. It may, of course, retard the recovery.'

Suddenly Alice opened her eyes, looked wildly around and cried out 'Cynthia! Oh, Cynthia!'

'I'd better give her a sedative,' murmured the doctor. 'She must be kept as calm as possible. I'll look in again later in the day. Where is Mr Gale? Has he been informed?'

'Indeed,' said Cynthia, stroking her friend's hand. 'He'll be here quite soon. I'll speak to him myself when he arrives.'

And she did. Alice, quite broken down, sobbed and raved until the doctor's draught took effect. She had been quiet for about fifteen minutes when Cynthia heard Howard's voice on the stairs. She got up quickly, tucked her friend's hand under the quilt and went out to meet him. They almost collided outside the bedroom door.

'She's asleep now,' said Cynthia, pulling the door shut behind her.

'But I must see her. I was called back urgently. I was told she'd had some kind of accident.'

Cynthia simply marched past him, stepped into his study and waited for him to join her. He followed in a rising temper and stood looking down at her sullenly. What a dumpy, bad-tempered looking little thing she was, he thought, though her eyes and skin were all right.

'What exactly has happened to my wife?'

He asked the question like a man trying to keep patience with a hysterical child so that Cynthia's colour rose.

'She fainted over there by your desk and hit her head on your chair. You can see the blood on the carpet.'

'What on earth was she doing in here?'

'So far as I can make out she came to see what had become of a poem that she'd written for you and left on the desk. I suppose she noticed that you'd screwed it up and thrown it into your wastepaper basket. When she went to pick it up she found a letter that you'd written—a letter to a woman, arranging an assignation, a woman who appears to be your mistress. That's why Alice fainted.'

Howard was lost for words. Cynthia went on staring up at him with her bright brown eyes, the whites of which were as pure as those of a young child.

'She went grovelling in my wastepaper basket!' he burst out at last, flinging away to fetch up by the desk.

'Oh yes! Abuse Alice! Don't you realise what you've done to her? Why don't you ask how she is? If she's badly hurt? Don't you care for her at all?'

'That's absolutely nothing to do with you. I'll thank you to mind your own business, Miss Campion.' He swung round like a bull baited by dogs and shouted, 'A great deal of this is your doing. You've done nothing but make trouble, coming between my wife and myself, turning her against me.'

'Turning her against you! How could I when she loves you as she does? Did you bother to read what she wrote? She loves you to distraction—or she did until you did this wicked, wicked thing. Am I to blame for your adulteries?'

Howard looked across at the door, struck by the awful idea that all his servants could hear every word of the quarrel. Cynthia pounced at once.

'What's the matter? Are you frightened of people knowing what you are? What you've done to that good sweet woman? You're not fit to touch the ground she walks on.'

'And you think she wants it shouted from the housetops?'

At this Cynthia banged the door shut.

'There! I'll say nothing to anyone until Alice can tell me what she means to do. But if I were her I'd never spend another night under the same roof.'

'But fortunately you're not. And I'll thank you in future to keep away from Alice.'

'Indeed, I shan't. I shall come here every day to look after her. D'you think I'm going to leave her to your mercy? I shall come and make quite sure she's properly treated. And if you try to stop me I'll proclaim your vile conduct in the streets. I really will shout it from the housetops. I'll see to it no decent person ever speaks to you again.'

'And who d'you think would believe you?'

'I have your letter. I'll show it to half of Bristol if I have to. I'll tell them Alice is on the verge of brain fever. D'you think people won't see you're responsible? Hurt her again and I'll see to it you're ruined.'

'And Alice with me, I suppose. Oh yes, a fine friend.'

'Alice will never want for anything. I'm not a poor woman, Mr Gale. You know very well I could buy and sell you five times over. And Alice shall have every penny if she needs it. So, make your mind up to this. You will be a good husband. You'll give up this squalid liaison that you have and devote yourself to making Alice well. Or mark my words you'll regret it very much.'

They stared at each other, both red in the face and trembling with rage. Abruptly Howard swung round and stood facing the window, his hands clenched in his pockets.

'Perhaps you'll tell me, since you're such an authority on marriage, how I'm to pretend a love I no longer feel?'

'You managed well enough for ten years. If you can't love her at least you can be faithful and try to be kind.'

'And if she realises it's all a charade?'

'Then she'll have to leave you. It'll be up to her whether she publishes the reason.'

'What if she doesn't choose to leave me?'

'It'll be up to her, of course, when she's well again. But you must keep your part of the bargain.'

'Bargain! It's barefaced blackmail.'

'You must be good to her. I shall know at once if you're

360

not. And you must swear to give up this other woman. Now, at once.'

Howard said nothing. 'He's wondering,' thought Cynthia, 'how I'll know if he goes running back to his harlot.'

'I suppose,' she said, 'your word still means something. And I can always hire men to follow you. Will you swear?'

'I haven't much choice. Yes, yes I swear. Now get out of my house.'

'Oh no! I'm going to stay with Alice. The doctor's coming back shortly and I want to see him. You'll have to speak to him too. I don't think Alice will want to see you but, if she's strong enough, I'll tell her you're here and very, very sorry for what you've done.'

∽

Alice was ill for a long time. Her head was slow to heal. She lost over a stone in weight. Dr Jeeves was worried at one stage about her heart and at another about the possibility of consumption. Eventually, in late October, she went to Bournemouth with Richard and Beatrice to stay for a few weeks with her Cousin Mary.

'Dearest old girl,' she wrote to Cynthia, 'How I long for the steady reliable love that is not subject to the alterations of doubt and distrust, but which keeps one warm quietly without extremes of any kind . . .'

Howard had sworn to her that he had broken with the other woman. He had done his best to be kind to her, but she knew, of course, that never again could she adore him as she'd done in the old days. And he, even when he vowed that he still loved her, when he brought her flowers or grapes or hothouse peaches, seemed to look at her so coldly. She felt terribly alone. Even when Howard was at her side. Even when she

361

walked in the autumn wind on the Bournemouth front with Richard holding her arm and Bea scudding ahead, arms out, imitating the sailing gulls. She felt a constant sense of loss that took her back to the time when her father died. It had been windy then, too, and bitterly cold in the library where the men came to pack his books for sale. They rolled up the carpet, took down the pictures, hurried off with the chairs until there was nothing left of the snug retreat where she and her father had sat, one on each side of the fire, for hour after hour reading their books and looking up occasionally to smile at each other or read out some special passage.

Mary knew nothing of Alice's anguish. She only knew that Alice had had an accident and been very ill. She was a good deal older than her cousin, widowed and childless, so she was glad, she said, to have a bit of life in the house, glad to help poor Alice through her convalescence. She fussed over her patient, consulting with her cook over dishes to tempt a jaded appetite, arranging little treats, tucking rugs round Alice's knees and trying to make sure she didn't overtire herself. But she was secretly rather baffled by her cousin's low spirits. After all, Alice had everything a woman needed to make her happy—children and a handsome, attentive husband who wrote every week from Clifton and sent down packages of crystallised fruit, gloves, scarves and even a copy of the new biography of Lord Tennyson.

Howard, in fact, made a point of being to all intents and purposes the best husband that could be imagined. It was almost as though he were saying to Cynthia Campion, 'Look, you see! I'm doing everything a man can do and it makes no difference.' At the same time, of course, he raged every day at the hold Cynthia had over him. Sometimes he thought he could stand no more—being dictated to in his own house, spied on, blackmailed and confined. Naturally, he had kept in touch with Kate, dashing off a letter to her on the day of Alice's accident to tell her he couldn't come to Reading, and writing later to explain that his wife had gone searching through his private papers and found a note meant for Kate. He begged his darling girl to be patient. He was surrounded by jealous suspicion and spies. He thought it possible that his wife was having him followed. They would have to be cautious just for a little while. He said nothing about Alice's accident, only that she was always pretending to be ill so as to keep him dancing attendance, and he said nothing about Cynthia Campion because he could hardly bear the humiliation of being in her power.

About three weeks after Alice's fall, he decided that Cynthia's threat of having him followed had been an empty one. As he went to and from his office he watched closely for any sign of a figure on his tail and, once he was sure that the coast was clear, made another arrangement to meet Kate in Reading. Lying side by side in their rented bed in a back street hotel, they talked again about the future. Grindley Gascoigne was still keen to buy the manor at Coombe Bassett but was haggling with his cousin over the price. All the necessary repairs, especially the rebuilding of the stables, were likely to cost a fortune. But what was the use? thought Howard. Even if Grindley bought his manor house and the Old Forge was eventually made habitable, there was no escaping to Devon every week. Whenever he stayed away overnight his wife or the Campion woman would pry and spy and kick up an awful fuss.

'There's always Melbourne,' he said, reaching up to touch Kate's hair as she propped herself on her elbow to look down at his face. But when the prospect of throwing up his practice, his house, his tennis parties, his place in society, came rushing close, as the threat of scandal and disgrace had already done, the dreams of the chestnut horse and the white mare, the toy farm, and the leisured life in the sun seemed to waver and blur. He knew no-one at all in Melbourne. He'd have to build a practice up from scratch, all the time eating away at what capital he might manage to take with him. And what if Grindley's father and his churchy friends got wind of his divorce? He winced at the thought of what people would say, the way they'd sneer and turn away, lording it over him, flaunting their moral superiority, inflicting on him all sorts of indignities as Cynthia Campion had done. Idiotic, chattering women, weak fools, jumped-up hypocrites, vulgar, impertinent johnny-come-latelies, all whispering and turning the cold shoulder until, in the end, he found himself without a penny, friendless and destitute in a strange land with a family of four children—not his own—to fend for.

'You look so sad today,' said Kate, stroking his cheek.

He kissed her hand absently and sighed.

'Perhaps we could go somewhere else. Not Australia.'

'Ah, yes!' he said brightening. 'Canada. The West Indies. What about that?'

'Would it be hot there? Like Africa?'

'I expect so. But we'd swim a great deal and lie under the palm trees drinking milk out of coconuts. Jamaica might be the place.'

'Could you still be in the law in Jamaica?'

'Oh, I shouldn't bother with all that. I'd just lie under the palm trees all day long.'

And for the first time that afternoon he burst out laughing. Thrust away into the realm of impossibility, the dream began again to glow with colour.

But on the train home, watching the countryside roll by just as John Phillips had done on all his journeys to Chippenham, Howard's spirits fell. 'Jamaica!' he thought glumly. 'It must be a rundown, miserable sort of hole these days.'

There were plenty of people in Bristol whose forebears had made their money from the 'triangular trip'—goods to West Africa, slaves to the West Indies and cargoes of sugar back to the home port. His own father had sailed on such a voyage in the early eighteen-thirties before slavery had been abolished and King Sugar toppled from his throne. But now, estates in Jamaica once worth twenty or thirty thousand a year lay in ruins, their gravel drives and shaven lawns lost in the bush, their marble verandahs cracked and stained, their windows staring vacantly out on desolation.

He wondered vaguely if Barbados or Bermuda might be better possibilities. He was still passionately drawn to Kate and attached no value at all to the promise he'd given Cynthia—an oath made under threat to a meddlesome woman. In fact, he couldn't have lived with himself if he hadn't gone against her injunction. At the same time his romance—even Kate herself—seemed tarnished by what had happened, by the constant grating knowledge that Cynthia and Alice had broken in on the affair. And there was always the danger that, even if they thought he was toeing the line, one or other of them might let something slip and start a scandal. Though, when he thought about it, Alice had never really been one for washing dirty linen in public. This reflection, at least, gave a touch of comfort.

Howard had seen very little of his wife during the first weeks of her illness. On the day of the accident he'd sat by her bedside for half-an-hour or so and after a long silence had said, 'Look here, old girl, you mustn't upset yourself like this. That letter—I mean, well, it didn't mean anything, you know.'

But Alice had only given a great sob and turned her face to the wall.

After that Cynthia seemed to be there most of the time and, when Dr Jeeves thought Alice's heart was affected, a nurse came in for a week or two. Howard contented himself with sending up flowers and little gifts, putting his head round the bedroom door when he arrived home in the evenings and having grave conversations with the doctor. But a day or two after his visit to Reading he passed Alice's room on his way to his study and saw that for once she was alone, sitting limply among her pillows with a book open in front of her. He shuffled his feet on the boards by the door so that she looked up quickly, but when she saw him she turned away, pressing a handkerchief to her mouth.

'How are you feeling today?'

'Oh, I'm better I think.'

'You mustn't fret over that business,' he said, coming to squat by the bed and take her hand. 'Can't we put it behind us?'

'I don't know. Can we?'

He stood up frowning. 'I don't suppose Cynthia thinks so.'

'Cynthia's been wonderfully good to me.'

'Still she does seem very set on telling our affairs to half the city.'

'I'm sure she'd never do that.'

'Well she told me in so many words she wanted to ruin me. Shout it from the housetops, I believe she said. I tried to tell her you wouldn't want that.'

'Of course not. It would be horrible.'

Alice began to cry and Howard sat on the bed to comfort her, reasonably certain that he'd managed to spike Cynthia's guns. Perhaps, after all, in time, life with Alice would get back on an even keel, Kate would move to Coombe Bassett and everything would be all right.

While Alice was in Bournemouth Howard went off to London, letting it be known that he had business with

Grindley Gascoigne. For a week he spent part of every day with Kate as well as two nights. They made love as fervently as ever but when he got back to Clifton, he felt fretful and sullen. Grindley's negotiations with his cousin were dragging on. The sale still hadn't been finalised and, even if the two of them ever managed to settle, the repairs Grindley meant to set in train were likely to take at least a year to complete. He'd admitted to Howard that Scallywag had let him down badly and he wasn't as flush now as he'd hoped to be. So when Kate began chattering happily about the Gloire de Dijon roses she meant to plant in the garden of the Old Forge, and then tried to draw Howard into the game of deciding how long their dining table ought to be—because one day there might be more than six people sitting at it—he felt for the first time that she was making demands on him. How, after all, had it happened that he was expected to provide for four children he'd barely set eyes on? Four! And there might indeed be others later on—his own—but it wouldn't be possible to make any distinction. All of them would have to have the best. A vista of bills for nursemaids, ponies and school fees opened before him. Cartloads of groceries! Butcher's bills as long as your arm! Mountains of pinafores and sailor suits and knickerbockers! Did Kate imagine the house in Clifton ran on air, or that Alice's illness was costing him nothing at all? Or that his son, Richard, and little Beatrice could simply be forgotten as of no account?

When Howard seemed uninterested in the dining table, Kate turned to another game. What about India? Or Ceylon? Or, South America? But Howard snapped that it had to be a common law country. How on earth did she think he could practise in some Spanish place?

〜

367

For a few months Kate had been free of her dream of the woman on the beach, but towards the end of 1897 it began to recur again, night after night. It was much the same as it had been at the beginning before her father died, only now as she ran along the beach towards the hump on the sand she felt that there was somebody behind her. She wanted to turn her head to see who it was and how close he was on her heels. She knew it was a man. She heard his thudding feet and his muttering voice. Sometimes she seemed to feel his breath on her neck and his hand scrabbling at the waistband of her skirt. She ran and ran, and although she dreaded coming up to the drowned woman, seeing her open eyes and her sand-laden hair, she knew as she flung herself down that now she was safe, at least, from chance. Something that had to be had been accomplished. She had reached a goal set out for her. She never knew what became of her pursuer, only that if, by falling prone on the sand with her face in the woman's skirt, she put herself in his power, then there was nothing in the whole world that could alter her fate.

In her waking hours she wondered who the man could be. She thought it might be John but couldn't understand why, in the dream, he should terrify her so much when, in real life, she despised him. Could it be Howard? She could imagine being terrified of Howard if he became angry with her—or rather she was terrified of reaching a point where such a thing could happen. But why should she run away from him when all she wanted was that he should catch and hold her, and her real fear was that he might tire of pursuing her? Going about the house she would close her eyes and pray that there would be a letter waiting at the post office. Her lucky numbers were seven or seventeen. She went to the post office on the seventh of January and then, unable to wait until the seventeenth, called in on the eighth because when she added all the parts of the date together—the eighth day of the first month of 1898—they totalled thirty-five which was a multiple of seven. She tried again on the tenth of January because, by then, the total was thirty-seven, and three, though not as potent as seven or seventeen, was also lucky.

She looked constantly for omens. If there were seven leaves floating on her tea, seven sparrows quarrelling in the yard, seven people in the post office, then a letter would be waiting; if she was disappointed, she told herself that today Howard had written or posted a letter which would arrive tomorrow. In the early part of the year he wrote quite often so that some, at least, of the omens seemed reliable. She puzzled over those that had failed her, trying to work out whether three or seventeen was to be trusted and fancying that somehow she had missed or misread a sign. She counted up the days since she had first met Howard. The date on Julia's tombstone was 22 June, but, in fact, she had died in the early hours of the 23rd, and this, it seemed to Kate, was proved when a letter from Howard arrived on 16 January, 207 days after that date.

With all this in mind, Kate chose the days for writing and posting her own letters as carefully as a Roman soothsayer, but since she wrote at least once a week she had to exercise all her ingenuity. If she wanted to write on a date that wasn't a multiple of seven or seventeen then she justified her action by working out that it came exactly twenty-one days after she and Howard had last met, or even seventeen days after his thirty-fifth birthday.

All this not only occupied her mind, helping to keep her prowling fears at bay, but also served to make everything Howard did seem as though it had been decided by forces as mysterious and ungovernable as those that shaped the weather. She could try to find a pattern and adapt herself to it

369

but she had no more responsibility for what occurred than the villagers who chanted,

Red sky at night shepherd's delight
Red sky at morning shepherd's warning;

or the old women who shook their heads when it rained on St Swithin's day.

If on St Swithin's there be rain
For forty days it shall remain.

All the same, every time she met Howard, she spent days raking through what he'd said and what she'd said. Had she been too pressing about this or that? Or not pressing enough? Had he showed himself as ardent as last time or the time before? Did he really mean, when all the games were played out, to take her away from Beaumont Street? She thought that if he failed her she would die. And she thought how, if she did, everyone would fold their lips and avert their eyes because she was, after all, a fallen woman, an adulteress, another example of the ruin awaiting those who offended against the laws of decent people. But then she'd think to herself, 'How would they know?' If Howard left her and she pined away no-one would know what ailed her. And if everything went as she longed for and she escaped to live in Devon or some foreign place no-one in her new life would know that she was a kept woman. All her new neighbours would think she was a respectable young widow with four children who'd married a second husband, handsome, prosperous but often away on business.

She never gave a thought to any divorce although Howard had spoken about it several times. She'd never met a divorced person and couldn't see why anyone would respect her marriage to Howard after she'd admitted being his mistress in a court of law. Instead, she dreamed of life in the Old Forge where everything would be clean and fresh—muslin curtains at the windows, the rooms filled with sunshine, the garden a riot of roses. And there Howard would kiss her and hold her, lie with her in a big white bed that was all their own—not paid for in a seedy hotel in Reading—and make love to her for hours and hours on end.

Sometimes in his letters he sent her money, which she used in ways she thought John wouldn't notice. Not that he noticed anything much these days; if he asked a question she could always say she'd had something from Aunt Martha. She paid off all the bills she'd run up at the shops so that she could walk in and out with her head held high, not scared to death the grocer would refuse her credit with all the other customers looking on. She paid Mrs Figgis to come in every day to do scrubbing and black-lead the range, she bought some lengths of good, warm cloth which she had made up into winter clothes for the children and secretly she began to lay in stores for her new life, gradually replacing some of the treasures that had been sold off when she left Hampstead.

She went to a smart dressmaker and ordered a walking costume trimmed with velvet and fur, chiffon blouses, silk skirts, a crépon tea gown with a deep lawn collar edged with lace. She hid all this away in a locked trunk, reverently lifting out one garment or another when she was planning to meet Howard or slip away for a shopping expedition in the West End. She would pack her new finery in a battered suitcase, change in the ladies' cloakroom at Paddington station and leave the case, stuffed with her old clothes, at the left luggage counter. Her greatest joy was shopping when Howard was with her and she could sit in some elegant establishment while obsequious assistants brought her parasols or muffs or Indian shawls to inspect. They saw her through Howard's eyes—an object of adoration for whom, it seemed, nothing was too good. And for one afternoon she could wave aside bits of finery that cost more than she spent on housekeeping in a month, and toy with something even more expensive. Sometimes she thought of pawning or selling such presents and using the money—said to come from Aunt Martha—to help pay off John's debt. But Howard's gifts had a special magic about them. They were portents of the life she would lead one day and she couldn't bear the thought of giving them up.

Usually she went shopping alone in secret—sometimes for velvet or silk, gloves or stockings—but more often for things that would decorate some corner of the Old Forge. When she got them back to Beaumont Street she would hide them away in a packing case in the shed behind the house and whenever she could creep out, undiscovered, she would kneel by the case, unwrap one of her treasures and hold it up to the light: a silver cream jug with pure curves, little legs and a fluted edge, a silk pincushion, a paperknife with a mother-of-pearl handle, two ebony elephants with ivory tusks, a handpainted French clock . . .

FOURTEEN

When Louie woke in the morning Ian was already in the bathroom, shaving, gargling, briskly flannelling his torso as he did at exactly this time every working day. Susan was downstairs making the tea and when Louie appeared in her dressing gown at the kitchen door she looked put out. Louie's tray was ready on the bench, laid with one of old Liza-Jane's embroidered traycloths and a red rose in a little Swedish vase.

'I was just going to bring you up a cup.'

'How lovely,' said Louie, sniffing the rose. 'You shouldn't go to all this trouble, Sue.'

Then the telephone rang.

'Oh dear, Noel,' said Susan. 'Oh dear, how awful!'

It was the manager of the chemist's shop at the bottom of Willowdene Drive where Susan had helped out on and off for the past twenty years. He crackled volubly from the receiver as Louie moved around behind Susan's back, peering into the teapot and quietly opening drawers to look for spoons.

'Poor Jenny. She hasn't! Oh, I knew she was doing too much. But what about Maureen? Oh no! He isn't! I thought it was just his leg. But I can't. Did you try . . .? But she's only just arrived. Are you sure Mrs Patterson couldn't . . .? Yes, I see. And you're absolutely certain Maureen'll be back on Wednesday? Just today. Well, I suppose . . .'

'I can't believe it!' wailed Susan when the manager rang off. 'Just the minute you've got here. I'm so sorry, Lou.'

One of the regular pharmacists had had a miscarriage last night. The other had gone rushing off to see her father who had rolled his tractor on a hillside near Aberystwyth.

'He's really badly hurt apparently, much worse than they thought. But Noel says Maureen's coming back tomorrow. Today there's just nobody else available. He knew you were coming but he says he's tried everyone else he can think of. And I even rang up Redland High to ask if they'd mind if we went round the school this morning . . .'

Breakfast was eaten in a rush that made Ian sigh. He called out to the kitchen, 'Are we not having marmalade this morning?'

Susan saw him off at the front door holding her sandals in one hand, and then blundered about in a panic trying to find her reading glasses. When she was ready to leave she crouched down to peer fondly into Louie's face.

'I'm just so sorry I can't get back for lunch, Lou. Help yourself to anything won't you? Or d'you think you'll go out? Why don't you go down and see the *Great Britain*?'

When she had gone Louie strayed about the house remembering the feeling of guilty power that had come over her whenever she'd found herself at home alone in Howard Road. She used to creep up into other people's bedrooms—even old Liza-Jane's—ease open drawers, poke about among underwear and bills, try on earrings and frighten herself with the sight of her own image, caught in the act of trespass, in someone else's dressing table mirror. Forty years later she was tempted to take a look through Ian's belongings, went upstairs, pushed open the door of the master bedroom and stared at the McAlisters' quilted satin bedspread, net frills and Axminster carpet. She went over and picked up Susan's hairbrush, part of a set with tortoiseshell backs and silver handles. The groom's present to the bride. Only now the silver had worn away in patches, exposing the yellow metal underneath. She put down the brush, chastened by the thought that she was doing exactly what Ian would expect, what, no doubt, he would do himself. When he came to Tasmania she would have to lock away everything she didn't want him to see. Or she could copy out famous love-letters and leave them tied with red ribbon in her desk. *For sixteen nights I have listened expectantly for the opening of my door . . . and tonight I am alone. How can I sleep? I can't go on. We must once and for all take our courage in both hands and go away together. What sort of life can we lead now? Yours an infamous and degrading lie to the world, officially bound to someone you don't care for, perpetually with that someone. And I, who don't care a damn for anyone but you, am condemned to lead a futile existence.* Violet Keppel to Vita Sackville-West. That'd put Ian in a spin.

Louie went downstairs again and stood at the window watching the buddleia in the garden flaunting the pale undersides of its leaves in the wind. It was very like the one that had grown in the corner by the coalhouse wall in Howard Road—grew there still, perhaps, its mauve blossoms covered, summer after summer, with Cabbage Whites and Red Admirals. It would take less than half-an-hour to walk to the old house. It was just a couple of miles away on the far side of Redland Green where the Bishop's Palace had been set alight by incendiary bombs during the Blitz. Louie and Susan had gone up after breakfast to see the smouldering ruins. They'd found puddles of molten lead from the mullioned windows congealing all over the footpath. The metal had shone in the early sun, lavish and bright as silver, and Louie had crouched down, trying to prise it up with her fingernails so that she could take some home and add it to her shrapnel collection.

She had half a mind to set out at once on a pilgrimage back to Redland Green and the streets where she'd pedalled her tricycle, walked to and from school and lingered with early boyfriends after dances at The Glen. But Susan was so eager to act as guide on a sisterly tour of all the sacred sites—the old home, the old school, the playing fields next to the enclosure where Bessie the Barrage Balloon had been tethered during the war—that it seemed quite treacherous to rob her of the pleasure of watching the exile's first reactions on returning at long last to the native heath.

So she decided to do what Susan had suggested, and caught a bus to the Centre to see Brunel's ship, the *Great Britain,* found derelict in the Falklands, towed back across the Atlantic and now restored in the very dock in which she had been built. But when Louie arrived at the quay she changed her mind, turned round and walked through to the Horsefair to look at the site of the watchmaker's shop her father had inherited from old Bert Duke. The shop, she knew, had been pulled down, but she expected to be able to stand and gaze at the place where it had been, just as long ago groups of passers-by had stopped to peer at the crater that had once been Miss Wesley's house. Only when she reached the Horsefair everything was so changed that she couldn't be certain where the old pavements had been or any of the shops or the *Evening Post* offices which, in 'The Brown Photograph', had been transformed to Mr Bertoli's photographic studio. This unnerved her, raising doubts about memories that had seemed quite clear and reliable. She hung about in the gritty wind, looking resentfully at the traffic, worried by the idea that all her memories might be delusive, that the only certainty was the present moment, gone as she drew breath.

Back in Willowdene Drive she poked about in Susan's pantry, made herself a cup of packet soup and a sliced cheese sandwich then settled down to write the letter she would have liked to be able to send to Tim, a letter which assumed they understood and cared for each other. It was a good chance to get on with 'The Brown Photograph' but after last night's stint she wanted a break before carrying on to the ending. She was almost sure now what would have to happen, just as Kate knew eventually what she would find when she walked along the beach in her dream, but like the grandmother she'd invented, Louie found herself shrinking away from the preordained conclusion.

Being back in Bristol is very confusing, she wrote. *This is partly, of course, because I've been away for so long and partly because I've been in a foreign country that isn't foreign enough. Coming down here on the train I thought the countryside—if you can call it that—looked horrific but I'm not sure if this was because I want to cling to the scenes of childhood or because I'm used to Tasmanian wilderness and can't forgive England for looking so humanised.*

In this city where I lived until I was eighteen and visited on and off until I was twenty-eight, some places are changed beyond recognition. Others look neutral at first then flicker into remembered shapes, only usually smaller and meaner than the images I've stored away. The people here make this worse. They hurry about, completely unaware of any change, making me feel that I'm moving in a different dimension, that I'm invisible like the vanished scene in my head which may in any case be all a dream.

Sue says I don't sound Australian. Everyone seems to think I'm simply English. Yet I feel like a foreigner. I have trouble with the money and the language. It's like that time when I came back from hitchhiking in Scandinavia feeling words were just little counters that you pushed back and forth—lorry, coffee, youth hostel—that there was no hope of conveying anything but the very simplest ideas. Now I feel the same sort of clumsiness because I don't know enough about the texture of life here—the TV quiz shows that we don't see in Oz, the jokes, the shared assumptions about VAT or personalities like Nigel Lawson. Sometimes when I say things people look as though they want to snigger. Last night I wasn't sure whether the radiator was still called an electric fire in England.

Louie put down her pen. Nobody, apart from Ian, had looked as though they wanted to snigger at her. As usual, when she started to write, she was slipping away from the truth, throwing herself into a role which made its own demands. It was the same in 'The Brown Photograph' where the characters had developed a logic of their own which had carried them far away from their real-life counterparts. Their fates, in the end, would tell her something about the world she'd invented, perhaps even about betrayal or passion in general. Perhaps they would show her a little about herself, but she couldn't expect any more that her fiction would end by pouring a flood of light on her family's history and solving riddles like her grandmother's disappearance.

In Tasmania, wrote Louie, picking up her pen again, *I built up, as foreigners do, certain images of England. One was based on all the grim news reported with so much relish in our media—strikes, the Falklands, riots, crime, homelessness, drought and tempest. The other was a rosy idyll, part childhood memory and part Victorian novel mixed up with Sue's chatty letters and* Homes and Gardens. *Neither has much relevance to life in Willowdene Drive. London and Bristol look much cleaner and more prosperous than they did in the fifties. Streets, docks and pubs have all been gentrified and hung with baskets of lobelia and geranium, but somewhere behind all this people are seething with anger and getting beaten up by the police. I've seen no violence at all in the centres of the cities, though that just makes everything more eerie than ever.*

Louie picked at the remains of her sandwich. *It's odd,* she wrote, still chewing, *how much of the rosy picture has to do with food. I suppose it's because my generation grew up on rationing, all the time devouring those children's stories about pale little creatures from the towns going to stay in Devonshire farmhouses. 'Oh don't you worry,' beamed Mrs Merryweather. 'We'll soon put some roses in her cheeks.' And then it's all clotted cream and speckledy eggs from the speckledy hens and pasties and spotted dick until poor little Betty is busting at the seams. I suppose my dresser at home with all the jams and things owes something to Mrs Merryweather. You know how people always said 'How English!' Well it isn't. If all that easy farmhouse plenty ever existed it seems to have given way to bare, shiny plastics, fish fingers, cup-a-soups, tiny tins of baked beans, miniature joints and Marks and Spencer quiches.*

That, of course, was quite unfair to Frank who had fed Louie very well and walked miles to find organically grown apples. It was even unfair to Susan, despite the sliced cheese in Louie's sandwich. She stretched out her fingers to crumple her letter, just as Howard Gale had done with Alice's poem but changed her mind and went on:

On Saturday we're going to Lyme Regis. Frank says the south coast isn't what it was. Apparently there are nuclear power stations and sewage farms all over the place as well as acres of caravans and bungalows. But I really must try to enjoy it. Sue is working as hard as she can to make me happy and all I do is whinge—to you anyway. I must sound like the whingeing Poms one kept meeting in Australia in the sixties, when you were little. They used to spend all their time complaining about the beer, the weather, the fish and chips, the nasty, straggly gum trees, the rude, unfriendly Australians and the use of corrugated iron for roofing houses. At home, they said, they'd had nice brick and tile. In England you never saw a real house with a tin roof, only chicken coops and pigsties. If they'd known they'd have to live in sheds they'd never have paid their ten pounds to migrate Down Under. You don't meet many of them nowadays in Oz. Perhaps most of them have come back to England and are living in caravans down on the south coast, gazing longingly out to sea and telling everyone that if they'd known about the blacks rioting and the strikes and the Arabs buying up London they'd have stayed in Melbourne or Broken Hill where anyone can afford to buy a lovely place of their own for a tenth of what it would cost these days in Eastbourne.

For a long time Louie looked at the empty half page on which she could still add something. Eventually she wrote: *When you were young I was jealous of the tie between you and your father. I felt excluded and wanted to force the two of you apart. I regret this now, though I doubt if you can ever forgive me. Perhaps we can talk about it when I get back to Hobart.*

Louie had never meant to post this letter, but having come so far she stuffed it into an airmail envelope and hurried out to the post office at the end of Willowdene Drive.

FIFTEEN

Susan had arranged a trip to Bath on Saturday. The morning was wonderfully fine—a golden autumn day as warm as high summer.

'And we could go to Chippenham,' said Susan, 'to see those graves you told me about, you know, great-grandfather Barker.'

'Genealogy fever,' said Ian, crisply buttering toast. 'Hunting down the ancestors. The brewer and—who was it?—the horse dealer.'

How on earth, wondered Louie, had Susan managed to stay married to this man for over thirty years? Despite the invitation to Tasmania he seemed to spend half his time devising ways of irritating Louie. He would glide around in the background carefully rearranging objects she'd disturbed, straightening forks after she'd laid the table, hanging up a coat she'd left lying on a chair. He always handled her possessions with a sort of mocking reverence as though he knew them to be very expensive, the kind of thing he and Susan had never been able to afford—at least until now when James's money would make them better off than Louie had ever been.

'The baths have all been done up beautifully,' said Susan, happily ladling marmalade. 'Not a bit like they used to be.'

She munched and beamed, absolutely unaware that her sister was bristling with rage because Ian was at his old game of treating her as a spoiled snob who needed to be taken down a peg.

All the same, once Susan had found the camera and made a Thermos of coffee, he waved the Peugeot off with ironic gallantry before settling down to a day of polishing his pristine windows and barbering his little square of lawn.

'We went to Bath with the school to see some Shakespeare play,' said Susan. 'They did it in the baths. D'you remember?'

'Yes. It rained all day.'

Bath had been grey and tatty after the war. Georgian terraces veiled in rain, crumbling stonework, cavernous tea shops for the County. Girls from the fourth, fifth and sixth forms had been bussed to a performance of *Julius Caesar*. All through the downpour the actors, sheeted in dripping togas, had come and gone like wraiths at the far end of the Great Bath or paced, blurred and inaudible, in the gallery overhead. The audience, mostly school parties, had cowered shivering in the arcades round three sides of the pool while all across the opaque, green, faintly steaming water the raindrops had spurted in millions of tiny fountains.

Later, reading *Julius Caesar* for A levels, Louie had been amazed to discover what had been going on all through the boredom and the rain. The play, she'd suddenly realised, was about the dangers of seeing people as stereotypes, as Brutus does when he murders Caesar. By ignoring the man, so much like himself, who lives in the skin of Caesar, the politician, Brutus not only kills his own humanity but also ushers in a world in which people are reduced to political counters, traded to and fro in bloody power games. Looking down at her text, she'd felt shocked that the weather and her own bad temper had cheated her of something so important.

Susan, for some reason, had started talking rather fast about the garden Ned had made at Ten to Three. A beautiful courtyard on one side of the house with wisteria growing all over the wall and old-fashioned roses in raised beds all round.

'And then you go through an arch and there's this wonderful herb garden. He put in lots of thyme and tarragon and basil in pots, of course, all the culinary herbs really. And he's got a few medicinal ones for looks, evening primrose and foxgloves and that sort of thing. It's just a picture and the scents in the evening when you're eating at a table outside are just out of this world.'

They seemed to arrive in Bath very suddenly. The city was a complete surprise to Louie. The greyness had evaporated, giving way to creamy stone, sunshine and colour. A fuchsia in crimson bloom spilled over the gate of a tea garden. There seemed to be some kind of festival going on with street musicians, jugglers, a man in a striped topper, clowns, someone on a penny-farthing bicycle. It was all quite Mediterranean with the crowds in their bright, summer clothes standing around outside the abbey, clapping the performers, laughing and clicking cameras. Louie began to smile, enjoying the warmth of the sun, the light, colour and bustle. But as she strolled about with Susan she began to experience the same odd sense of disorientation that she'd felt in the Horsefair. She couldn't remember quite how the streets to the south of Abbey Green had looked in the old days, but the hulking Woolworth's building running parallel with the abbey was certainly new.

'What's been happening here?'

'Oh they've knocked down quite a lot of the old city. There's been an awful fuss about it. Ian says we've got to keep up with the times but it seems a pity really.'

Louie's spirits sank. The seeming cheerfulness of the new Bath had been produced at too high a cost. In any case it was hard to see why the old streets couldn't have been cleaned and restored instead of being replaced by hunks of seventies concrete.

She felt better when they went into the abbey and walked about in the cool gloom under the fan vaulting, gazing at the stained glass, alabaster tombs and memorial tablets. They found an Australian flag overhanging a plaque commemorating Admiral Arthur Phillip, 'Founder and First Governor of Australia', who, like hundreds of other Empire builders, had come home to spend his declining years in Bath.

Next they visited the Roman baths, all bright and orderly now with a well laid out museum and sparkling water. Then they walked back to the tea garden with the fuchsia for lunch at a table under a blue umbrella.

Susan started talking again about Ten to Three, only now she had moved inside from Ned's garden and was trying to describe the dining room curtains—a kind of deep blue, more of a peacock really.

She's nervous that I'm going to get intense, thought Louie, then said, 'Sue, I wanted to tell you how sorry

384

I am that I didn't get home to help when Mum and Dad were ill or see them before they died.'

Susan stopped in mid sentence and looked down at the paving stones.

'I'm sorry you had to cope with it all on your own.'

Susan went on looking at the stones, then fidgeted with one of her sandals. Eventually she said, 'You couldn't help it. I know you'd have come if you could.'

A waitress brought open sandwiches and apple juice.

'Actually I've been a bit worried about the money,' said Susan. 'The will. It seems a bit unfair really.'

'Oh no, I don't think that. It's absolutely fair. You mustn't worry about that.'

Susan, picking away at the wiry sprouts on her sandwich, was on the verge of tears.

'I was so excited at first. For a long time really. It was such a thrill getting the Peugeot and feeling you could go out and buy things like a tape recorder without worrying about the price too much. I mean, we've been all right with me working, and Dad helped us now and again. But it was really expensive with Sandy and Colin at uni and helping them all get started and Ian's never earned as much as he liked people to think. But then when I saw you I began to wonder about it. I mean it could have been us that went to Australia couldn't it, and you who stayed and looked after Mum and Dad?'

'No. That wasn't just luck. That's the way we are, Sue.'

'Well, I don't know, but I thought maybe you ought to have more of the money.'

'No, it's lovely of you to offer but I couldn't take it. I don't need it. I don't feel quite as guilty as I did and if I took your money I'd just feel dreadful again. And Tim's doing very well. It's not as though I have to give him a hand. I think Dad did the right thing.'

'It wasn't that he didn't care about you. He used to talk about you all the time.'

'I loved him too, though I don't think I understood him very well.'

'You couldn't really could you? Not when he kept such a lot of things to himself. We couldn't believe it, Ian and I, when Cissie and Jane turned up like that at the funeral.'

'And there's more to it, I think.'

Louie went on to explain the noble lover theory, which, despite her first resistance, had begun to take root in her mind. She pointed out how James and Annie had been watched over by Grandpa Gale and the Gascoigne family and provided with money in a way that suggested there was some special tie between them and Bathurst Hall. Susan was aghast.

'But that can't be right, surely!'

'You listen to Violet's tape again.'

'I couldn't make head or tail of a lot of that, but then she is over ninety. I thought she must be a bit gaga.'

'She sounds pretty sane to me.'

'I s'pose she was amazing. She had that place absolutely immaculate. So if this were true, if those two had a different father from the others, who could it have been?'

'I think it must have been Sir Henry, the one who was drowned in his yacht. He was the grandfather of Frank's friend, Teddy. Very dashing. He was one of the Prince of Wales's set. But I think Frank's come up with some other idea.'

Susan's colour rose at the mention of Frank but she refused to be distracted.

'And d'you think Dad knew about this?'

'I think so, because he must have known Annie was getting the same treatment as he was.'

'And is this what you're writing about in your book?'

'No. I thought that idea was too farfetched so the book's going along in a different direction. I'll have to finish it, though. I've got to see what happens.'

Susan looked puzzled. 'Don't you know?'

'Not really. All I know is some of the people let guilt screw up their own lives and other people's. They're un- lucky in some ways but they don't have the strength to pay their dues and go on. Or perhaps they do in the end. I'll have to find out.'

After they had finished their lunch Louie and Susan went down to the river and sat on the grass in the sun. They talked about Howard Gale, Alice's unhappy letters and Uncle Richard's elopement with Norman Judd. Then Louie described her visit to Gladstone Gardens. Susan was rather miffed about this because she'd expected to go with Louie to visit Aunt Annie at the Eveningtide Home. She pulled hard at the grass, breaking off stems and twisting them round her finger.

'We can still go,' said Louie. 'Frank and I never met her. She was in hospital. But to be honest, she sounds so ghastly I'm not sure I want to go and see her.'

Susan was so interested in this, in the way Dennis and Cissie had been neglected, and how Mad Jack Quant, the conjuring footman, had burnt his pile of money on Giant's Tump that she forgot to be annoyed.

They talked on and on. It was a day for being open in a way that had been impossible when they were young.

By common consent they abandoned the idea of going on to Chippenham. Neither was in the mood for tombs in a rundown graveyard. In any case, Louie's curiosity was subsiding. She was mildly intrigued by Frank's new theory and the mystery of the real Kate's disappearance but these riddles absorbed her less than the onward march of 'The Brown Photograph' which she felt she had to finish before she could make any clear decisions about the present, her home—wherever that might be—her living family, the future course of her life without George.

∽

'I can't understand how I never realised the situation with you and Frank,' said Louie at last. 'I know I was pretty wrapped up in my own affairs—in both senses—but it's incredible that I never noticed anything.'

Susan sat up. 'Oh well. You were out a lot of the time and Frank wasn't there that much.'

'Haven't you ever wondered why he never married?'

Susan went a deep red. She fixed her eyes on a party of ducks scudding downstream and muttered something Louie couldn't hear.

'You didn't think he'd turned out to be gay, did you? Like Uncle Richard?'

'Well, I suppose . . . Ian thought . . .'

'It's because all these years he's been in love with you. A genuine grand passion, Sue.'

'That can't be right.'

'He told me.'

Susan was close to tears again. She scrambled to her feet, saying something about getting a cup of tea. It was late, time to go home.

SIXTEEN

Winter came on suddenly. One morning Louie drew back her bedroom curtains and saw that Ian's square of lawn was white with frost. She thought at once of the day when she had first seen the brown photograph and had wandered about her house in Hobart, staring out at the frozen plants in her garden. It was summer in Tasmania now. All her roses would be in full flower. In the long afternoons there would be cricket teams practising on the oval across the road. The hills on the far side of the Derwent estuary would turn the colour of sand under the sun, and sometimes at dusk the smell of smoke from a bushfire in the foothills of Mount Wellington would float through the city streets.

At slatted tables behind the river beaches families would be unpacking their Eskies and the air would be full of the smell of barbecued chops. After Christmas they'd all be driving away from the city for holidays near some beach where the sea rose in waves as clear as glass and broke in boiling snow beyond the dunes. As you came to the crest of the hill above the neck of land that led to the Tasman Peninsula you could see breakers like this streaming into the bay, while away to the south the ocean faded into milky mist. There was nothing between that coast and the shores of Antarctica but the wind and the wild sea where whales swam and albatrosses rode the southern gale.

When she went downstairs for breakfast Louie found a postcard from Tim on the table by her plate. Emma had sent several bland little notes folded around letters from Oliver, letters full of drawings and jokes: 'What goes 99 bang 99 bang? A sentypeed with a wodden leg.' But this was the first time Tim had written to her since she'd left Hobart. The postcard showed a picture of some park in Brisbane. He was there, he wrote, for a conference— mostly marketing people and merchant bankers. Emma and Oliver were well. They were all going to New Zealand for a break in January. Then he thanked her for her letter and asked when she was planning to come home.

It wasn't much but to Louie the card meant a great deal. There was nothing snide in it. Tim hadn't mocked at her apology or ignored it. He had even signalled an interest in her return, which meant perhaps that he was prepared to let her talk to him honestly, prepared even to speak openly himself. Coming so soon after her bout of longing for Tasmania's summer it seemed like a sign. Her resolution to try to repair the rift she'd made between Stuart and Tim, which had seemed to require her to step away, to hide herself in England, was pulling her, after all, in the opposite direction.

'I must go,' she thought. 'I'll go to London and see Frank and then I'll go.' She got up at once and went to the kitchen to tell Susan her decision.

'But you'll stay for Christmas! Oh, Lou, it's all arranged!'

'I really can't.' She began to talk very rapidly about work she had to do, about Tim and Emma and Oliver expecting her, about her tenants moving out so that there would be nobody to water the garden.

'But they don't go till January. You told me.'

Louie had no ready reply. She muttered something about having a week or so with Frank before she left England. Susan was getting red in the face. Her voice rose. Ian who had started on his breakfast in the dining room next door looked expectantly at the serving hatch. He saw Louie's torso in dark blue cable stitch shifting about.

'I know all that,' Susan was saying. 'But that's not till early January. That's what you said. That's what you led me to believe.'

Louie was beginning to wish she'd been less impetuous, but she felt irritated at being covertly accused of plotting to escape from Willowdene Drive.

'You've sent Oliver's present. Why did you do that if all the time you meant to go back for Christmas?'

'Look, I'm sorry. It was just I thought I might be outstaying my welcome.'

'I don't know why you should think that. I thought you were quite enjoying it. If you weren't happy you only had to say. And now I've made all these arrangements.'

To Louie's horror Susan snatched up an apron and pressed it to her face.

'So the cat's out of the bag is it?' Ian, peering in through the serving hatch, looked like a cat himself, lean, grey, prowling in search of tidbits.

'What cat?'

'The gathering of the clan on Boxing Day.'

Susan banged the table, sat down with a clatter and began to cry in earnest. 'I asked you not to tell her. It's all spoiled now. Oh, Ian, I did ask you.'

'Well, if she's going back Down Under it hardly matters.'

'But I'm not. I'm not. It was just a thought. I really didn't mean to upset you, Sue.'

'It's not that it's anything much,' wailed Susan. 'But I wanted to surprise you. I thought it would sort of round things off for the book and everything.'

Ian vanished. For once Susan made no attempt to see him off. He called, 'I'll see you this evening, then,' from the hall but when nobody appeared to open the front door for him he let himself out and left the sisters together.

It took most of the day to reassure Susan and revive some of the easy fondness that had grown up between them. Louie got so desperate at one stage that she offered to show Susan part of 'The Brown Photograph'.

'I thought you said it was just notes,' said Susan suspiciously.

And, of course, Louie had said that, because she knew very well that Susan would be baffled by the web of invention that she'd woven and probably shocked at the affair between Kate and Howard.

'Actually there's one part I've started writing up. I haven't shown any of it to anyone yet—well, Frank read a little bit—but I'd really appreciate your opinion.'

She went upstairs and dug out the piece about the butterfly hunt. Susan, pleased and flattered, fetched her reading glasses and settled solemnly at the kitchen table. But almost at once she wanted to know if Mr Bertoli was real or not. After that she read dutifully on, brightening up whenever she came to a recognisable fact.

'Those butterfly cases! Mum was always trying to get rid of them. D'you remember? We had them up in the attic at Howard Road for years. Of course, there were only the two but Dad said Grandma Duke got rid of a lot. He always hung onto those last ones. He even had them in the flat after he moved. Still, it turned out for the best in the end. You'll never guess where they are now. Ned's got them at Ten to Three. They suit, you see, being Victorian, and they look lovely there in the dining room. He's got them against the wall between the windows and some of the colours go just beautifully with the curtains—that's the peacock blue ones I told you about.'

In the afternoon Colin rang up. Louie crept out of the room and left Susan weeping into the telephone but when the call finished she sighed once or twice, wiped her eyes and seemed quite calm and cheerful.

'He's a good boy really. People say he's always had everything his own way because he never had any trouble passing exams and that kind of thing. Not like poor old Ned. And then he's always had the looks, too. Nobody could resist him when he was little. I used to worry he'd grow up spoiled but I don't think he has. I mean, look at the way he's worked on that business. People think it all just fell into his lap but it wasn't like that at all. He worked like a Trojan for years. He never had time for a family like the others. He must've been dreadfully lonely out in the States with nobody of his own, so I suppose when Jill started making up to him he couldn't resist.'

'So they're in Houston are they?'

'Oh, yes. And he seems happy enough except that he's worried about upsetting us all. He really is sorry about that, but I told him "You can't expect Ned to get over something like this in five minutes." I know Ned and Jill

393

didn't really get on but just to be left like that with the twins and the restaurant and everything! Anyway, Col says he wants to help if he can. He wanted to know what Ned owed and he says he'll pay it off. Well, Ned's got his pride, of course, but it would be a great thing. If he didn't have all that interest to pay, Ten to Three would go ahead like anything. And I don't see why he shouldn't take it because it was Jill who ran up those bills in the first place. And she ought to contribute something for the twins, anyway.'

'Is Jill coming back to see them?'

'Not just yet. It's probably best to let them get properly settled first. They're getting on really well with Jill's mother. It's been good for her, I think. I mean, Jill's father died years ago and now Norma's retired she didn't have a lot to do except go on these package tours all the time. Col says she's thinking of living at Ten to Three permanently and that's partly why he and Jill thought they'd put in money. Not that it's Jill's money, of course.'

'So they won't be here for the party?'

'Oh, no. And Ned can't come either, I'm afraid. He's always absolutely flat out at Christmas. Thank goodness he's got that friend of his, Gervase, there. He's very good apparently. Much better than Jill.'

'Who is coming? D'you mind telling me?'

'It can't hurt now you know all about it. Oh, I was angry with Ian this morning. I asked him specially not to say anything. Anyway, there's Sandy, of course, and Gail and Duncan. They'll be here on Christmas Eve. And there's Cissie and Jane and Dennis and Dennis's wife and son. He's got three boys but just one's coming home for Christmas. The other two are married, Cissie said. And Auntie Violet's coming with Bart and his wife. And there's Frank. We thought if he came you could go back with him, you see. I did ask Auntie Annie but she doesn't feel up to it.'

'Probably just as well if Violet's coming.'

'Oh dear, d'you think that's what it is? I should've remembered they didn't get on. I just didn't want to miss anybody out. Except I didn't bother with the Chubbs, Cissie's husband's people. There are dozens of them, apparently, and I didn't see the point.'

Louie had mixed feelings about the party. She was touched by all the trouble Susan was going to on her behalf and intrigued by the prospect of meeting people she had heard about but never seen, especially Dennis, the daft son of Mad Jack. At the same time, she felt a fraud in letting people think she would use their scraps of family history in her novel. She'd tried to explain this to Susan but the idea that Louie was writing a true record of the Phillipses was so firmly planted in Susan's mind that nothing was going to uproot it. And it did seem perverse, thought Louie, to turn her back on the truth. Why, after all, had she come to England if not to discover facts about her family? She began to reproach herself for not being a more vigorous researcher, for letting information that would soon be lost forever slip away. In a few weeks she would be going home and yet she had made no effort to meet Teddy Gascoigne or even visit Coombe Bassett, where her grandmother had disappeared. She'd done nothing about hunting for any newspaper reports of her death or locating her grave. Instead she had simply invented Coombe Bassett from memories of walks in the lanes beyond Blue Anchor and installed Grindley Gascoigne in a manor house which might bear no resemblance to the real thing.

Eventually, about two weeks before Christmas, she suggested to Susan that they might go down to Coombe Bassett for a weekend. Susan gaped at her.

'Now? In this weather? And look what we've got to get done! Oh, Lou, you go if you must but I couldn't possibly.'

So Louie contented herself with telephoning the vicar of the parish which included Coombe Bassett and asking if he knew anything about a Kate Phillips who might have met with an accident in about 1900. He sounded incredulous, almost amused that she should expect him to have a record of this event after more than eighty years. But, humouring her, he said that there were several tombs of interest at Coombe Bassett, a number dating from the seventeenth century, but no Phillipses. And he certainly couldn't recall any reference to the long-ago accident. Fishermen, of course. Quite a number lost at sea. And an occasional yachting tragedy. Perhaps the woman in question had been lost on a yacht. If so, almost certainly she would have been taken back to her own parish for burial, provided, of course, that the body had been recovered.

That evening Louie reported what the vicar had said when she telephoned Frank. He had gone searching for parish records in Islington but had found that the Phillipses' local church had been destroyed in the Blitz. Yet he seemed determined to carry on with his detective work and said something about going through the records of the *Barnstaple Courier*.

After that Louie set about getting ready for Christmas. In Tasmania this had always been quite a leisurely business. Louie had long ago given up serving roast turkey and Christmas pudding on what was usually a hot summer's day. Instead she had made feasts of crayfish, prawns and salmon with fresh salads, or ham and smoked chickens, or barbecued steaks and kebabs, eaten under the trees in her garden. Afterwards there were plates of strawberries and cream with pavlovas, those huge, soft, circular meringues, piled with fruit, that seemed to turn up at every family party in Australia. Last year they had all gone to Tim's house, near the beach in Sandy Bay, and had lolled about in deckchairs watching Oliver and several other children splashing around in a paddling pool on the lawn. People had wandered in and out in their bathers or T-shirts and shorts while she and George lay back, talking idly about the holidays. For teachers, students and anyone who could get away from work, Christmas was the gateway to summer freedom. Louie and George had planned a couple of weeks on the Peninsula, fishing for flathead from their aluminium dinghy, lazing on the verandah of their shack and bodysurfing in the bay near Eaglehawk Neck. It was all utterly pagan, of course. Pure pleasure, taken casually. But here, in Britain, everything was different. Christmas had a necessary quality. The days were so dark, the weather, as time went on, so miserably cold that the coloured lights of Christmas trees, all the glitter, bustle, and preparation of hot food seemed an essential defence, a promise, like the cribs in the churches, of an eventual end to deprivation.

In mid December Susan and Louie set to work. Susan wanted the whole house spotless because she was nervous about Aunt Violet looking for specks of dust in every corner.

'She won't look under the beds,' said Louie, exasperated.

'That's just the sort of thing she would do.'

So they scrubbed and vacuumed and polished, aired

the spare bedroom, put up a camp bed for Duncan and then spent a day dressing the tree and hanging paper chains that looked exactly like the ones James had put up every year in Howard Road. The whole event began to seem uncannily like the Christmases that Louie remembered from childhood—except that nearly all the people for whom she'd once bought presents had disappeared and been replaced by a swarm of new relations. All the party guests were to receive gifts. Susan suggested toiletries and boxed handkerchiefs which she could get at wholesale prices from her chemist but Louie was doubtful about giving Bart a set of Old Spice. In the end they decided to dispense photo albums and jars of crystallised ginger at the party and buy separate, more elaborate presents for those who would be at Willowdene Drive on Christmas Day.

'And I want to get something nice for Frank,' said Louie.

She looked sideways at Susan. Since the day of their visit to Bath she'd tried several times to get Susan to talk about Frank but this was the one topic from which Susan always backed away.

'What d'you think he'd like?'

'You'd have more idea than me. D'you think I ought to send Cissie and Jane something extra?'

The party was to be at noon on Boxing Day so that the visitors could get home before bedtime and Frank and Louie could arrive in London at a reasonable hour. Susan was planning to serve savouries followed by a buffet lunch. She and Louie had just started shopping for provisions when a hamper arrived from Ten to Three packed with Gervase's specials—terrines, pâtés and salsas—along with two of Ned's pigeon pies and an assortment of cheeses. Louie ordered a dozen bottles of champagne as a surprise and no sooner had the wine merchant's van driven away than a man in a brown overall came knocking at the door, asking for Mrs McAlister. Susan came out of the kitchen with flour on her nose and tried to tell him there must be some mistake. By this time the garden path was filled with cardboard boxes.

'It's a stereo system. We haven't ordered a stereo system.'

'It's all paid for. Look here. McAlister.'

Susan and Louie peered at the delivery note.

'My husband would never've bought this. You'll have to take it away.'

'No, wait,' said Louie. 'It's from Colin. It's a Christmas present, Sue, to you and Ian.'

Kate and John hardly ever spoke of Jimmy. Even John had given up writing to him now. Kate, once she had become Howard's mistress, felt nervous of having dealings with Mrs Duke because she was the only person who knew both the Gale and Phillips families and could recognise both lovers if ever she happened to meet them face to face. Sometimes Kate still felt guilty about what she'd done to Jimmy but now always she managed to turn things around in her mind so that John was to blame. He had driven her to it. It was his fault that she'd been robbed of her firstborn. She brooded on this, heaping up her grievances. In the end, when the heap was high enough, she would be able to take his other children and leave John with no remorse at all.

Kate had more time to brood as the year wore on. Howard's letters came less frequently. When they met in Reading in March he seemed preoccupied and depressed. At one point, as he was dressing in their bedroom, he stuck his hands in his trouser pockets and stood there by the window, frowning down at the rainy street below.

'Oh, what's the use?'

Kate scrambled up in bed, her skin prickling with terror.

'Gascoigne still hasn't bought that place.'

'But he will, surely?'

'Oh, I don't know. It's been—what?—eight months now. You never know with these racing fellows. One minute they're going to do wonders, the next they're scratching for sixpence. Say he did buy it. He'd probably lose it again in six months.'

Kate thought of bringing up Australia but didn't dare say a word.

'I can't just up sticks and go off to the other side of the world,' said Howard as though she'd spoken after all. 'Not with four children in tow.'

But she couldn't leave them with John. Not one. If she did, the guilt she kept at bay would overwhelm her.

'What about somewhere else in Devon? Or Somerset? Somewhere nearer Bristol.'

'Possibly. Yes, that's possible.'

He cheered up then, turned back to her and took her in his arms, but when they parted on the station platform there was no date set for their next meeting. Howard said he would write and let her know when he could get up to Reading again. Things were difficult just now. Alice wasn't well, he had a great deal of work on hand . . .

The weeks dragged on. Sometimes Kate would wake from the dream of the woman on the beach and find that she was sobbing aloud while John, roused from his usual lethargy, was jerking his pillow in a fury. Then she would lie quietly in the dark, listening to the plaintive sounds of the night, while the ghostly pain of her dream flowed into the multiple pressing forms of loss that afflicted her daily life. Often in that chilly spring she would lie like that for an hour with the withering cold on her face until, bitterly, she would turn on her side with her back to the turned back in the bed beside her, and breathe and breathe, recalling the old days of love and pleasure that had been taken from her. There must, she thought, be better times ahead. Surely, surely Howard couldn't have raised her hopes only to dash them again.

Howard, for his part, couldn't make up his mind what he wanted. Alice had come back from Bournemouth looking pale but self-possessed. She was less effusive and clinging than she had been and spent more time with Cynthia Campion, but otherwise he couldn't see much change in her. He watched for signs of jealousy, suspicion, reproach but there was nothing he could put his finger on. It began to get on his nerves. Supposing she suddenly up and left him? She'd said she didn't want a scandal but if she went off for good, tongues were bound to wag. He couldn't see her suing for divorce but if Cynthia started egging her on she might do anything. And then where would he be? He'd have to go to Melbourne after all—give up everything, start again at the bottom just to put bread in the mouths of another man's children. He was still captivated by Kate and determined not to be dictated to by a woman who'd had the gall to threaten him in his own home but sometimes these days he wondered if the game was really worth the candle. It was the four children that made things so impossible. One, two, even three would have been different but four was asking too much. It wasn't as though he hadn't been generous to Kate. He smiled to himself at the thought of how overcome she was when he bought her some little necklace, how grateful for a pretty dress or a pair of gloves. But the upkeep of four children was another thing altogether. He watched the girls who rode bicycles through the leafy streets of Clifton, looking speculatively at their bloomers and twinkling calves. Perhaps the best thing would be to make his peace with Alice and later on look about for a cottage out at Nailsea or Almondsbury, some quiet little place at the bottom of a lane where a pretty girl with a bicycle and no children at all could be hidden away.

So one night at dinner he said to Alice, 'Are you quite well now, my dear? Not still worrying over anything?'

'I'm pretty well thank you, Howard. I shall be better when the summer comes, I think.'

'And you're not brooding at all on that other business

because, Alice, I swear to you, I absolutely swear it's all in the past. Not that it was ever of any consequence as I told you at the time. It's you I love. I've always loved you. You must know that.'

Alice stared down at her plate. Tears began to pour down her cheeks.

'I wish I could believe you. I go on as calmly as I can for the sake of the children but sometimes I think my heart will break thinking of how things used to be.'

'And will be again. Often, you know, a setback like this can make a bond stronger than ever.'

'A setback? Is that how you see it?'

'You won't think of leaving me, Alsey, will you? You won't let Cynthia spirit you away?'

'I can't bear to think of it. But nothing, nothing could be worse than living on here in absolute coldness and mutual contempt—to feel your indifference, to know you resent me as a shackle that keeps you prisoner . . .'

'Oh, come now, Alsey. What nonsense! A shackle! How on earth would I ever manage without you?'

❧

All at once Grindley sold Scallywag and paid his cousin's price for the manor of Coombe Bassett.

'Well,' he said, 'it's still a bargain. I've beaten him down no end since last year. Now why don't you bring your girl down and have a look at the Old Forge? Once I know what you want, I can get that done up at the same time as the stables.'

He was so cock-a-hoop, so sure that he'd done Howard a good turn, that Howard couldn't bring himself to admit that, after all, he meant to abandon the idea of bringing Kate to Devon. As Grindley chattered on, making it plain that he was prepared to let Howard have the Old Forge for next to nothing, Howard's interest in the scheme began to revive. His affair with Kate wasn't quite dead. It was now May and he hadn't seen her since March, but she still wrote—sometimes playful, sometimes pleading—and from time to time he wrote back. Only last week he'd sent her twenty pounds to salve his conscience. He thought of her joy when he told her that, at last, their dream of life in Devon could soon come true. And as he pictured her, laughing, weeping, adoring, his desire for her began to flare up again.

'You know she's got four children? You won't mind them running about the place?'

'Good Lord, no. I don't mind kids. It'll liven things up a bit. There's an old pony out at grass there they can ride if they want to.'

It was very tempting. Alice had settled down pretty well. She wasn't likely to kick up much of a fuss when he went off to give Grindley a hand with his affairs. As for the children— perhaps, when all was said and done, they wouldn't prove much of an expense living simply in the country. They weren't used to a lot of luxuries. After Beaumont Street the Old Forge would seem like a paradise. They could play on the beach and ride the pony. There was no need for them to go away to school. Kate could give them all the lessons they needed. It would give her an interest, something to keep her busy while he was away in Bristol.

Howard wrote off that night, summoning Kate to Reading on the following Thursday. He had, he told her, 'great news' and underlined it three times. But Kate, to her chagrin, had to put him off. Aunt Martha had died in Cobham and on Thursday she was going down for the funeral.

It was strange, she thought as she sat in the Cobham train, how the number of people she truly loved had shrunk so much. Once she had loved her father, Aunt Martha, Julia—in a way—Jimmy and John as well as her other children as they came into the world, one by one. But now there was nothing but her towering passion for Howard, drawing all her violent love up into itself like one of those whirling columns of sand out in the desert. But didn't she then love Violet and Gilbert, Charlie and Baby Annie? She sighed and closed her eyes, leaning her head back against the padded headrest. She wanted to love them. She felt wicked for secretly wishing they had never been born. She pitied them sometimes with all her heart when she thought of the grime they played in every day and the tears they shed in the little black world of Beaumont Street that was all they knew. She would take them away from Holborn to a better life—she was sure Howard's great news must mean that soon she could escape to Devon— she would keep them with her, never let them be lost to her like Jimmy, and protect them always like a tigress. Failing love, this was the best she could do.

She began to think about the money Aunt Martha would have left her. It was strange that after all this time of scrimping and scraping when a few hundred pounds could have transformed her life—even, perhaps, kept Julia alive—she no longer cared much about it. John's debt was nearly paid off. Soon he'd bring in nearly double what he earned now. But by then, if all went well, she would be gone. And at the Old Forge she would belong entirely to Howard, depending absolutely on his generosity as he loved her to do. But then she thought, 'I'll keep it for the children.' Although Howard was so openhanded, the support of her family seemed to be a touchy subject with him. Over the last two months as she'd become more and more desperately afraid that his passion for her had burnt itself out, she'd thought more than once that if it wasn't for the children she could have won him back—

simply gone to him and made him love her again. But now everything was all right, changed by the letter with the promise of good news. Soon she would see him, soon they would be together nearly every weekend. Only it was a relief that she wouldn't have to worry him by asking for money for the children's clothes and such things. It would be a weight off his mind, too, but she would have to find a way of telling him about the legacy that wouldn't belittle him or make it seem that he'd ever been anything other than utterly generous.

Kate and the Burnes were the only mourners at the funeral. They stood together at the graveside while the birds whistled in the hawthorn hedges around the churchyard and the young leaves on the elms glowed in the sunshine. After the service they all shook hands with the vicar and walked away, the Burnes moving ahead towards the gate. Kate hung back a little, half hoping they would go straight on up the lane to their house, but at the gate they stopped and waited for her. She flushed, wondering if they meant to let bygones be bygones and ask her to take some refreshment with them. Should she apologise for the way she'd flung out of their drawing room on her last visit and thank them for all they'd done for Aunt Martha? But before she could say anything Mr Burne took an envelope and a small box from his coat pocket and handed them to her. Mrs Burne, looking frostier than ever, cleared her throat.

'Mrs Phillips, your aunt wanted you to have this brooch. And we knew, of course, that you would be anxious to see a copy of her will. Everything, you'll find, is quite in order, but if you wish to discuss the terms with Miss Barker's solicitors, I'm sure they'll be happy to advise you.'

Mr Burne put his hand to his black hat without actually raising it from his head, then the pair turned and left Kate standing alone. She opened the box and stared at the cairngorm pin. Divorced from Aunt Martha it seemed a heavy, ugly-looking thing. She could never think of wearing it herself. She shut up the box, wondering what had become of the mourning ring with its casket of hair cut from the head of the young man who'd died in the Crimean War. Perhaps Aunt Martha was still wearing it now in her grave, down in the pitch darkness under the mound of freshly turned earth on the far side of the churchyard. The idea that the sun would never shine again on the tiny brilliants in the spray of asphodel seemed to Kate unspeakably sad. There was no-one left to mourn the young soldier now, no-one to remember what he and his promised bride had said to each other forty-five years ago back in the old days, the time of Tobias's boyhood stories when he'd seen a woman hanged in public for murdering her husband down in Dorset. A crime of passion he'd said it was, a quarrel over the man running after another woman.

Kate opened the envelope and ran her eye over the lines of copperplate. At first she had trouble making sense of it, but when she read it again she saw that Aunt Martha had divided nearly all her money between the Burnes and some missionary society. Kate was to receive one hundred pounds. She began to tremble with rage at the way Aunt Martha had made off with money her father would have wanted his daughters to have, and then given it away to strangers. Julia had been quite right about the Burnes. No wonder they'd made themselves scarce in such a hurry. They must be ashamed to look her in the face. But they needn't think they could dupe and rob her just as they pleased. She would tell Howard all about it and he would make them give her money back. But then her hands fell. She sank on to a bench and gazed at the ground, seeing all at once that if Howard were to act for her everyone would realise that they knew each other, that John might guess where she'd gone when she ran away.

Elizabeth-Jane or Howard's wife might start poking and prying until they stumbled on the secret of the Old Forge. She looked again at the will. What did it matter now? What use would she have had for all those thousands? A hundred pounds was still a lot of money, close to what she, John and the four children lived on for a year. With what Howard gave her she could make it last for longer, probably until all the children were off her hands. Perhaps, she began to think, Aunt Martha's meanness was a blessing in disguise. If she had inherited a great deal John would have laid claim to part of it. As things stood she was convinced he'd barely lift a finger to find her or get her back when she ran off. But if losing her had meant losing a small fortune he might well have roused himself and hunted her down.

As she walked back to the station she gave herself up to the relief and joy of knowing that after all the weeks of doubt and fear, the computation of favourable dates which failed again and again, Howard was still true. She would see him on Monday and hear his 'great news'. Meanwhile he was in Bristol, working in his office, perhaps, or walking about the streets in his well-cut clothes. It excited her to think of other people—the men he worked with, the tobacconist who sold him cigars, the waiter who brought him a plate of food—treating him as quite an ordinary person, as Mr Gale, someone they'd known for years, when all the time he was like a prince in disguise, transfigured by a love of which they knew nothing, wrapped in a glow to which they were totally blind.

At supper that night Kate kept expecting John to ask about Aunt Martha's will, but, as usual, he said next to nothing. In the end she broke out,

'You know what she's done with her money—the money that should've come to Julia and me?'

He shook his head.

'She's left it to those Burnes and some missionary society. If Pa only knew he'd be sorry he ever gave her house room.'

'And you get nothing?'

'Well, a few pounds.'

John gave a bark of laughter. 'You might've known. It's always the way isn't it?'

He sounded so savage and defeated that Kate stopped short.

'Still, you'll be bringing in more soon won't you? Next month, isn't it?'

'I won't get four pound, though. No-one thinks I'm worth more than three pound ten.'

'You've been looking around then?'

'I've got a place. Pears in Oxford Street. You didn't think I'd stay on with Nutting did you?'

'Pears the soap people?'

John nodded. He dropped his head and went on eating. Kate looked at his black hair brushed back in a stiff wing. She felt suddenly uneasy that she had so much to look forward to when he had nothing.

'It'll be a new start for you. You'll get on all right now. And we don't owe anything, you know.'

He looked at her in astonishment.

'Yes, well, I told you Aunt Martha was sending money. Maybe she thought she'd done enough . . .' Kate flushed, confused and nervous of getting tangled up in lies about how she'd managed to pay off all the tradespeople.

'Well then, we'll get another place straight off.'

It was Kate's turn to look amazed. She hadn't thought John would think of leaving Beaumont Street so soon. There was no point in it now. All her thoughts were concentrated on the Old Forge. She had no interest at all in hunting about for a better house in London.

'That's what you want isn't it?'

'Oh yes. But there's no hurry. We'll have to be sure and get the right place.'

For the first time since she'd fallen in love with Howard, John looked her straight in the face as though, all at once, he'd become aware of how much she'd changed and was trying to search out the reason.

'You always said you couldn't wait to get out of here.'

'I can't. Of course, I can't. I just mean we'll have to be careful. Not take on anywhere we can't afford to keep up.'

'If everything's paid off we can pay double what we pay here. That's all about it. There's plenty of places.'

'I'll look around. I'll start looking around.'

She turned away, twisting her hands together under her apron. She found she was even more averse than she'd imagined to making the move John thought she'd been longing for. Ever since she and Howard had first begun to talk about the Old Forge she had been picturing how it would be to go straight from Beaumont Street to the sweet, spacious rooms of the new house with the smell of roses wafting in from the garden and the green Devonshire countryside all around. To go there from somewhere different, somewhere better, a place, perhaps, with a garden of its own, took away somehow from the magical promise of the new home. And there was a feeling, too, that if she were to gather up all her belongings and go with her children to some house in another part of London, then that would be the only move she'd make. It would take the place of escaping to Coombe Bassett as though a fortune teller had told her she would change houses, and for months she'd believed this must mean moving to the Old Forge only to find, in the end, it meant no more than shifting again with John.

410

'I'd like to get a daily in to do more of the cleaning. That's it you see. I'd rather that than move.'

'I daresay we can manage both.'

'You'll want to give up doing all those books at night though won't you?'

'Makes no odds. I'll go on with it if I have to.'

'Well then I'll look around.'

John pushed back his chair and stood up with a clatter.

'You've been down on me like a ton of bricks for bringing you here. Ever since we set foot in the place. And now you can get away you're making out you're hard done by having to give it up.'

He went banging out of the room and after a moment Kate heard the front door slam behind him.

Upstairs Violet lay in her truckle bed in the room that had once been Julia's. She could hear voices down in the kitchen and wondered if a visitor had arrived because usually her mother and father hardly spoke at all when they ate their supper. She couldn't hear any words of course, just a dull murmur, a bit like the bee in the box. Mickey O'Reilly had given her the bee yesterday, holding the dirty little paper box up to her ear first and grinning all over his monkey face when she jumped away from the angry, fizzing sound. The bee had been a lot more lively then.

'What's it doing here?' she asked. 'There aren't any flowers for it.'

Mick thought it had followed his Ma home because she had a bunch of violets in her hat.

Violet felt sorry for the bee. Mick opened the box with his quick grubby fingers and they both inspected its folded wings and the stripes on its abdomen. It crawled about with a swaying, staggering motion.

'What do you give it to eat?'

Mick shook his head.

'It'll die if you don't feed it,' said Violet severely, so Mick gave her the box and ran off home, leaving Violet to decide how the bee was to be kept alive. When she asked her mother what bees ate, Kate said they sucked nectar from flowers and ate honey as well but there were no flowers and no honey in the house. Violet made do with a pinch of sugar but the bee stumbled blindly over the grains as though it had no idea it was meant to eat them. Sometimes it made a faint buzzing down in its box under Violet's bed. She began to be afraid that when she picked the box up in the morning there would be no sound at all, except for the rattle of the stiff little corpse, slipping about in its prison with its crooked black legs in the air. This picture alarmed Violet so much that she decided to let the bee go. If it gathered all its strength it might still be able to fly over the rooftops to the market where all the flower-sellers were, or to one of the parks or gardens up West.

Violet got out of bed and pushed up the window. When she turned around she saw that Annie had woken up and was lying in her cot, sucking her thumb and watching. It made Violet furious that just when she'd been given a room of her own the baby had been moved in with her. Annie made horrible smells and clutched at the things on Violet's night table. She pulled pages out of picture books and had snapped the string in Violet's coral necklace. Molly was always making Violet give Annie her pappy food and watch over her in the kitchen. Ma was always brushing Annie's pretty dark curls and calling her a little fairy. Even Pa seemed to like her better than anyone else, now that Jimmy had gone away. Sometimes he took her on his knee and dangled his watch for her to play with or, late at night, he'd put his head round the door, without a glance in Violet's direction, just to see that Annie was safe and sound. Annie laughed at silly things like

412

somebody clapping their hands and wanted them to go on doing it over and over again. And she cried for no reason so that people blamed Violet for upsetting her when she hadn't done anything.

'Nasty little fool,' said Violet. 'Horrid little beast.' She forgot the bee and went and stood by Annie's cot. 'What are you staring at then?'

Annie just smiled and giggled. Violet let down the side of the cot and clambered up. She swayed to and fro, itching to pinch Annie's satiny plump arm. Then she went and got the bee.

'Look at this,' she said in a cooing voice. 'Look at the pretty bee.'

She tipped the insect onto Annie's coverlet. It laboured feebly over the quilting. Annie wriggled up onto her pillow and pressed herself against the bars behind her.

'Look,' said Violet. 'Touch the pretty bee.' She began to shiver with excitement. Could she be found out? She ran back across the room and pushed the paper box under her bed. Perhaps her mother would forget she'd had the bee. Even if she remembered nobody could really blame Violet for letting it escape. When the bee stung Annie's finger and she started to scream Violet would pull up the side of the cot and jump back into bed before everyone came running to see what the trouble was. She flew back to the cot, gripped Annie's hand and pulled it towards the bee. Annie tried to twist away and started to whimper. All at once the bee shot into the air and cannoned against the window pane. It bounced back, flew through the open space and in a moment was lost in the bright evening.

'Now look,' hissed Violet. 'You frightened it away.' She banged the side of the cot up and pulled a terrible face at Annie through the bars. Annie's bottom lip dropped. She

413

made a tentative mewling sound like a frightened kitten. Violet rushed to shut the window and get back into bed.

'Go on. Scream, do. Nasty, dirty, little monkey.'

Annie wailed again with more conviction. There were footsteps on the stairs and Kate appeared at the door.

'What now?'

'Oh is she crying again?' said Violet, making a great show of waking up in surprise.

'Perhaps she had a bad dream.'

'Poor little thing,' said Kate and took Annie downstairs to comfort her.

∾

Kate's reunion with Howard was almost as ecstatic as she'd imagined it would be. The only trouble was that when Kate asked when she could move to the Old Forge—next week? the week after?—Howard laughed and said, as though he thought she was joking, that, of course, the house had to be done up. And then he suggested that they might go down to Devon together to meet the builder Grindley had engaged to do his work.

'You can show him how you want things done,' said Howard, smiling down at her, expecting excitement and grateful delight at his thoughtfulness in letting her have her say in the improvements. She tried as hard as she could to play up to him, but secretly she was bitterly disappointed. She had pictured moving into the Old Forge in high summer, sitting out on the lawn in the dusk, wandering through a landscape as bountiful and smiling as Howard himself, breathing the scent of flowers as she lay in her lover's arms. But now it looked as though it would be autumn before she could begin her new life and all the pleasure would be tempered by rain

414

and wind, the sadness of falling leaves and shortening days. Meanwhile she would have to drag through months of stifling heat in Beaumont Street, making up one story after another to stop John hauling them all off to a different house. Still, once Howard had fixed on a date in late June for their meeting with the builder, Kate's spirits began to rise again. She started to hope that she might, after all, escape from Holborn before the end of August.

In the event the transfer of the property proved much more vexatious than Howard had anticipated. The estate was on several different titles and encumbered by a mass of mortgages. The day of the meeting at Coombe Bassett had to be put back several times and then put back again because of Grindley's racing commitments. Finally Howard wrote asking Kate to meet him in Barnstaple early in September. He explained that she was to change trains in Bristol and Taunton and that he would come in Grindley's brougham to drive her from Barnstaple station to Coombe Bassett. The letter, which arrived on 17 August, should have filled her with joy. Instead it raised a flock of doubts and fears.

It wasn't simply that, by now, she half expected the meeting to be cancelled. What really irked her was that Howard, who had always talked about them travelling down to Devon from Bristol together, now meant to go ahead of her. 'He's afraid,' she thought, 'of running into someone he knows on the platform at Temple Meads. Or in Taunton. Even in Taunton.' She saw sense in this but the furtiveness of the arrangements and the realisation of how ashamed Howard was to be seen with her in public made her miserable. How would life be in Coombe Bassett?

For months she'd drifted along, picturing an idyllic existence in the Old Forge. Everyone would call her Mrs Gale. Howard would be with her very often. They would drive about the lanes together, make trips to Taunton or Ilfracombe, walk arm-in-arm down the village street and be known through all the district as a happily married couple. They would have friends—people they met in Grindley's house—who would call at the Old Forge and invite them to their homes for dinners and dances, even balls. Most of the time she and Howard would just luxuriate in each other's company but all these other pleasures—the delights of her lost girlhood—would be there for the taking. Only as the wife of the wealthy, gentlemanly Howard, bosom friend of the lord of the manor, her social standing would be higher and more secure than it had been in Chippenham. There would be no more snubs of the kind she'd endured from old Lady Gascoigne when Henry had started making sheep's-eyes at her—the daughter of a man in trade, a brewer—at one of the balls at Bathurst Hall.

Now, in a flash, she saw that all this could never be, that Howard had always known it could never be and, all the time, had been picturing quite a different sort of life for her. County people weren't like cottagers who never moved from the villages where they were born. Grindley Gascoigne's friends would go shooting in Somerset and travel up to Bristol without thinking twice about it. They would know some of Howard's clients—they might even be clients themselves. They might well know all about the real Mrs Gale in Clifton. Kate would have to be kept out of the way. She could never masquerade as Howard's wife. She would be left alone with her children, day in and day out, until, on the occasional Saturday night, Howard came under cover of darkness to make love to her.

In fact, when Howard arrived at Barnstaple station he had worked out what he saw as a capital scheme.

'We'll have to begin as we mean to go on,' he explained as

they clopped along the dusty lanes towards Coombe Bassett. 'I've talked it over with Grindley and we think the best idea is for you to be introduced as my sister. You'd better drop the Phillips, though.'

'In case John tries to find me?'

'Well, you know . . .'

Howard was in a great good humour. He began suggesting the names of famous beauties whose photographs were on sale in the stationery shops of Bond and Regent Streets.

'Terry. What about that? Or Hanbury? That's got a good ring. And, of course, there's the Duchess of Portland.'

'And am I to be a widow?'

'Better if you have a husband in the navy. Just in case of any additions to the family.'

He laughed and gave Kate a kiss. She smiled, much cheered by the plan he'd devised. At least, as Howard's sister, she'd be able to go about with him now and again, though they'd always have to be careful that nobody carried word of this new relative back to the jealous Alice, who would know, of course, that Howard had no sisters.

They began to talk about the Old Forge, which Howard confessed he'd seen only from the outside. It emerged, in fact, that the house had been locked up for months, possibly years, and that it wasn't until this morning, after Howard had left early to transact some business, that Grindley had gone down with a locksmith to open the door.

It was almost time for their appointment with the builder, so instead of driving in at the manor gates they went on through the village and turned into a lane by the church. This, Howard explained, led to another entrance to the manor grounds, barely a stone's throw from the Old Forge. Kate admired everything—the stone griffins on Grindley's gate-posts, the village green, the church spire, the beeches overhanging the walls of the manor grounds, and, when they finally alighted among meadowsweet at a wicket gate, the home of her dreams. It looked exactly as she had pictured it, standing back from the track that led on to the manor house, with its own little garden path lined with roses and lavender.

At first they thought there was nobody about, but as they drew closer to the Old Forge they saw that the front door stood open and heard voices inside. All at once there was a crash, a sound of splintering wood, a thud and clatter of feet. When they came up to the door they almost collided with an angry-looking man in a bowler hat who was half supporting, half dragging another person, covered from head to foot in dust and cobwebs.

'Stairs gave way,' said Fielding, the builder. He dumped Grindley among the lavender and brushed himself down. 'You were lucky not to break your neck, sir.'

Howard was very put out. He had been looking forward to ushering Kate into the house, to saying 'Well now, what have we here?' as he did when he watched little Bea unwrapping a present he'd given her.

'It's a death trap, that is,' said Fielding. 'You'd do better to pull it down and start again.'

Grindley didn't know where to put himself. He couldn't look Howard or Kate in the face though he was very taken indeed with Kate's appearance. He felt he'd made a fool of himself and let everyone down. The house had seemed all right from the outside—pretty enough and solidly built, its windows carefully protected by strong shutters—but when, this morning, the door had finally been opened and the shutters pulled back he had been appalled. He'd set four men to cleaning out the rooms, knocking down the old swallows' nests and shovelling up barrowloads of rubble, but by the time they'd finished the Old Forge looked more depressing than before. It was nothing more than a shell. The ceilings were falling down. Patches of narrow red bricks laid in the seventeenth century stood out like sores where the plaster had crumbled from the walls. The roof leaked and half the floorboards in the bedrooms were rotten, as the stairs had proved to be. And the place was alive with rats, so that all the time the labourers were clearing out the house, the farm dogs yelped and scratched at holes in the skirting boards.

'Was you thinking of living there, ma'am?' asked Fielding when Howard had managed some snappish introductions. The builder spoke as though this was the best joke he'd heard in a twelve month.

Kate blushed. Her lips trembled. She looked down at Grindley's dusty boots, while he, brushing himself off, began to assure them as cheerfully as he could that there was nothing wrong with the house that couldn't be put right. Howard refused to meet his eye. He stared away into the beech trees, pale and furious, dissociating himself from the whole débâcle.

Limping slightly and trying not to think what the putting right was likely to cost, Grindley led them all back to the front door. Dust from the broken stairs still hung in the hall.

'Come on now, look here. That's a really fine old chimney piece. Just imagine that with a good fire on a cold night. And look, this'd make a capital dining room. View right across the park . . .'

The others trailed after him. Fielding brought up the rear, providing a commentary of his own.

'All this needs coming out. There's doors gone. You'd need half a dozen new doors. Those stairs'll have to come right out. There's timbers in the roof gone. Then there's the floors upstairs . . .'

Kate could've wept. She had expected to wander about on

Howard's arm, discussing whether a wallpaper might be changed or a small conservatory added. She couldn't bring herself to think about additions like a scullery or a wash-house. The place was a hundred times worse than Beaumont Street. There was no range in the stone-flagged kitchen, just a big old fireplace with a sooty chain and a hook dangling down. Fielding flicked the chain with his stick and laughed contemptuously.

'No water, of course,' he said. 'Except for that.'

He pointed to a helmeted pump next to a stone sink.

And Kate had forgotten that there wouldn't be any gas so far from a proper town.

Mrs Duke had put herself in charge of a committee whose main business was to invite people of note to visit her local Sunday school. In June she was able to announce that, thanks to her own powers of persuasion, old Lady Falcombe had agreed to present the prizes at the end of the school year in late July. There would be a prize for every child who knew its catechism and could answer a list of questions which Mrs Duke had devised ('Name the seven plagues of Egypt'; 'Why did the prophet Elisha summon two she-bears to eat up the bad children?'). The prizes, which all had titles like *Tales from the Mission Field* or *Old Testament Stories for Young Readers*, had been selected and inscribed, but at the last moment, Lady Falcombe, who was nearly eighty and rather lame, found herself indisposed. The committee, apart from Mrs Duke, would have been happy to invite the vicar's wife to present the prizes, but Mrs Duke insisted on a post-ponement until classes were resumed in early September.

'No running off after butterflies today,' said Mrs Duke.

James, although his attendance record was not good, had been thoroughly drilled in the knowledge required to win a prize. Well scrubbed and buttoned up in his best suit, he was presented to Lady Falcombe on the appointed Sunday. Mrs Duke murmured in the visitor's ear. This, she explained, was the child she had rescued from the London slums and reared herself.

'A brand plucked from the burning,' smiled Lady Falcombe, handing James a copy of *Men of God Among the Heathen*.

Afterwards there was a tea for the children and their teachers in the church hall and a more elegant repast for Lady Falcombe and Mrs Duke's committee at the vicarage. Lady Falcombe ate a quantity of seed cake and then showed a tendency to nod off, so that she had to be gently roused in time to catch the train home to Weston-super-Mare, where, since her son's marriage, she had lived quietly in a private hotel on the front.

At such times Mrs Duke found the lack of a carriage of her own very galling. She had to stand by while the wife of the alderman who had misled her over the Jubilee banner offered to drive Lady Falcombe to Temple Meads, although she reasserted herself by carefully dusting the carriage seats with her handkerchief before she and Lady Falcombe took their places. Perhaps because of this Lady Falcombe seemed to assume that, after all, Mrs Duke was the owner of the vehicle.

'I'm very glad,' she said, smiling and nodding, 'that you haven't gone in for one of those motor cars. Such dreadful dust and noise. I told my son I'm sure it can't be natural to go rushing about at such awful, giddy speed. But he says people used to complain in the same way about trains and soon everyone will be going about in motor cars and think nothing of it.'

At the station Mrs Duke and the vicar led Lady Falcombe onto the platform. The other members of the party, including the alderman's wife, had to fall behind them so that Mrs Duke began to feel that the day had been entirely satisfactory until, glancing to her right, she noticed a very smartly dressed young woman speaking to one of the porters. She noted the elegant little hat decorated with swirling ostrich plumes, the well-cut jacket and skirt and the expensive-looking gloves. She took all this in a second before she realised that the person wearing these clothes was uncannily like Kate Phillips. The same height and figure, the same hair, and when the woman turned for a moment to look across the tracks where the porter was pointing, the same profile. Mrs Duke turned her back. She bent over Lady Falcombe and began to hurry her off towards the train for Weston but as she turned she heard the young woman behind her say something about her bag and the London train. It was undoubtedly Kate. Her voice quite unmistakably. Mrs Duke was badly shaken. Kate could have only one reason for coming to Bristol. Something had happened. The Phillipses had come into money. They wanted their son back.

Through all the business of finding Lady Falcombe a suitable window seat facing the engine and helping her wrap shawls around her shoulders and over her knees, Mrs Duke's mind was busy with the crisis that had arisen. Her interest in James had waned over the past eighteen months. Sometimes—when he contracted measles in the spring, for example—she had found him a burden, and always, although she practised the strictest economy, he was a drain on her resources. But, as against all that, he enhanced her reputation with people like Lady Falcombe. Much more importantly he had gradually established himself in Mrs Duke's mind as the prop on which she would lean in years to come. She no longer

422

thought much about how he would devote himself to the business and to herself as he grew older. He was simply there now, like the roof over her head. She was annoyed when slates blew off the roof, when it needed special attention that cost money, but obviously one had to have a roof. The idea that anyone should sweep down like a tornado and snatch away what was hers, depriving her of what even the meanest creature needed and claimed as a right, filled her with outrage.

Kate hadn't written to tell Mrs Duke she was coming to Bristol. She had arrived like a thief in the night, appearing unbidden as her husband had done two years ago. She must have gone to the Dukes' house and prowled about, peering through windows, trying the handles of doors. But, thought Mrs Duke, vengeful and triumphant, none of that would have done her any good. For once Cook and the maid-of-all-work had been given the same afternoon off. The house had been locked and nobody home. Herbert had gone off with Mr Bertoli. She and James had been at the Sunday school since two o'clock.

James had been left in the church hall, under orders to help clear away the tea things and then go straight home to wait in the porch until Mrs Duke arrived from the station with her keys. How fortunate that Kate hadn't lingered on at the house. Otherwise she might have met James at the garden gate, and then, as Mrs Duke led Lady Falcombe to her train, there he would have been! In his mother's grip, ready to be whisked away to London.

It was possible, of course, that he would have resisted Kate. After all, he had refused to visit her. Perhaps he would have turned and run away from her, just as he'd run from the room when Mrs Duke had talked about taking him to London to see the Diamond Jubilee procession. But ah! thought Mrs Duke, Who could tell what wiles the mother

423

would've used, what blandishments she had hidden in the bag she was carrying?

Something would have to be done. Providence on this occasion had saved the day. Kate's plot had been foiled, but now that their circumstances had changed, the Phillipses would no doubt set about planning another attack.

That evening after James had gone to bed and Herbert had retired to his study to mount butterflies, Mrs Duke sat down at her bureau to write a letter. She explained that she had caught sight of Kate while seeing Lady Falcombe into her carriage, but that when she had turned back to find her, Kate had vanished.

'It is such a pity,' she wrote, 'that you did not let us know you meant to visit us . . . I quite understand that you are anxious to see James occasionally even though he is still not at all happy about meeting you.'

She underlined 'not at all happy'. Then, after a moment's thought, she added, 'And it is quite settled that he will remain in Bristol.' She drew two heavy lines under 'quite settled'. After that she found herself in difficulties. Neither she nor James had heard anything from the Phillipses for months. It had been all too easy to imagine that they were prepared to forget any idea of trying to reclaim their son. Mrs Duke had even come to think that there was no longer any need to worry about taking James on a visit to Beaumont Street. When she had gone up to see the Jubilee Procession she and Herbert had left James with Mr and Mrs Ffoulkes and had made no attempt to meet the Phillipses in London. Mrs Duke frowned. The memory of the Jubilee visit still rankled. She and Herbert had stayed with Elsie Dickens in her villa at Lee but Elsie, always indecisive, had taken so long getting ready to drive to London on the great day that they had lost the places Mr Dickens had booked and after being terribly jostled had ended up in a crush of common people unable to see anything but the plumed helmets of the passing horsemen.

Since that time Mrs Duke's relationship with the Phillipses had, it seemed now, undergone a change. For a long period Kate had been her ally against John Phillips, but now it looked as though husband and wife had joined forces and were working together to upset Mrs Duke's arrangements. How was she to outwit them? Perhaps she should make a concession—propose taking James to see his family and then let the parents discover for themselves how strongly he clung to his foster mother, how utterly he rejected his blood relations. The danger, as always, was that he might find out that his parents hadn't abandoned him as easily as he imagined. If he heard about those early letters, the birthday presents and his father's attempt to see him two years ago then, despite all the good Mrs Duke had done, the whole lot of them would turn on her and James would be snatched away.

'If you want to see James I shall be very happy to bring him up to London,' she wrote. 'It may take a little time to persuade him that this has to be, so I think we should leave it until a little later in the year . . .'

Christmas, perhaps. In the intervening months, very gradually, she would drop a hint here, a sigh there until eventually she would come right out with something like, 'I think you ought to know, James, your Papa and Mama have decided you must go back to them. Yes, leave me and Uncle Herbert and Mr and Mrs Ffoulkes . . . Yes, now you're a big strong boy they want you to go and work for them, carrying coals and blacking boots and so on. And I'm afraid, dear, I have to tell you they aren't being quite truthful. Do you know they asked me to tell you that they've been writing to you all the time and all the letters have got lost? And that they've come here to see you when we've all been out? And when

I told your Papa about your beautiful boat, d'you know what he wanted me to do? He wanted me to pretend that he sent it to you . . .'

But it would have to be a short visit and one so crowded with outings that there was no time for a lot of talk. They would go to Madame Tussaud's and Kensington Gardens. Perhaps, since the Phillipses were so anxious to become a united family, they would have a photograph taken, a family group with James in the middle, making it plain that he was hating every moment. The parents could keep it as a memento after they had come to understand that it was too late to lure James back to them.

When Mrs Duke began to address her letter it struck her that, if Kate's clothes were anything to go by, the Phillipses would have moved away from Beaumont Street. Still, there was nothing she could do about that, apart from writing 'Please forward' on the envelope. Even if the letter never reached the parents she could at least rest easy in the knowledge that she had done what was right.

∾

One warm evening in October John was walking home from the City when he came to a public house called the Three Tuns. Someone pushed open the door as he was going by so that a breath of cool air, rich with the dark brown scent of beer and wet sawdust, caught him in the face. He thought he might go in for a pint, though in the normal way he never touched a drop and had no time for fools like old Lovatt, his drunken neighbour.

'But where's the harm,' he thought, 'on a day like this?'

It was a quiet place. He leaned one arm on the bar and looked around. Although Beaumont Street was only a stone's throw away, he didn't recognise anyone, except for one fellow sitting by himself in a corner—a queer fish with longish hair and a sketching block who went past sometimes when John was smoking a pipe in his doorway late in the evening. Some sort of artist. Just now he seemed to be making a drawing of a little group, who looked like cab drivers, drinking at one of the tables.

When his beer was almost finished John picked up his bag and would have been back in the street in less than a minute if the artist at that moment had not met his eye and smiled. He put down his work, came across to the bar and shook hands. His name, he said, was Pendennis St Clair and he had a request that John might find quite strange.

'It's your head, you see. Well, not just the head, the whole figure. The world-weary air. I want you for my Lancelot. My painting of the Last Tournament.'

'You think I'm like Sir Lancelot?'

'Absolutely, my dear fellow. Now, it wouldn't mean many sittings. Just now and again on a Sunday, maybe, and I'd expect to pay you for your trouble, though it wouldn't be much—I'm not too flush at the moment.'

'You paint for a living, do you?'

'Well not exactly. I'd paint all day if I could but to earn a crust I teach young ladies to draw and I do a little of this and that for the illustrated papers. Just now I'm doing a series on The Cabman's Lot, which isn't so bad at all. The cabbie I'm following doesn't care for the heat. He's a sensible man who knows the importance of frequent liquid refreshment in warm weather. Speaking of which, might I buy you another drink?'

He talked and talked in his pleasant, Irish voice. He harked back to his boyhood in Mayo and his father's passion for fox hunting, 'the unspeakable in pursuit of the uneatable'. This made John laugh. He began for the first time since Jimmy had left home to enjoy himself. He ordered more drinks but Pendennis, saying he had to keep a steady hand, refused and lit up his pipe instead.

'But don't let me stop you. Never let it be said I came between a man and his pleasure.'

So John had another beer and then several more.

'You must meet my wife,' said Pendennis. 'You will meet her when you come round on Sunday. I've tried to paint her a hundred times but I've never pulled it off. No not once. It'd take a Botticelli to get that golden hair and the look in the eyes. But with you, now, it'll be plain sailing. There we'll have the "double-dragoned chair", bright gold, very heavy, though I'll get the sense of corrupted power by picking up the gold in the autumn leaves—"And ever the wind blew and yellowing leaf." A stormy sky behind you, with the blowing leaves, a pillar to each side and the dark pavilion roof arching over. Then there'll be a group to the right and left, a maiden or two in white samite but a dulled, shadowed white, and the fool, Dagonet, whimpering and cringing, and on the steps—dark red steps—the knight cast down before the throne of arbitration cursing the follies of King Arthur, arm outstretched, helmet tumbled off. And you'll be the heart of it, wrapped in a dark cloak, dark, dark red, leaning across where the steps and the pillars and the back of the throne are all verticals, so the body's like a bend sinister. One hand gripping the gilt dragon to your left and the face, very white, staring out, 'As one / Who sits and gazes on a faded fire / When all the goodlier guests are past away.' You'll not see the knight at your feet— nothing—you'll stare out over the lists like a man in a dream. And then there's the rubies, the carcanet, the prize for the victor in the tournament. I think they might be dangling from the left hand, where they'll show against the throne like drops of blood. Now what d'you think? Tell me frankly.'

'What was that? "As one / Who sits and gazes at a dying fire"?'

'Faded. "When all the goodlier guests are past away."'

'I know how that is, anyhow.'

'Mind you, I think Tennyson's a good deal overrated in the general way—I'm more of a Swinburne man myself—but he knows how to paint a melancholy scene. Autumn leaves, the moon on water, slumbrous rivers, all that kind of thing. D'you know Verlaine at all?'

It was nearly dark when they left the Three Tuns. Pendennis led John to his lodgings so that he'd know where to come on Sunday and tried to persuade him to walk upstairs there and then to meet his Mimi and take a bite of supper, but John shook his head and swayed around the corner to his own home.

'There!' said Kate. 'Your pie's as dry as chips. You never told me you'd be late tonight.'

She banged down his plate and straightened up quickly when she caught the whiff of beer.

'You've never been drinking! Whatever's come over you?'

She was quite astonished because she knew how John despised his old father for squandering his money on ale and making a beast of himself. But she had to admit that John seemed better tempered. He even laughed once or twice while she was tidying up before bed.

'Who were you with then?'

'That artist chap that lives round by the church.'

'Him! The one with the hair all down on his collar? He gives me the creeps. He looks just like that awful Wilde man.'

'He's not so bad. He wants to paint my portrait as Sir Lancelot.'

'What are you talking about?'

'Sir Lancelot in that poem Tennyson wrote. I read a bit of it once.'

429

'I can't understand a word you're saying,' said Kate who had never cared much for poetry. She sighed, wondering if this kind of thing was going to happen again. In a way she almost hoped it would because, even if John started throwing money away in the public house, at least he'd have something to do in his spare time besides sitting about brooding. Since he'd paid off his debt and moved to Pears he'd given up bringing work home every night. Often he'd just sit by the range after supper staring at the floor and never saying a word. His silence made her uneasy. She felt he must be totting up a list of charges against her—taking Jimmy from him, trying to hang on in Beaumont Street when he'd slaved night and day to get her out of it, lying to him, leading him by the nose. Sometimes she felt sure he'd guessed that she had a lover, that someone he knew had seen her going with Howard into the hotel near Paddington station. Or perhaps he'd managed to open her trunk when she'd been away and had realised in a flash that she wore her secret finery for another man.

The letter from Mrs Duke had shaken her, making her feel that there were eyes everywhere. What would have happened if Howard had been with her at Temple Meads? And although it was a relief that Mrs Duke had leaped to the conclusion that Kate had come to Bristol to see Jimmy, she felt guilty at never having even considered breaking her journey to visit the child she'd rejected. She dreaded facing him when he came to London. She feared the way he would look at her and what John would say to her after he'd gone. Yet she couldn't admit to Elizabeth-Jane that she'd been in Bristol on any other errand. She had to pretend she was anxious to see her boy, and so had written back welcoming the proposed visit to London and saying she hoped Jimmy would come to Beaumont Street very soon.

When John went off on Sunday afternoon to sit for the painter, Kate was pleased to have something to hold against him—going off, just as she did, to enjoy himself with no thought for the one left at home. And it soothed her to think that when, at last, Howard found a house for her and she left for good, John would be able to find a bit of company at the lodging house by the church or in the Three Tuns.

Yet now, of course, ever since the horrible fiasco of the day at Coombe Bassett, her flight seemed further off than ever before. Now that she'd seen the ruinous state of the house she'd dreamed of for so long she couldn't imagine it ever becoming habitable. But it was hard to know what Howard had in mind. He had been so furious at what they found in the Old Forge, so outraged at the failure of the treat he'd planned, that she'd been afraid to press him, to ask whether they might look around for something else. Once again she was on tenterhooks, unsure, as she'd been back in March, whether Howard would stay true to her. By now, although she never consciously admitted such things to herself, she knew at a more canny, instinctual level that Howard hated nothing more than being made to look a fool, especially when his liberality was called into question. So she wrote to him, pouring out praise of the beautiful countryside round Coombe Bassett and marvelling at his generosity in thinking of finding her a home in such a place. She said nothing about the Old Forge and left it to Howard to suggest that they might turn their attention to some farm on Grindley's estate or a cottage in the village.

But Howard was slow to respond. He was sick to death, he told himself, of the whole business. He had come very close to quarrelling with Grindley and set no store at all by his repeated assurances that all would be well, that he'd set the builders to work at once and have the Old Forge looking like new before spring.

'I'll believe that when I see it,' he thought. And, by now, he had convinced himself that, unless he did see it, the whole idea of bringing Kate away from London must come to nothing, that it was only Grindley's offer of a peppercorn rent that gave the project substance. Money for a few gewgaws that made Kate look at him as though he were a prince, even banknotes slipped into an envelope now and again were one thing—spontaneous gestures that committed him to nothing. A substantial weekly rent, paid out month after month, year after year, on top of a great list of household expenses was another thing altogether. It wasn't reasonable to expect him to find that kind of money on and on for years with no respite, no escape, whatever other calls he might have to meet—school fees, doctors' bills, whatever Alice might take it into her head to demand of him. He crumpled Kate's letter, looked darkly at his wastepaper basket and threw it on the study fire.

The weeks slipped by. As Howard had expected, Grindley started to shillyshally again. He'd found the bill for repairs to the stables was double what he'd been quoted in the first place. Kate wrote again and again. Howard sulked. He spent more time in his office and complained of overwork. He sent Kate five pounds and a note saying he was run off his feet. Then, in the first week of December, Grindley, very cock-a-hoop, came bursting in upon him as he sat at his office desk.

'What d'you think, old man? I've just heard my guv'nor's coming over to see the ancestral home. I told you I'd make him sit up if I got it. He's pleased as Punch. Wants to get the whole place in apple-pie order. Not that he's throwing his weight about. Very respectful! Says he'd be honoured to assist me. And Mother wants to help with doing up the house. Look here! Screeds of stuff about tapestries. And, of course, the thing is they don't care tuppence what it costs.'

'I'm delighted for you, of course. But aren't they going to cramp your style a bit?'

'Oh, I don't know. I'll have to watch my step, I suppose, but I've still got my place in town, and I'll still get away to the races. I live pretty quietly down there as a general rule. Of course, a couple of times, there's been a bit of a row. There was a girl with some sort of a grudge against me—that one I told you about I kept for a couple of years. She came down once and kicked up the devil of a fuss. I was at Newmarket at the time but old Prosser, my head groom, got her away and put the fear of God into her. Never seen her again. I'll have a word with the servants. Just tell 'em to be cagey of strange women. But, now, look here, old man, the thing is we'll get the Old Forge done up in no time once my guv'nor gets here.'

'But I can't bring Kate down when your parents are there.'

'I don't see why not. Respectable married woman with four kids. Friend of the family wants to rent the place. And you're the brother, dropping in to stay. That won't bother 'em.'

'They'll know I'm your solicitor. And from what you say I'm bound to have dealings with them. What if they come in here asking after my sister?'

'Where's the harm in that? You're allowed to have a sister. Plenty of chaps have 'em.'

'The people here've known me for donkey's years. They know very well I was an only child. Most of them knew my uncle.'

'But my guv'nor's not going to come up here. That's the point of you coming down to Devon. We'll do all the business there. You're just making difficulties, old man. Good Lord! I say you haven't gone off her, have you?'

'What? No, no. Of course not.'

'Well, look here then. My guv'nor's arriving in April. We

should have the Old Forge good as new by August at the latest.'

'August?'

'I know I said spring but now, you see, I've got to get the west wing done up for the honoured guests. Nothing fancy. I'll leave all that to Mother, but they'll have to have decent plumbing and the roof's in a bad way. And I shan't finish paying for the stables until well into the new year. But once my people get here we'll start on the Old Forge right away.'

The next day another letter from Kate arrived. Howard hadn't much faith in Grindley's new promise but he thought he might as well pass on the news if only to keep Kate quiet. He wrote at once, asking her to meet him in Reading on the following Thursday.

In the cab that took them from the station to their usual hotel Kate looked up at him tremulously.

'Have you anything to tell me, dearest?'

Howard smiled, his moustache bristling. He began to feel more cheerful.

'Perhaps we'll talk about it later.'

So when they had made love and Howard had slept for a couple of hours he recounted what Grindley had told him. He spoke very confidently, as though he were offering her a gift and daring her to be disappointed in it. But, despite the warning voice of her instinct, tears came into her eyes.

'That's another eight months at least. It'll be over two years by then since we first met.'

Howard got up and started putting on his shirt, fastening his collar stud, tying his tie. He made a business of putting in his cufflinks and then began studying his teeth in the mirror.

'I wondered,' said Kate, picking at the fluff on a blanket, 'if we couldn't rent another place—a cottage somewhere—until the house is finished.'

'A cottage?'

'Just a small place.'

'It couldn't be particularly small if it's to hold you and four children.'

'We don't take up much room really.'

'But you'd need three bedrooms, I take it. A three-bedroomed cottage. And a servant's room. D'you realise what it costs to rent a place of that size? Do you? During the holiday season? Have you any idea at all?'

Kate said nothing. Howard's voice grew louder. He felt ill-used. He'd lavished money on this woman but nothing was ever enough. All the time she wanted more and more.

'You seem to think I'm absolutely made of money. Don't you understand I'm already supporting one family? And obviously I'm going to have to pay out something towards the repair of that Forge place. Hundreds very probably.'

He paused since he'd never before considered this possibility. The idea that he might end up paying for improvements to a property he could never own startled and then infuriated him. He felt like hurling his watch at the wall or smashing the mirror with his fist. He turned on Kate, looking so savage that she let out a cry, put down her head to avoid his eyes and rushed to him, gripping him in her naked arms and cowering against his chest as though she were seeking protection from a brutal stranger. He looked down at her with his hands held out like hooks, taken off balance, jerked from rage against her stupid greed to a furious desire to crush and hurt her slippery white body. He broke from her arms, threw her onto the bed and fell on her, digging his fingers into her flesh and sinking his teeth in her breast. Then he drove into her, pressing her shoulders down into the bed with the heels of his hands.

'You need a thrashing,' he said. 'Say it. What do you need?'

435

Afterwards he seemed embarrassed. He sat on the edge of the bed and patted her thigh without looking at her.

'We'll just have to be patient.'

'Yes, yes. I'm sorry.'

Howard went back to his dressing, moving in a slow, absentminded way, and Kate, turning to the mirror in the wardrobe, covertly examined her bites and bruises, wondering how she was going to hide them from John. On the way back to the station they hardly spoke. They kissed goodbye quite solemnly. Howard said he would write soon and, when Kate's train drew out, stood on the platform, waving, until she was out of sight.

On the journey home he was very thoughtful. He had always considered himself a decent, normal man with ordinary appetites. Although from time to time he had engaged in odd fantasies and felt his skin prickle at rumours he'd heard of a woman in Clifton who was hired by certain parents to discipline their erring daughters, he had brushed these inklings aside. He had heard vaguely of the Marquis de Sade and thought him disgusting—above all, alien—largely because he talked about what he did. At school, Howard and all his fellow prefects had dutifully punished the younger boys in their house and occasionally had done other things to them, but because nobody ever discussed these activities—leave alone labelled them—Howard saw no connection at all between his own conduct and that of a man like Oscar Wilde.

Sitting in his railway carriage, looking out at the wintry countryside, he was, at first, disconcerted by the fierce excitement he felt when he let his mind go back to the hotel bedroom. He even began to rage against Kate for driving him to such lengths. But that, of course, only excited him more as he began to think of how he might punish her. At once he reared back again, frightened by the force of a need he'd never acknowledged before. He wondered if all the worry she'd caused him had made him hate her. Was that why he longed so much to hurt her? But no, no! The thought of losing her now drove him nearly frantic. Eventually he began to regain his balance. She was like a child, he thought, a dear little thing who had to be kept in order. His little rogue, his sweet little rogue.

∽

'They're bound to ask a lot of questions,' said Mrs Duke, 'but there's no need to say much. We don't want other people knowing all our little secrets do we, James? We won't stay long anyway. Uncle Bert's taking someone I know to Madame Tussaud's this afternoon, isn't that right?'

The cab drew up outside number forty-six. James saw faces at the downstairs windows then his father opened the front door. His mother came close behind with one little child in her arms and another hanging onto her skirts. Violet, looking very neat in a clean pinafore, rushed into the street dragging Gilbert by the hand.

'Well, here we all are,' called Mrs Duke, clambering down to the pavement. She shivered dramatically.

'Oh, what a bitter wind! Do let's get inside.'

This had the effect of confusing the welcoming party. Kate backed away from the door but John came forward and, bending down, tried to speak to James, only to find him whisked from under his eyes into the house.

Uncle Bert and John ended up face to face on the pavement. They shook hands though neither could think of much to say to the other. Bert Duke believed that the Phillipses had sent their son off to Bristol and taken no further interest in him, while John assumed that Bert must have had some part in turning James against his family.

'It's James now, not Jimmy, isn't it, James?' Mrs Duke was saying as they all squeezed and shuffled along the passage to the parlour. 'And now take my coat, dear. That's right. Fold it nicely and put it somewhere safe, away from sticky little fingers.'

'Our fingers aren't sticky,' said Violet loudly. 'Mother washed Annie and Charlie. And I washed Bertie. And I don't get my fingers sticky even when I make jellies.'

'That'll do, Violet.'

'At least,' said Mrs Duke, settling herself in the best chair, 'I'm glad to see, Kate dear, that you took my advice and started training the little ones to help you.'

'I helped clean up in here,' said Violet. 'And I helped get dinner.'

'I did too,' piped Gilbert.

'You!' snapped Violet. 'You went picking at the chicken and knocked the pickles over.'

Once James was free of Mrs Duke's coat, Kate put out her free arm to give him a hug but he looked so pale and stiff that she faltered. He kissed her quickly on the cheek, as he'd been told he must do, and stepped back. He didn't like this room which seemed much darker and smaller than the place he remembered. He thought the house had a nasty smell and his father, when he tried for a second time to look into James's face, smelled even worse. His breath was like the sour air in the cobbled alley at the back of the Irish Packet where the brewers unloaded their drays. When Uncle Bert had a drink with Mr Bertoli he always sucked a peppermint to take the smell away before they went home to Aunt Elizabeth-Jane.

'Where would you like to go tomorrow then?' asked John. 'I've got the day off so we can have an outing.'

438

James looked at the carpet.

'I'm going to the theatre with Uncle Bert and Aunt Elizabeth-Jane.'

'Oh, yes indeed!' cried Mrs Duke. 'Gilbert and Sullivan! James has been looking forward to that for weeks, haven't you, James?'

There was an awkward silence. After a moment Mrs Duke leaned across and gripped Kate's arm.

'You see how it is, dear. I don't think any good can come of forcing him.'

She straightened up and beckoned James to her, smiling brightly.

'Look, James! There's someone here you haven't met yet. Your new, little, darling baby sister.'

'She's nearly two,' said Kate, lifting Annie into a sitting position and pushing the shawl away from her face. 'But she's not well at the moment.'

'Oh, nothing infectious I hope?'

'No, it's only a cold, but her chest's not strong. She often gets like this in the winter.'

'Well, perhaps, James, we won't kiss Baby after all. We don't want nasty colds and coughs spoiling our holidays, do we? Just take her little hand and stand well away.'

So James touched the baby's hand, carefully avoiding his mother's eye, and Kate, feeling she couldn't bear to stay in the same room as Elizabeth-Jane for another minute, muttered something about seeing to the lunch and hurried away.

'I'm afraid we can't stay very long today. James is going to Madame Tussaud's this afternoon.'

'But he's staying here tonight,' said John. 'His bed's made up.'

James looked quickly at Uncle Bert who fiddled with his hat and cleared his throat.

'He asked to stay with us at the hotel so we've got him a room.'

'But we've got a special supper for you,' said Violet. 'With a big cake. And we've got your Christmas presents ready.'

James looked at her sideways. His mother came back into the room, saying lunch was on the table in the kitchen, but he wouldn't look at either of The Liars. They were just big black holes in the air. He didn't want to know they were alive. He had expected to feel the same about his brothers and sisters, the ones who hadn't been sent away. He had thought they would stand in a line like little fenceposts and smile proudly and sneer at him. But they weren't like that at all. They were very small. They didn't know anything. Perhaps soon they would be sent away too. He felt sorry for them. He thought, all at once, that if, instead of arms, he had big wings like an angel he would stretch them over the children and shield them from harm.

Once they were settled at the kitchen table, Mrs Duke explained that she could never touch cold meats in the winter months and would just take a mouthful of soup and a tiny slice of hot pie, but as the meal wore on she murmured something about abhorring waste and allowed James to put half a cold fowl and several slices of tongue on her plate. James himself ate very little. Almost at once John turned on him.

'So you won't be here this afternoon or tonight and you're going to this theatre tomorrow. When are we going to see you then?'

James hung his head.

'It *is* a short visit this time,' said Mrs Duke, 'with *so* much to fit in. But we will be here tomorrow morning early—long before we have to be off to the theatre. I've arranged something very, very special. You might say it's a present from our little family to all of you here at number forty-six.'

Mrs Duke looked enquiringly around as though she expected eager interest and gratitude. When nobody spoke she put down her knife and fork and clasped her hands.

'I have made an appointment with somebody not very far from here. Does the name Burton mean anything, I wonder?'

'There's Burton's the photographers,' said Kate as coldly as she could.

Mrs Duke clapped her hands.

'Oh, James, she's guessed! She's guessed our lovely surprise! There now! Isn't it thrilling! We're to have a beautiful portrait done of the whole family with James in the middle. Then he'll have a lovely keepsake and so will all of you.'

'You want to remember us, do you then?' said John.

James said nothing.

'Why put him in the middle of the family when we never set eyes on him?'

'Well of course,' said Mrs Duke, 'if you don't care for our little surprise we'll say no more about it. We really thought, James and I—and Herbert, of course—it would give you pleasure. I don't suppose, by the time you've finished paying for one thing and another—new clothes and so on—there are too many pennies left for photographs.'

She looked meaningfully at Kate. The situation wasn't at all as she had thought. The Phillipses were only slightly better off than they'd been before. Probably there had been some little legacy which featherbrained Kate had squandered at once on a fashionable outfit. And, then, with just a few shillings left, she'd gone rushing down to Bristol to try to get hold of James, never stopping to think of how it would be now her windfall was all spent, never realising the wickedness of tearing James away from his lovely home and dragging him back to this horrid, dingy place.

'Oh, come now,' she cried. 'I'll pay every penny out of my

own pocket. Now, you can't refuse, not after everything.'

This was too much for John. He got up, banged out of the room and walked round to the Three Tuns. But the next morning, feeling nothing was of any consequence, he allowed himself to be shepherded down the road to Burton's Photographic Studio. When the photographer ducked under his black cloth John stood very stiffly behind his wife's chair. He was dressed in his best suit instead of a length of dark red velvet, but his expression was the one he wore in St Clair's painting of 'The Tournament of the Dead Innocence'.

∽

On the way home to Bristol Mrs Duke leaned back in her seat and closed her eyes in exhaustion. The visit to London had been a splendid success. There had been no awkward questions and the Phillipses had made only the feeblest effort to reclaim their son. She had managed the whole thing wonderfully well. The only galling reflection was the cost of the exercise—the amount she'd been forced to lay out on James's hotel room and the various treats required to keep him away from his family. Still, a period of strict economy would soon restore her losses.

'Well, James,' she said, 'we have had a lovely time, haven't we? But we can't have treats all the time, can we? We'll really have to buckle down to work when we get home again. You're a big boy now and it's quite time you did more to help your Uncle Herbert.'

'Won't I go to school any more?'

'Perhaps for a little while, but really I think if you were to work in the evenings on your sums and read something from the Bible every day you'd learn quite as much as Mr and Mrs Ffoulkes could teach you.'

442

'He's not ten yet!' burst out Uncle Bert, shocked into rebellion.

Mrs Duke, thinking of all that could be saved if James's school fees could be eliminated instead of just reduced, pursed her lips.

'I didn't say immediately, Herbert. But I have doubts about that school. They seem to me to be far more interested in all those heathen stories—shameless gods, all kinds of wickedness—than in proper Christian teaching. I shall certainly speak to the Ffoulkeses before very long.'

But she never did. Somehow Howard Gale—jovial, handsome Mr Gale—heard about her intention. One day when she was sitting in his office, laughing and simpering, he asked her about James's education. When she began to prevaricate she saw his smile fade, his blue eyes grow hard and cold. She felt her own ham-pink cheeks turning pale. He reminded her of her responsibilities and the provisions of the Education Act. He rose from his chair and towered over her. The plumes in her hat began to quiver with a fine nervous tremor.

∾

'So James will remain at school until he starts his apprenticeship,' said Elfrida Gascoigne. 'I hope, Mr Duke, that is clearly understood. Of course, if there is any financial difficulty, I shall be happy to make some contribution.'

SEVENTEEN

'Hoo!' said Violet. 'I thought we'd never get here.'

Bart and his wife Moira began to unwrap her, unwinding scarves and trying to pull her arms out of the sleeves of her sealskin coat.

'Don't you touch my hat!' she snapped, shaking them off. The hat, like a blue flowerpot, covered her eyes so that she had to tilt her head to see who was in the hall.

'There you are, then,' she said to Susan. 'This is my son I told you about. And his wife. Who's that there?'

'That's Ian, Auntie Violet.'

'He's the one came in that black jumper. My bees would've taken to him if he'd gone near them. And that's the other girl is it?'

Louie squeezed through the crowd and shook hands. Violet didn't look as though she held with kissing. Taking the knobbled old hand gave Louie the strangest sensation as though, like somebody drowning, she was seeing a whole life flash past in a few seconds. Here was the child with the bee in a paper box, the housemaid picking a love letter from the day's flowers, Harry's wife, Bart's mother, suddenly there in the flesh at the age of ninety-five.

'You're a lot more like Jim than that Susan. Take's after the mother, I s'pose. Bart, you got those parcels there? I brought you both a bit of honeycomb.'

Bart poked about in a basket, found the honeycomb and presented it, smiling with embarrassment. Louie was surprised at how old he looked—a little, gnarled man with spaniel eyes and strands of grey hair trained over a bald head. His wife was a good deal younger and seemed excited by the outing. She was dressed up in a bright green suit with what Beatrice used to call a peplum—a frilled jacket-skirt—standing out stiffly from a nipped-in waist. Was this the woman who washed her floors with a dirty mop and left a grimy line all round the walls? She put her mouth to Louie's ear and broke into a spate of whispers.

'I brought a cake. It's not much really but I thought you could do with it with so many coming. It's nice here, isn't it? Modern place like Mum's got.'

'Where do we go now, then?' asked Violet. 'Got a chair, have you?'

She hobbled quickly into the sitting room and settled herself next to the imitation logs glowing in the fireplace.

'Now they're good. No dust and mess with them. Got a sherry there, have you? Nice dry one. "Keep sweet sherry for the trifle", old Mr Cripps used to say.'

'That was the butler at the place she worked in,' whispered Moira. 'Donkey's years ago but she's always on about it.'

Duncan, who had spent most of the morning with his father drawing a family tree, considered her carefully.

'You are Mrs Moira Stringer. You are Bart's wife and

Great-great-Aunt Violet's daughter-in-law. You live near Williton and grow vegetables.'

Moira giggled and wagged her head as though to say 'Whatever will they think of next?' She seemed to think Duncan was some kind of entertainer hired to break the ice by playing a new version of 'This is Your Life'.

'Actually,' she whispered to Louie, 'it's nearly all tomatoes now. Bart's getting into the hydroponics.'

'I won't have one of those trees,' announced Violet. 'Dropping needles all through the house. I got a nice, clean, silver one.'

Ian moved about with a tray of drinks. Louie slipped out to the kitchen where Susan was banging plates and dishes around in a panic.

'It's all going very well,' said Louie soothingly and took a tray of miniature vol-au-vents back to the company.

'You're the one writing the book then,' said Bart. 'I never met any of Mum's people except your Dad. You'll have to ask Mum. Mum knows all about it.'

'She's amazing really. You'd never think she was over ninety, would you? Bart's right though. We don't know much at all, do we?'

Sandy, shepherding Duncan out of the throng, looked irritated. He was planning an announcement, explaining that Louie would move round the room with her notebook interviewing each family member in turn.

'Why don't some more come?' asked Duncan. 'Where's Mr Dennis Quant and Mrs Nettie Quant and their son Graham Quant? And where's Mrs Cissie Chubb and Miss Jane Chubb and Mr Frank Gale?'

'They'll all be here soon,' said Gail. 'There's the bell now.'

The five newcomers made a tremendous noise. Ian

glanced quickly at Sandy and raised his eyebrows. Susan rushed out of the kitchen and found the hall jammed with people peeling off coats and juggling crates and parcels. In the middle of the melée was a very tall man with a vacuously amiable face, wild white hair, and no chin. There was something weirdly uncontrolled and dangerous about him. Louie could imagine him flailing about in innocent fun and starting a pub brawl, upsetting a boat, detonating a bomb. His voice was a loud shrill neigh that incited those around him to extremes. Cissie and Jane were already in fits of laughter, screeching and holding each other up. His wife and son, on the other hand, looked as though they would like to murder him.

'Oh, it's Susan is it?' he shouted, reaching out over the others' heads. 'Dennis here! Here's the old trouble and strife! Here's our little blue-eyed boy, young Graham!'

Graham, who was twenty-four and dressed in a tightly buttoned dark suit, curled his lip. He shouldered his way up the hall and looked disdainfully round the sitting room. Cissie and Jane, still laughing and squealing about Dennis the Menace, came in behind him. Finding he had room to manoeuvre, Dennis decided to make a spectacular entrance, grabbed his wife round the waist and dashed her along, shouting, 'See me dance the polka!' Erupting through the sitting room door he collided with Ian who was just raising a glass of champagne to his lips.

'Greetings!' cried Dennis, lifting his arm and setting the central light swinging madly on its chains. A plump red and green paper chain fell heavily onto Violet's hat.

'That's Annie's boy is it?' she asked testily. 'Doesn't surprise me.'

Gail managed to get Dennis to sit down. Ian went off to change his shirt and tie. Bart helped Susan provide all the new arrivals with drinks. Sandy climbed on a stool and carefully tied the fallen decoration back in place while Louie began to move around with another plate of savouries. Order, it seemed, had been restored but within a few minutes Dennis was up again.

'There's nothing like a drop of bubbly!' he shouted. 'And very good bubbly it is. Don't get me wrong, but I've got something out there'll really get the old joint jumping.'

He dashed into the hall and returned with a milk crate full of cider bottles. He ripped the top off the first one and began sloshing the cider into every glass he could get at.

'Best drop of scrumpy you'll ever taste! Come on, Grandma! Give it a go! There, squire, that'll put some hair on your chest!'

'A very select gathering,' muttered Ian, carefully putting his glass of cloudy cider on the sideboard and pouring another measure of champagne.

'Got any other tapes, have you?' asked Graham. He jerked his head at the new stereo system which was gently pouring forth carols from King's College Chapel. 'Need something to drown him out. Daft old bugger.'

'You'd better ask my wife.'

But Susan was out in the hall talking to Frank who had just arrived.

'That's gone straight through me,' said Violet, looking darkly at Dennis. 'I'll have to go to the toilet now.'

So Louie had to steer her along the hall, interrupting Susan and Frank, and on up the stairs.

'That Frank, he's your cousin is he?'

'Yes. He's Mum's brother's son. We had the same grandparents.'

'That's it. That Howard Gale. The lawyer chap. Oh, I could tell you a thing or two about him.'

'Yes, I heard what you told Sue about him.'

Violet shut the bathroom door. Louie could hear her cackling happily to herself. In a minute she was back, poking her blue hat out into the landing.

'He had a fancy piece down in Coombe Bassett for years and years. Course old Gale was years older than she was. Must've been pushing fifty when he met her—when he started on with her anyway. Thought he was God Almighty just because he was errandboy for Him'

'What Him was that?'

'I could see Jim'd never said when that Susan came. Never heard a word about it, have you? Him as went through the alphabet more than once. That's who.'

Back in the sitting room Susan, looking very hot and flustered, was trying to make sure Frank had been introduced to everybody else.

'You are Great-uncle Frank Gale,' said Duncan. 'You live in London but I don't know what you do.'

Dennis thought this was uproariously funny.

'Just as well, eh? Just as well! Never know what they get up to in London! Here, Frank, what you been up to then?'

Cissie and Jane screamed with laughter and Nettie looked disgusted. She had started knitting with some kind of plastic yarn and gave the unreeling strand a furious tug. Graham leaned against the wall, smoking a cigarette. Louie, trying to draw him out, asked about his mother's wool.

'Not wool. Plastic bags she uses. Bread bags and crap like that. Won't throw anything out. You should see the dump. Stuff everywhere.'

'Is that what her dress is made of? Plastic bags?'

'Some crap. Here, can't you see about getting a bit of music?'

Jane, who seemed to regard Graham as her private property, came rushing up to stop Louie taking him over.

'Yeah, go on Auntie. Gray and me want to have a dance.'

'But I think we're just going to have lunch.'

Dennis, now rather drunk, was making another round with a cider bottle.

'You're splashing that everywhere,' snapped Violet. 'Look what you done to that carpet.'

Louie hurried after Frank and Susan who had gone out to the kitchen.

'For heaven's sake let's get them into the dining room. That cider's absolutely lethal.'

She went back and alerted Sandy who tapped briskly on a bottle with a knife.

'Ladies and gentlemen, lunch is about to be served in the dining room. After lunch, our guest, Louisa Gresham from Down Under, better known as Aunt Louie, will be coming round to ask you some questions about the family. As I'm sure you all know by now Aunt Louie, who is quite well known as a writer in Tasmania, is writing a book about the Phillips family and would appreciate any material any of you can contribute. Thank you. Now if you could just line up there you'll find plates and cutlery just inside the dining room door.'

The line, which quickly became a scrimmage once Dennis joined it, lurched away. Ian and Sandy brought up the rear. Violet remained in her chair waiting for Moira to reappear with a plate of food.

'What's this then?'

'It's the chicken curry, Mum. If you don't like it there's other things. A nice sort of stew and pigeon pie and cold meat and that.'

'That'll do. I'll have a bit of the pie after.'

Ian and Sandy stood aloof, nibbling terrine. Graham, his plate piled high, settled near them on a free chair. Jane got down on the floor next to him and started trying to tempt him with tidbits of her own.

'Come on, Gray! Have a taste of this spicy stuff!'

When he snarled and shook his head she turned her attention to Sandy.

'Doesn't know what he's missing does he? Did Sue make all this?'

'I believe a lot of it came from my brother's restaurant.'

'Oh did it? Well I'm not touching that then.'

Jane banged her plate down on the sideboard and went off to find her mother who started and gazed at her lunch as though it had turned to serpents before her eyes.

Together they complained to Dennis who bent down his head to listen.

'You know, where that Ned went off his head and called me for everything after Mum and me went all the way over there to help him out . . .'

'Serving all this raw stuff . . .'

'Throwing out all this lovely custard I'd made specially . . .'

'Meat half raw. Janey tried to tell 'im . . .'

'I said to 'im, "I was in the catering game when you were in short pants, kiddo".'

'She's been doing the food at the Eveningtide for donkey's years.'

'It's a bloody insult expecting us to eat this muck!'

'What are they on about?' asked Aunt Violet, turning on Bart.

He shook his head. 'Something about the meat.'

Violet raised her voice. 'No manners some of them.

Kicking up a fuss over what they're given. That's good pie that is like Cook used to make at the Hall there. 'Course, not everybody's used to things like that.'

'Away with the fairies, she is,' muttered Jane but she and Cissie subsided into whispers. Dennis, who had no idea what they were talking about and wanted to enjoy himself, raised his head and began to sing, 'Oh! Oh! I love a bit of pie! Hey diddley-ay! Smack 'em in the eye . . .'

'Christ!' said Graham.

'Dessert!' cried Louie brightly. 'Dessert's all ready now!'

'There's a lot of waste on them dinner plates,' said Nettie appearing in the doorway, dour and sallow in her strangely glittering frock. 'Got a bag have you so I can take it?'

Louie went off to find a plastic carrier bag and came on Frank and Susan hurrying a Christmas pudding onto the dining room table. Frank, now in tearing spirits, doused it in brandy and threw a lighted match.

'Oh!' wailed Susan. 'I wanted them all to see!'

'Leave it to me!'

And Frank snatched up the plate, raced with the flaming pudding into the sitting room, did a quick lap round the guests amid shrieks and guffaws and returned panting to the dining room.

'God!' said Sandy. 'I'm not surprised we've always steered clear of him before. Frankly, Dad, when you look round it's hard to believe they're all related to Duncan in some sort of way.'

But Susan thought Frank's Olympic run was the funniest thing she'd ever seen. She collapsed onto a dining chair and still couldn't speak when Cissie and Jane appeared, demanding to know who'd made the pavlova and the mince pies.

'My pavlova. Sue's pies,' said Louie.

'That's all right then.'

Sandy arrived to help Duncan choose his dessert. Why was the big white thing called a pavlova? Louie thought it might be because the ballerina had been fond of it.

'She was a Russian lady,' said Duncan crossly. 'And you said that's an Australian pudding.'

'Well, I expect she went to dance in Australia and somebody made one for her.'

Duncan wasn't convinced by this explanation. He was getting tired and fretful.

'Why not have a nice nap, Dunkie?' suggested Gail. 'I'll come up with you.'

'Then I'll miss the Christmas tree and all the presents.'

'That won't be for ages yet. Auntie Louie wants to ask everybody questions about the family first.'

'Really, I don't have to.'

'Best to keep to the programme I announced,' said Sandy.

EIGHTEEN

When Louie went upstairs to fetch her notebook she lingered by her bedroom window, looking out at the chilly clouds over Willowdene drive. Despite Aunt Violet's tantalising hints and the chance of learning more about Coombe Bassett and Kate's disappearance, she wished that Sandy had just forgotton the interview idea. She felt more of a fraud than ever because 'The Brown Photograph' was nothing like the family history everyone, apart from Frank, expected. And all of them were going to wait in vain to see their contributions included in an account she could never let them read. After setting out to uncover the truth she'd ended by creating another secret. But there was no escape. If she didn't go back to the party very soon, Sandy would come rapping at her door.

Things were much quieter now, largely because Dennis had fallen asleep on the sofa, his mouth wide open and his long legs sprawled across the hearthrug. Even so, Louie decided to conduct her interviews in the dining room, where interruptions would be less likely. She began with Bart and Moira who explained all over again that the only one they'd met was Louie's Dad. Violet was the one to ask, they said.

'It's not that Bart isn't grateful,' whispered Moira. 'It was your Dad started him off with the combine harvester. He used to go round all the farms after the war. That's how we expanded you see.'

Bart, who hadn't heard a word of this, looked uneasily at his hands.

'I expect you both know the area very well,' said Louie. 'I was wondering if you could tell me something about a village called Coombe Bassett.'

'Coombe Bassett! That's where Bart's Mum's sister was—the one she can't stand at any price. Those Quants and Chubbs all come from round there. I've been over that way a few times and Bart knows Coombe Bassett, don't you, Bart?'

Bart agreed that he did and enquired huskily what Louie wanted to know.

'I daresay your mother's told you our grandmother— her mother—is supposed to have had some accident near Coombe Bassett. I think she may have drowned.'

'Really? Well, I never knew that before. I've never heard a word about it. Did you know that, Bart?'

'Might've been by the Tump there. Several's got caught there by the spring tides.'

'Cissie and Jane said something about the Tump.'

'Giant's Tump they call it. Great lump of rock up one end of the beach with a bit of a cove right next to it.'

'That's where it would've been you see. That's where people've got caught before. But fancy Bart's granny being caught there and us not knowing a thing about it.'

'Mum might've said something,' mumbled Bart.

'You never said a word to me! However did it happen then? Of course, she didn't come from round there, did she? Down on holiday was she or something like that?'

'Look,' said Louie, 'I really don't know. I'm not even sure the story's true. What I really need to know is something about Coombe Manor.'

'Oh, yes. Lovely great place, Coombe Manor. Lovely gardens with a lake and everything.'

'The old squire did a lot to it. People still talk about him. Did a lot in the village.'

'It was a real showplace, Coombe Bassett. They had these new model cottages and a new school and all, didn't they, Bart? Course, they're not new now. That was back when Bart's mum was a girl. But they were strict, mind. You wouldn't go up to the front door unless you were quality or the butler'd see you off with a flea in your ear. And there was this head groom there—a real terror he was. Mrs Morris at the pub was in service there for years and she said one day this chap went after a girl with his whip just because she came up to the front door instead of going round the back. Imagine that! You'd get had up if you did that nowadays. Just some poor kid from the village sent up with eggs or something.'

'Loved anything newfangled, the old squire.'

'That's right! They had electric light years before anyone else and water pumped up to the house. And there was this boat on the river by the Home Farm you could pull over and back on a rope. Everything ran like clockwork, Mrs Morris said, up in the house, in the garden, on all the farms, everywhere.'

'The farms were a sight. And lovely orchards.'

'But the young squire wasn't a bit interested was he, Bart? Course, he's not young now. Must've died years ago. He went off to Australia or somewhere, didn't he? So when the Old Squire died it was all sold up.'

'Were there many farms?'

'There was the Home Farm and that one behind the beach, Marsh Farm.'

'And there was Willow Farm over past the church, though that was let out, wasn't it?'

'And Biggadike's all along the back there.'

'Of course it's all different now. The Manor's a big hotel and Marsh Farm's some sort of riding school. And what've they got at Willow Farm, Bart?'

'That's all arts and crafts. Spinning and that. Biggadike's is about the same though. Retired doctor chap's got Biggadike's now.'

Cissie and Jane came in, still giggling. They seemed to have got over the shock of being confronted by Ned's food.

'Oh, Den's a card, isn't he?' sighed Cissie, shaking her head.

'Hey, Louie,' said Jane, 'is that right about Frank being engaged to Sue?'

'Well, yes.'

'Mum said, but I couldn't believe it. And is that right they haven't met for years and years until today? And she broke it off and married Ian?'

'You seem to know all about it.'

'Perhaps they'll get back together again. He's got a bit more life in him than that Scottish git.'

Louie looked away. She felt furious that Jane should pick up her own thought and flourish it about so casually. Cissie, seeing Jane had overstepped the mark, started nudging and whispering. 'We had another word with

Mum,' she said at last. 'We asked her when her Mum died. That was what you wanted, wasn't it?'

'Didn't tell us anything really, though. Just laughed at us like she always does.'

'She said, "Violet thinks she went down on the Arry-something but Jimmy and I know better." Then she said we'd better ask you if we wanted to know about that.'

'Me? What on earth did she mean?'

Cissie and Jane shrugged. They wanted to get back to the party. When Louie went out to look for Dennis and his family she found Dennis was still asleep and Graham, who was too young to be much use anyway, had shut himself in the bathroom with Susan's portable radio.

'Best leave him,' said his mother. She folded her knitting and stumped along to the dining room by herself. 'There wouldn't be much we could tell you,' she said, settling herself at the dining room table and starting to knit again.

'I just wondered if you had any special memories of Dennis's parents or grandparents.'

'His mother—that Annie Quant—was a flighty bit of goods. Carrying on with this older chap all the time. Not that you can blame her altogether. Heard what the husband did, did you? Mad, he was. Stark raving mad, burning all that money. Should've known better, shouldn't I? Marrying into a family like that.'

She shook out her twinkling knitting in disgust.

'My poor mother nearly had a fit when I got engaged. "He's a great gaby," she said. "You can see he's wasteful." But you don't listen when you're young, do you? Wasteful! I've never known anyone like him for smashing things and just chucking them out. Thinks money grows on trees. And the boys take after him. They all go on at me,

459

making fun of what I do to make ends meet, but I tell them, "You'll regret it one day. Don't care was made to care." That's what I tell them.'

Louie fiddled with her notebook, wondering how to stem the flow.

'Your dad was all right,' Nettie went on. 'He used to come down and see us quite a bit. Helped us out. "Don't give him anything," I said. "You know what'll happen." So he used to give it to me. "Are you sure you can manage?" I said. I didn't want him to leave himself short. He just smiled. "It's money that comes to me from on high," he said. "What? From God?" I said. "That's right," he said, "and from the bounty of my earthly father." Well, I thought that was queer because from what Auntie Vi said their father died of drink years ago. Threw away every penny he ever had.'

'So what could Dad have meant?'

'Ask Auntie Vi. She might know.'

Louie didn't want to disturb Violet and went through to the sitting room to talk to her by the fire but Violet insisted on being treated like everyone else.

'I don't want all that lot listening in,' she said shutting the dining room door on her relations. 'What d'you want to know then? I told the other one most of it.'

'Why should my father say his money came from his earthly father? I thought the Phillipses were really poor.'

'So we were. And what we had all went on beer in the end. It was that St Clair chap got Father started on the drinking. But then, Father wasn't father to Jim and Annie, was he? Didn't you ever cotton on to that?'

'I had begun to wonder. But then who was? Sir Henry Gascoigne?'

'You better look higher than that. I know she went off

with the Gascoignes on that boat but that was only to see Him, wasn't it? Him who went through the alphabet— Preston Phillips, Annie Anjoulème. All of them called like that, one after another, all the ones he fathered out of wedlock. Some of those women thought it was an honour, but not Mother. She'd never've let Him have his way if it hadn't been for that Gale pestering. But He saw them all right, I'll say that. Sent people to watch them, sent them plenty of money. And it went on after He'd gone, just the same. Course, they always made out it came from somewhere different. That St Clair made out he'd come into family money though the father wouldn't give him house-room. And Jim's was supposed to come from Miss Gascoigne and that butterfly chap.'

'Mr Bertoli?'

'That's it. That butterfly chap. Supposed to have left Jim a fortune. But where would he ever get that sort of money? That's what Jim said. Where would he get it if it didn't come from him?'

NINETEEN

Driving back to London in the dark with the head-lights of an unending stream of cars rushing towards them, Frank was almost intolerably cheerful. He'd had a lovely day and even though Ian and Sandy had made themselves as unpleasant as possible when the other guests had all gone, nothing could cloud the pleasure of his time with Susan. Louie, on the other hand, felt confused and depressed.

'They must have been having me on. Violet, anyway, and that loony in the frock made of plastic bags.'

'Well, stranger things have happened.'

'Have they? Not much stranger, Frank. You realise what Violet was hinting at with all that stuff about Him who went through the alphabet? Are you seriously suggesting that my father and his youngest sister were the illegitimate offspring of Edward VII?'

'That's what I decided a while ago. Teddy thinks so too. It's quite true about him going through the alphabet.

Teddy ran into a couple of them in Scotland ages ago. Hector Harland and Roderick Ross. Oh and, by the way, I don't think Old Howard had an affair with Grandmother Kate.'

'Why not?'

'Teddy found a photo of him with "To my beloved Elfreda" written on the back.'

'Oh Frank, you're such a romantic! Howard wasn't like you. He could've made love to Elfreda before, after or during the Kate affair. Anyway, Elfreda didn't die in 1900. She can't be the woman Howard was so distraught about when Alice left him.'

'But that's when the *Ariadne* sank. When Elfreda decided to devote herself to the orphans. Seems to have been a very dramatic person. Changed in a flash and part of it was dropping Old Howard. As for the other business, it all adds up, Louie. I've been reading away about His Royal Highness. He could very well have been at Bathurst Hall in October 1888. He'd been roaming around in Europe, shooting chamois and trying to shoot Transylvanian bears but he was back in Paris by late October. Went to a circus to watch a mimic seafight and visited Pasteur's laboratory, then came back to England. Same sort of thing nine months before Annie. Definitely in England in March 1896 writing letters about Kitchener subduing the Sudan.'

'But I thought he ran his affairs by strict rules. No single girls. No middle-class mistresses. No uncooperative husbands as far as possible. Just actresses and aristocrats like Lillie Langtry and the Countess of Warwick.'

'Kate was the exception. Knocked him off his feet I think. Took him back to his youth. Couldn't get her out of his system even after he met Alice Keppel. But she or

John or both tried to break away. Well they did for a long time but he caught up with her again when she was getting pretty tired of Beaumont Street I suppose. Then there was another swaying battle with Old Howard pressing the Prince's suit and eventually she agreed to take the children down to Coombe Bassett for a few weeks' holiday while she went off on the *Ariadne* to meet HRH in Denmark.'

Halfway to London they drew off the road to have a drink in a pub called the Bunch of Grapes, hidden away up a side road near Reading. When they were settled at their table Frank felt in his pockets and pulled out an envelope containing another cutting from the *Barnstaple Courier*. This one carried a date: 21 April 1900.

TRAGIC LOSS OF
SIR HENRY GASCOIGNE'S YACHT

On Thursday last residents of the district awoke to the dreadful news that Sir Henry Gascoigne's new ocean-going yacht, the *Ariadne*, had foundered in the sea off Bideford with what is feared to be great loss of life.

It is understood that the catastrophe occurred on the afternoon of Tuesday 17 April when the *Ariadne* was observed at the mouth of Bideford Bay sailing calmly in the direction of Ilfracombe. The weather was perfectly fine and the sea smooth yet within a matter of seconds the yacht plunged beneath the surface of the waters, giving the passengers and crew no time to launch a lifeboat or take any other measures to save themselves.

So unbelievable was the tragedy that those observing the *Ariadne*'s progress from the shore could not accept the evidence of their eyes and hesitated to raise the alarm in the belief that their senses had played them false. Captain Abel McDevitt (R.N.retd.) of 'The Crowsnest', Bideford, who had been keeping track of the yacht's progress with the aid of a telescope, was at first convinced that his eyesight or his instrument was at fault, while others attributed the disappearance to a trick of the light or the sudden rise of a sea-fog. After a restless night, Captain McDevitt finally raised the alarm on Wednesday morning. The coastguard from Bideford agreed to put to sea and made towards the spot where the *Ariadne* had last been sighted. Here a quantity of debris, including lifebelts, dressing cases and articles of clothing were discovered floating on the surface of the water, and a solitary survivor, a young apprentice to the *Ariadne*'s French chef, was found clinging to a broken spar, almost at the end of his endurance.

Coastguards from every station in the region were at once called out and began to search every inch of the sea for survivors. Unhappily, so far none have been discovered although there are still hopes that some who may yet be alive have been swept away by the current to a great distance from the wreck. A thorough search of the beaches all along the coast has resulted in the recovery of the bodies of a number of those who lost their lives in the tragedy, but the possibility of finding the living among the dead has not yet been discounted.

Sir Henry Gascoigne, who last year commissioned the building of the *Ariadne*, was well known in the region of Barnstaple as the former owner of Coombe Manor in the village of Coombe Bassett. His prowess in the yachting fraternity and on the turf is acknowledged nationally, while, as a close friend of the Prince of Wales, his station in polite society could not have been higher. We may still hope that Sir Henry and Lady Gascoigne will be found safe and well as the loss of this brilliant young couple would be a heavy blow to their family and all their friends who are especially numerous in the West Country.

It is not yet known how many others were aboard the *Ariadne*. Sir Henry had set out from Plymouth earlier in the month with the intention of sailing north through the Irish Sea and east through the Orkney and Shetland Islands to join the Prince of Wales in Denmark, where he and the Princess of Wales are recovering from the dastardly assassination attempt made upon them in Brussels. Sir Henry and Lady Gascoigne were accompanied by seven or eight companions, whose names are not yet available, as well as members of their domestic staff and the captain and crew of the yacht. It is understood that Sir Henry intended to rendezvous with other guests at Bideford although it is not known whether this additional party had yet boarded the yacht or whether Sir Henry had elected to take advantage of the fine weather by sailing out to view the beauties of Bideford Bay while awaiting the arrival of his friends.

Speculation as to the cause of this terrible event continues on every side. It is attributed by some to a fault in the design or construction of the yacht, by others to a collision with a submerged object such as a whale and by still others to the actions of some deranged person who deliberately opened an aperture below the waterline. An anarchist outrage of the kind so recently perpetrated by the villainous Sipido has not been ruled out.

It is the lack of certainty which is proving such a strain on the nerves of all those throughout the West Country and beyond who can at this time only wait and pray. We

extend to the relatives and friends of all those on board
the ill-fated yacht our very deepest sympathy in this time
of anguish and pray with them that the objects of their
apprehensive affection will yet be restored to them.

'So,' said Louie, sipping her whisky, 'you think Kate
boarded the yacht in Bideford to go sailing off to Denmark
for a holiday with the Prince. Despite the Princess.'

'She was often there when Alice Keppel was about. But,
no, darling, I don't. I think she saw a chance to escape
from an impossible situation and went off with Grindley.
Let everyone think she'd been drowned. It meant leaving
her children behind but she seems to have made contact
with James and Annie later.'

'You mean she went to Australia? So that's what Annie
meant when she said Cissie and Jane ought to ask me
what happened to her!'

'See what you can find out when you go home.'

'Well, I'll look up Grindley's marriage, but I doubt
Kate would've used her real name on the certificate. How
odd. The quest that brought me away leads me back.'

'But there were other reasons for coming to England
weren't there?'

'Oh yes. And I'm very glad I came.'

Frank suddenly reached out and pressed Louie's hand.

'Sue's coming up to London for a bit. And we might
have a holiday in Scotland. Ian's planning a couple of
golfing trips so she thinks she might just leave him to it.
She actually suggested it herself.'

'Oh Frank, I'm so glad.'

'It may not come to much but it'll be wonderful while
it lasts.'

'I was looking today at all those people. Duncan's just so much like that photo of Dad in the velvet frame and Bart must have been a lot like my grandfather, John, when he was younger—shorter and stockier, but just the same eyes and expression. I was trying to work out whether the new generations made up for whatever happened to him and my grandmother and Dad being sent away and Alice's misery. Cissie and Jane, leave alone Dennis and that ghastly Graham didn't seem to redeem too many sorrows. But if you and Sue can be happy even if only for a little while that's really something.'

Frank just smiled at this so Louie began again. 'D'you think some terrible events—the Holocaust, say—just go on breeding evil and hate forever?'

'Not necessarily. They shouldn't happen. Nothing can ever make them less dreadful. But you can make good come out of bad sometimes. As long as you don't just sit around waiting for the sunrise.'

'Perhaps we just have to learn to keep our eyes open.'

'I'd rather say we have to make our own light.'

'Well, I'll tell you something. When I came to England I felt nothing good could ever possibly come out of George dying. That it was just black loss, but now I think I've gained a bit by being without him and coming here and trying to write this book. And meeting you again, of course. And Sue.'

Back on the motorway Louie said, 'All my life I've wanted to discover some wonderful secret about Dad's parentage. It's very tempting to start revelling in the thought of royal blood. Sue and I would be cousins to George VI, wouldn't we? Along with a few hundred others, of course. If Dad was Preston Phillips then, presumably, Edward managed to father Quentin Quilp

469

through to Zuleika Zebidee before he started off again with little Annie Anjoulème. I can't believe it, Frank, but I think Dad did. I suppose he heard the stories about the Prince of Wales at Bathurst Hall.'

'How he danced at the ball with pretty Miss Barker?'

'Well, maybe. That sort of thing. So it wouldn't have been hard to convince himself that there was somebody higher than the Gascoignes looking out for him and that Old Howard was this earthly father's agent.'

'Where did the money come from then? Elfrida wouldn't've produced much. Not with all the nieces and nephews to think of.'

'According to Violet it came from Mr Bertoli, though Dad, of course, made out he was behind all that.'

'But if the King story isn't true why didn't Howard simply say so?'

'You don't imagine Dad could ever ask him, do you? Frank, we're talking about the Phillips family. They tend to keep things to themselves. I'm sure now Dad convinced himself he was Edward VII's son. That's why he took the breakup of the Empire as a personal affront, but he never said a word about it to Mum or Sue or me. Bert Duke might have been in the secret but I'm sure Old Liza-Jane didn't know what Dad believed. She just couldn't have resisted dropping hints if she'd thought she'd reared a princeling. She'd heard the story about the sinking of the *Ariadne*, but I can't remember her saying anything else about the Gascoignes. She probably felt miffed because Bert and James went to Bathurst Hall but she was never invited.'

'Violet and Annie knew all about it.'

'But only because Dad fed them the story. There's no real evidence for the King theory except what those two think, and I'm sure Dad made them think it. No wonder he liked visiting them so much. He turned into a prince down in Devon with them.'

'It's weird he kept the whole tribe such a secret.'

'I think he was really scarred by being the one chosen for rejection and sent away to awful Liza-Jane. So he pretended he'd never known his family at all and once he'd denied them it just became impossible to admit to their existence. That's one of the things I discovered through writing the book.'

'D'you think you'll finish it?'

'Oddly enough I feel better about it now. My version of what happened can't be all true but I trust it more than I did. I'll see it through. And then I'll go home. I'll miss you, and I'll miss Sue but I must go. Why don't you come out for a visit? Sue wants to do that one day soon. It'd be marvellous if you came with her instead of Ian.'

'Steady on. I'd love that but I don't want to wreck things by rushing them.' Then after a moment he said, 'I'm glad you'll have Oliver and Tim.'

'I'm going to try to think more about them having me.'

'Will you tell them the King story?'

'Oh yes, I think so. Oliver would like that.'

Yes, she would tell that story. But she wondered if she would ever show Tim 'The Brown Photograph' with the story of the stolen boat folded inside it. Or would she let her descendants discover the book packed away in a box of manuscripts as a piece of the puzzle she'd one day leave behind?

Old Mr Gascoigne had a passion for order, which had served him well in every aspect of his life. He was fond of telling everyone, especially his son, that all his success on the land and the flourishing of his Melbourne business interests were due to method. On the day after his arrival at Coombe Bassett he got Grindley to take him around the remnant of the Gascoignes' estate: the gardens—now half wild—the park, the Home Farm, the stables, The Willows—occupied by the sole remaining tenant farmer—and Marsh Farm, where the previous owner had lived for several years. Grindley had now taken over the fields of Marsh Farm for his horses and had installed his head groom and general factotum in the house. There was also a string of tumbledown cottages in the lane leading down to the village green, a small gatekeeper's lodge and, of course, the Old Forge.

The tour took all day. Old Mr Gascoigne pried into weedbeds with his stick and turned over broken flowerpots in the garden sheds. He jotted down the names of unpruned roses in a notebook and attempted to count the fallow deer in the park. He tapped the boles of oak trees, sniffed at pinches of soil and paced around the lake to find its dimensions. Down by the river that flowed between the Home Farm and the manor park he came upon a brick tunnel let into a mound which contained the water pump for the house. Then nothing would do but that he must creep into the tunnel to see the pump at work and assess its efficiency.

There was an old, flat-bottomed boat, operated by ropes

and pulleys, which Grindley reeled into the river bank so that they could cross to the Home Farm. This, too, had to be minutely inspected. On the far side of the stream it was the same. Every tree, every hedgerow, sometimes, it seemed to Grindley, every blade of grass was scrutinised.

'And who lives here?' asked the old man, peering over the gate at the farmhouse.

'Nobody at the moment, but I'll get a manager in before long.'

'It certainly needs some management. Very well. If there's no-one there we can look right through the house. Have you got the key?'

All the time, as they went over the Home Farm, questions came thick and fast. How much hay did the place produce? How many cattle had it carried? How many pigs, ducks, chickens, geese, bees? Grindley floundered. His father began to frown.

At The Willows and Marsh Farm things went rather better because first, the tenant, and next, the head groom, acted as guide and drew Mr Gasgoigne's fire. The Willows was in fair order, though the tenant, scenting an opportunity, kept pointing out improvements he'd like to see. Marsh Farm, all put down to pasture for Grindley's new stud, could hardly be faulted. It seemed, then, the inspection would end on a high note, when, just before sunset, father and son set out along the track that led from the head groom's house to the freshly renovated stables. They passed by a belt of pines planted to keep off the sea wind and were just crossing the lane that led to the village when Mr Gascoigne noticed the cottages away to his left.

'What are these?'

'That's where the farmhands live. And a few old people.'

'D'you mind if we take a look?'

Grindley tried to protest. It was getting close to dinnertime. Before they finished inspecting the stables it would be dark. But his father was already pushing at the gate of the nearest cottage. Unhappily, it was the most dilapidated of all. The thatch had a great hole in it, roughly covered by a bit of old sailcloth. The chimney lurched. The front door was askew. The man of the house was in no better case, lame ever since his foot had been crushed by a wagon wheel. His wife looked half starved, his pack of children had tangled hair and streaming noses. Mr Gascoigne was appalled. He was a devout man and, in Melbourne, had interested himself in the work of several charitable institutions. He was also much in love with the idea of the beneficent squire, who cared for all those who depended on him, and was universally admired for the way in which he discharged his responsibilities. Above all, he hated muddle. The ruinous cottage and its doleful inhabitants shocked him not only because people were living in confusion but also because their condition had been produced by a wretched muddle in his own son's ideas.

'Under your nose!' he barked as he and Grindley made their way back at last to the manor house. 'You show me horses living in the lap of luxury when all the time your people live like dogs. Worse than dogs!'

'Not all of them. It's just that chap. He hasn't worked for a year. But I've let them stay. And the gardener takes them things.'

'Gardener! A cabbage patch and half a dozen carrots! You're a fool. Which might not matter so much if others didn't suffer for your folly. That place should be torn down. The whole lot of them very likely. We'll go tomorrow and make a thorough inspection. And then we'll have plans drawn up for model dwellings. Treat people properly and they'll treat you properly. How can they work when they live in those conditions? And from what I've seen today there's no shortage of work crying out to be done. Where's the sense in spending money on horses when you haven't raised a finger to get your Home Farm in order? You could feed your whole household from there if you took the trouble. What d'you do now? Buy everything in, I suppose, pouring out money you could spend on putting a decent roof over those poor wretches' heads. D'you think I made Murrimbah what it is carrying on like that?

After this there was no more talk of the father being honoured to advise the son. The cottages were to be attended to first, then the Home Farm and the vegetable garden. Mr Gascoigne's temper cooled over the next few days but his mind was made up.

'Of course, we want the place to look dignified,' he said. 'I came here once as a boy. It was a picture in those days. But all in good time. We can get those reeds out of the lake and attend to the flower garden later. And your mother's making a list of repairs she wants done to the house before she gets her decorators in.'

'There was one thing. This house they call the Old Forge. I didn't show you that the other day. It's a pretty place but it needs a good bit of work done. As a matter of fact I've promised a friend I'd let him have it for his sister.'

'But where will you get your men? The builders can't be everywhere.'

'I thought, perhaps, once the cottages are done . . .'

'The Home Farm has to come next.'

'What shall I tell him, then?'

'I wouldn't promise him anything before next year.'

When Kate heard about this she nearly despaired. The only thing that kept her going was the rekindling of Howard's interest. He wrote more often now, arranged more meetings.

Yet, while she was glad of that, she was baffled and frightened by the way he treated her these days once they were locked away in their hotel bedroom. She tried not to think about what he did, to remember only kisses, presents and protestations of love, but sometimes at night she would wake and wonder in terror whether, with half his heart, he had come to despise and loathe her. Why else should he want to hurt and shame her so? Perhaps, in secret, he blamed her for deceiving her husband and thought her love for himself was false and worthless, that, having betrayed one man, she could never again be trusted. And then it would strike her as odd that she had turned against John because of a single blow that had never been repeated, while, again and again, she went back to a man who had taken to beating her soundly every time they met.

Her dream still came at intervals over the months of 1899. Still she laboured along the beach towards the hump on the sand, still she felt a pursuer thudding behind her, still she fell beside the dead woman and buried her face in the damp, sea-smelling cloth of her blue skirt. John, meanwhile, had given up any idea of leaving Beaumont Street. He still went to work, came home again, ate at the kitchen table, slept by his wife at night and spoke occasionally to his children. Once or twice on a Sunday, he took little Annie around the corner to visit the St Clairs.

'Be careful with her,' said Kate. 'Don't you get drunk and let her fall.'

'I'm only going up to the studio.'

'I thought he finished that painting he was doing.'

'So he did. He's on to another now with a little girl in it.'

'And she'll be there, will she? Mrs St Clair? What's she like?'

'All right. She's fond of children.'

'That's easy enough when you haven't got any. I suppose she's pretty, is she?'

'Lovely.'

Kate bit her lip, jealous in spite of everything.

'And you sit there making sheep's eyes at her, I suppose.'

John made no reply. He simply lifted Annie onto his shoulders and walked out. It wasn't Mimi who attracted him so much as the St Clairs' marriage. Although his own seemed bleaker than ever in comparison, it gave him a kind of comfort. He warmed himself at it, like a man frozen to the bone from walking miles on a bitter night. And he liked the way they spoke to him as though they realised he wasn't a common fool but had read books and turned ideas over in his mind. He even took out a few of the books he'd kept from the days in Hampstead and started telling Pendennis what he thought about Marx or the wrangle over the gold and diamond mines in South Africa. He looked at paintings Pendennis put in front of him and borrowed an edition of Swinburne's poems. Sometimes he left the St Clairs' lodgings thinking that talk was cheap and nothing any of them said to each other would make any difference to what went on, but sometimes he felt quite buoyed up. Whatever his mood he usually ended his outing by dropping in at the Three Tuns.

❧

Although one and nine didn't add up to one of her lucky numbers Kate welcomed the new century. Things would be better now, she told herself. From now on, everything would change and go well. Grindley Gascoigne's parents had gone back to Melbourne, leaving the village of Coombe Bassett dazzled and dazed. Everywhere the villagers looked there were gleaming brass plaques: on the new horse trough by the green, on the new font in the church where the memorial tablets of bygone Gascoignes gazed down from the walls, on the new parish hall and on a curiously shaped piece of stone, like a granite lectern, which stood at the corner of the lane where the model cottages had been built. All these plaques recorded the generosity of Edward Moreton Gascoigne, but they represented no more than the tip of the iceberg. The 'Old Squire', as people called him, had left his mark on everything about him. The smith, the carpenter, the wheelwright, the saddler and the stonemason had never been so busy or prosperous. Young people who had drifted away to Taunton and Exeter came tumbling back to work alongside their parents or go into service at the manor. The village shop was given a coat of paint and the public house, though Mr Gascoigne had no wish to increase its trade, put out a new sign. The children, trotting along to their refurbished schoolroom, looked plump and clean. Even the ducks on the village pond seemed larger and whiter than other ducks and preened themselves with a more confident air.

'And he's coming back next year,' groaned Grindley. 'Selling up and coming back for good. And Mother's got this idea I ought to marry. It's all very well. I grant you he's got the place back on its feet but I can't call my soul my own any more.'

Howard, sitting back in his office chair, did nothing but laugh.

'I can't see you've got much to complain about.'

'You don't have to put up with my guv'nor chasing up and down from morning till night. And on Sundays I get dragged off to church. Twice. Twice in one day. You'd better warn Kate about that. She'll have to turn up, too. And so will you when you're in residence. Which reminds me, old chap. The Old Forge is nearly done now. She can move in sometime in April if you like.'

In March 1900, rioting against the Boer War broke out in Scarborough. The following day Lord Roberts took Bloemfontein while Colonel Baden-Powell remained besieged in Mafeking. In Paris, which was visited in the course of the year by a nineteen-year-old painter called Picasso, the Théâtre Français burned to the ground. Pope Leo XIII celebrated his ninetieth birthday. Cambridge won the Boat Race and, to Grindley Gascoigne's delight, the Prince of Wales's horse, Ambush II, won the Grand National. Kate made a flying visit to Coombe Bassett and found the house filled with sunlight and the smell of newly planed wood. Electricity, from a generator that old Mr Gascoigne had ordered for the manor, had been installed, and the house had been connected to the water supply serviced by the pumping apparatus by the river. There were even some handsome carpets and pieces of furniture which Grindley's mother had banished from the manor because they were too modern in design.

'All you have to do,' said Howard, beaming and patting her hand, 'is let us know what else you need and we'll see that the carpenter makes it up for you.'

She went home dizzy with joy and prattled about curtain materials she would buy in London, crockery, mirrors and pianos all the way to the station.

Once back in Beaumont Street she began laying her plans. She and Howard had agreed that the move she had yearned for so long would take place on 17 April. On that day, as soon as John had left for work, she would finish packing her own boxes and all the children's baggage. Meanwhile she would stow some of her hidden treasures in a crate, along with anything she could take from the cupboards in the house without arousing John's suspicions, and send the whole lot off to Devon. Then, on the great day, she would go with Violet, Gilbert, Charles and Annie to Paddington station. Howard had agreed, for once, to meet her at Temple Meads so that he could help her find a porter and see everything safely stowed in the luggage van. Afterwards, all together, they would travel to Coombe Bassett, moving into the light of a new and radiant future.

It all seemed astonishingly simple and straightforward. At the same time there was a good deal to be done. Whatever John or anyone else might think of her, she would never let it be said that she left her house in a bad way. She would see to it that all the tradesmen's bills were paid, the pantry stocked and every room scrubbed out, before she left. As it happened, she was glad to have plenty to do. It helped her to keep her excitement in check so that, to John, she would seem no different from her usual self.

In Bristol, Howard was feeling less ecstatic. Although he'd laughed at Grindley's gloom over his parents' return to Coombe Bassett, when he settled down to think about the news he found it disturbing. A year ago the Old Forge had been the most secluded place imaginable. No-one, apart from the occasional gardener, passed along the track leading up from Church Lane to the Manor House. But, once old Mr Gascoigne and his wife had appeared, the situation had changed. The village had begun to hum with activity. Servants and workmen bustled about the manor grounds every day of the week, and since the track was a shortcut between the church and the manor, on Sunday when the Old Squire was in residence the entire household went trooping up and down. Soon these processions would begin again. Old Mr Gascoigne had cut short his visit to Australia and summoned Grindley to Melbourne to finalise the sale of his property. The Gascoignes would come calling, asking questions, and would go about discussing their charming neighbour, young Mrs Portland, Mr Gale's sister. And sooner or later the tale would come to Bristol where someone who knew very well that he had no sister—or someone who thought it strange that they'd never heard of one—would carry the gossip to Alice or Cynthia Campion.

Just as Howard was reflecting on all this Alice said one morning at breakfast,

'I thought, Howard, we might go away for a few days at the end of the month.'

'I'm sorry, my dear, I can't possibly manage that. I'm rushed off my feet just now. But you go, by all means. Where were you thinking of going? Bournemouth?'

'No, I don't think so. I'd like a change from Bournemouth. I was thinking of Devon—you know, where we used to go. Mrs Riddle's cottage. I used to love it there and we haven't been down for years.'

'It's probably not let out any more. Probably changed hands.'

'Oh no. It's still available. I wrote some time ago to ask about it. Cynthia was interested. She used to go on sketching tours all round that part.'

'You're going with Cynthia?'

'Well, if you can't get away I think perhaps I will. Of course we'll take the children. Richard's been looking rather peaky lately. I expect the country air will do him good.'

'Isn't it rather early in the year for Devon? Far too cold for the seaside surely.'

Alice looked surprised.

'It's too early for sea bathing, of course, but it's quite as warm down there as it is in Bournemouth. I thought we might hire a trap and do some exploring. Cynthia knows some wonderful little villages.'

This threw Howard into a state of panic. The holiday cottage was no more than seven or eight miles from Coombe

481

Bassett, further down the coast. What was more likely than that Cynthia would lead an expedition to view the fine old church, the village green with its oak tree and duckpond? He imagined Alice straying about and catching sight of one of Mr Gascoigne's plaques.

'Gascoigne! But how extraordinary! This must be where Grindley Gascoigne lives, Howard's client. I thought he said it was in Somerset. How strange that he never told me it's so close to the cottage. So this is where he spends so much of his time. Shall we call at the manor and introduce ourselves? Shall we walk up past the church? Oh, Cynthia, what a pretty house! The Old Forge! I wonder who lives there. Shall we ask that man over there, raking the grass?'

The whole thing had been an absurd mistake. He should never have let himself be coaxed into it. The whole point of getting Kate a place away from London was to enable him to enjoy her in peace without having to scheme and lie and look over his shoulder all the time as he had to do when he stole off to meet her in Reading. But it looked now as though he'd jumped out of the frying pan into the fire, that he'd be in far greater danger of discovery with Kate in Devon than he'd ever been before. He decided to write to her and arrange a meeting so that he could tell her their plans would have to be changed. She'd be disappointed, naturally, after waiting so long to become entirely his, but she'd have to trust his judgement, obey his order, accept that he was her master.

'So you see, my dear,' he said as, four days later, they lay in their bed in Reading, 'it's altogether too risky. I'm sorry, but there it is.'

'What shall we do then?'

'Well, I daresay I might be able to scrape up enough for a cottage somewhere a bit later on. But we'll have to make sure it's well out of the way where nobody knows me.'

'After all this time? After two-and-a-half years?'

'It can't be helped.'

'Can't be helped? Is that all you have to say? It can't be helped?'

'Don't talk to me like that,' said Howard, propping himself on one arm and gripping her chin with the other hand. He looked down insolently at her face, excited by her rebellion. Then suddenly she burst into hysterical sobbing, bit madly at his fingers and leaped out of bed.

'I've bought the curtains!' she shrieked. 'I bought the curtains yesterday and I'm going! I won't wait! I won't wait any longer! I don't care if you come or not. I'm going down there.'

Howard was amazed. He simply lay on the bed and gaped. Kate snatched up her clothes and began pulling them on anyhow, shaking, sobbing, pouring out a breathless tirade.

'I've waited all these months, on and on, night after night, day after day in that hole because I thought you loved me. I believed you. I believed you'd take me away from there. And now when it's all settled and the work's done and everything's ready you turn round and try to take it away. Well you won't! I'll go to Grindley. He'll let me stay there whether you're there or not. Don't come! I don't want to see you again. You're nothing but a liar—a great hulking liar and a cheat and a bully. Go back to your wife! Keep away from me!'

'Go to Grindley?' Howard shot upright, kicking furiously at the bedclothes. 'You whore! What've you been up to behind my back?'

Kate snatched up her coat and fled to the door but, before she could turn the key, Howard was on her, shaking her violently back and forth, shouting, 'What's this? What's this about Gascoigne? What's this?'

483

'Nothing! I've done nothing! But I will! I will if you try to stop me now!'

'I'll smash you to atoms first!'

Howard drew back his arm to hit her but Kate wrenched herself free and ran across the room crying, 'Ah! Ah! Ah!' Such loud, guttural screams that Howard was frightened. He thought everyone in the hotel would come running and, realising he was still stark naked, tore at his heap of clothing, hunting for his trousers.

Kate stopped screaming and sank to the ground, sobbing, 'Of course it's you I love. Of course it is. But I can't go on as I am. I can't! I can't!'

Howard tried to get her onto her feet.

'Stand up. Stand up when I tell you!'

'I don't care what you do to me. You can do what you like. But I must get away from London. I can't go on.'

'And you haven't been seeing Gascoigne on the sly?'

'I've told you. Of course I haven't. I only meant he was kind and would let me stay.'

'Does it mean so much to you? Having that house?'

'How can you ask? You know. Of course it does.'

'But what,' said Howard, beginning to stroke her hair and purr over her like a lion, 'if someone who knows I have no sister hears about you?'

'Couldn't you make something up? Say I'd been kept out of the way for some reason? Because of some scandal or something?'

'A little bastard, smuggled away at birth and revealed to me in a deathbed repentance?'

'Something like that.'

'Or a bad lot disowned by her sorrowing parents?'

'If you like.'

'Well, we'll see.'

'Then I can go on the seventeenth? We can go on after all?'

'Provided I can trust you with young Gascoigne. What about when I'm away all week?'

'You know I'd never look at anyone else. I'm sorry if I made it sound like that.'

'I don't think you're penitent enough by a long chalk.'

~

Old Mr Gascoigne had dreams that went beyond the improvement of the existing estate at Coombe Bassett. He also wanted to restore it to its original size and was already negotiating, through Howard and Grindley, for the purchase of Giant Tump's Farm which lay to the north of the manor and owed its name to a curious knob of rock on its eastern boundary. Giant's Tump, its domed top sparsely covered with bracken and grass, projected into the sea, closing off the western end of the beach which flanked Marsh Farm and part of the manor grounds.

'Here it is,' said Grindley, spreading out his map. 'It's a queer shaped property. Look here, it goes all along the coast behind the manor and then on past Home Farm and The Willows. It was sold off about twelve years ago. Can't say I care much for the chap who's bought it. He's kicking up a fuss now about shooting rights. Anyway, I said we'd go over to see him on the seventeenth.'

'That's the day Kate's coming down,' said Howard. 'I'm to meet her at Temple Meads.'

'But I can't put Pollinger off. You told me the seventeenth weeks ago. We've got to get this settled, old chap, before I leave, or I'll have my guv'nor down on me like a ton of bricks.'

'Won't the eighteenth do?'

'Pollinger's an awkward old devil. If he thinks we're playing fast and loose he'll very likely call the whole thing off.

485

Look here, can't you meet Kate in Barnstaple? She won't get there before two-thirty. We'll thrash out the shooting-rights business and try and get old Pollinger nailed down in the morning and then we'll have a bite of lunch and you can go straight to the station.'

'I suppose I could.'

Howard had always felt uneasy about appearing with Kate in Bristol and although she seemed contrite enough about turning against him he felt it would do her no harm to be reminded that he was the one who gave the orders. So he wrote her a note, addressed as usual to her local post office, explaining that business prevented him from coming to Temple Meads and that he would meet her instead in Barnstaple. He posted this on Friday 13 April, quite sure that it would reach her before she set out on the following Tuesday. She was certain, he told himself, to call at the post office on Monday to see if he had sent any last minute instructions.

But Kate did nothing of the sort. She made her final round of the local shops on Friday afternoon. On Monday she stayed at home, feverishly sorting the last of the clothes and packing what she could. She washed the windows, polished up the range and stood at the parlour window, staring out at Beaumont Street and trying to grasp the fact that after tomorrow morning she would never stand in that spot or look out at that street ever again in her life. Such thoughts gave the whole day a dream-like quality. Knowing that soon she would never again go back and forth from the kitchen to the scullery, or climb the narrow stairs to the bedrooms, she became aware of sounds she'd never listened to before—the tap of her steps, the swish of her dress—and saw for the first time nail-holes in the walls, a stain like a dog's head on the scullery ceiling, so that, as in a dream, the familiar things of everyday seemed mysteriously changed.

She wondered if she should run up to the post office but decided not to partly because she feared more than anything that Howard might try yet again to keep her in London. She was going to Devon whatever happened. If he ordered her to stay where she was she was better off knowing nothing about it.

Late in the afternoon she went into the parlour and wrote a note to John:

> Dear John,
> I have gone away with the children to a safe place. I am at the end of my tether. Please do not try to find us. We are better apart I am sure. I hope you will go on well.
>
> Kate.

There seemed to be no more that she could say. She put the letter in her apron pocket ready for the morning when she would leave it propped against the kitchen clock.

∾

At Temple Meads Kate looked out anxiously over the crowd on the platform. At every second she expected to see Howard, standing a head taller than anyone around him, watching the carriages sliding to a halt or waving his hat to show he'd caught sight of her. When she failed to find him she got down from the train reluctantly, afraid that he might have trouble seeing her once she was hidden in the throng. Annie clung to her neck, Charlie hung onto her skirt but Gilbert began hopping about, jigging in and out of the crowd. Violet ran after him, shouting, 'Come here, you Bertie! Don't run away! You're a bad boy!'

She wanted her mother to hear, not to get Gilbert into

trouble so much as to show how helpful she was being on this great, surprising day of the sudden holiday and the ride on the train.

'I'll have to get the boxes off,' said Kate faintly. She turned this way and that, looking for a porter, still hoping that Howard would come bursting through the crowd and be there, strong and commanding, to protect her. She stared up at the station clock. The Taunton train was leaving in twenty minutes but she didn't dare have the luggage taken to another platform. Instead, she got the porter to leave it piled up around her like the blocks of a fort. Gilbert began scrambling over the heap at once, reached the topmost box and jumped up and down chanting, 'I'm the king of the castle! You're the dirty rascal!'

Charlie, dressed in his best blue serge frock trimmed with white braid, left his mother and ran to join the game. Violet, looking sideways at Kate, called out, 'Get down, Bertie! Don't do that! Don't Charlie! You'll spoil your pretty frock.'

She caught hold of Charlie and led him back to Kate.

'Bertie's being naughty. He won't get down.'

Kate, still nursing Annie, hardly heard. The crowd had thinned now. She gazed from the station entrance to the clock and back again. What was she to do? She tried to think calmly. Perhaps Howard had been delayed at the last minute by some accident. His wife might be ill again or one of his children. Perhaps a letter, warning her that he couldn't be at Temple Meads had come yesterday to the post office in Holborn. Perhaps, then, nothing much had changed. Howard still loved her and still wanted her to come to Devon. He would be waiting at Taunton or Barnstaple or, if something had prevented him from leaving home, he would come to her at the Old Forge as soon as he could. But as she ran through these comforting, sensible explanations Kate became convinced they were all false. The real reason for Howard's failure to meet her had to be linked in some way with what had happened in Reading, with Howard's announcement that the Old Forge was too open to discovery or his rage at the thought of her being unfaithful to him with Grindley Gascoigne, his resentment of her defiance of his will.

Kate began to pace up and down, holding Annie's silky dark head against her cheek. Violet trotted after her calling, 'I got Charlie down, Ma!'

If they were to catch the Taunton train they would have to move at once.

'Are we going on another train now?'

'I don't know. Just leave me alone a moment.'

One thing was certain. They couldn't go back to London. They had to go forward. The hands of the clock clicked on. Again she looked towards the entrance, willing Howard to appear, to come running towards her. If he came in the next minute and they all hurried off at once they might still catch the train and the day would go on as she had imagined it. But, no, he wasn't there. They had missed the train. Everything she'd dreamed of was falling in ruins.

'What can I do?' she asked aloud, sinking down on her trunk.

She looked so pale and distraught that an elderly woman, passing along the platform, stopped to ask if she felt faint.

'Can I fetch you something, my dear, from the refreshment room? A little brandy?'

The children came crowding round to see what was happening.

'Don't you feel well, Ma?'

'We're going on our holidays,' said Gilbert. 'At the seaside. And Ma says there's a pony we can ride. I'll ride 'im! I'll gallop everywhere.'

And he started galloping and snorting among the boxes to demonstrate his intention.

'I have to get to Taunton,' said Kate to the stranger.

'But the train's just gone. There's not another till two o'clock.'

'We'll catch that then.'

'It's a long time to wait with the children. Shall I get a porter to put your boxes in the cloakroom? Then you could get away from here. D'you know anyone in Bristol? Somewhere you could go and lie down for a while?'

Kate shook her head. Since the encounter well over a year ago she had seen nothing of either Mrs Duke or Jimmy, though Mrs Duke had written once or twice to remind the Phillipses that James was all hers and, as a result, doing very well. Jimmy himself, to everyone's surprise, had sent Violet several accounts of butterfly-hunting expeditions, with instructions to read them out to the other children. Since Violet was slow to learn her letters, Kate had read them instead, though afterwards Violet would sit with the pages in her hand, mouthing over the words she couldn't read.

'Why don't you come over to the ladies' waiting room, dear?' urged the stranger. 'You'll be more comfortable there.'

Kate, who was beginning to find her new friend's attentions oppressive, roused herself to say firmly that she was quite well now and would stay where she was for a time. When the woman had moved away she found some pennies in her purse and told Violet to take the younger ones to the refreshment room and buy them each a cake. At this even Annie allowed herself to be prised loose and led away. Kate watched the four of them running along the platform, so intent on their cakes, so oblivious of everything else that it nearly broke her heart. She felt a spurt of fury against

Howard. It was all very well for him to punish her but how could he vent his spite on her little children?

She got up and began to pace about again. She was in a fever to know what was going on. She longed to be at Coombe Bassett where she would find the answer to the riddle. Yet, at the same time, she was fearful of what might be waiting for her. She couldn't believe—not quite believe—that Howard had actually left her so cruelly, so abruptly, after all that had passed between them. Perhaps he was simply demonstrating that he would meet her where he, and not she, chose and would be there at Taunton or Barnstaple or Coombe Bassett when she arrived, angry at her having missed the Taunton train and having kept him waiting. But he would be there after all, so that in a day or two everything would flow on calmly as she had dreamed it would and this interval at Temple Meads, the awful uncertainty and fear, would dwindle away into the past and be forgotten.

It was more likely, though, she thought, that he was standing by what he'd said to her in Reading, that he regretted letting her break down his resolve and had written to tell her to stay in Beaumont Street. If this was so he might not be in Devon at all, and, if he was there, he would be absolutely enraged by her arrival. It would look as though she was carrying out the threat she'd made, defying him, coming to throw herself on Grindley's mercy.

She began to tremble. She had never really faced the consequences of actually doing what she had threatened. The very idea took her breath away. She knew that Grindley admired and liked her. On the two occasions they had met he had gone out of his way to please her and make her welcome. He had a kind heart and liked children. But would he be willing to harbour her and her brood if it meant defying Howard? Would he sacrifice an established friendship and lose his man of business for the sake of a woman he knew so slightly? There could be only one reason powerful enough to sway him. And how could she even think of that when she loved Howard? Had Howard been right to call her a whore? When it came down to it, if she had to choose between Grindley and the Old Forge and Howard and who-knew-where—the cottage he'd said he couldn't afford, the foreign place she knew they'd never reach, Beaumont Street to which she could never return—what would she do? Could she really think of making love with Grindley? The round red face and paunchy little body in her bed? The round black eyes and grinning clown's mouth? How could she even think of it? But if Howard spurned her, ordered her back to London, shouted that unless she obeyed he was finished with her for good, what else could she do? She was adrift in the world with four children, a mound of baggage and a hundred pounds. She had to find a home and a protector.

Far down the platform the children were emerging from the refreshment room. Annie seemed to be crying. Violet, standing over her, stamped her foot. Gilbert capered about, waving his arms. Charlie, in his blue frock, stood holding his cake in both hands. How on earth was she to manage? How could she take them down to Coombe Bassett when she had no idea what she'd find when she arrived? Whatever happened she'd have to give all her mind to winning over one man or the other. How could she do that with Annie clinging to her neck, Charlie sticking like a burr, Gilbert running wild and Violet watching every move she made? And what if, when she got to Barnstaple, there was nobody to meet them and the station fly was taken? She could walk to Coombe Bassett if need be but it was much too far for the children. Night would be coming on. It would be dark and cold. And what if the Old Forge was locked and barred when they reached the end of their journey? What if Howard turned her away and Grindley wouldn't help her? No, it was impossible. For one night at least, just until she had made sure she could find a roof to put over their heads, the children would have to stay in Bristol.

∿

'Splendid!' said Grindley. 'Splendid! The guv'nor'll be no end pleased. And I can go off to Melbourne knowing everything's as it should be.'

He beamed and hooked his thumbs in the armholes of his waistcoat. Some of the village wiseacres had prophesied a storm but the day had turned out gloriously fine. The manor grounds had never looked better. Beyond the gravelled semicircle in front of the house gardeners were busy among the rose bushes. The oaks and beeches in the park were in new leaf and beneath their boughs the first bluebells showed as a faint blue mist.

'Not a bad morning's work at all. I'm no end grateful, old boy. You handled old Pollinger like an out and out champion.'

'I think we did pretty well.' Howard pulled out his watch. 'Where's that carriage?'

'Be here in a minute. Now when you get back I'll have a few chaps ready to take the baggage in. D'you think a drop of champagne would be in order?'

'Very good of you.'

Something in Howard's tone made Grindley look up.

'I just thought I'd walk down to welcome her, old chap. I won't stay long.'

'I'm sure she'll be delighted to see you.'

Grindley laughed. 'She won't want to be bothered with me. Not with you about.'

Howard nearly snapped back, 'And when I'm not about?' but managed to keep silent. From time to time the suspicion Kate had planted in his mind rose up to irk him, but he knew very well in his heart there was nothing in it. He could read Grindley like a book. If there had been anything between him and Kate it would have shown at once in his look and manner. Women were always making up such stories to stir up trouble. He doubted that he would ever quite forgive Kate for stooping so low.

When the carriage horses came jingling round the bend in the path to the stables Grindley gave an exclamation and rushed forward.

'What the devil are you doing there, Tilly? Where's Pitcher?'

The young coachman, in a fluster at being late, said Mr Pitcher had felt poorly after his dinner and gone back home.

'We can't have this,' said Grindley to Howard. 'That lad'll never manage the new wheeler. Get down out of that, Tilly. I'll drive myself. Sorry, old boy, to come barging in like this but the chap's just not up to it. He'd have the whole lot of you in the ditch as like as not.'

So poor young Tilly went trailing back to the stables and Grindley, with Howard up on the box beside him, set off at a spanking pace down the drive. Despite the skittishness of the new wheeler they made good time to Barnstaple, arriving only a minute or two after the train from Taunton had pulled in at the station. But Kate, of course, was not there. After a few minutes Howard came back to the carriage with a face like a thundercloud.

'After all that she seems to have missed the train.'

'Oh, Lord!' said Grindley. 'I daresay it's my fault. She might not have got your letter in time, old chap. Probably waited for you at Temple Meads. D'you think she'll be on the five-thirty?'

'She'll come. Wild horses wouldn't stop her. But what on earth are we to do for three hours? It's hardly worth going back to the manor.'

'We could go to the Crown, I suppose. Have a glass of something.'

'I don't fancy kicking my heels in an inn all the afternoon. What about that friend of yours with the yearling you wanted to see?'

'Jerry Falcombe? I don't know. It's a good eight miles to his place from here.'

'We can manage that, surely. It'd be better than waiting about. And it's a capital day for a drive.'

Grindley was uneasy. He remembered what he'd heard about a storm before nightfall but he thought a decent stretch with himself on the box would help settle the flighty young wheeler so he fell in with Howard's suggestion. At first everything went very well. The sun shone, the wheeler behaved himself and Howard became more affable.

'Isn't Falcombe the fellow who's mad about motor cars?'

'That's the one! Selling off half his horses. He's off to Italy soon to see some race and he's just got this Dion something-or-other sent over from Paris.'

'Well, they're the coming thing. No horse can go at twelve miles an hour all day long can it?'

'Don't know as I'd want to, old chap.'

They drove on and were within sight of the gates of Falcombe Hall when a strange noise caught their ears. Suddenly out of the drive, tooting madly and enveloped in smoke, burst Lord Falcombe in his new Dion-Bouton. The wheeler attempted to rear. The other horses panicked and, before Grindley could get them under control, shot through a

495

gateway on the left, whacking the carriage wheels against the gatepost.

∽

'What is it, Polly?' asked Mrs Duke. None of her maids-of-all-work gave much satisfaction but Polly, the latest in a long line, was worse than most. 'Is there somebody at the door?'

'Yes, mum. There's a lady and four kids with boxes.'

'Did you ask her name?'

'No, mum. She wants you.'

'But you must always ask the name. Go back and find out who she is.'

There was a commotion in the hall outside the morning room door. Gilbert had escaped into the house, with Violet in hot pursuit.

'What on earth is going on?'

Majestically Mrs Duke moved to the door and flung it open. She saw a small boy rolling on the carpet and a solid child with her hat knocked over her eyes tugging at his arm. Beyond, at the front door, Kate Phillips, with two more children and a heap of boxes, was making frantic gestures. Mrs Duke stared at her. She was even more extravagantly got up than on her last visit to Bristol.

'Oh, Elizabeth-Jane,' she said, 'I'm sorry to come like this without any warning. I'm taking the children down to the country but I've just heard the cottage isn't ready. I'll have to go ahead and sort it all out. So I thought, perhaps, you wouldn't mind if the children stayed with you tonight.'

'What? Stay here?'

'Tomorrow if you wouldn't mind taking them to Temple Meads and leaving them with the guard they can catch the eleven-thirty to Taunton. Here. This is the money for their tickets. Get down, Annie dear. Now Violet come to me a minute.'

'But I can't possibly undertake . . .'

Mrs Duke was cut short by Gilbert who was trying to edge past her in order to explore the morning room. She seized him and gave him a shake.

'Haven't you any manners, little boy? Don't you know you must never push uninvited into someone else's house?'

But Kate, who was meant to hear this, was tucking some money into Violet's pocket.

'When you get to Taunton ask the guard to put you all on the train for Barnstaple,' she whispered. 'But it's a secret. Don't tell the lady. I'll meet you there. Will you be all right? Can you remember the name? Barnstaple?'

Violet nodded.

'Are you going away now, Ma?'

'I have to go. Thank you, Elizabeth-Jane. Their boxes are here with all their night things. And if anything should happen, if there's a change, I'll telegraph. Goodbye. Thank you. Annie, go to Violet.'

And she left. Mrs Duke, throwing dignity to the winds, ran after her, but Kate was too quick. She had a cab waiting at the gate and was inside with the door slammed before Mrs Duke could reach the pavement.

∾

Lord Falcombe was extremely apologetic. He did everything he could to make amends. The horses, one of them lamed in the accident, were taken off to his stables. A wheelwright was sent for to look at the wrecked carriage.

'The devil of it,' said Grindley, 'is we must be back in Barnstaple by half-past five.'

Lord Falcombe offered to drive them in his Dion-Bouton and when it was explained to him that this wouldn't meet the case, that there was a lady, four children and a mass of luggage to be conveyed to Coombe Bassett, he suggested that Grindley and Howard should take his own carriage. The only trouble was that old Lady Falcombe, who had come from Weston to visit her son, had driven off in the carriage to pay an afternoon call.

'Don't worry,' said Lord Falcombe. 'I know where she'll be. It's no distance at all. I'll dash over now in the Dion and get her back. I say, why don't you fellows come too? Or d'you want to stay and take a look at that horse?'

Grindley and Howard decided to salvage what was left of the afternoon by doing what they'd planned so they walked up to the stables to watch a stableboy put the yearling through his paces. Grindley was disappointed. He told Howard he wouldn't give tuppence for a horse like that and, pulling out his watch, pointed out that it was nearly half-past four. It was high time they were starting back to Barnstaple but there was no sign of Jerry Falcombe, his mother or the carriage. They went back to the house and waited. The sky was clouding over now and the maid who brought them some tea prophesied, like the Coombe Bassett villagers, that a storm was coming. It was black as ink over Ilfracombe way, she said.

'This is absurd,' snapped Howard.

He stood at the window in a rising temper. Five o'clock had come and gone. Eventually, at a quarter-past five, Jerry Falcombe came chugging up the drive, leaped out of his motor car and erupted into the drawing room full of fresh apologies. Lady Falcombe had turned aside from her intended path to speak to the vicar and, seated in the vicarage, had fallen into a light doze. It had taken much longer than he'd expected to run her to earth and get her back into the carriage. Even then, she'd refused to allow the coachman to whip up his horses since she was absolutely terrified of speed. But when the carriage finally arrived neither Grindley nor Howard could imagine that she would have been in much danger. In contrast to Grindley's dashing turnout, the Falcombe carriage was a heavy, solid vehicle with a team to match and a bowed, lugubrious coachman.

'Of course,' said Lord Falcombe, noticing his visitors' looks of dismay, 'I'm getting rid of it soon. My wife and I hardly use the thing now we've got the Dion.'

The coachman was not pleased at the prospect of turning around, driving to Barnstaple and then going on to Coombe Bassett. He pointed his whip at the darkening sky and said his horses couldn't stand lightning. But at last they got away, jogging sedately through the louring evening. It was half-past five. Kate, at that very moment, was arriving at Barnstaple station.

All the way from Bristol in the train she had tried to convince herself that there was nothing seriously wrong, that Howard had simply been delayed in Devon, that he'd realised she'd missed the morning train and would be there at Barnstaple waiting for her. If he failed to come it would mean that he'd written, asserting again that any idea of the Old Forge must be abandoned, or, worse still, that he'd decided to have done with her for good. But could he do such a thing? Let her come away from home with her children and then simply leave her to fend for herself? Was it possible that he'd been so angry at what she'd said about Grindley that he'd thought to himself, 'Then let him have her'?

She could hardly bear to look out at the platform when the train came to a halt. She bowed her head as she climbed down, thinking that when she looked up she would see Howard close to her. And when she saw that he wasn't there she clung to the hope, as she'd done at Temple Meads, that he was late, just a few minutes late and would come running up just as she was showing the guard her luggage and getting it stowed away in the cloakroom. She stood out on the platform until all the other passengers had gone. Then she sat in the waiting room for a time. At last she went out and asked the stationmaster if she could hire the station fly but he said it had gone off towards Falcombe and, since the driver lived out that way, wouldn't be back till morning.

'Can I leave my luggage here? I'll just take the carpetbag and come for the rest tomorrow.'

The stationmaster nodded. 'You got far to go?'

'Not very.'

'Cause if you have, ma'am, I'd not try to get there tonight. Stop at the Crown. There's a storm coming.'

Kate said nothing. She couldn't bear to wait a moment longer. She thought of walking up to the inn to see if she could hire a gig or something of the kind but she couldn't endure to delay even for that. She had to get on the road to Coombe Bassett to find out once and for all what had happened, what awaited her there. So she walked as quickly as she could out through the station gate, down through the end of the town and on to the coast road. Thunder muttered in the distance. The sky grew darker and darker, the sunset blotted out by a bank of cloud. Where the road wound through a patch of woodland she could hardly see her hand in front of her face. The wind was getting up. A few raindrops pattered on the brim of her hat. Lightning flashed far out over the sea. Kate began to walk faster and faster. She looked back over her shoulder, hoping that someone in a cart or a pony and trap might come along. It began to rain in earnest. The thunder rolled closer and when she next glanced back she was horrified to see a flicker of lightning, like a white hot wire, dancing in the looming curtain of grey that shut off the world behind her. And then the downpour increased to an absolute torrent. She was deafened and blinded. She might have been standing under a cataract. She felt her clothes contract to a clinging sodden weight, pulling her earthwards, dragging against her legs. Her feet squelched in her shoes as she staggered along with her eyes screwed up and her mouth open, crying and wailing.

Gradually the roaring of the rain began to abate. The thunder rolled again but further off. When she opened her stinging eyes Kate could see the outline of hedges rising against the sky ahead and, far away, a light that might be the window of a house or someone with a lantern on the road. She could hardly get along. Her skirt, plastered against her thighs, trailed behind in the mud, hauling against each step she tried to make. The bag had become a sodden lump, four or five times its previous weight, so that every so often she had to rest it on the ground and bend over gasping with one hand pressed to her side. The feather in her hat had become a dripping rat's tail whipping against her neck. At times she thought of pulling off her skirt and hat and throwing them with the bag into the ditch but she felt that to do that would be like stripping herself for death, giving up any idea of meeting people again. How could she appear before anyone else in her petticoat, hatless like a farmgirl, with no luggage to prove her station in life?

She had strange thoughts as she crept along in the dark. She remembered stories her father had told of old times when they used to get hold of women in the villages—scolds or old hags thought to be witches—and duck them in the millpond. When she was a girl she'd seen a ducking-stool in a village near Chippenham. She imagined the loneliness under the dark water, the cold piercing the clothes, the roaring in the ears.

And the men high and dry up in the sunshine laughing. Punishment, as she was punished now, all alone in the wet, cut off from everybody. She thought of all the other people in the world who were not her and had never heard of her—people living far away in the places she'd talked of with Howard where it was a bright day now, or where there were lights in the streets and cafés and men in evening dress going up and down contentedly with women in dazzling gowns and diamonds.

Had she known of it she might have thought of the opening of the Paris Universal Exhibition where visitors were touring the site on moving platforms powered by electricity, exclaiming over X-ray photography and wireless telegraphy, or gazing at the Art Nouveau furniture, Tiffany lamps, jewellery by Lalique or landscapes by the once-controversial Claude Monet. Right now, across the Irish Sea Queen Victoria, in the year before her death, was expressing appreciation of the valour of the Irish regiments in the Boer War, and far away on the other side of the earth on a fine warm morning in early autumn, the inhabitants of the little isolated colony of Tasmania were looking forward with mixed feelings to the era of Australian Federation.

The light that Kate had seen came and went as the road dipped into hollows or ran past thickets of trees, but at last it established itself as a small square, the window of a cottage. After what seemed to be hours Kate arrived, exhausted and chilled to the bone, at the cottage gate. It was a poor little place with only two or three rooms. The path to the front door was half closed by dripping bushes. Kate pushed her way through and, dropping her bag, banged on the door. There was dead silence for a time then a quavering voice called, 'Who's there?'

'I've been caught in the rain! Please can I come in for a minute?'

The door opened a crack and a very old woman peered out. When she saw Kate in the lamplight she pulled the door back and stared in amazement.

'Oh, my dear, you have had a wetting!'

She looked doubtfully at Kate's muddy skirt.

'I'll get a sack you can stand on.'

She vanished for a moment then beckoned Kate in and motioned to her to stand on a sack by the door. Kate unpinned her hat. The old woman put out her hand for it and stood looking from the bedraggled object she was holding to its owner and back again.

'However did you come to be out in that storm like that?'

Kate, stepping out of her skirt, peeling off her jacket, was shivering so violently she could hardly speak. The cottager, shocked and mystified that a lady in a feathered hat should get into such a pickle, saw that explanations would have to wait.

'You'd best get those shoes off and come over to the fire.'

It was only a little fire but Kate crouched down before it, holding out her hands.

The old woman made small, uncertain movements as though she wanted to test the wetness of Kate's underclothes but didn't dare touch her. In any case, since water was still dripping from her petticoat on to the floor, it was clear that the mysterious visitor was soaked to the skin.

'I'll get you something to dry yourself and something else to put on. Dear, oh dear, what a thing!'

Kate began to pull off the rest of her clothes. Now that her hands were warmer, the wet skin of her thighs as she peeled away her stockings felt icy to the touch. The cloth on her shoulders clung like a second skin, coming away with a sucking sound from the flesh.

The old woman had hobbled away upstairs and was bumping about in the room above. Eventually she came back

503

down again with an armful of clothes and a square of clean cloth to use as a towel.

'These were my sister's,' she said. 'I've always kept 'em ever since she went. That'd be nineteen years now. Nineteen years I've been here on my own.'

When Kate had rubbed herself down and put on the drawers, skirt and bodice she was given, the two of them gathered up the wet clothes from the floor, wrung them out and hung them on hooks in the walls or rafters to dry. Then they sat down by the fire to wait for the kettle to boil for tea.

The old woman's name was Selina Biggadike. Her husband had been lost at sea when she was young. She had two sons, one in the army and one a fisherman. After her boys left home she'd moved with her unmarried sister into this cottage. 'Thirty years ago that'd be,' she said. 'Eleven years we were here before Lucy passed on.'

Kate looked around. The place was very bare—a table, a dresser, a rag rug, a tin bowl on a packing case. Mrs Biggadike's sons couldn't have sent her much. As she sipped her tea Kate felt tearful and weak. She would have liked to tell the old woman her whole story and ask her advice but she knew very well that any respectable woman, even the poorest of the poor, would regard her with scorn if she ever confessed the truth. So she said only that she was taking the Old Forge as a tenant and that the people who were meant to meet her in Barnstaple had missed her somehow at the station.

'A carriage went by about two. I looked out but I couldn't see much for the bushes. I think it was Squire's, though, with the grey horses.'

'They expected me to get the earlier train,' said Kate. At news of the carriage, hope leaped up. She felt a great rush of energy, longing to be on her way again, as though for an hour or so she'd been washed aside into the shallows of a river and was back now in midstream. She stood up and asked if she could borrow a shawl. The rain had stopped altogether but the wind was rising. She could hear it in the trees around the cottage.

'You're never going on there tonight! It's a good three mile.'

'They'll be worried about me. I expect they're looking for me.'

'I don't know that carriage went back. Course it might've done when I was out with the bees. But you'll never walk all that way on your own in the dark.'

In the end, though, Kate had her way. She took a few things out of the carpetbag—her purse, a brush and comb—and because Mrs Biggadike had nothing else to lend her, tucked them into a chaff bag on a string. She would have liked to take a change of clothes but, as Mrs Biggadike said, everything in the bag was as wet as muck and would have to be hung up to dry with the walking costume. As she was leaving Kate took ten shillings from her purse. The old woman looked at the money in amazement.

'Whatever's that for?'

'The tea and everything. You've been very kind.'

'Tea don't cost ten shilling.'

But in the end Mrs Biggadike took what she was offered and put it away in a tea caddy on the dresser.

Although her shoes were still damp and the night was cold, Kate went along much more cheerfully than when she'd first started out. Mrs Biggadike's glimpse of the carriage going towards Barnstaple had changed everything. Grindley's parents used the carriage but he himself preferred the gig. The carriage had been brought out expressly to meet her, to carry her four children and all her luggage. When she hadn't appeared at two-thirty, Grindley and Howard must have driven home again. It was strange that they hadn't realised that she would be on the later train, but she had no doubt now that Howard was at Coombe Bassett, wondering what had become of her, longing for her to come to him.

∽

About halfway to Barnstaple the party from Falcombe met the station fly on the road. Grindley spotted it driving towards a bend up ahead, jumped out and spoke to the driver. Howard, leaning from the carriage window, saw the man shake his head. No, there weren't any children on the train from Taunton, not at half-past five. He was sure of that because his fare had engaged him beforehand and he'd gone on to the platform to wait for him. There wouldn't have been more than a dozen got off at Barnstaple. An artist chap, the local doctor, a few ladies he'd never seen before, but no children.

'I can't imagine what she's done,' said Howard. 'I'm sorry she's putting you to all this trouble.'

'No trouble, old chap. Anyway, that fellow might have missed them somehow. Ten to one we'll find them at the station wondering what on earth's become of us.'

They jogged on. The sky darkened. The rain began. A mile out of Barnstaple the storm that had broken over Kate's head burst upon them. The coachman, with considerable presence of mind, managed to get off the road into a farmyard where he drove straight into an empty barn. He clambered down from his box, his coat hanging about him like a dripping cassock and went to his horses' heads, calling, 'Whoa! Steady there! Whoa!', as if the whole team were about to bolt. In fact they merely shifted their feet uneasily when the thunder rolled, meek as four fat donkeys in their sodden harness.

Grindley and Howard got out of the carriage and stood gazing at the teeming rain beyond the barn door.

'I told 'ee a storm was coming,' shouted the coachman. They could hardly hear him above the roar of water. Grindley took out his watch and showed it to Howard, tapping the dial with a forefinger. It was nearly a quarter to seven. Howard spread his hands in exasperation.

'We can't go on in this.'

'At least if they're at the station they'll be under cover.'

When the noise abated Grindley suggested to the coachman that he might find a dry coat at the farmhouse, but the old man with a bitter look said the place was empty. Once the rain had eased they went on again. Grindley, anxious about mistreating another man's servant, assured the coachman they'd find him a dry set of clothes at the Crown in Barnstaple but asked him to look in at the station first. The coachman said nothing. He drove at a snail's pace through the wet streets, coughing and groaning piteously, and while Howard hurried into the station to speak to the stationmaster, sat hunched on his box, the picture of ill-usage.

The stationmaster confirmed all that the driver of the station fly had told them.

'I can't understand it,' said Howard. 'She must have missed the train at Taunton. If she hadn't left London she'd have telegraphed.'

'We'd better get this poor old chap up to the inn.'

'And have a bit of dinner. I don't know about you but I'm ravenous.'

'Oh Lord! Cook'll be in a state. I told her dinner for three at eight sharp.'

At the Crown Grindley saw to it that the old coachman was made warm and dry and dosed with hot toddy. Afterwards, over the chops and boiled potatoes, he told Howard that he couldn't see them getting back to Coombe Manor before tomorrow.

'We can't drag Falcombe's chap all out there tonight. They'll give us a bed here. Then if Kate comes in from Taunton in the morning we'll be here to meet her.'

❦

When James came home with Uncle Bert he was astonished to find a girl in a frilly blouse and a straw hat swinging on the front gate. It was getting dark so that he didn't at first recognise his sister.

'Is your mother here then?' asked Uncle Bert.

'No. She's gone to Taunton. But she's going to meet us off the train tomorrow.'

'Taunton?'

'We're going for a holiday. Bertie and Charlie and Annie and me. I expect you could come too if you like, Jimmy. If she'd let you. That lady, Aunt Elizabeth-Jane.'

'Well,' said Uncle Bert, 'we'd better get inside and sort this out.'

'I can't come in. She said I was rude and I'd have to stay out here. I said we ought to have some dinner because we only had a cake at the station.'

'Quite right,' said Uncle Bert unexpectedly.

'Charlie was crying because he was hungry. And Annie. But Annie always cries. She's been crying all the time since Ma went.'

Inside they found Polly standing in the hall and gaping up at the ceiling. They could hear faint yells and thumps from somewhere upstairs.

'It's that boy Bertie, sir,' whispered Polly. 'Just listen to 'im!'

'Where is he?'

'Missis shut 'im and the little boy in Master James's room. They was running round the house like a pair of mad things. And now Missis's in bed with a sick headache and Cook and me's afraid 'e'll 'ave the door down.'

'And where's the little girl?'

'Cook's got 'er in the kitchen giving 'er a bit of bread and milk.'

'Good Lord!' said Uncle Bert, stripping off his coat. 'And where's the key to Master James's room?'

'Missis left it on the morning room table.'

'Better get them out, James. Then we'll have to see about some supper. I don't suppose Cook could find something?'

Polly shook her head. 'There's just that bit of mutton for the three, sir. And the Missis's things. But Cook wouldn't like to touch them.'

'Well then, we'd better get some pies and buns hadn't we, James?'

So James went off to the pie shop in Zetland Road. He wasn't really surprised that his brothers and sisters had been sent to Mrs Duke, and although he pitied them, he felt enormously elated. He didn't believe the stuff about the holiday because talk about holidays was nearly always some sort of blind or trick. Even if Violet got all of them to Taunton they'd soon be shunted back to Bristol. He'd have to teach them ways of staying out of trouble while he was away with Uncle Bert in the daytime and if, when he came home at night, they were locked in the cellar, Uncle Bert would let them out.

He tried to reassure Violet on this score after supper when Polly was getting bolsters from the linen cupboard and making up beds. But she didn't seem to understand what he was saying. She kept on about James going to Taunton and after that to another secret place.

'I can't,' he said. 'I've got to help Uncle Bert.'

'Don't you go to school?'

'Yes, I go to Mr and Mrs Ffoulkes. I used to just do reading and writing and sums but now I do the same as the other boys. Only after school I go down to the shop and on Sundays we go out after butterflies.'

'The ones you said about catching in the letters?'

'I've got a lot now. All properly mounted and everything. Except for one I keep here—the first one I ever caught.'

'Can I see it?'

Nowadays James kept the Ringlet in a tin that had once held cough lozenges. He took the tin out of a drawer and opened it.

'It's dead,' said Violet.

'It's at peace. I think its soul has gone to Jesus.'

'I had a bee once but Annie made it fly away. It was still alive. I had it in a box.'

'It wouldn't want to be in a box if it was still alive.'

James tipped the Ringlet into his hand so that Violet could see it better, and rocked it to and fro, a thing like a beautiful leaf or feather, an empty shell.

❧

Everything in the servants' hall at the manor was at sixes and sevens. The young master had been expected back at about half-past three with Mr Gale and the lady with the four children who was taking the Old Forge. Two men had gone down to help with the luggage and had hung about in Church Lane for over an hour.

'They'll be here at half-past six,' said the butler. 'You go back down there then. She's caught the later train.'

But at half-past six the heavens opened. The footmen ran

for shelter in the kitchen of the Old Forge where two house-maids were sorting out the supper Cook had put up for the children.

The four of them went about the house exclaiming at the sight of the torrent from different windows. They made up the fires the maids had lit in the late afternoon and stood round, rather awed and awkward at having the place to themselves, cut off from everyone by the fury of the storm. The girls set out the supper dishes on the dining room table and the young men started to tease them by snatching pieces of bread and butter, chicken legs and sugared biscuits.

'Who's to know? Move 'em all up close again. Let 'em snuggle up like, see, like this.'

There was a lot of giggling and squealing. A junket was spilled on the floor, which meant that a bucket and cloth had to be fetched. One of the maids cleaned up the mess, helped by one of the footmen who crawled under the table. The other couple scampered off to the kitchen where a dozen bottles of champagne were waiting on ice.

'They won't miss one,' said Jack. 'Look, move 'em all up close again. Good and close.'

'What if they come?'

'They won't come in this weather. They'll wait, won't they?'

'Not if they was in the open, and nearly here. They'd just drive on, surely to goodness.'

'Come on, don't worry about that. Come to Jack, me little darling dear.'

Just after seven o'clock, when the rain was starting to ease, Mr Bradstock, the butler, took his umbrella and hurried down to the Old Forge to see if the party from the station had arrived. What he found on opening the back door put him in a towering rage, though Jack hadn't yet started on the champagne and the couple under the table, concealed by the tablecloth, hastily put themselves to rights and emerged with a story about chasing a cat.

Then the generator failed. Oil lamps had to be brought out from cupboards, filled and carried here and there. When this had been done Mr Bradstock marched the young footmen back to the servants' hall.

Everyone had begun to speculate. The train had been late. The lady hadn't come. The party had stopped to shelter on the way home.

'But where'd they shelter between here and Barnstaple?'

'Mr Grindley might've got down out of the rain and left the rest in the carriage.'

'Got into the carriage with 'em.'

'Got under a tree.'

'Never a tree, you great jackass. My gaffer had a pony struck dead under an oak over at Falcombe.'

'That wheeler might've played up.'

'They could be in the ditch.'

'Whole carriage could've gone over.'

'Dinner at eight sharp, Mr Grindley said. I can keep the soup but what about the sole? What about my green sauce? What about the ducks?'

'Never mind ducks, Cook. They should've been here over an hour ago. Summat's not right.'

'The rain's nearly stopped. They wouldn't be sheltering now.'

'Whatever's happened to 'em? Pray God they aren't all smashed to smithereens.'

'They might've put up at the Crown. Thought better of driving all out here tonight.'

'They wouldn't do that. Not Mr Grindley wouldn't. He'd drive in any weather, Mr Grindley.'

'Somebody ought to go and see what's happened.'

'What about Mr Prosser? He can take the gig.'

'Jack could run over and ask 'im what 'e thinks.'

'I been up and down all day. Let Esau go.'

'You do as you're told. Any more larks from you, you'll be out on your ear. Get over to Marsh Farm, give Mr Prosser my compliments and ask him to step over here quick as he can.'

'He'll want the gig. Young Tilly can get the gig.'

'What about that lovely supper for that lady's children? Them jellies'll all be melted. Everything all dry and spoiled by now.'

'You go straight there and back. Don't you go fooling about where you got no business.'

At the Old Forge Nancy and Millie put damp cloths over the bread and butter and laid plates over the savoury dishes. They put the jellies in the pantry, then hung about giggling over Mr Bradstock looking around for the cat, and what Jack had said to Nancy in the kitchen. At about eight o'clock they agreed it was too late now for anyone to arrive from Barnstaple. They damped down the fires, pulled shutters over the windows, put out the lamps and set out through the windy, wet-smelling darkness back to the big house. By the time they reached the servants' hall, Jack, to Nancy's secret chagrin, had left to find the head groom. Everyone was looking solemn. Most of them were rather in awe of Mr Prosser who was a tough little man with a cutting tongue and a quelling eye. The decision to rouse him from his fireside so late in the evening sealed the non-arrival of the carriage as a much more alarming event than Cook and some of the others had allowed.

Prosser arrived very quickly and stood with his arms folded and head bowed while Mr Bradstock added to Jack's explanation of the afternoon's events. He had been away from the estate until nightfall on some business about a stallion and had the air of a man thoroughly irritated at finding chaos had come as soon as he turned his back.

'It makes no odds,' he said, cutting Mr Bradstock short, 'whether the lady got to Barnstaple or not. Either way Mr Grindley should've come back. Ten to one there's trouble with the carriage. Five to one he's stopping the night at the Crown. But then again if he went in the ditch on the way back here the whole lot of 'em could be out on the road with their legs broke. And I'd like to know why nobody went looking two hours ago.'

Mr Bradstock, angry at being spoken to like this in front of his staff, went red as a turkey-cock. Everyone else started to explain they'd thought Mr Grindley was just sheltering from the storm or had stayed at the inn like Mr Prosser said.

'Well, never mind that now. I'll get on. If he's at the Crown I'll stop there with him. He'll very likely want the gig first thing. If there's anyone hurt I'll send word in the next hour so if you don't hear by ten you can get to bed. Young Tilly's bringing the gig round the front. Can someone come and lock the door behind me?'

He looked at Mr Bradstock but the butler merely signed to Nancy to go. They went out through the green baize door, down one dimly lit passage and up another. All at once the front doorbell rang.

'Oh, it's the master!' cried Nancy. What would he think having to ring at his own door? There should have been someone watching for him from a window. She went forward in a rush, straightening her apron, patting her hair, glancing in the drawing room as she went by to make sure Esau had seen to the fire there. Her heels clicked across the polished boards in the hall, over the rugs, past the stags' heads on the walls and the lamp on the table with the silver

514

salver for letters, until she came to the big oak door and turned the key.

'Oh, sir,' she was going to say, 'we've all been that worried.'

Because Mr Grindley didn't mind them showing they cared about him, didn't expect them to hide their feelings and never say a word like they did in a lot of places. And he'd tell her what had happened, how the new wheeler had gone lame or how he'd got caught in the storm and soaked to the skin.

It was still blowing when she pulled open the door. A great gust swept into the hall and set the lamps swinging. She saw the trees in the park tossing their branches back and forth against the sky, but the smile faded from her face because instead of the master and his friend, solid and lively, filling the doorway with their shoulders and stamping their feet, there was nobody there. Or so it seemed at first. And then she saw a woman huddled to one side of the wide step against the ivy branching away from the wall. She knew they had to be careful about women who came asking for the master. There had been several before now. One, with paint all over her face and showy clothes, had shaken her fist at Mr Bradstock and made a terrible scene. He'd said the master wasn't at home. It had been quite true. He'd been in Taunton at the time but the woman had shouted, 'Liar! Liar!', until Mr Bradstock slammed the door in her face. Afterwards they'd all agreed Mr Grindley was too soft-hearted so that trollops like that would always come hanging round to see what they could get out of him. When Mr Prosser had heard about it he'd gone all around the park to make sure the woman had gone. He'd found her in the summerhouse by the lake and given her such a fright she couldn't get back to London quick enough.

This caller wasn't overdressed like the other one but she didn't look any sort of lady. She had an old shawl round her

515

head and old draggled clothes like some zany thing. And a chaff bag! Nancy stared at it. She couldn't get over the cheek of the woman, coming up to the front door at nine o'clock at night with a chaff bag.

'She don't look right in the head,' whispered Nancy to Mr Prosser, glad that he was there behind her and that Mr Bradstock, having heard the bell, was hurrying down the hall towards them.

Prosser gripped Nancy's arm in his hard hand and drew her out of the way.

'Now then, my girl,' he said, stepping out to face the woman. 'What are you about? Looking for Mr Gascoigne are you?'

'Yes I am. And Mr Gale.'

'Oh, Mr Gale as well, eh? From London are you?'

'That's right. I am.'

She seemed about to say something else but Prosser broke in.

'Well you better get on back there, you baggage. We don't want your sort round here.' And he flourished his whip at her.

Mr Bradstock, standing tall in the doorway, thundered, 'Get on, you brazen thing! Coming after gentlemen like that! Coming to the front door! You shameless piece of goods!'

The woman fled, running down the steps and blundering into the dark towards the stables.

'Now where's she gone?'

'It's all right,' said Prosser. 'The lads know not to let strangers near the horses. They'll see her off.'

He went to the gig, jumped up to take the reins and sped away down the drive. Nancy could see light from the gig lamps sliding under the branches of the oaks as the gig moved down the avenue.

'Where d'you think she'll go, Mr Bradstock? Where'll she sleep?'

'That sort'll sleep anywhere. That's what happens to them who's too free and easy, Nancy. You remember that.'

Kate ran down the track towards the stables, saw lights and veered away to the left across grass, through trees, on to a little path. There she stopped. She couldn't believe what had happened. She stood absolutely oblivious to everything around her—the torn clouds streaming across the moon, the gusting wind, the black pines—with every particle of her being drawn into a knot around the words she'd heard. It was as though a knife had been driven into her side and all her blood was welling up in the wound. She saw now what she had become, saw too that Howard had abandoned her, that she'd forced herself on him when he was tired of her and no longer loved her. He had never meant to meet her anywhere today. He was far away in Bristol with his family, hoping he'd never set eyes on her again. She'd run after him like a woman of the streets and he'd cast her off like the drab that she'd become. And Grindley Gascoigne, his friend, had told all his servants to drive her away when she came to his house, drive her off into the night with a whip.

She began to walk down the path, the wind flattening her skirt against her thighs, filling and tugging at her bodice, dragging at her shawl. She dared not think of John who flickered momentarily in her mind as a lean, black judge who stared at her with the bitterest contempt. She thrust away all thought of her children because they too seemed to stand in judgement over her, all betrayed, loveless and cold as ice. Not knowing at all where she was going she moved on between the threshing trees until she came to a wicket gate and felt soft sand under her feet.

On her left, far down the beach, rose the Giant's Tump, the

line of its dome black against the cloud wrack. It seemed like a great monkish head with the chin sunk on the breast and the eyes averted. She began to weep, wailing and holding her hands clutched to her face while her skirt cracked like a sail in the wind. There were tears on her fingers, their saltiness smelling of the sea. Dropping her hands she saw the moon gleam on a chilly waste of waters and heard waves plunge and spread on the dark sand.

She had no idea what to do. She felt only that she must get away and hide herself. She couldn't bear to think of going back through the gate and wandering about on Grindley's land where the man with the whip or some other servant might catch her trespassing and drive her off again. Most horrible of all she might meet Grindley, or Howard, who could be at the manor after all. She felt no resentment against him. It was as though he had simply stepped back into the world of respectably married couples where he belonged and was looking down with all the other moral people at her burning, annihilating shame. It seemed plain now that he had always meant to do this. Only she had been mad and wicked enough to abandon her marriage and drag her children off to share the degradation of a kept woman.

She began to walk towards the Tump, then broke into a run. It was strange to be running along the beach at night. Always before it had been bright day, with the dark lump up ahead quite clear to see. And yet, despite the darkness, she knew now that the trees above the beach were windblown pines, and wondered why she'd never realised this before. Inland the ground began to rise towards the great ridge behind the Tump. She strained her eyes, thinking she could see something black on the sand, out in the glimmering moonlight where the monk's chin dropped towards the sea. She passed a rocky spur, the near side of a little cove, curling like a hollow shoulder from the Tump's base. At the back of the cove was a steep, slanting cliff, dry for much of the year, although a few strands of weed on its rocky face showed where an occasional neap tide had risen in springtime to a height of seven or eight feet.

Suddenly Kate was out of the wind, sheltered by the mass of rock above her. She sank down and lay panting, confused, as can happen in dreams, as to whether she was the watcher or the watched. She raised her head to look up at the hurrying clouds above the cliff. And then it dawned on her— something, it seemed, that had always been plain as day—that the face of the blue-eyed woman with sand in her hair was inevitably, inescapably her own.

❧

In the morning Howard went up to the station to see if Kate and her children had arrived from Taunton on the early train. While he was waiting he wandered about, sat for a few minutes in the waiting room, glanced into the cloakroom and turned his head idly to read the name on a large trunk. Portland, Barnstaple. Portland? He went quickly to find the stationmaster who told him about the lady—a very smart, well-dressed lady—who'd taken a carpetbag, said she'd call back for the rest of her luggage, and gone walking off last evening about half-an-hour before the storm broke. Howard demanded that the stationmaster open one of the trunks. The stationmaster indignantly refused. Eventually they compromised by looking in one of the smaller, unlocked bags. Under the stationmaster's eye, Howard drew out a tissue-paper package, unwrapped it and saw, with mingled triumph and alarm, the handpainted French clock.

'Think!' said Howard. 'She goes off—God knows why—all

alone—God knows where the children are—with a carpetbag. Where does she go?'

'Not the Crown. Some other place. That's it, old chap! She's gone to a boarding house.'

They searched for most of the morning, visiting all the boarding houses in the town and driving in the gig to outlying farms and cottages with rooms to let. When they arrived back at the Crown, baffled and on the point of quarrelling, they found a message from the stationmaster. Four children belonging to the lady they were looking for were waiting at the station for their mother to collect them. Violet, it seemed, had identified the trunks. Grindley and Howard cheered up immediately.

At last something that had been arranged had actually occurred. The children were in Barnstaple and where the children were the mother would surely appear before long. They went down to the station in good spirits, commandeered the station fly, loaded both gig and fly with luggage and passengers and set off for Coombe Bassett.

Annie was crying again. Howard dandled her on his knee, thinking her a pretty little darling, while Violet looked sullenly on.

'Ma said she'd meet us at the station,' she said accusingly.

'Yes, well, we're not quite sure where your mother's got to at the moment but we'll probably find her waiting in your new house.'

This view was soon confirmed. Prosser pointed out a cottage, close to the start of the Coombe Bassett road, which took paying guests, a place they'd overlooked in the morning's search. The owner had noticed a very elegant lady in a grey walking costume trimmed with black bows and a hat with an ostrich feather walking past just after six o'clock last evening. She'd thought it queer that the lady should be going out that

520

way because there was nobody anyone like that would want to visit until you got right through to Coombe Bassett village. The men conferred again. They concluded that Kate must have taken shelter when the storm came and ended up staying the night with some hospitable farmer or cottager who didn't in the normal way let rooms.

'There's not many places she could've got to in the time,' said Prosser. 'Jeeveses', Packenhams', Griggs'—though that's well off the road. Old Mother Biggadike, maybe. But that's a fair step.'

'That don't matter now,' said Grindley. 'She'll have gone on to the manor this morning and be wondering what the devil's become of us. Get a move on, Prosser. That kid's up on the box again.'

The whole party went on quite cheerfully. When they reached the manor they were startled at finding Kate still hadn't arrived but, for a time, everyone was so busy doing what they'd expected to do yesterday, there was no serious alarm. Jack and Esau unloaded the luggage. Mr Bradstock opened up the Old Forge. Nancy and Millie found that the jellies were still in good shape and laid out a refurbished spread for the children. Cook whipped up a hasty lunch for Grindley and Howard, and two stablelads were sent off to catch the pony. But soon Howard began to frown and tap his foot.

'I can't understand it. What in God's name is she up to?'

'Perhaps she caught a chill. That's it! She's probably been put to bed at Jeeveses' or somewhere.'

'You'd think she'd have the sense to send a message. And what about the children? Apparently she said she'd meet them at the station.'

'We'd better get back. Go and call at those places straightaway.'

This time they left Prosser behind. Anxious again, they

drove at a great pace, hardly speaking, until they reached Mrs Biggadike's cottage.

'Oh, sir,' she said. 'I been that worried about her going off like that but she would have it. Off she went in those old things I had up in Lucy's box. Look here!'

And she showed them all Kate's clothes laid out on the table, dried and brushed with the mudstains sponged from the skirt and the curl restored to the feather in her hat.

'She give me ten shilling. She would have it. I'm glad to do summat for her.'

Howard stared at the fashionable outfit, lying limp and flat. He even put out his hand and touched the jacket as though he wanted to make sure it was completely empty. It was as though some malevolent conjurer had whisked the living woman into thin air, drawing her out of her clothes like a puff of smoke.

Millie Morris always told the tale in the same way: 'It was a terrible time just before Mr Grindley went away. It's no wonder he never came back. That yacht went down with his cousin and all those others, but for us the worst was what happened up at the manor. Nobody there ever forgot that day. Mr Grindley came back, driving like a madman and shouted he wanted everyone on the place out looking. He went down to the servants' hall and stood there with his friend, pale as death. He asked if anyone had seen a woman in old clothes with a shawl and a chaff bag. Nancy burst out crying and ran off. Mr Bradstock looked like he'd seen a ghost and Mr Prosser who was finishing his dinner went white as chalk. But he spoke up. He was a brave man for all his nasty tongue. Mr Gale—Howard—went for him like a lion and knocked him down, got his hands round his throat and would've throttled him if Mr Grindley and some of them hadn't pulled him off. Mr Grindley shouted at Mr Bradstock to get out of his sight and he did. He left soon after though Mr Prosser stayed on in the end. But he wasn't the same man. He used to stop with the horses all the time and never hardly spoke a word to a soul.

'Everyone went running about—some down to the village, knocking on every door in the place, some up in the woods and out along the roads, some going round the park, some poking about in the lake and the river where the boat crossed over. Mr Grindley went all through the stables, because that was the way she went when she ran off. He got all the lads going through the haylofts and everywhere.

'I was told off to see to the children, poor little mites. The young ones didn't know what was going on but there was a girl about nine or ten kept asking and asking after her mother. Esau told her, "We mustn't give up hope." Then Howard, just after that, went down to the beach.'

❧

Kate had never told Howard about her dream. He came through the pine wood and stood by the wicket gate, looking up and down, recognising nothing until he saw the shawl on the hard, shell-studded sand near the edge of the sea. He went quickly, picked it up and, gazing round more wildly, caught sight of the hump far down the beach. He tried to tell himself it was only a rock, though against the beetling wall of the Giant's Tump it looked too light in colour. Holding the shawl, he walked towards it, moving between the sunlit sea and the quiet trees. As he came nearer he saw that the hump was made by the swathed hips of a woman in a skirt of washed-out blue material. He began to run.